Onslaught

Onslaught

The Centurions: Volume II

ANTHONY RICHES

HODDER &
STOUGHTON

First published in Great Britain in 2017 by Hodder & Stoughton
An Hachette UK company

1

Copyright © Anthony Riches 2017

A CIP catalogue record for this title is available from the British Library

Hardback ISBN 978 1 473 62875 5
Ebook ISBN 978 1 473 62877 9

Typeset in Plantin Light by Palimpsest Book Production Limited,
Falkirk, Stirlingshire

Printed and bound by Clays Ltd, St Ives plc

Hodder & Stoughton policy is to use papers that are natural, renewable
and recyclable products and made from wood grown in sustainable forests.
The logging and manufacturing processes are expected to conform to the
environmental regulations of the country of origin.

Hodder & Stoughton Ltd
Carmelite House
50 Victoria Embankment
London EC4Y 0DZ

www.hodder.co.uk

For Helen

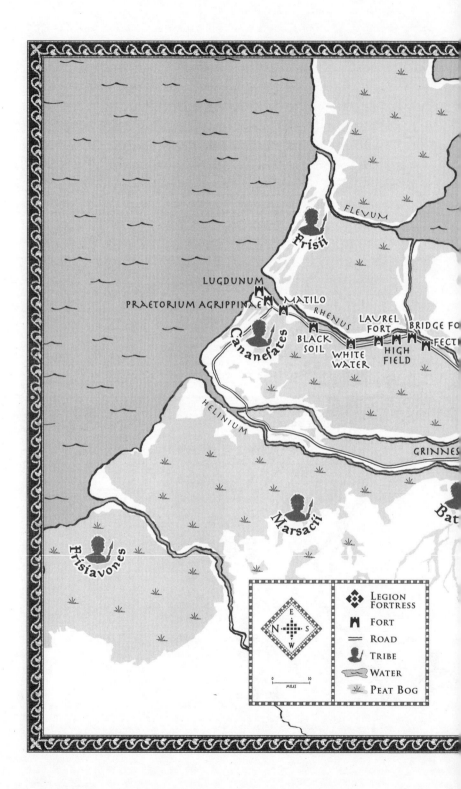

FLEVUM

Frisii

LUGDUNUM
PRAETORIUM AGRIPPINAE
MATILO
RHENUS
LAUREL
FORT
BRIDGE FO
FECT
Cananefates
BLACK
SOIL
WHITE
WATER
HIGH
FIELD

HELINIUM

GRINNES

Marsacii

Bat

Frisiavones

◆ LEGION
  FORTRESS
🏰 FORT
═ ROAD
👤 TRIBE
〰 WATER
🌿 PEAT BOG

N E S W

0   10
  MILES

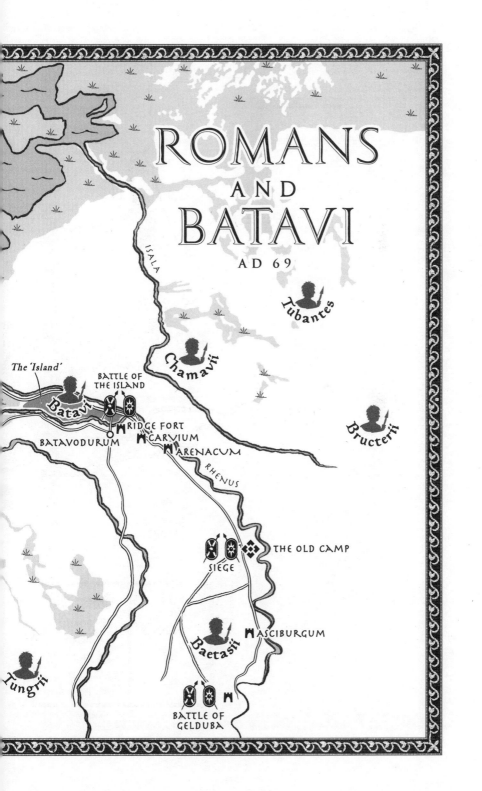

ROMANS
AND
BATAVI
AD 69

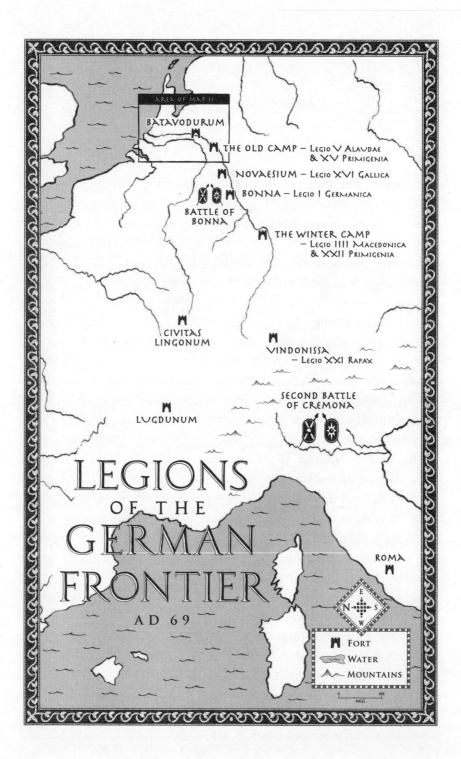

AREA OF MAP II

BATAVODURUM

THE OLD CAMP – Legio V Alaudae
& XV Primigenia

NOVAESIUM – Legio XVI Gallica

BONNA – Legio I Germanica

BATTLE OF
BONNA

THE WINTER CAMP
– Legio IIII Macedonica
& XXII Primigenia

CIVITAS
LINGONUM

VINDONISSA
– Legio XXI Rapax

SECOND BATTLE
OF CREMONA

LUGDUNUM

LEGIONS
OF THE
GERMAN
FRONTIER
AD 69

ROMA

N E S W

FORT
WATER
MOUNTAINS

0   100
MILES

ACKNOWLEDGEMENTS

As ever, I am indebted to the patience of my editor Carolyn and the smooth facilitation of her assistants, Abby and now Thorne, the indefatigable publicity efforts of Kerry and Rosie and the constant encouragement – only occasionally backed up with the use of force – of my wife Helen. My thanks to all of you who encouraged, cajoled and generally helped me to deliver a readable book.

Jona Lendering, owner of the fantastic *Livius* website (*livius. org*) very kindly agreed to cast an eye over the manuscript and point out any gross errors. His comments have proven immensely valuable in more than one respect ('there were no trees there so your character can't run off and hide in them', for example), and I am hugely indebted. Thank you, Jona.

And thank you, the reader, for continuing to read these stories. Please keep reading. We're only taking a temporary break from the *Empire* series, by the way, and once this story of the Batavian revolt as seen through the eyes of the men I've imagined fighting on both sides is done Marcus and his *familia* will return.

One last thing. There's a gold aureus from the time of Vespasian – yes, a real Roman gold coin – to be won by one lucky reader in my *Centurions* competition. All you have to do is go to my website and enter the answers to three questions that you'll find there, the answers to which are contained in *Betrayal*, *Onslaught* and *Retribution* as each book is published. There's no restriction on when you enter each answer, multiple entries are allowed; but the last answer given will be taken as your definitive entry, and all answers will be invisible to everyone except myself and my trusted webmaster (who's not allowed to enter). I'll be offering separate raffle prizes shortly after this book is published for entries received for each question – details on the website. Don't hold back: get your entries in early to win unique *Centurions* artwork and other goodies. Please do get puzzling, think cryptically, and the very best of luck – someone's got to win it, so why not you?

LIST OF CHARACTERS

AD43
In Britannia
Titus Flavius Vespasianus – legatus, imperial 2nd legion Augustan
Gaius Hosidius Geta – legatus, imperial 14th legion Gemina
Sextus – senior centurion, imperial 14th legion Gemina
Julius Civilis – centurion, allied Batavian cohorts
Draco – prefect and commander, allied Batavian cohorts

AD69
In Rome
Aulus Vitellius – emperor
Aulus Caecina Alienus – consul and army commander
Fabius Valens – consul and army commander
Alfenius Varus – praetorian prefect

In the Old Camp (modern day Vetera)
Marius – senior centurion, imperial 5th legion Alaudae
Munius Lupercus – legatus commanding imperial legions 5th
    Alaudae and 15th Primigenia
Marcus Hordeonius Flaccus – legatus augusti commanding all
    Roman forces in Germania
Claudius Labeo – prefect commanding the 1st cohort Batavian
    Horse

In the Winter Camp (modern day Mainz)
Dillius Vocula – legatus commanding imperial legion 22nd
    Primigenia
Antonius – senior centurion, imperial legion 22nd Primigenia

In Bonna (modern day Bonn)
Herrenius Gallus – legatus commanding imperial legion 1st
  Germanica

With the Batavian cohorts in Germania Superior
Scar – prefect, commanding the eight Batavian cohorts
Aelius Verus – tribune, sent to order the Batavian cohorts to return
  to Italy
Alcaeus – centurion, 2nd century of the 1st Batavian cohort
Banon – chosen man, 2nd century
Grimmaz – leading man
Egilhard (Achilles) – soldier
Andreios (The First One) – soldier
Andronicus (The Other One) – soldier
Adalwin (Beaky) – soldier
Levonhard (Ugly) – soldier
Lanzo (Dancer) – soldier
Wigbrand (Tiny) – soldier

On the Island (the Batavi homeland)
Aquillius – former senior centurion, imperial legion 8th Augusta,
  defeated commander of detached auxiliary forces
Kivilaz – (known as Julius Civilis by Rome) – prince of the Batavi,
  commander of the tribe's revolt against Rome
Hramn – decurion, commander of the Batavi Guard (formerly
  the Emperor's German Bodyguard)
Draco – former prefect of the Batavian cohorts, tribal elder
Brinno – king of the Cananefates tribe, allies of the Batavi
Lataz – retired veteran and father of Egilhard
Frijaz – retired veteran and brother of Lataz

Preface

It is August of AD 69, and the Roman Empire is staring disaster in the face. A period of little more than twelve months has already seen three emperors: Nero, hounded to suicide by an enraged senate; his successor Galba murdered on the streets of Rome by praetorians in the pay of the usurper Otho; and Vitellius, his path to the throne cut by the bloody swords of the German legions. In the east, Vespasianus, the only potential challenger for imperial power left alive is gathering legions to himself, preparing for an invasion of Italy that must result in yet another climactic battle for domination.

And at the lowest point of Roman rule for a hundred years, just as things could apparently be no worse, the Batavi tribe of Germania Inferior and their German tribal allies have risen in revolt, driven both by Roman duplicity and the ambitions of their war leader Kivilaz, Civilis to his former allies. Through a combination of cunning, ferocity, betrayal and the duplicity of officers with loyalty to Vespasianus, eager to foster an uprising to deny his rival critical reinforcements from Germania, the revolt's first engagements have ended in comprehensive defeat for Rome's overstretched frontier army. The Batavi are seemingly poised to take their war onto imperial territory and attack the legionary fortress that watches their homeland, the Old Camp, if they can be assured of the support of their powerful cohorts.

As a former ally of Rome, and having participated in the brutal suppression of Britannia's Iceni tribe a decade before, Kivilaz knows only too well the devastation that Rome has historically visited on any tribe that dares to challenge the empire's military might – enslavement, resettlement and genocide. And yet Rome has never looked more vulnerable to a knife in the back.

Prologue

Britannia, June AD 43

'It won't be long before they attack us again, First Spear.'

Legatus Vespasianus's voice was deliberately pitched low, and he glanced with fatherly sympathy at the two young tribunes sleeping fitfully under their cloaks in a corner of his legion's improvised field headquarters.

'What an introduction to battle, eh Julius? I'd hope to blood our men with something a little less horrific than a full day of barbarian savagery followed by a night of arrows and infiltrators. And once the sun's up we can expect those blue-faced maniacs to come down that hill at us with fresh fire in their bellies. And while they lack any real quality when it comes to swordplay, I think we both know that overwhelming numbers have a quality all of their own.'

The Second Legion's commander looked out into the darkness that surrounded his men, his body tensed against the weariness of having been on his feet for more than a day with only the briefest moments of snatched sleep. He shook his head in continued disbelief at the seemingly limitless number of tribal warriors that had been continuously thrown into battle against his legion's tenuous bridgehead on the river Medui's western bank throughout the previous day.

'And we're victims of our own hubris, it has to be said. How the gods must have laughed when I agreed that we should attempt to force a crossing of the river with just one legion! Come on, let's do the rounds of the front line shall we, and give the men something to laugh at before it starts all over again? You can do some motivational shouting, and I'll tell them that they've "all done very well" in that voice the emperor uses when he's inspecting his praetorians. I'll just have to find a marble to put in my mouth first . . .'

His first spear chuckled softly.

'I've served under seven legion commanders, Legatus, and I have to say you're a first. With the greatest of respect, of course.'

Vespasianus snorted his own cynical amusement.

'If that's your way of telling me that you're not sure whether to laugh with me or at me, you'd probably better hurry up and make a decision on the matter, hadn't you, Julius? Because we all might very well be cracking jokes in the Underworld before we know it.'

A messenger stepped into the circle of torchlight that illuminated the headquarters, the light concealed from the enemy by heavy leather tent skins erected on spears to form a protective semi-circle around the squatting men who were its occupants, saluting punctiliously and holding out a message tablet.

'A dispatch from the senior medicus, Legatus.'

Vespasianus took it from his hand, snapping apart the wax seal that held the tablet closed, a reckoning of the casualties that had been evacuated from the tenuous bridgehead's line of battle to the improvised medical station on the river's eastern bank.

'Now there's one of the very few men in the legion who'll have slept less than us since we crossed the river. Let's see what he has to say . . .' He turned the tablet to the torch's flickering light, holding it out at arm's length. 'Bugger these eyes . . .' He squinted again, shifting to position the tablet better to catch the light. 'I suppose I ought to thank the gods that my manhood hasn't gone the same way as my eyesight. The senior medicus informs me that we have five hundred and six men dead or likely to die, and another two hundred and thirty-three treatable wounded.'

The first spear shook his head in disgust.

'In battle with any other people I'd have expected the numbers of dead and wounded to have been the other way around, but these madmen will throw their lives away to allow one of their mates to put a spear into one of ours. So we've lost the best part of two cohorts with nothing much to show for it apart from a few hundred paces of riverbank. And I thought these people were supposed to be ripe for conquering? Nothing better than underfed peasants, and no threat to Roman discipline and aggression?'

The legatus snorted derision.

'Oh, they're no threat alright, *if* you're a wealthy senator with a fortune invested in invasion ships and several legions between you and the "underfed peasants" in question. They may be ignorant, stinking barbarians, fit only to die on our swords, but by Jupiter's hairy balls they're *brave*.'

His senior centurion sighed.

'And even if every man in the legion has killed five of the bastards there are still another hundred thousand of them waiting for their turn. I'd say you learned gentlemen have bitten off more than you can get in your mouths.'

Vespasianus laughed without any trace of his usual good humour.

'You can cross me off *that* list. I class as the hired help in this particular enterprise, just a humble servant of the emperor's imperial ambition . . . that, and the senate's collective purses.' He shook his head in dark amusement. 'I remember only too well the briefings to which you're referring, all confidence and encouragement, and by the gods I'd like to have had those smooth-faced men for company when the Britons came storming down the hill at us as we waded out of the river. I thought for a moment we were about to get pushed straight back into the water. It's a bloody good thing young Geta's Batavians managed to deal with their chariots before we came across the ford, or we'd have had a face full of their best and nastiest swordsmen too, and that might have been all it would have taken to stop us dead, with most of the legion still on the other bank. Even without their intervention you can be sure I'll be awarding every centurion who survives this horrible mess their torques and phalerae after the battle. If, that is, any of us actually manage to survive this horrible mess!'

★

'Like all the best plans, gentlemen, my intentions for this morning's actions are simple and direct.'

Legatus Hosidius Geta looked around his senior centurions, his usual pugnacity clearly combined with the frustration of having watched the men on the far side of the river struggle to make any headway against their tribal opponents for most of the previous day.

'Without wanting to go over the events of yesterday at any great length, since we all saw what happened, we must nevertheless be honest with ourselves. We failed, gentlemen. And by we, for avoidance of doubt, I do not mean my colleague Vespasianus and the men of his Second Augustan. The gods know they fought like men possessed in the teeth of overwhelming enemy strength. No, *we* failed. *We* sat and watched while the Second fought their way into the very teeth of the barbarian counter-attack. *We* waited for Vespasianus to cut out a bridgehead into which our men could advance, while all the time it was evident to anyone with eyes to see that it simply wasn't going to happen. The Second were never likely to prove strong enough to push these Britons far enough off their ground to allow for an orderly leap-frog advance by the rest of the army, not on their own. Every time we thought our brothers-in-arms were making some progress another wave of wild-eyed maniacs washed down that slope and pushed them back on their heels, which means that the bridgehead is barely big enough to give us the room we'll need to cross the river and pass through them to take up the fight. And, may my ancestors forgive me, by the time it was clear to me what needed to be done it was deemed too late in the day for an alternative line of attack to be launched.'

He shot a swift glance at Vespasianus's brother Sabinus, who was standing to one side as the army commander's representative at the orders conference, knowing that his role was to ensure Geta stuck to the script that had been agreed in the army commander's tent the previous evening.

'And so last night Legatus Sabinus and I rode back to consult with Legatus Augusti Plautius, and presented our proposal for what needs to happen this morning, at first light, if our comrades of the Second Legion are not to be thrown back across the Medui in disarray. I'm delighted to be able to tell you that he agreed with us, and has given us permission to carry out an attack from first light. We're going to cross the river and pass through the Second Legion, march straight up the hill through their bridge-head and attack the Britons with the advantage of being fresh into the fight. And if I know Titus Flavius Vespasianus as well as I think I do, he'll know what to do when our men take over the fight . . .'

He paused theatrically, drawing a small smile from Sabinus who, while he tried to hide it from his comrades, was both charmed and slightly amused by the younger man's fire-eating attitude to whatever life threw at him. Geta turned to gesture for him to speak, as they had agreed, and the older Flavian brother stepped out of the tent's shadows.

'My brother Titus will attack on either flank. He'll muster his legionaries to make one last titanic effort and, combined with the fresh men of your legion, a legion with a peerless reputation for bravery in battle, the attack the Britons must intend to send down that hill this morning will be pinched off before it can be launched. Your time has come, gentlemen of the Fourteenth . . .' He paused with equal theatricality to Geta and flashed the younger man a quick grin. 'Or should I perhaps call you by the name you prefer – "The Fighting Fourteenth"? Whichever, now is your time to shine once more, and show these barbarians that we can wipe them from the map before we've even taken our *breakfast*!'

The centurions gathered around them laughed, most of them knowing just how keen Sabinus was to take a morning meal before doing anything else.

'Will you be coming with us, Legatus?'

He grinned easily back at the speaker, a senior centurion commanding one of the legion cohorts, and if he lacked his brother's effortless ability to communicate with the common soldier as an equal, he knew from their upbringing by the outspoken daughter of a retired camp prefect just how important it was to hit the right note with men like this hard-bitten officer.

'Do you think I'd miss the opportunity to dine out on my small part in one of the greatest victories since Caesar got his men to dig a little bit of trench work at Alesia? Not to mention the chance to watch you fine gentlemen in action.' He smiled wryly with just the right degree of self-deprecation, patting the hilt of his gladius. 'Who knows, I might even get the chance to use *this* for a change, instead of spending all my time chasing legions round the countryside to make sure they're in the right place.'

The jaundiced tone of his voice drew an amused laugh from the assembled centurions, who knew well enough that his service record was more than respectable. Geta nodded, clearly too preoccupied with the coming battle to join in their levity.

'Very well. Sextus, this is your legion by rights, you should be the man to issue the orders that set this attack in train.'

He stepped aside, allowing the veteran first spear who had been waiting patiently behind him to step forward. Cohort commanders who until then had been attentive but relaxed were abruptly all business, hard eyed and stiff backed, as he started talking in the matter of fact way that demonstrated the lightness with which he wore his authority.

'It's been a few years since we put down the last tribe to challenge Rome, so some of your men will be new to all this, and most of them will be rusty, but *all* of them are going to perform to my satisfaction or some of *you* are going to be discussing their failings, and your own, with me, once this matter has been dealt with to my liking. And wine will most definitely not be served.'

He paused, looking around at them, and several big, hard-faced and combat-experienced men, whose first instinct would always be towards violence, looked down at their feet momentarily with the memory of short and meaningful discussions with him that they had no desire to repeat.

'So make sure your centurions know their orders, and make sure they also know that I expect them to deliver the legatus's plan to the last detail.' He paused for a moment, but any theatricality that might have been implied by the moment was dispelled without trace by the hard, unmoving line of his mouth as he looked round at them. 'Or at least have the good manners to die trying. Questions?'

After a moment's silence he turned to look at the legion's officers, gathered behind the broad-stripe tribune who was their leader, and second-in-command to Geta.

'Tribunes.'

In the mouths of some men of his rank the word might have carried a faint edge of scorn, the dismissive hint of superiority felt by a man with half a lifetime of service for officers whose qualification for command was family wealth rather than experience or ability. The experience of working with his new legatus, a man of only twenty-four years and yet the most disturbingly competent legion commander he had ever served under, had somewhat softened his attitude. To a degree.

'Tribune Abito. You will, of course, stay close to Legatus Geta and the eagle, in order to take command in the event that some enemy warrior gets lucky and sends him to have dinner with his ancestors?'

The legion's only broad-stripe tribune nodded confidently. A man of the senatorial class like Geta, and therefore his second-in-command, his certainty of his own ability to step into the young legatus's shoes was so self-evident that it was all the more experienced Sabinus could do not to shake his head in amusement.

'Tribune Pulto?'

The oldest of the narrow-stripe men of the equestrian rank looked up, a square-jawed man of thirty with two auxiliary cohort commands under his belt and a self-declared career soldier.

'I would be grateful if you, sir, were to accompany me with the first cohort. I should very much appreciate your advice and quite possibly your assistance when the fighting gets vigorous.'

Pulto nodded, ignoring the awed stares of his younger brethren. It was tacitly understood that in the event the senior centurion was killed or seriously wounded that he would assume tactical control of the legion, and none of the cohort commanders present would have considered disputing that plan.

'And the rest of you young gentlemen will march with the second, third, fourth and fifth cohorts. May Mars himself stretch his hands over you and keep you safe when the time comes to fight. I look forward to hearing your stories of the battle over a cup of the legatus's wine once the Britons have turned tail and fled.'

He waited a moment for any of them to ask a question, then turned to look at the last group of men in the room.

'Prefect Draco.' The Batavi commander raised his gaze to meet the first spear's appraisal. 'Are your men ready to fight again?'

Draco nodded tersely.

'As ready as any other unit on this battlefield, Centurion. Do you have a place for us in the line?'

'No.' The legion officer shook his head briskly, and waited a moment as if challenging the other man to comment before continuing. 'I want your men at the back of the approach column, and I want you to stay on the eastern bank of the river until I give the signal.'

Draco's face remained as stubbornly imperturbable as before.

'And when you give the signal?'

Sextus smiled thinly.

'That, Prefect, will depend very much on what we manage to achieve in the teeth of a hundred thousand screaming barbarians, won't it? But given that I'm potentially denying you the glory of another day spent biting out the throats of Rome's enemies, your command can have the honour of taking the news of our impending arrival to Legatus Vespasianus. I presume you have a man to whom you can entrust that task?'

'Hear that?'

The Second Legion's first spear looked at Vespasianus for a moment, then turned to stare back across the river, no more than a dark line in the thick mist that had risen in the last hour before dawn.

'It sounds like someone shouting the odds.'

The distant voice, albeit muffled by the thick curtain of moisture in the air, was just loud enough for the two men to hear, and the legatus shook his head in disagreement.

'You're almost right. Whoever that is isn't angry though.' He waited for a moment, cocking his head to listen. 'That sound, First Spear, is *you*, with the legion on parade and not doing what you want them to quickly enough. They're not sounding any trumpets, it would give the barbarians too much warning, but there's something going on over there. You mind the shop for a short time while I go and see what's being cooked up.'

He walked swiftly down to the river's bank with the men of his bodyguard in close attendance and stepped into the water. He was barely calf deep as low tide approached, wading across to the narrow island that divided the stream in two for fifty paces of its course and then back into the cold flow, stepping out onto the eastern bank and grimacing at the muffled sounds of agony coming from the waterside grove in which his medical staff had set up the legion's field hospital. The centurion commanding the crossing sentries, set to ensure that any legionary seeking to run from the fight on the far bank was apprehended and punished with summary execution, came out of the darkness and hailed him, snapping to attention halfway through the challenge as he realised who it was he was facing.

'Legatus!'

Vespasianus returned the salute with the casual ease of long practice.

'Relax, man, I heard the shouting of a bad-tempered centurion and thought I'd best come and see what all the fuss is about. Any ideas?'

'None, sir. It sounds like a legion getting ready to move, but we've had no . . .'

The officer fell silent as he realised that his legatus was staring up at the sky over the shallow hills behind him, the older man's musing a quiet murmur as he calculated the circumstances.

'One legion mired in a sea of barbarians on the other side of a river that will shortly be at its lowest ebb for the next eight hours, and half an hour until dawn. And another legion on this side, intact and mad with frustration at not having been allowed into the fight yesterday. If I were a fire-breathing young legatus planning to intervene in this fight in force, then now would be the time.'

His eyes narrowed as the barely discernible figure of a man walked towards him out of the darkness, powerfully built and clad in the armour of an auxiliary officer, his helmet crowned with a centurion's crest. Ignoring the men of Vespasianus's bodyguard, he approached to within touching distance before saluting. His voice was hard and confident, pitched low to be heard only by the man to whom he was talking.

'Greetings, Legatus. I am Kivilaz, centurion of the first Batavi cohort. It seems you have spared me the need to get my feet wet, as I am carrying a message for you from your fellow legatus, Hosidius Geta. He has requested me tell you that he is coming, now, with the full force of his legion and that of the tribes who fight in his service. He plans to immediately and directly assault the Britons facing you, and asks you to make ready for his arrival at dawn. You are requested to provide support on the flanks, once his advance has engaged the enemy.'

Vespasianus nodded.

'He plans to take his legion straight up the middle, does he? That young man is nothing if not direct. And does his plan include your own people, Centurion?' He smiled knowingly. 'Or perhaps I should call you *Prince?*'

The German bowed his head in recognition of Vespasianus's point regarding his status within the tribe.

'Yes, I am a prince of my tribe, but centurion is an adequate title. No man of my family has ruled my people since the days of Augustus. And yes, the Batavi will march in the Fourteenth Legion's column, although at the rear and not, as we would have wished, at its head.'

The Roman chuckled quietly.

'You are typical of your tribe, Centurion. As if your exploits in the dawn yesterday weren't enough, now you yearn for yet another chance to throw yourself at an enemy whose overwhelming numbers might yet be our undoing.'

Kivilaz nodded sombrely.

'It is the nature of my people, Legatus, to seek to prove ourselves against our enemies. And now that we serve Rome, that need for victory has been provided with a larger selection of enemies to defeat. We knowingly exchanged a squalid life of cattle raids and the occasional opportunity to put one of our neighbours in their place for the chance to test our martial skills against those of Rome's enemies. The name of the Batavi will come to be feared across this land the Britons currently call their own.'

Vespasianus inclined his own head in respect.

'Those are noble words, and I fully expect that you and your people will live up to them, Centurion. But don't mistake the position of the rear guard in my colleague Geta's column for an attempt to deny your people the blood and glory you so badly desire. If I had close to a legion's strength of your people at my command, I'd want the maximum flexibility as to their employment. I suspect that when your boots touch the far shore of the Medui there will be a pressing opportunity for you to demonstrate that martial prowess you're so keen to visit upon the men facing us. Although by the time that moment comes you might well find the task for which you are needed less about glory and rather more about blood.'

He turned away from the Batavi officer with a parting comment called back over his shoulder as he stepped back into the river's cold water.

'Tell Hosidius Geta that the Second Legion will be delighted to make some room for him on the western bank of the river. We will be ready to cede our centre to his legion, and to fight alongside him like men who slept soundly in their beds rather than standing alert for an attack all night, after a day of death and horror. And tell him that there are more than enough of those blood-crazed animals for everyone.'

'First cohort! *Halt!*'

The leading centuries of the Fourteenth Legion's first cohort had climbed the shallow slope that led to the Second Legion's front line in a column twenty men abreast, each double-sized century compressed into a frontage barely twenty paces wide, a thick ironclad snake of men climbing the slope from the river as the successive cohorts deployed to either side. Geta and his most senior officers had pondered their best approach to the coming battle in the small hours of the previous night, eventually coming to the conclusion that their centuries would be best arrayed eight men deep in order to avoid the need to re-order their march formation before joining battle, leaving their men nothing more complex than the switch from column to line, difficult enough in itself given the circumstances. Before dismissing them to their cohorts, the grizzled first spear had looked around the command tent at his senior centurions with the air of a man who knew that he was about to throw the dice on the gamble of a military lifetime.

'This is it then. No more training, no more drill, no more polishing the blade. The next few hours will tell us whether we've built a legion that can stand comparison to the men who stood alongside Caesar. When we reach the back of the Second Legion's line the first cohort's first century will hold position, ready to attack, while even-numbered centuries will deploy to the right and odd numbers to the left. I'd imagine that should be within the grasp of even the dimmest of our centurions.'

The men gathered around him had smiled at the well-tested joke, intent on his words as he spelt out the way in which they would approach the battle that would define their legion's reputation for decades to come.

'We will extend from column to line at the double march, because that will be the moment of our greatest vulnerability. Pray to your gods that the Second can hold off the blue noses for long enough that we're in battle line before the fighting starts, because if they manage to break into the bridgehead while we're getting ready it could turn into a goat-fuck quicker than Quintus there can put a jug of the good stuff down his throat.'

The centurion in question had smirked at the compliment while his commander continued.

'Get them into line and get them set to attack, quick as you can. If we get it right we'll have a front six hundred paces wide, which is just about the size of the bridgehead the Second have managed to hang on to. When I blow my whistle we go. We go fast and we go hard, as hard as we can, because if we hesitate or falter those bastards have the high ground, and you can be sure that they'll use it to push us back down the hill to where we started. We need momentum, we need to keep moving and not stop until we have those tribal sheep fuckers on the run. As for our own domesticated long-hairs . . .' He had grinned at Draco, the friendly insult well worn and likely to be reciprocated soon enough, and the prefect had in turn kept his face admirably straight.

'The Batavian cohorts will follow up, ready to reinforce or exploit as appropriate. Detach your horsemen, Prefect, and keep them in reserve on the eastern bank, because there'll be no room for cavalry on this battlefield, not until we have them broken and running for their lives.'

The Batavi officer had nodded his understanding.

'We will be ready for any eventuality, First Spear. We will do what is ordered and at every command we will be ready. Although my men will be more than disappointed if your legionaries hog all the glory. Maiming horses has left us with a bad taste in our mouths.'

Sextus had smiled wryly.

'I wouldn't worry about that, Prefect. There are more than enough of them for all of us.'

The legion's first spear stepped out in front of his men with his sword drawn, his gravel-edged voice ringing out over the increasing chorus of hate from beyond their sister legion's line, where the Britons were gathering in ever greater numbers as word of the newcomers' arrival spread through their host.

'Fourteenth Legion! The time has come for every man here to prove himself worthy of our legion's proud name! Are you ready for war?'

The long line of armoured men erupted in a clamour of assent that quickly died away in readiness for the second asking.

'Are you ready for war?'

The shouted response was louder this time.

'Ready!'

'ARE YOU READY FOR WAR?'

'READY!'

He fell silent for a moment and a soldier of the Second Legion shouted the inevitable insult, expressing the impatience of men who had been fighting for twenty-four hours with little respite.

'Fucking get on with it, you shower of c—'

The veteran's barked command effortlessly overrode his protest, its power raising the hairs on his men's necks as they readied themselves for what was to follow.

'Ready! Spears!'

The men of the Second Legion's battle-weary cohorts, fore-warned of the Fourteenth's battle plan, sank behind the cover of their own shields to reveal the enemy warriors who had been baying at their line a moment before.

'Throw!'

Even as the Britons gathered themselves to exploit the sudden lack of resistance from the soldiers who had faced them throughout the previous day, springing forward to hurdle the dead and dying bodies of their fallen, a wave of deadly iron-shanked spears arched up into the cold dawn light and fell onto their poorly protected bodies. It reduced their hasty advance to blood-soaked chaos and wrenched a chorus of screams and curses from the barbarian mass as hundreds of men fell dead or horrifically wounded, the stink of their blood and involuntary bodily emissions strong enough to make Geta, standing at his men's rear with Vespasianus, wrinkle his nose in disgust.

'I can see why you're so keen to fight your way out of this bridgehead, colleague. The neighbours smell positively disgusting!'

While the enemy warriors milled in confusion, the legion's first spear was swift to ram home his momentary advantage.

'Ready! Spears!' He waited for the legionaries to transfer their spare weapons from left hand to right, and ready themselves to throw again. *'Throw!'*

The second volley was thrown higher than the first, to fall out of the dark dawn sky onto men behind the Britons' front rank who would never see what had killed them, only recoil in sudden agonised shock as the missiles' long iron shanks transfixed their bodies. Putting his whistle to his lips, he drew breath and blew a long blast, the Second Legion's men going from kneeling to lying flat at the chorus of whistle blasts that greeted the command, shouting encouragement as the Fourteenth's legionaries strode forward across their prone bodies, cursing at the bite of hobnailed boots on unprotected legs and arms as the fresh troops hurried forward to take the fight to the enemy, individual soldiers stabbing down with their swords to kill the wounded Britons in their paths. Before the reeling tribesmen could recover, the legion had reformed barely five paces from them, a very different proposition from the exhausted legionaries of the Second they had faced a moment before, fresh soldiers standing with swords drawn and shields raised in an unbroken line, ready to fight.

Geta turned to the young tribune standing behind him.

'Go and bring the Batavians across the river, would you, Gaius? I want them well placed to launch the pursuit when we've broken this barbarian scum.'

The officer, little more than a boy despite his rank, saluted and turned to hurry down the hill, while Geta turned to Vespasianus with his face alive at the prospect of a fight.

'If you'll excuse me, Flavius Vespasianus? I think it only fair for my men to see that I'm every bit as keen to get at the enemy as they are!'

'A good deal keener, I'd say . . .'

But the younger man was already gone, his sword unsheathed and gleaming in the dawn's meagre light as he hailed his first spear in the clipped, patrician tones that were widely imitated by his men when no officer was listening.

'Now then, First Spear, I think it's time to show this ugly mob what can be achieved by the application of Roman discipline and courage. Shall we?'

He took his place beside the legion's aquilifer, deliberately placed close to the first cohort's rear as an encouragement to the other cohorts to press forward with equal vigour once the advance began, and Sextus drew breath to bellow his next order.

'*Fourteenth Legion! With swords! Advance!*'

'If we have to stand here much longer I'm going to fall asleep standing up.'

Draco turned back from his place at the riverbank to shoot a pointed glance at Kivilaz, shaking his head as he admonished the younger man with a raised eyebrow.

'Fighting one action, *your highness*, especially a one-sided slash and run against a witless mob of sheep-worriers, hardly qualifies you to come it the veteran. You're no more likely to be able to sleep than the youngest warrior in the tribe, although I'll concede that in your case it would be less to do with fear than the urge to take the heads of as many men as possible to decorate the roof beams of your farm.' He turned back to the far bank, casting an expert eye on the scene that was gradually being revealed by the daylight that grew brighter with every minute. 'Besides, we'll be moving in a minute, most of the Fourteenth is engaged.'

'It's about time, Draco. Anyone would think this Roman legatus Geta considers us to be no better than the Nervians . . .'

Kivilaz fell silent as a legion tribune came splashing across the river, whose waters were on the rise and already calf deep. The Batavi officers snapped to attention while the young man gasped out his message.

'Prefect Draco! Legatus Geta requests you to advance across the river and into place behind the Fourteenth Legion! He wants you ready to pursue the enemy once we have them on the run!'

Draco saluted.

'At once, Tribune. Please tell the legatus that we will be ready for his command.'

He turned back to the gathered centurions.

'Back to your cohorts, brothers.'

As they hurried away to re-join their commands, he shouted the order for his own cohort to follow him, and stepped into the river in the wake of the tribune who was already close to the far bank. Leading his men across the Medui, he took them up the hill on the far side at a swift march, looking up the slope at the line of legion cohorts fighting their way forward into the barbarians, the screams and bellows of men in combat an unending cacophony of violence, bloodshed and death. By contrast, it seemed that the left and right-hand sides of the bridgehead's perimeter were almost silent, only the occasional bow shot serving to remind the Second Legion's men that the Britons were still lurking on the slope around them. Seeing the Second Legion's legatus, Draco walked across the hillside and nodded, knowing better than to advertise their status by saluting when there were sharp-eyed archers on the other side of their men's shields.

'Legatus.'

Vespasianus turned from his critical consideration of the Fourteenth Legion's advance.

'Ah, Prefect. Your men are ready to take whatever part is required of you?'

The Batavi warrior nodded briskly.

'We are. The boy sent to fetch us mentioned a pursuit, once the fight is won?'

The Roman nodded distractedly, watching the Britons still streaming down the slope from their camp to join the fight in growing numbers.

'My colleague Geta may have been a little premature in that assessment of his current position.'

The two men shared a moment of silent understanding.

'You think he's bitten off too big a mouthful, Legatus?'

Vespasianus shrugged.

'My legion came across the river at dawn yesterday, just as you were pulling back from dealing with their chariot horses. We barely had time to get our perimeter established before they came at us in tens of thousands. At first there were three of them for every one of us, and my men killed them at such a rate that the wall of their dead became a hindrance to them, but even when they were climbing over the corpses of their own people to get at us they still bayed for our blood, an unending torrent of blue-painted warriors with no other aim than to hurl themselves onto our swords in the hope of taking one of us with them. Their priests have them whipped into the same frenzy now, and I fear that Geta may be pushing his luck a little too hard. Look up the slope to the top of the hill.'

Draco craned his neck and stared for a moment, his practised eye taking in the cluster of barbarian standards on the hill's crest with groups of warriors gathered about them.

'They're gathering more men to attack.'

Vespasianus nodded dourly.

'Not only that, but you see those men gathered around their tribal standards?'

The Batavi prefect looked again, nodding slowly.

'They wear iron helmets and carry shields with heavy iron and bronze bosses. And they wear swords while most of these warriors have nothing better than spears.'

'They are the royal guards and champions of the kings of Britannia. The best fighting men of the Cantiaci, Trinovantes, Regni, Catuvellauni, and so many other tribes that I cannot remember their names. The finest warriors their peoples have, lavishly equipped, and every one of them an accomplished swordsman who has spent most of his life preparing for this moment. A thousand trained swords or more, and the key to victory on this battlefield for either side, our victory if we can send them away with their tails between their legs, theirs if they can concentrate their force and strike us such a blow that we are unable to recover from it. Those are the men at whom your dawn attack yesterday was aimed, not to strike them directly but to deny them their chariots' speed into action, speed that might have thwarted our river crossing by putting those swords right in our faces as we waded out of the water. Their leader has wisely preserved them, kept them out of the fight and spent his peasant levies lavishly to wear us down, but now young Geta has thrown his legion into the fight I suspect the man up on that hill knows that to delay any longer might be his undoing. If the Fourteenth manage to get his peasants running then they won't stop for anyone, and his swordsmen will either find themselves alone with two very angry legions or just swept away in the mob like twigs on the flood.'

The legatus looked up at the host of swordsmen clustered around the enemy king's standard, tipping his head to one side in calculation.

'Yes, I'm as sure of it as I know that I'll need to piss in the next hour. Any time now he's going to send them down this slope, gambling that they can cut the head off the Fourteenth and leave the legion leaderless and adrift on the tide of battle. He can see the eagle, and he can probably even see Geta, and he'll expect the legion to be so devastated by the loss of both that the fight will go out of them. And he might well be right. And so I suggest, Prefect, that you take your men up that hill and get close in behind my colleague's leading cohort, ready for whatever it might be th—'

His musing was cut off by the blare of a horn, loud and clear above the angry buzz of the Fourteenth Legion's drive into the mass of the enemy.

'They're coming.' The legatus turned to Draco with fresh urgency. 'Viewed from up there, Geta's legion is a beast with its head in a trap of its own making. And now their king has slipped the collar on his wolves and sent them at us to bite that head off. If you can stop them from doing that, I'll swing my legion's blade at the throat they expose in making their attack.'

The two men nodded at each other, Vespasianus turning away and calling for his first spear as Draco gestured his centurions to join him, ordering them to gather round in a tight knot so that every man could hear him.

'For decades now we have fought as the Romans do, ignoring our urge to fight as heroes and wielding our swords and spears from behind a wall of shields instead, like the Greeks of ancient times! But there were heroes in those days, men like Achilles and Hector, gifted with skills that made them seem almost divine among their fellow warriors, and there are heroes still in these days! Our enemy has such men, trained all their lives to fight man to man just as we are, and a thousand of them and more have been sent against our parent legion!' He pointed up the slope, aiming his finger at two spearhead formations that were advancing to meet the Fourteenth Legion's first cohort. 'They come to kill the legion's legatus, and to capture the legion's holy eagle standard and carry it away in shame, taking the legion's spirit with them! They believe that to do so will be to win this fight. But they reckon without the Batavi!'

He looked around them, his face hard.

'There will be no skulking in the night this time, with no one to see our ferocity and tell their children tales of the fell-handed horror we will inflict on Rome's enemies! This time the heat of our fury will start a fire that will burn in men's minds for a hundred years and more! Make gardens of ash poles with your men's spears, for there will be no spear fighting today! This day, my brothers, is a day of swords! A day for blood! A day for heroes! A day for wolves to fight wolves! Bring your men as the warriors they are, and be swift about it! Today we fight not as cohorts, in tidy ranks, but as we truly are! As . . . The . . . *Batavi!'*

He waited impatiently as his centurions mustered and arrayed their men ready to fight, while the battle within a battle unfolded before him exactly as Vespasian had predicted. Storming down the hillside with all the speed and purpose of men held back from fighting for far longer than they felt fitting, the Britons drove the points of their wedges into the Fourteenth's line at two carefully chosen points, swordsmen spending their lives extravagantly to wreak havoc among the legionaries facing them, fighting furiously to separate the legion's first cohort and those to either side. Their onslaught first penetrated the legion's line in a furious whirl of swordplay that felled two Romans for every warrior lost, then pushed deeper, pressing the legion's severed line away from their intended victims, as the struggling soldiers lost cohesion and allowed their tidy ranks to splinter into groups of two and three men fighting for their own survival, the freshly encouraged peasant warriors flooding in to reinforce the swordsmen who had broken through the invaders' dogged resistance. The tips of the two horns fought their way through into the open space behind the first cohort and then turned to engage the Roman rear. They forced the first cohort's legionaries to go back to back, isolating them from their fellows, the men on either side too busy fighting for their own survival to have any hope of assisting their encircled comrades. As the Batavi hurried forward to take their places behind him, Draco shook his head at the speed with which the legion's spearhead had been stopped and then trapped, turning to his men who had fallen silent at the sight of their parent legion's eagle in such deadly trouble. He drew his sword and raised it high above his head, then flashed it down to point at the enemy host.

'Batavi! As warriors! With me!'

Running up the hill's slope at the Britons, the prefect had covered no more than a dozen paces before the younger, stronger men of the tribe overtook him, and he shot a disgusted glance at Kivilaz as the centurion and a dozen of his biggest and most dangerous men arrayed themselves to either side of him, adjusting their pace to match his own.

'I don't . . . need babysitting . . . Centurion! You get on . . . with your . . . own fight . . . and leave me . . . to mine!'

The prince shook his head, grinning back at his superior as they pounded up the hill.

'Just this once . . . Prefect, royalty outranks you! If a prince . . . of the tribe . . . says he'll fight alongside you . . . that's how it is! It was you . . . who asked us . . . to fight . . . the old way!'

They were close enough to pick opponents now, a few of the Britons having realised the danger at their backs and turned to meet the oncoming wave of Batavi swordsmen, yelling at their heedless comrades who were, for the most part, lost in their individual battles with the encircled legionaries. As he covered the last few paces, Draco fixed his attention on a big man whose back was still turned, wielding his blade in wild chopping strokes at the legionaries clustered around the Fourteenth's eagle. Most of the beleaguered soldiers were too cowed by their unexpected peril and too heavily outnumbered to do much more than defend themselves against the tribesmen hammering at their shields, and even as the prefect poised his blade to strike, the Briton hacked his sword down into a legionary's helmet, felling the man with its stunning impact and opening a gap in the shrinking circle of shields. He swung the sword up again, but before the blow could fall Draco was upon him with his men on either side, plunging the point of his gladius deep into the warrior's back before twisting it savagely and wrenching it free, stepping back against the men pushing in behind him to thrust the point down in a swift death stroke.

'Batavi!'

The men around him echoed the war cry, and Draco felt something unravelling in his head, decades of military training and conditioning falling away, suddenly acutely aware of the stink of blood and excreta and the bellowing, screaming, weeping chaos of hand-to-hand combat roaring in his ears as he momentarily exulted at the sight of his warriors assaulting the Britons with all the savagery of the tribesmen they still were at heart, bellowing a command over the tumult to give his men the last order they would need.

'The eagle! *To the eagle!*'

Kivilaz's men were already ripping into the ranks of the Britons, the swordsmen either turning to face them or dying without ever seeing their killers, while the Batavi fought with deadly purpose, focused only on killing the men in front of them and carving a bloody swathe through the enemy warriors. The man to Draco's left died with a sword thrust through his throat, and Kivilaz, fighting alongside him, smashed away another tribesman's sword with his shield before pivoting to ram his gladius into his killer's belly with a bellow of rage at his comrade's loss. While his men pulled their dying comrade's body back into the protection of their ranks, uncontrollably coughing and spluttering bloody spittle in his choking death throes, the centurion abruptly threw himself into the fray with berserk speed, hacking to left and right as he carved his way deep into the host of Britons.

'With him!'

Draco led the press of men in the prince's wake, realising that the younger man had lost himself in the rage that was coursing through him. As each man he encountered fell, whether stabbed through or simply smashed aside by a shield punch, the arrowhead of Batavi warriors close behind him put them to the sword without compunction, the prefect at their head realising that he was experiencing something that he had only ever heard in the tribe's songs of wars and heroes from days long departed. Feeling the blood coursing through his body as a dull roaring in his ears, he took advantage of a momentary lull as Kivilaz fought shield to shield with a quick-handed warrior, pushing his sword's point down into the turf, switching the shield to his right hand and then taking the weapon's hilt in his left in the way he had been taught by his father, drilled through hour upon hour of practice until his skill with the other hand was almost as good as with his right. Kivilaz put his man down with a sword thrust to the thigh that left the Briton staggering, staring stupidly as blood sprayed from the wound, and Draco stepped up alongside him, tapping his shield's boss with his own as he slid into position.

'See the eagle?'

The centurion looked up, nodding. The first cohort's embattled remnant was holding, just, and the golden standard was a flicker of the morning's pale light as it bobbed with the exertions of the men surrounding it. The two men shared a moment of understanding before glancing around them at the warriors behind them on either side, set and ready to attack again, and Draco lifted his shield in readiness to move forward into the press of the enemy.

'This time we go all the way through them! And we don't stop until we reach that standard!'

Kivilaz nodded, his face hardening.

'For Hercules!'

Draco grinned.

'Not this time! This one's for our own god! For Magusanus!' He lunged forward, the men at his back baying for blood as he led them into the enemy. *'And for glory!'*

I

River Rhenus, August AD 69

'Did you hear that?'

'Hear what?'

The oldest of the four men around the fire shook his head, then stood, spitting onto the ground and walking a few paces away from the flames' dim light. He lifted his tunic and grunted a sigh of pleasure at the sensation of the first flow, addressing the youngest of his tent party comrades over his shoulder with a note of scorn.

'You're in the country, you idiot!'

The murmuring voices of the men gathered around the neighbouring fires was the only sound to be heard over the quiet eddies and ripples of the great river. In the wake of the battle by the Rhenus, the scene of a complete defeat for several Roman auxiliary cohorts in the face of treachery by the Tungri, whose camp fires now studded the riverbank, the corpses of the men killed in the brief, one-sided fight had been dragged onto a pyre and burnt with minimal ceremony. The reek of burning flesh hung over the Tungri camp, and many of the soldiers had found the meat they had been given to roast over their fires hard to stomach, preferring instead to drink heavily from the beer supplied to them by their Batavi allies, in whose betrayal of Rome they were now complicit. The surviving five men of the tent party had positioned their own fire as close to the river as possible and as far from the pyre's still glowing remnant as they could, a good twenty paces from the closest of their comrades, their proximity to the water helping to mitigate the stench of burning flesh. Their centurion, had he been present, might well have ordered them to relocate further from the bushes that lined the river, but in his absence their choice of location had gone unchallenged. The cohort's remaining officers were too tired and drunk with success to care, several centurions having chosen not to join the Batavi cause but instead to return home. With the camp sunk in the impenetrable darkness of a moonless night, most of its occupants had surrendered to the oblivion of exhaustion and alcohol, leaving only the few who were unable to sleep to while away the night hours with desultory conversation. The urinating soldier, the de facto leader of the five men who remained of their tent party after the battle, snorted derisively at his younger comrade.

'And in the country there are animals, right? Pigs? Deer? Badgers? And they all make noises, don't they, which might scare a man raised in Tungrorum but don't mean a thing to us country boys. Ain't that right, Tritos?'

The fifth member of their group had vanished into the darkness a moment before with the bald statement that he needed to defecate, and since he was a man of few words nobody was especially surprised when he failed to respond to the question with anything more eloquent than a muffled grunt. The tent party's leader shook his manhood to make sure that he wasn't going to spot his tunic with urine as he continued his monologue, a knowing hint of sarcasm creeping into his voice.

'Good old Tritos, now he's got no imagination so he ain't worried. He's not going to let a pig's snuffling put him off curling out—'

With an almost imperceptible rustle of metal, a massive figure rose out of the bushes behind the three men he was addressing, scale-armoured and bareheaded, his eyes hard points of reflected firelight in a face whose brutal lines were accentuated by a thick crop of black stubble. Striking with sudden, whiplash speed, he thrust the full length of a bloody-bladed, army-issue dagger sideways into the throat of the nearest soldier with his left hand, driving the weapon's wide blade through his neck to sever the dying man's windpipe, arteries and vocal cords in a spray of blood. Spinning through a half-circle so fast that the gladius in his other hand was an indistinct silver blur in its lethal arc, he punched its blade though the armour of the soldier on his other side, the scrape of its iron length sliding through the rent torn in his mail by its point, and his agonised grunt as the weapon stopped his heart was no more than brief punctuation in the havoc. Leaving the blade where it was, he reached out and snatched a handful of the third man's mail at the collar without even looking at him, his attention fixed on the urinating soldier who was yet to realise the depth of his predicament, then wrenched the hapless Tungrian towards him, turning at the last moment to punch his victim in the face and knocking the hapless soldier senseless. Then, as the stunned soldier's legs crumpled, his weight held up only by his assailant's brute strength, the big man lowered him to the ground and turned back to the last of them who, having eventually woken up to the horror being visited upon them and, with his hands still on his penis, was drawing breath to scream a warning when the dagger's blade snapped through his spine at the base of his neck and dropped him twitching to the ground.

'No better than children . . .'

He sheathed the knife and retrieved his sword from the corpse in which it was embedded, the dead man's ribs cracking as he stamped down to free the iron blade. He then hoisted the unconscious soldier over one shoulder and withdrew from the fire's faint circle of illumination, hurrying silently away through the darkness. Finding the hide that he had cut into a thicket of bushes a hundred paces from the camp's edge, he dumped the unconscious soldier into the dew-slick grass and pulled on his campaign cloak, a carefully chosen shade of dun that the officers of his previous legion had treated with lofty disdain, their own garments tending to favour brighter, showier colours, but which faded easily into the night's monochrome landscape.

'You wouldn't be laughing now, would you? Not that any of you would even have got off that battlefield alive.'

His face hardened at the memory of his small army's abject defeat the previous day. In less than the space of a hundred heartbeats his command of three apparently loyal cohorts of auxiliary soldiers and five hundred loyalist Batavi cavalrymen, fresh formations arrayed in a defensive position made seemingly impregnable by the protection of heavy naval artillery support from a fleet moored at their backs, had been reduced to little better than a rabble. Aquillius grimaced, as he recalled the moment at which their cohesion had been shattered by one cohort's treachery, another's terror-stricken disintegration under their former comrades' swords and the third's abject surrender under attack from both foe and alleged friend. The one cohort that had remained loyal and steadfast despite the Batavi's exhortations to them to desert had been flayed by bolt throwers turned upon them by the mutinous crews of warships moored behind them, while their more unsteady Frisian comrades had disintegrated under the assault of the treacherous Tungrians. Tungrians with whom, Aquillius had little doubt, the Batavian prince Civilis had long since agreed the moment and nature of their betrayal. The crowning insult had been the swift retreat that Labeo, the apparently loyal commander of the Batavian cavalry, had ordered in the face of the sudden catastrophic defeat. Not that the Roman would have blamed him for protecting his men from certain defeat, if he had not already been utterly convinced that the prefect's true sympathies lay not with Rome but with his countrymen, the very rebels he professed to despise. The soldier at his feet began to stir, and the big man drew his pugio, putting the dagger's bloody blade across the groaning soldier's throat.

'Quiet. If you cry out, I'll cut your throat.'

He waited a moment for the threat and the weapon's overpowering smell of blood to sink in, tensing to rip the dagger across his captive's throat as the soldier drew breath to answer.

'You'll kill me anyway.'

The dull certainty in the boy's voice bought a smile to his captor's face.

'I won't. If I have one weakness, it is my sense of honour. It is the reason why I am here, cowering under a bush with a knife to the throat of a boy young enough to be my son, rather than commanding the five thousand men of the Eighth Augustan

Legion far from this barbarian Hades. So when I tell you that I will let you live, *if* you tell me what I want to know and don't try to attract your comrades, then that is what will happen.' He yawned. 'I'm tired and irritable, so make a decision whether you want to live or die quickly, before I make it for you.'

The Tungrian looked at him for a moment, seeing the certainty of his death in the older man's hard eyes.

'You'll spare my life?'

'You'll talk?'

'What do you want to know?'

The big man nodded, withdrawing the dagger and sliding it back into the intricately decorated scabbard on his belt.

'Your cohort betrayed us. Why?'

The soldier shrugged.

'We have served Rome since before my grandfather was born. And Rome has given us much in that time, but of late . . .'

He looked up momentarily, and the other man's lips creased in amusement as he realised that the boy was trying to remember the arguments he'd heard in the Tungrians' barracks, discussions that must have raged briefly as his older colleagues turned away from the empire's service and plotted the momentous step of rising in rebellion against their imperial masters.

'Your people have treated us more like subjects than allies. And when you ordered us to kill Kivilaz of the Batavi—'

The Roman leaned forward, the speed of his movement disconcerting the boy enough to make him shrink back into the bush behind him.

'I have heard this story. You were there, when the Batavian prince talked his way out of his own assassination?'

Transfixed by the older man's stare, the Tungrian shook his head hurriedly.

'No! But I know men who were. Kivilaz persuaded them not to end him. He told them that they were being used by Rome in a way that would result in war between our tribes.'

'And that it would be better for the Tungri and the Batavi to unite against Rome?'

The boy nodded.

'He came to our barracks in the Old Camp in secret, and met with the centurions wearing a tunic marked with the blood of the officer who had been sent to kill him, murdered by one of his own men when Kivilaz pointed out that to take his life would sign all their death warrants.'

The big man nodded reluctant respect.

'He must have balls the size of apples, to confront the very men who had accepted our gold to remove his threat to Roman rule. And the betrayal yesterday – it was agreed in advance?'

The boy nodded.

'Yes. We were told the previous night, in camp, but the centurions had agreed with Kivilaz months before that when the time came they were his men.'

His captor fell silent for a moment before asking his next question.

'And what happened after the battle? What did Kivilaz do with your prefect? I suppose he was tortured, as you Germans like to do with Romans you capture?'

The soldier shook his head.

'The prince had already issued orders for him to be disarmed, but not to be harmed. The prefect was freed on condition that he return home and take no further part in the war, and the rest of us were offered the choice between serving under Batavi command or leaving with a share of the spoils of your defeat.'

'And?'

'Most of us chose to stay and fight with our brothers the Batavi, although some of our older centurions decided to go home.'

The other man nodded.

'They have enough money saved to be comfortable in retirement I'd imagine, and if they fought in Britannia they'll know what happens when you pull Rome's nose.' The young soldier looked at him blankly. 'What happens when you pull Rome's nose, boy, is that Rome gets a hard-on the size of a tent pole, rolls you over and takes you dry. You people have chosen their side cleverly in the short term, while the empire's attention is fixed on the war for the throne, but when that's settled you have a rude awakening in store. Rome doesn't tolerate rebellion. Now close your eyes.'

'But you promised . . .'

His captor snorted mirthlessly.

'I'm not going to kill you. Not unless you try to work out which direction I'm heading in when I leave you here.'

The soldier shut his eyes, and the big man pulled the scarf that protected the Tungrian's skin of his neck from the bite of his mail's collar rings, tying it around his head as a blindfold.

'I'll be watching you. Count to five hundred before you remove that scarf unless you want to meet your ancestors with your throat cut. Just tell anyone that asks who killed your tent mates that Centurion Aquillius isn't done with you treacherous scum yet. Not by a long way.'

The sound of his withdrawal from the hiding place died away to absolute silence, but just as the soldier was starting to feel the temptation to remove the blindfold a voice spoke quietly in his ear, so close that he lost control of his bowels in an irresistible surging rush of foul-smelling liquid.

'I'm still watching you.'

Aquillius smiled to himself as he turned and padded away from the bush, knowing that his former captive would stay where he was for far longer than the count of five hundred, pacing carefully away through the darkness to the west and making what he knew only too well would be the dubious safety of Roman territory.

Germania Superior, August AD 69

'Fighters . . . are you ready?'

Egilhard looked across the fighting ring's sandy floor, scuffed and marked by thousands of hobnailed boot prints, and raised his blunt-edged sparring sword as a signal to the arbiter that he was ready to fight. The soldier facing him did the same, his cruel, scarred face set hard as he stared directly at the young soldier facing him in a naked attempt at intimidation. The man standing between them raised his voice again to remind the men of their respective centuries, gathered in the heat of a late summer's afternoon to witness the bout that would decide who was the First Batavi cohort's champion swordsman, of the rules they already knew all too well.

'Three touches on arm or leg wins the fight! One touch on the chest and one on arm or leg wins the fight! One touch on the head wins the fight! If there are no touches by the time the count has run out, then the winner will be decided by me! Fighters, prepare to fight!'

He smiled at the older man, feeling his eyes narrow in genuine amusement not just at the comically serious look on the other man's face but with the sudden memory of something his uncle Frijaz had told him one evening, shortly before his departure from the Island to join the Batavi cohorts.

'There'll always be some prick who tries to get one over on you in the ring by giving it the eyes, right? Two things to remember when that happens . . .' Frijaz had taken a sip of his beer before continuing. 'First thing is that they're not half as hard as they'd like to have you think, or they wouldn't need to be giving it the eyes in the first place, would they? And the one thing that really pisses off a man that's trying to stare you out is just to grin back at him, a nice big smile, like you haven't got a worry in the world.' He'd drunk again, shaking his head and smiling at some memory or other. 'The usual reaction is some stupid fucking comeback like, "I'll have that smile off your face" or "You won't be fucking smiling when I'm done with you, boy", giving it the hard man voice too. And when they do that, that's the moment when you put the knife in, good and quick, right?'

The scar-faced soldier spat on the sand, shaking his head at the younger man.

'You'll lose the smile soon enough, pup!'

Egilhard raised an eyebrow and cocked his head to one side, feeling the tight grin broaden to a quizzical smile.

'Seems to me that given you're the only one here slow enough to have had his looks spoiled, I'll probably still be smiling when this is done.'

His opponent's face darkened, his lips pursing tight with anger at the jibe's failure and the insult to both his prowess and his appearance.

'I was going to go easy with you, boy! But perhaps I'll just play with you for a while instead! You ain't got the strength in you for a long match, so I think I'll take my time breaking you in!'

The younger man laughed aloud, unable to prevent himself rising to the other man's bombast.

'And the fact that you imagine you'll have any choice in the matter of how fast this bout ends means I can add stupidity to ugliness, I suppose!'

That got a laugh from the watching soldiers of their two centuries, and the older soldier hammered the flat of his training sword against his shield's flat surface.

'Let's fight! I'll put this upstart in his place soon enough!'

The arbiter looked at them in turn, satisfying himself that both men were ready to begin the match, then nodded and stepped out from between their swords and shields.

'Fighters . . . fight! Start the count!'

Egilhard's opponent stormed straight in, bulling at the younger man's shield with his own and following up with an attempted stab over its metal rim, going straight for his opponent's face in a strike calculated to split the skin with the weapon's rounded end and leave him scarred for the rest of his life. Swaying to his right, the young soldier watched the blade as it swept past his head, time seeming to slow in the way it always did for him when battle commenced, flicking his own blade up to catch his opponent's fingers with a sharp tap that bared his teeth in pain and ensured that the arbiter spotted the strike.

'One touch!'

They stepped apart, as the rule of the contest demanded, the scarred soldier staring at Egilhard with a predatory focus as he crabbed around to his left, looking to put his blade on his opponent's unshielded side, the younger man turning to face him with every step.

'We can go round in circles for the rest of the afternoon if you like.'

The other man was silent now, his previous show of anger replaced by the cold calculation of a man who had realised that rage could only result in his defeat, and he ignored the jibe, continuing his slow circle to the left while his eyes ceaselessly searched for an opportunity to strike. A bead of sweat ran down Egilhard's temple and into the corner of his eye, and as he blinked away its salty prickle, the other man was in motion, swinging his blade up and round to hack a ferocious backhanded blow at his opponent's unguarded side. Stepping back, Egilhard angled his own weapon to parry the blow upwards, pushing their two swords high and wide even as he swung his shield round to the right, smashing the metal rim into his opponent's sword arm hard enough to make him drop the weapon, then swung his own blade low to find the grimacing soldier's left knee, his strike hard enough to make his opponent shout with the pain.

'*Two touches! Trainer!*'

The scar-faced soldier's second hurried forward, only to be waved away by the now openly furious soldier as he retrieved his sword and turned to face Egilhard.

'You can fuck off! I can still fight, and I can still do this little cunt! All it needs is one tap on his helmet! *Come on!*'

He sprang forward, cutting furiously at the younger man in a wild-eyed attempt to put him on the back foot, punching with his shield in a manner calculated to push his opponent off balance and open him up for his sword, a continual rain of attacks with boss and sword, which Egilhard rode with relative ease as he backed away from the ceaseless attack. Beginning to tire, the scar-faced soldier stumbled slightly and the younger man took his opportunity, punching back with his shield while his opponent was momentarily off balance to open up his left side, then spinning away to the left, ducking a wild sword swing and cutting with his own weapon at the other man's ankles. With a yell of agony his opponent fell heavily to the ground, throwing his weapons aside to clutch at his leg as he rode the pain of the dull iron blade's impact.

'*Three touches! The winner is . . .*' The arbiter stepped forward and took Egilhard's sword hand, raising hand and weapon into the air above their heads. '*Egilhard of the Second Century! Champion of the First Cohort!*'

The men of his century, silent until that moment in respect for the rules of the contest, erupted into cheers and whistles, his tent mates rushing forward to engulf the bemused champion and lift him onto their shoulders despite his protestations. Their leading man Grimmaz turned to face the men of the other century with clenched fists raised in celebration, the tendons of his neck standing out as he roared at them triumphantly.

'*Victory to Achilles!*'

His comrades lowered Egilhard to the ground, and he turned to salute his defeated opponent who had waited patiently for the celebration to quieten. The two men saluted each other, the older soldier nodding with a wry smile now that his pain-born rage had burned out to be replaced with the dull ache of defeat, calling out the words that were expected of him.

'I respect the tribe's traditions! Enemies until the last touch, brothers again from that moment.' He limped forward, the ankle still painful, holding out a hand. 'You're good, young 'un, and not just with the sword either. You can stand next to me in the line any time.'

The younger man bowed his head, the gesture drawing surprised stares from the men around them.

'This is one thing, but battle is another matter. I saw you fight at Cremona, and standing alongside you would be an honour.'

His opponent's dour face cracked in a slow smile.

'You really *are* good, aren't you? And not just with your father's sword either. I predict big things for you, lad. Now go and get pissed with your mates, the way it's supposed to be when you become champion.'

Watching from the edge of the ring, Banon, the Second

Century's chosen man, mused quietly to his centurion without taking his eyes off the young soldier as he was reclaimed by his ecstatic comrades and hoisted back onto their shoulders. Taut muscles moved under his tunic as he leaned against the rough wooden fence, watching the scene through hard blue eyes with his blond bearded chin resting on a scarred fist.

'A good match. And there's not another man in the cohort who could have offered him any more of a fight.'

Alcaeus, half a head taller than his subordinate, and with brown eyes, which, along with his black hair, tended to lead to good natured accusations of there being a Roman somewhere in his ancestry, nodded with an approving expression. Long experienced at gauging the temper and quality of his men after twenty years' service that had lifted him to the ranks of both centurion, deputy to the cohorts' prefect Scar, and wolf-priest, the most senior of the men who provided spiritual leadership to the tribe's warriors, he watched with an expert eye as the young soldier laughed and joked with his tent mates, raising his hands self-deprecatingly and shaking his head when his comrades feigned adulation by bowing and fawning over him.

'It doesn't seem to be going to his head.'

Banon nodded.

'Couldn't blame him if it had. He's done things on the battle-field I couldn't begin to understand, never mind emulate. Remember that axeman he put down at the battle of Cremona?'

Alcaeus grinned at the memory of the wiry soldier, little more than a recruit on the day that two would-be emperors' armies had met in a titanic clash of arms at the river Po, despite the fact that he had already killed for the tribe. In the course of the fighting he had stepped forward to face a giant of a marine with a viciously hooked boarding axe, seeming hopelessly over-matched against a rampaging monster of a man who had already torn a gap in their century's line with the terrible speed and ferocity of his attack. As the men around him had involuntarily cowered away from the terrible weapon's bloody rending blows, Egilhard had stepped in close, first raising his shield to expertly disarm the marine and then, with two swift and clinical spear blows, leaving him dying in the battlefield's blood-foamed mud.

'How could I have forgotten? And it's not as if he looks the part either.'

Banon nodded.

'Deceptive. That's the word you're looking for. So he's got all the makings of a hero but he doesn't ride the high horse, not ever. That's partly your doing, of course.'

His centurion shrugged with a small smile.

'His father gave him a good talking to before he left him, I believe, and warned him what happens to men who try too hard. All I did was take him aside, after the battle at the farm, when he'd killed his first—'

'And his second.'

'And his second. I told him what usually happens to heroes, how long they tend to last once the expectations on them become too much for any man to live up to without taking risks that the rest of us could never consider. I told him that Lataz and Frijaz were no fools for all their joking, and that Lataz's son and Frijaz's brother-son won't be any sort of fool either. Seems like he was listening.' Banon nodded silently. 'He'll have the chance to use those skills in anger again soon enough though. Another few weeks' march will see us over the mountains and back in Italy, and then the fun will really begin. The latest messages from Rome to the young tribune they sent to fetch us back to rejoin the legions say that Vespasianus's army is coming west from Judea and Syria, picking up the legions of the Danubius along the way. There's a battle coming, Banon, another one like Cremona except with a real enemy rather than a young fool with less between his ears than that boy over there, so I don't expect we'll won't get off so lightly next time, not if we take our rightful place in the line. A lot of us will go to meet Magusanus that day.'

The chosen man shrugged.

'It's what we do, Centurion. You know that better than anyone. You've had the dream again, I presume?'

'The dream. Yes . . .' He fell silent for a long moment, staring blankly at the horizon. 'Yes, I dream of battle, of death and blood. And the dream always ends with that same image of young Achilles there. But yes, Banon, it's what we do. So I should stop complaining and get on with it?'

His friend grinned.

'With all due respect to your august place in the tribe as a wolf-priest . . . yes.'

Alcaeus shook his head with a wry laugh.

'Very well, Chosen Man, since you insist. Get that miserable old bastard Hludovig off his arse and chase this lot back to their tents. Now that we've crowned Egilhard as master of all he surveys, just as long as he has a sword in his hands, we can get back to being ready to march first thing in the morning. Rest days are all very well, but they won't get us over the mountains before the passes close for the winter. And Scar tells me he has no intention of trying to emulate Hannibal. We march south at first light.'

The Winter Camp, Mogontiacum, August AD 69

'A good turnout, First Spear. You are as usual to be congratulated on both the appearance and the efficiency of your men.'

Centurion Antonius nodded briskly in acknowledgement of his superior's compliment, careful to invest the gesture with sufficient respect without appearing overly obsequious. Shorter than most of his colleagues, he lacked the bulk that many of them used to command respect, as in consequence his nose had the appearance of having been broken and reset too many times to have retained its original lines, but if the men who served under him knew one thing with crystal clarity, it was that while affable enough under the right circumstances, he was by dint of his hard route to the top of his profession a dangerous man to cross.

'Thank you, Legatus. It is our duty to ensure that the men we have been left with are as capable and ready for war as those who were selected to march south with the emperor.'

His superior had cut a frustrated figure since the bulk of his Twenty-Second Primigenia had marched south under the command of the Fourth Legion's legatus, but had quickly channelled that frustration into a single-minded drive to ensure that his command was capable of meeting any threat to the massive fortress's weakened garrison, and his men had responded well to their leader's brisk no-nonsense approach to his responsibilities. With Antonius as his new first spear, promoted from the legion's centurionate on the recommendation of his predecessor Secundus, who had himself marched south to war with six cohorts, they had settled into a routine of training and aggressive patrolling intended to demonstrate their readiness for action both to the local tribes and any doubters within their own ranks. Freed from the petty restrictions of peacetime soldiering by a legion commander interested only in results, Antonius had seized his opportunity to build a reputation as a no-nonsense seeker of military effectiveness, riding his centurions hard enough to ensure that he delivered what was expected of him and yet not so hard as to foster discontent.

Legatus Vocula held his stare for a moment, nodding sagely at his senior centurion's words.

'Indeed it is. These ten cohorts that remain carry a heavy responsibility, as do we. The Winter Camp is the nail that holds the entire German frontier together, First Spear, which is ironically the *stated* reason I was asked to accept the duty of remaining here to command what remains of these two legions, rather than being given the honour of leading the other ten cohorts south to fight for the throne. Although the fact that I'm something of a new boy to the ranks of the purple-striped and weak-chinned might also have been a factor.'

Antonius inclined his head slightly, knowing better than to comment on matters he had little chance of fully comprehending, and the legatus flashed him a hard grin. The son of an equestrian from the province of Hispania, and the first man in his family to ascend to the godlike heights of the senatorial class, he had consequently needed to be better than his fellows to enjoy the same degree of respect, a challenge to which he had risen with considerable success.

'I know, you can hardly be expected to comment. But I'd wager good money that while you agree with me as to the importance of our responsibility, you still wish you'd gone south to challenge Otho?'

The senior centurion nodded, carefully controlling the urge to smile back at his superior.

'Yes, Legatus. I do have my . . . reservations about remaining here while the rest of the army marches over the Alps in search of glory. They will return here in due course, whether they've won or lost, in possession of one massive advantage over the rest of us. They will have seen battle, Legatus, which will make them—'

'Unbearably smug? I expect so!' Unable to control his expression, Antonius smiled at his superior's perfectly timed interjection as the legatus continued. 'Yes, they'll come back here with torques and phalerae and the self-satisfied air of men who've seen the face of the battle and lived, although whether they'll have distinguished themselves in that fight will be entirely another matter. But they may not be the only men who'll see battle this year. You might well greet them back into the camp with honours of your own to display, and won in more arduous circumstances than a single battle on a warm spring afternoon.'

'You think we'll see combat? But . . .'

'How? Not in the civil war, that's pretty much certain. The last that I heard, Vespasianus's army was marching for Italy, collecting friendly forces along the way. The decisive encounter will probably happen somewhere on the plains of the Po valley, just like Cremona back in April. And who knows which way such an encounter might go? But that's not what's on my mind.'

'You're thinking of the revolt of the Batavians?'

Vocula nodded.

'Yes. It's easy to imagine that they'll pose no more of a threat to us here than Vespasianus's men, given the distance between us, but such a view might well be . . . near-sighted.'

'They are almost two hundred and fifty hundred miles distant, Legatus. I fail to see how they're likely to offer us battle from that far away.'

The legatus nodded his understanding, lowering his voice to a conspiratorial tone.

'That, strictly between you and I, First Spear, is because you're not privy to the intelligence that I see. The official story is that the Batavians have been pinned back in their tribal lands next to the sea, with two legions to keep them in their place. It's being painted as a local rebellion, to be contained until our detachments return from the south and we have sufficient strength to deal with them with the appropriate vigour and make an example of what happens when subject nations choose to revolt.'

'But that isn't all there is to it, Legatus?'

Vocula shook his head.

'No, Antonius, that's far from all there is to it. For a start, there are the eight cohorts of their troops that were camped here until a few days ago, sent north to their homeland by Vitellius as a reward for their leading part at Cremona. Now they've been ordered south again, to rejoin the army that will face the challenger Vespasianus's legions. Although whether they'll do that as formed cohorts or simply as scattered battle replacements is another matter. I'd break them up if it were my decision, and remove the threat that they might mutiny. But more importantly than that are the things we're *not* telling the troops about the rebellion to the north. We're not telling them that it's not just the Batavians who are up in arms. Half a dozen other tribes have risen with them, and the Germans across the river are flocking to their leader Civilis's banner. There are probably twice as many of them as we have men in the Old Camp, and if they get it into their heads to destroy that fortress then we really will have problems.'

Antonius nodded slowly.

'So you think we might see action?'

The legatus shrugged.

'I couldn't say, in all truth. But keep your men ready to march at an hour's notice, boots shod, rations ready and iron sharper than a swindled whore's tongue, eh? Because when the time comes, I don't think we're going to get all that much warning.'

Germania Inferior, August AD 69

'You're certain this is the place?'

Kivilaz answered his companion's question without looking up from the lines he was drawing in the dust with the point of his dagger.

'I'm certain. The officer who carried the legatus augusti's message was very specific that the meeting would take place at dawn, at the fork in the road where the two roads from Batavodurum lead to the Old Camp or Tungrorum. So unless there are two such locations, this is where Hordeonius Flaccus wanted to speak with me.'

'That, or have an assassin put a poisoned arrow into you.'

The prince laughed out loud.

'You really were in Rome too long, weren't you, Hramn? Perhaps we should start calling you by your Roman name again? Would you prefer to be Julius Victor among the men of the tribe?'

He raised a hand to deflect Hramn's ire.

'I'm joking with you, man! Every boy in our family has been *gifted* with a Roman name since Julius Caesar took a shine to us all those many years ago, and I can't say that I find *Victor* all that bad a name for you to be carrying – if you can live up to it!'

His nephew shook his head with a sour expression.

'I've sworn never to use that name again, not after what Galba did to our honour by sending my men of the German Bodyguard home. The fool. And if he fell victim to assassins, so can you!'

'Galba was killed because that fool Otho managed to bribe two dozen praetorians to do the job for him. But assassins with poisoned arrows don't do very good business out here on what the Romans call "the edge of the world", because in these parts most men who want someone dead tend to pick up a sword and try to make it happen themselves.'

The younger man shook his head in amusement, scratching at his scalp through a thick mane of dirty blond hair, blue eyes flashing in evident disbelief.

'With all that they've put you through, how can you still underestimate the Romans? Three years commanding the Bodyguard in Rome taught me everything I'll ever need or want to know about those cunning, devious, murdering bastards. They're all at it, from the emperor himself to the lowest beggar, all thumbing their blades and wondering who to kill next for their money, or their woman, or even just for sport. They put tens of thousands of men to death in their arenas every year, and that's just the gladiators, expensive property that their owners can ill afford to lose. The gods only know how many poor innocents die for the entertainment of the scum that populate Rome, rich and poor alike.'

Kivilaz looked up from his doodling in the dirt at the roadside.

'I asked the same question of my host, Petillius Cerialis, Vespasianus's son-in-law, while I was enjoying the hospitality of his home, in the days after Galba found me innocent of the charge of treason that saw my brother executed. He told me, proudly, mind you, that the games consume fifty thousand lives a year: slaves and Jews who die on the sand for their entertainment. So no, Hramn, despite the fact that my time in the city was limited, I don't underestimate their murderous ways. But neither am I willing to overestimate their capabilities. And besides, the land to either side of the road is crawling with your guardsmen, I presume?'

The big man smiled smugly, looking about him with a proprietorial air.

'I did take the opportunity to send a century of my men out here in advance of our leaving Batavodurum. You can't be too careful when it comes to—'

'There.' Kivilaz pointed down the road to the south. 'There are your devious murderers.'

Hramn turned and looked down the road to the Old Camp, pulling a face at the small cavalry bodyguard that accompanied a horse-drawn carriage. Kivilaz sheathed the knife and waited for the newcomers to reach the spot where the two men stood, while Hramn summoned a tent party of his guardsmen, formerly proud members of the emperor's German Bodyguard, nodding his approval as they stepped out in front of the prince with their shields raised. Halting twenty paces distant, the carriage swayed as a heavily built Roman dismounted with painful care before turning to address them.

'Prince Gaius Julius Civilis, known to his countrymen as Kivilaz, I presume? And that must be your nephew Julius Victor, who I believe prefers to be known as Hramn, former commander of the emperor's bodyguard. I see the centurion bearing my message reached you, and that since you're here, you are presumably agreeable to the idea of our indulging in some . . . shall we say . . . *undocumented* discussion with regard to our mutual problem?'

Kivilaz grinned back at him.

'Legatus Augusti Marcus Hordeonius Flaccus, commanding general of the legions of Roman Germania. And that's not a presumption, it's a cast-iron fact. There couldn't be two men of your stature in positions of command on this frontier.'

Flaccus shrugged equably at the jibe.

'I sincerely hope not. I cut a unique figure and I intend to keep it that way.'

The Batavi leader turned to his prefect, dropping into their own language while the Roman listened impassively.

'I'm going for a walk with the Legatus Augusti. Try not to start anything vigorous while we're away, eh, Hramn? You'll have the chance to work off that sense of righteous indignation on the battlefield soon enough.'

Flaccus nodded briskly to the decurion commanding his escort and strolled forward to meet the prince, extending a hand to point down the road back towards Batavodurum.

'I think, given the degree of trust you've shown in coming out here to meet me, that I should reciprocate and stroll a little way further into your tribe's lands. Shall we?'

The two men walked in silence until they were out of earshot of their escorts, Flaccus looking about him at the neat, well-ordered fields.

'But this is just like Italy, if a little colder. And how unlike all that nonsense the writers tell us about the far north, the edge of the world with impenetrable forests, unclimbable mountains and bottomless marshes.'

Kivilaz smiled at the conversational gambit.

'I had plenty of time to consider the obvious similarities during my journey to Rome after my first arrest on the charge of treason, once the bruising from several beatings had subsided enough that I could see. And you're right, this is nothing like the way it's portrayed to your people. Of course if you want to see forests, mountains and bogs, all you need to do is take a boat across the water to Britannia.'

'You fought in Claudius's campaign to bring the Britons into the empire, I believe?'

Kivilaz laughed curtly.

'Claudius's campaign? The war I fought in was mainly prosecuted by a pair of legion commanders by the names of Gaius Hosidius Geta and Titus Flavius Vespasianus. But then you know Vespasianus, don't you? The man the eastern legions have declared to be their emperor must surely be an acquaintance of yours, given the small circle you senators move in?'

Flaccus echoed his barking laugh.

'Your countryman Claudius Labeo said you were sharp! I'll—'

The Batavi turned sharply, his eyes narrowed in anger.

'Leave that treacherous fool out of this discussion! And you can warn him that I'll have his head the next time I see him across a battlefield, whether the men of the Batavian cavalry wing stand between us or not.'

Flaccus raised a conciliatory hand.

'I understand your anger at your countryman having chosen Rome as the side he'll take, if this comes to serious fighting. We all have to make our choices and then live with the consequences, don't we? And yes, I know Titus Flavius Vespasianus well enough, from the difficult days of Nero's court. Well enough to trust him implicitly. Well enough, in fact . . .' he looked around himself reflexively, 'to know that he'll make a better emperor than Vitellius could ever hope to be even if he lived to be a hundred years old.'

He waited for the other man to respond, a slight smile his only reaction to Kivilaz's evident disbelief.

'You're trying to tell me that you favour Vespasianus over your own emperor? That you'd prefer the victory of a challenger from the distant east rather than the man who put you in the position you hold and who is somewhat closer to hand?'

Flaccus shook his head.

'In all truth I said no such thing, Prince Kivilaz. I simply pointed out the relative merits of the two men, without ever denying the loyalty I am of course bound to declare for my imperial master.'

'And . . . ?'

The Roman looked away across the farmland.

'I believe you received a visit from an old friend of mine recently? A man by the name of Gaius Plinius Secundus? I expect that he made a promise to you on behalf of Titus Flavius Vespasianus, a solemn undertaking that, in the event of his victory over Vitellius with your active support here on the German frontier, he would grant your people irrevocable self-governance over their own affairs.' He paused for a moment, fixing the German with a knowing smile. 'That, and the right to appoint a king if that were the tribe's will, of course. You would be allied to Rome, but independent of Rome. Am I right?'

Kivilaz nodded slowly.

'I met with Plinius. And yes, he requested certain favours on the behalf of Vespasianus, in return for certain assurances as to imperial policy in the event of his master becoming emperor.'

'I expected that would be the case. He and I met in Colonia Agrippina several days before he rode on to your city, and reached an accommodation of our own.'

The Batavi frowned, his expression wary.

'You actually agreed to take Vespasianus's side?'

Flaccus smiled disingenuously.

'We discussed how the German legions might best be employed over the next few months, while Vespasianus's legions make their way from the east to join with the legions on the Danubius which have declared for his cause. We discussed how disappointed Vitellius would be, were he unable to draw any further reinforcements from the army on the Rhenus. And we hypothesised, Prince Kivilaz, purely speculatively of course, as to how even the most short-lived rebellion on this frontier would be enough to prevent that reinforcement.'

'Did you also speculate on the impact the loss of the Batavian cohorts would have on Vitellius's army?'

The Roman shook his head in evident admiration.

'Straight to the point, eh, Kivilaz? We might have discussed the potential for that risk to become a reality, and what it would mean . . .'

The two men stood in silence for a moment.

'So in short,' Kivilaz shot a piercing glance at the Roman, 'the two of you spent your entire time together speculating as to what might be the impact of a tide of events here in Germania flowing against Vitellius's plans, something which, *strangely* enough, has now come to pass?'

Flaccus smiled again.

'You have the nub of it.'

'I see. And this is all very interesting. But tell me, Legatus Augusti, would I be correct in my expectation that, were you to be questioned on the subject later, your purpose in inviting me here was clearly *not* that of inviting me to join you in a plot to make it appear as if the Batavi are revolting, while in reality our armies would do little more than posture at each other?' He looked at Flaccus questioningly, and the Roman spread his hands in silent comment. 'I see. So, given that this meeting is apparently *not* an invitation to collude with you in such a way, my only question is just what guarantees you *might* have offered me, if you *had* come here to make such an invitation?'

Flaccus pursed his lips, and made a show of thinking for a moment.

'Guarantees? I have nothing to offer by way of any sort of guarantee. But I can perhaps make a suggestion? When my legions march into your territory, as must be my next step given your brilliant victory over the auxiliary cohorts I sent to deal with you, there is a particular response on your part that would perfectly fulfil the need for you to defend your land and people without resulting in an all-out war with Rome.'

Kivilaz nodded.

'I'm listening.'

The Old Camp, Germania Inferior, August AD 69

'Enemy tribesmen to the front! Form line of battle!'

Marius watched with professional detachment as the men of his leading cohort switched from their routine marching gait to the double pace, the leading century spreading out to either side of their front rank and each successive century hurrying to left and right across the Old Camp's parade ground as they converted the Fifth Alaudae's marching column into a battle line four men deep, the two cohorts following in their train marching to the left and right respectively at the same urgent pace and moving to take up their positions on either side of the rapidly widening line. Behind them came the six cohorts of their sister legion the Fifteenth Primigenia, also under the command of the legatus who had been left in sole command of the double legion fortress that was the closest base of Roman military power to the rebellious Batavi tribe's territory. Their stand-in first spear was shouting his own commands to hurry his men along as they too split the line of their march to either side, taking up the positions on both flanks of the Fifth to provide Marius's soldiers, many of them still little better than raw recruits, with a reassuring presence safeguarding their flanks and, if he was being honest, acting to prevent their sliding away to left or right in the event of their actually having to fight a battle. Which, he mused unhappily, looked ever more likely in the light of the recent catastrophic defeat of the force sent to put the German tribesmen back in their place.

A big man, if not as tall or broad as some of the heftier specimens who had been recruited to the service from the close-by tribes in the last few months, he unconsciously radiated a dark-eyed menace as the result of having spent much of his off-duty time over the previous ten years leading the Fifth Legion's harpastum team, loving the brutal game of ball possession too much to ever consider giving it up even as he had ascended the ranks to the point where the potential loss of his dignity on the pitch might undermine his ability to command. Inwardly continually unsure of his own suitability to provide the Fifth with the leadership expected of him, it was the facade of hard-faced competence he had grown through playing the unforgiving game that had taken him to the point where it was both second nature and completely indispensable, as much a part of his act as the vine stick he was rarely forced to wield in his exalted position as the legion's senior centurion.

The line was almost formed now, the Fifteenth's cohorts literally running for their places at each end of the battle formation with all of the urgency that would be required in the event of an unexpected contact with the Batavi, when, as Marius believed was almost unavoidable, the two legions were sent to deal with the rebel tribe. The last of the men at both ends of the line fell into their accustomed places, and for a moment the simulated battlefield was quiet, as the shouts of encouragement and bellowed imprecations of the centurions whose task it was to create order out of chaos died away. It was the moment he enjoyed the most, when his men were arrayed ready for battle, six months of intensive training having knocked enough of the rawness out of them that they knew where they needed to be and how quickly they needed to be there in almost any circumstance that might befall them. Looking across their line he felt a surge of pride at the degree to which they had improved of late, under the constant lash of merciless training in all weathers and times of the day and night, and had changed from a dispirited collection of sullen individuals into a collective entity, trained and conditioned to a hard-edged fitness that would stand them in good stead in the horror of battle that was almost certainly looming before the two legions.

'Your thoughts, First Spear?'

He turned to the speaker without a second thought. A month or so ago he would have paused for an instant to process the fact that the legatus was indeed talking to him, and not to the legion's real senior centurion, now many miles distant in Italy along with the other eight cohorts of the Fifth, which he had led away to fight for the throne on behalf of their former commander, and now emperor, Vitellius.

'My thoughts, Legatus?'

His superior Munius Lupercus nodded encouragingly, and, not for the first time, Marius thanked whichever god had been smiling upon him when the experienced career soldier had been left in command of what remained of the two legions, while his younger and more politically favoured colleague Fabius Fabulus had been selected to command the twelve cohorts that had been stripped from their strength to march south. Well into his forties, and at a time when most Roman gentlemen would have abandoned the legions for an altogether easier life in the capital, he was still as lean and well-muscled as a man half his age, the result of a punishing daily exercise routine with the men of his bodyguard. His visibly greying hair had been clipped short of late, and he wore his helmet over a thick woollen liner whose weight and tendency to encourage sweating seemed not to matter to him. He occasionally rubbed at a thick white scar that ridged his left cheek which was, he had confided to Marius, a souvenir of his time fighting in Britannia with the very Batavian warriors they now faced. Marius looked up and down the line of legionaries again before speaking, nodding his head in satisfaction.

'Well, they look like real soldiers, which is an improvement over the state they were in only a month or two ago. And they're starting to manoeuvre like real soldiers too. I just wish we had another month to get them properly used to doing it with an enemy facing them.'

He was referring to the mock battle his men had fought the previous week, the first time that most of them had faced something akin to a real enemy with two cohorts of auxiliaries set to oppose them, hurling themselves at the legion's shields with their practice swords alternately hammering and probing at his men's defences until the two sides were ordered apart, the Tungrians exhausted and the Fifth's men a good deal wiser as to what an attack by the men of the Batavi tribe might well entail. The exercise's realism had been somewhat brutally underlined by the same Tungrians' battlefield defection to the Batavi army shortly thereafter, in a battle that had resulted in total defeat for the auxiliary force sent to bring the rebellious tribe to heel. Lupercus shook his head tersely.

'So do I, Marius. I've fought alongside the Batavi tribe's warriors in my time, and I can assure you that my main impression of their way of going to war was gratitude that I wasn't having to face them. Some god or other must have heard that hubris and resolved to punish me for it, when the time was right. But . . .' He shook his head firmly. 'The time for practice is done, I'm afraid, whether they're ready or not. With the news from the west being so disastrous it was only ever going to be a matter of time before we were ordered to go and deal with them. Of all the times for your counterpart from the Fifteenth to break his blasted leg, with the fact that he did it slipping off a wet step only adding insult to the injury—'

He fell silent as one of their commander's freedmen hurried up the path from the fortress to its massive parade ground, making a beeline for the two men. Reaching the place where they stood, he bowed deeply to both before recounting the message he had been given.

'Legatus Lupercus, the legatus augusti requests your presence in the principia, and that of the First Spear.' The messenger pursed his lips apologetically. 'Legatus augusti Flaccus asks that you attend him immediately, Legatus.'

On reaching the headquarters building the two men found the general commanding the legions of Germania waiting impatiently for them. Even if somewhat corpulent for a soldier, and seemingly aged beyond his years, Marcus Hordeonius Flaccus had nevertheless proven himself to be a direct and pragmatic commander. Having moved his headquarters downriver to the Old Camp the best part of a week before, he had then ordered the rescue of the outlying garrisons as they came under attack by the Batavi tribe's allies the Cananefates, sending his aide Centurion Aquillius to direct their withdrawal and establish a defensive position with heavy naval support, a rock on which it had been hoped that the rebellious tribesman's army could be broken. When his plan had turned sour, with the small force's abject defeat by the ferocious tribesmen whose attack had been apparently been abetted by a treacherous betrayal, he had ordered Lupercus to be ready to move forward and engage the rebels, declaring it self-evident that the Batavi's nascent uprising had to be crushed before it spread to the tribes on either side of the Rhenus.

'Munius Lupercus . . . First Spear.' Marius saluted with punctilious care, only too well aware that Flaccus's demeanour had been harder edged since the unexpected defeat of his initial attempt to deal with the problem. 'I summoned you from your preparations for war with the Batavians because we have fresh intelligence as to what's happening.'

He led them past the chapel of the standards, guarded as ever by a pair of hard-faced veterans, and into the inner office, where a small group of men were waiting in an atmosphere that could only be described as tense. In one corner stood the Batavi loyalist Claudius Labeo, studiously ignoring the brooding man whose muscular bulk dominated the office. Lupercus smiled, his expectations of the missing centurion's ability to evade capture and find his way back to the Old Camp having been proven well founded.

'Centurion Aquillius.'

The hulking officer turned to face Lupercus and saluted.

'Legatus.'

Flaccus stepped into the middle of the room and coughed loudly, all eyes turning to him as he put a finger on the smooth wooden surface of the map table and jabbed it down for emphasis.

'There will be no recriminations. There will be no posturing. There will be no backbiting. All we're going to do here, gentlemen, is establish the facts of what happened at the battle by the Rhenus, now that Centurion Aquillius has made his way back to us. Centurion?'

He gestured to Aquillius, who stepped forward a pace and began to recite the briefing he'd had several days to prepare.

'Legatus Augusti. In accordance with your orders to destroy the Batavian uprising, or failing that, not to jeopardise my own force while I awaited the arrival of the legions, I deployed my cohorts in a defensive formation close to the river Rhenus, with fifteen of the fleet's ships anchored behind me to provide artillery support. I placed the Frisian cohort, men whom I judged to be the weakest men in the army both numerically and morally after their loses to the Cananefates, in the centre of my line, with the Tungrians to their left and the Ubians to their right to make sure they didn't succumb to the urge to pull away to either side when the battle began. I placed Prefect Labeo's horsemen slightly behind my left flank, facing the Batavian cavalry formed by their men of the Bodyguard who were dismissed from the emperor's service last year, with the aim of preventing them from attacking my line's left flank. And I ordered the fleet to anchor behind us on either side, ready to use their bolt artillery to strike at the advancing Batavi forces. I determined not to attack the enemy, as I did not consider my force capable of sustaining that sort of pressure, and so we waited for the enemy to come to us. Which they did.'

'In what strength, Centurion?'

Aquillius turned to Marius, his answer crisp and professional.

'On their right were the Bodyguard cavalry. Five hundred men, highly motivated and with a score to settle with Rome. They looked like first-class troops to me, all veterans, and I considered that to be their main threat. In their centre were the men of the Cananefates. A ragbag of tribesmen, untrained for the most part, undisciplined but full of their recent victories in burning out the border forts. I deemed that they would come forward eagerly but without any particular formation, and that their threat would be only be critical in the event of a disintegration of our own line.'

Marius nodded. It was a central tenet of Roman military doctrine that well-disciplined men in a strong defensive formation were unbeatable by the same number of tribal warriors, a belief only strengthened by recent experience in Britannia.

'And on their left were their militia. One thousand men, more or less, and from the way they moved once the attack began I'd say they've been well trained, probably by the men of the Bodyguard. They looked a bit raw, but I suspected that they would perform well enough in battle, so I told my bolt thrower crews to focus their shooting on them, to thin out their line and give them something to think about as they came at us.'

Flaccus nodded his understanding.

'I see. That all sounds very well thought through, Centurion, and much as Prefect Labeo described it.' Aquillius shot the Batavi officer a hard stare, which Labeo completely ignored. 'So what went wrong?'

'What went wrong, Legatus Augusti? Everything that could go wrong. It was a complete disaster. One moment I was contemplating tactics, as the Batavi came forward to fight, the next I was unhorsed, and in the middle of a rout. There are no kinder words to describe it.'

'But how?'

'How did such a strong position fail? Treachery. Treachery on all sides. The naval crews mutinied, took their officers prisoner and turned their scorpions on the rear of my Ubian cohort. Thirty bolt throwers shooting into the rear of a formed infantry cohort, and at a range so close they couldn't have missed if they'd wanted to. The Ubians were broken with their third volley, and that was before the Batavian militia reached them and started fighting. The Tungrians . . .'

He paused, shaking his head at the memory.

'The Tungrians looked solid enough, until the Batavian leader stood up in his saddle, pulled his cloak aside and showed them something on his chest, something that looked like a handprint. He shouted something at them – *"Who will avenge him?"'*

Aquillius stared at Labeo for a moment.

'And what was *that* supposed to mean?'

The Batavi shook his head.

'I have no idea, Centurion. But what I do know is that Kivilaz was ambushed on the road back to Batavorum after he'd been freed from this fortress by the emperor, back when Vitellius was still getting used to the feeling of having his backside on the throne, and knew he needed to keep the Batavi neutral if he were to strip the legions from the German frontier for his attempt to deal with Otho. It seems that someone in this fortress bribed the Tungrians to deal with both Kivilaz and the men sent to take him home, one of them a respected elder of my tribe with a record of service in Britannia that would shame any man in this room. I didn't ever hear how he managed it, but by some means or other my compatriot not only talked them out of killing him but gave them a reason to revolt in support of his cause. Whoever it was that commissioned that attempt at murder did the empire no favours that day, in my opinion.'

He looked across the room at Marius, who returned the gaze in stony silence. Aquillius shrugged.

'Whatever it meant, the effect was immediate. The Tungrians turned to face the Frisians and tore into them, while their officers disarmed their own prefect and led him away. And just as this was all happening my horse was shot from beneath me by a pair of bolt throwers. By the time I was back on my feet my command was in pieces, and it was all I could do to escape.'

'You ran, Centurion?'

The big man turned to face Legatus Augusti Flaccus with a dour nod.

'I ran, Legatus. It was either that or be captured or killed, and useless to Rome in either case. I killed two men who got in my way and escaped on a stolen horse. And then early the next morning I went back, in that period before dawn when most men are at their least effective.'

'You went *back*? Why in the name of all the gods would you risk such a thing?'

The centurion smiled bleakly at his superior.

'Because I wanted a prisoner to interrogate, Legatus Augusti. Because I wanted to prove to myself that I am still a warrior. Because I needed to vent my rage upon them. I waited until the camp was asleep, all bar the few men still sitting up and talking, picked a tent party who had set their fire too far from their comrades, and sent them to meet their ancestors.'

Marius shook his head in disbelief.

'You killed a whole tent party of men?'

Aquillius shrugged, his expression unchanged.

'There were only five of them left, and one of them had already made the mistake of going out into the darkness to defecate, which meant he practically walked onto my blade. I killed three more and took the last one away with me, before their loss was discovered. Although they were so lacking in sentry discipline that there were still no sounds of any pursuit by the time I was done with him.'

'You killed him too?'

The big man smiled, his eyes hard with pride.

'No, I told him my name and let him live. Let them fear at least one Roman.'

Flaccus nodded, his expression expectant.

'Which is all very inspiring, Centurion, but given that you had the nerve to attempt such an exploit and succeed, perhaps you could share with us what it was that you learned from your prisoner that we can use to our advantage in the next stage of this campaign?'

Aquillius bowed his head slightly.

'Of course, Legatus Augusti. It seems that all three of the auxiliary cohorts under my previous command have decided to change sides, and have made common cause with the Batavians. Their prefects and any loyalist centurions have been offered their freedom, on the condition that they go home and take no further part in the war. Which leaves them understrength from their battle losses, and underled from the loss of those officers unwilling to join with the Batavians, but still with the best part of three cohorts to swell this man Civilis's army. You plan to attack them, Legatus Augusti?'

Flaccus nodded, pointing to the map.

'The Fifth and Fifteenth Legions will advance into Batavian territory from the south and east, and look to trap the rebel forces with the river at their back. We need to crush these scum before the disaffected tribes of the eastern bank flock to them in numbers too great for us to defeat.'

Aquillius turned to Munius Lupercus.

'And you, Legatus, you will command this attack?'

The veteran officer nodded.

'I will lead the nine cohorts that remain of my two legions, plus our loyal auxiliary cohorts and Claudius Labeo's cavalry, over the river with the intention of bringing Civilis to battle. We march tomorrow, at dawn.'

The centurion pursed his lips.

'My advice, from my recent experience, would be to leave the auxiliaries behind.' His lip curled as he stared at Labeo. 'And these Batavian horsemen. Their loyalties can only be viewed as suspect. March fast and strike hard, taking the war into the Batavian homeland with sword and fire, and force them to come to you on a field of your own choosing, but operate unencumbered by tribal soldiers who may well either sink their swords into your backs or simply run at the first sign of battle.'

Labeo's face darkened, and he raised a hand in protest only to be cut off by Flaccus's imperious gesture for silence.

'This matter has already been decided, Centurion. The maximum possible strength will be used to punish this uprising, and every prefect of the auxiliary cohorts who will march with the legions has personally assured me of their absolute loyalty, as have their First Spears.'

'And him?' Aquillius pointed at the Batavi prefect. 'What about the man who led his cavalry away from the fight unscathed?'

Flaccus looked at the outraged Labeo, raising a pacifying hand.

'Prefect Labeo did what was sensible and reasonable under the circumstances. As, I might further observe, did you, Centurion. So we'll hear no more of this, and instead concentrate on beating this rebellious tribe back into their proper place within the empire?'

Aquillius dipped his head in acquiescence.

'Yes, Legatus Augusti. We will do what is ordered and at every command we will be ready.'

'Good. Besides, we're going to need every experienced officer, including yourself, Centurion. And since it seems that the Fifteenth Legion has only this morning lost its first spear under somewhat farcical circumstances, you would appear to be a very timely and ready-made replacement. You can discuss the formalities with Legatus Lupercus, but as far as I'm concerned, we can let that be an end to such concerns and allow you to focus on ensuring that your new command is ready for war. Dismissed.'

2

'A good day's march, don't you think, Prefect?'

Scar looked at the young officer standing beside him, and then back down the valley where his eight Batavi cohorts' long snaking column was marching into their overnight camp, his face creased into a quizzical smile.

'I'm not sure the people of this province would be quite as pleased as you with the circumstance, Tribune Verus. This is the third time they've had a legion-sized force march through their land in the last year, and the first time it wasn't just us, but the Twenty-first Rapax on their way south. You heard what they inflicted on the people of the Helveti tribe, I presume?'

Verus nodded with a serious expression.

'I did. But when one trains a pack of war dogs I suppose one must expect the occasional innocent to get bitten?'

The Batavi prefect shook his head.

'I wouldn't have expected quite the degree of license that the Twenty-first seem to have been allowed. Indeed, they seemed to be beyond the control of even their own officers at times, killing, robbing and looting at will, and on the basis of a fairly thin pretext which was largely of their own invention.'

Verus looked at him with a raised eyebrow.

'It almost sounds as if you disapproved of the command decisions made by Legatus Augusti Caecina during his triumphant march south to victory? You do know the man can do no wrong in the eyes of our new emperor?'

Scar smiled mirthlessly.

'Disapprove? Of Legatus Augusti Caecina?' He drew the moment out, looking around the hills on either side. 'It's not my place to grant him approval, Tribune, or to disapprove of him for that matter. But were I to be asked whether I found the Legatus to be easily swayed, and with no real loyalty to any man, I might well be placed in a difficult position. The Twenty-first seemed to conduct themselves in whatever way seemed right to them, without reference to any of the Legatus Augusti Caecina's *command deci-sions*. You'll be aware that the legatus augusti was Galba's man, before that old fool dismissed the German bodyguard who were the only thing between him and the praetorians who were supposed to be his protectors, and heaped shame on our people while at the same time condemning himself to a very public and humiliating death at their hands?' He laughed sardonically. 'If ever there was a pack of hungry dogs it was the Praetorians. But we broke them at Cremona, after we'd recaptured the Twenty-first's lost eagle for them, despite Legatus Augustus Caecina's attempts to keep us out of the battle.'

'And in achieving both of those feats you made my sponsor Alfenius Varus's reputation in the space of an afternoon, since he was at least nominally in command of your cohorts. Not to mention gaining the eternal gratitude of the emperor.'

Scar laughed curtly.

'Our friend the new praetorian prefect was more than single-minded enough to make his own reputation without the Batavi's help. And if the emperor's grateful to us . . .' he smiled wryly at the Roman, 'I look forward to some sign of it. He promised us a donative after the battle, but we're yet to see anything more that the initial handful of silver that everyone who fought was given. And that wasn't all he vowed to do for us, while the joy of his victory was still fresh, but had he sworn an oath on those prom-ises there'd be a disappointed god somewhere in the pantheon.'

Verus frowned, but any further comment was forestalled by the growing thunder of hoofs, as a century-sized squadron of cavalry cantered up the road's wide grass verge, riding swiftly along the long column marching into the camp.

'Those horsemen look like your Batavians, but . . .'

Scar stared at them in puzzlement, momentarily perplexed at such an unexpected arrival, then broke into a beaming smile at the sight of the newcomers' leader as he leapt down from his saddle and strode towards the two men.

'Bairaz! Brother!'

He hurried to meet the other man, both of them throwing themselves into an embrace of genuine affection. Holding the rider out at arm's length, Scar looked him up and down.

'By Hercules you've changed! The last time I saw you, you were little better than a snot-nosed child, and now here you are with a beard worth shaving and wearing a sword like you have some idea what it's for!'

His sibling grinned back at him.

'And there you are, brother, looking like a proper prefect of the cohorts . . .' He paused before delivering the telling follow-up. 'Fat, old, and as ugly as only a man who's past the date at which he should be in the grave could be!'

They stared at each other for a moment and then burst into laughter, embracing again. Scar turned away and addressed the tribune.

'This, Tribune Verus, is my brother Bairaz. He left us for Rome five years ago, to serve among the emperor's bodyguard, and I haven't seen him in all those years. And now here he is, no doubt bearing news from home.' He looked back at his brother, who nodded. 'Will you forgive me then, Tribune, if I am a little pre-occupied this evening?'

Verus waved a gracious hand.

'Far be it from me to get in the way of such a reunion. I'll take my dinner in my tent tonight, thank you, Prefect, and wish you a pleasant evening.'

He turned away and walked through the gradually growing city of tents towards the spot where his slaves would be erecting his own shelter, leaving the two men looking at each other. Scar looked pointedly at the men of Bairaz's squadron.

'Never, in all the time that I've served with the cohorts, have

I ever seen a messenger from home at the head of a full century of horsemen. A few good men to scare away the bandits, that makes sense . . . but eighty of you?'

Bairaz looked at his brother for a moment before replying, his tone suddenly sombre.

'This news would be better shared somewhere a little less public.'

Scar led him away to the command tent in silence, dismissing his scribe and closing the flaps with an instruction to the men standing guard to rejoin their tent parties. Pouring a cup of wine, he offered it to his brother and waved a hand to a chair, taking a seat himself and drinking the wine with an expression of satisfaction.

'It's not as if we're likely to come under attack with the best part of a legion's strength of the most feared soldiers in the empire around us, and I suspect your news would be best heard by my ears alone, until I've had time to digest whatever it is you've been sent to tell me. So go on then, tell me.'

Bairaz took a seat, placing his helmet and sword on Scar's desk and draining the cup.

'That's good. Your taste in wine seems to have improved since the last time we drank together.'

Scar laughed.

'Which has got nothing to do with me, and everything to do with that tribune who's been sent to take us back south. It seems that the emperor needs the Batavi more than he thought when he sent us home, once we'd done our part to win the battle that gave him the empire on a plate.'

Bairaz nodded.

'We heard about it. And about the extra verse you added to the paean about what you were going to do to the praetorians. Quite touching . . .' He held out his cup for a refill, and waited until Scar had put down the jug before speaking again. 'And since there's no gentle way to break the news, here it is told straight. We're at war with Rome.'

Scar's mouth opened involuntarily, and it took him several heartbeats to voice a response.

'We're . . . *at war* . . . with Rome? Is this some kind of joke? How the *fuck* can we be at war with Rome, brother, when we're Rome's favourite allies? And what kind of madness would lead to our people starting a fight we have no chance of winning?'

'Who's the one person you think could persuade the tribe to do such a thing?'

Having asked the question, Bairaz stared at him in silence, and Scar's face hardened as the first hint of realisation dawned on him.

'Kiv?'

His brother nodded.

'Our cousin *Prince* Kivilaz. You know as well as I do that he was shipped off to Rome last year, accused of treason against the emperor Nero, and that his brother was executed without trial for the same alleged crime. And you know he was released by Nero's successor Galba, and given command of the German bodyguard when they were dismissed from the emperor's service and sent back to serve in Germania.'

Scar waved an impatient hand.

'All this I know. *And* the fact that he was arrested again by the commander of the army on the lower Rhenus, as a means of gaining favour with his legions' officers, and that he escaped execution only because Legatus Augusti Vitellius knew that the continued support of the Batavi was worth more to him than the moment's enjoyment for his centurions. Quite wisely, given the role we played in defeating his rival Otho and putting him on the throne. So, more to the point brother, what *don't* I know?'

Bairaz leaned closer, his voice lowering to a conspiratorial mutter.

'What you don't know is that while he was in Rome, Kiv managed to make some powerful new friends. Friends in very high places. And one of those friends visited him in Batavodurum a month or so ago, a former cavalry officer who served in the Old Camp a few years ago, a man by the name of Plinius, come to ask him to lead an uprising against Rome in order to distract Vitellius just as a certain legatus augusti in the east challenges the emperor for the throne. This man Plinius predicted that the Romans would resort to conscription of our youth, and he was soon enough proven right in that expectation.' He paused, taking another sip of his wine while Scar shook his head in bemusement.

'Conscription? But that's—'

'Against the terms of our treaty with Rome? Of course it is. That didn't stop them though. And it didn't stop them from grabbing old men and boys for ransom too, or from forcing themselves onto the boys either.'

Scar frowned into his face, reading the pugnacious set of his brother's jaw.

'They . . . *raped* our children?'

'Yes, Scar. They raped our children.'

'Gods . . .' The prefect shook his head in disgusted amazement. 'But all the same, to go to *war*?'

His brother nodded.

'I know. But Kiv did it right, in the Batavi way. He didn't try to climb aboard the high horse, he called a meeting of the tribal elders and officers and put it to them straight, what the Romans had done in breaking the treaty and the request that this Vespasianus had made of him, to put a dagger into Rome's back at the very moment when the emperor can least afford to divert men to fight us.'

'*You* were invited to this gathering?'

Bairaz grinned at his brother's disbelief.

'Of course not. I was just one of the men selected to make sure that the council meeting wasn't disturbed or overheard. But if my mouth was firmly shut that doesn't mean that my ears and eyes weren't open, brother.'

Scar grinned at his knowing smile.

'You little fucker, you always were the sneaky one of us, so light-footed that you could have bread out of the oven without mother ever noticing it and get the rest of us the blame. So what else did you hear?'

The younger man leaned closer.

'His argument was that we were damned whether we betrayed

the Romans or not. I forgot to tell you that our nephew Hramn ran their recruiting parties off our soil with nothing more than their tunics. He even took their belts, which meant that half a dozen of their centurions had to walk back into the Old Camp looking like women. The legions will be baying for our blood after that, not just his. He told the elders that if we stay true to Vitellius and help him defeat Vespasianus, then his legions will come home with revenge for that humiliation on their minds, and that Vitellius will have no particular interest in protecting us – whereas if Vespasianus wins, then he has a promise direct from the man himself that our tribe would be given the same independence that Tiberius granted the Frisii forty years ago. But if Vespasianus wins *without* us, he will probably send our cohorts somewhere distant as a punishment for failing to assist his cause *and* send the German legions home defeated, where they will have nothing better to do than persecute our defenceless families.

'So we fight for Vitellius and end up with the shitty end of the stick whatever happens, whereas if we get behind Vespasianus he'll be obliged to protect us from the German legions, *if* he wins.'

'And give us back our status as partners of Rome, rather than being their subjects.'

Scar sat back in his chair with a sigh.

'Let me guess. Kiv sent you, with enough men to bull through anything short of a legion cohort, to come and fetch us back to Batavorum. Trusting that the fact of our family ties to him will ensure that I turn the cohorts around and march to the tribe's aid.'

Bairaz nodded seriously.

'Of course. Without the cohorts all he has is the militia, a single mounted cohort of pissed off former members of the Bodyguard, and a horde of German tribesmen who are flocking across the river to join us. Perhaps too many of them for the tribe's safety. Whereas—'

'Why?'

'Why what?'

'Why are the German tribes suddenly so interested? I thought they learned their lesson after Arminius's uprising, and the way the Romans slowly but surely tightened the noose around their necks until they could hardly breathe?' His brother smirked, and Scar raised a jaundiced eyebrow. 'I see. What else is it that you know and I don't?'

'There's a priestess . . .'

Scar tipped his head on one side.

'A *priestess*? So fucking what?'

Bairaz shook his head at his brother in mock sympathy.

'How quickly we forget the old ways, eh? In days gone by we worshipped the older gods, not those the Romans have "encouraged" us to adopt alongside our own. Hercules Magusanus? What was wrong with Magusanus that he needed to have Hercules forced upon him? The Romans took a god of raiding and plunder, a god suited to our tribe, and they turned him into something from Greek legend instead.'

'And your point is?'

'And my point, brother, is that the tribes on the other side of the great river still worship Magusanus, and Thunraz, and all the other gods. And this priestess, this woman Veleda, she truly seems to have the power of those gods running through her veins. Men travel hundreds of miles just to hear her words, from both sides of the river, and she has so great an influence on Romans and Germans alike that she settled a dispute between the Ubii on the Roman side of the river and the Tencteri on the German side simply by sending them her answer to their dispute, which satisfied neither side completely and therefore allowed honour to be served for both.'

Scar shrugged.

'And?'

'And how does this bear upon the Batavi? It's simple, brother. Veleda has declared that the Batavi will be at the heart of an uprising that will result in their freedom, perpetual and unchallenged, leading the free German tribes and those conquered by Rome in a revolt that will break their power over us forever.'

'And the people of the tribes believe this nonsense?'

Bairaz regarded his brother steadily for a moment before speaking again.

'It is the curse of the soldier that he more than any other man will inevitably come to doubt in the reality of the gods, and their ability or even their willingness to intervene in our affairs, seeing as he does so much blood and death. Yes, Scar, the people of the tribe believe it. What you call nonsense they see as the voice of their real god speaking to them through a holy woman. The elders listened to arguments from Kiv for an uprising against Rome, and from Labeo against the idea, and their votes were given to—'

'*Labeo?*' Scar leaned forward, his eyes narrowing in an almost predatory stare. 'Claudius Labeo? I'd imagine that his contribution very nearly had our cousin reaching for his knife.'

Bairaz chuckled.

'You know Kiv just as well as I do. As a prince of the royal blood, he sees himself as the leader of the Julians, Augustans and Tiberians, now that his father's too old to do much more than sit in the kitchen of their farmhouse and curse the families granted citizenship under Claudius and Nero, and their ambitions to take power.'

'What happened between them?'

The younger man shrugged.

'It didn't come to violence, if that's what you're wondering. When the lots were cast and it was clear we were going to war, then the two of them went off into a corner, apparently to resolve their differences. But soon after that Labeo left without saying a word to anyone, and at dawn the next morning he led his entire cohort away to the east, and joined forces with the Romans.'

Scar shrugged.

'What else did Kiv expect? That two-faced bastard will put himself on the side he expects to win, we all know that, hoping to be the man the Romans show favour to when we've inevitably been ground into the mud by half a dozen legions. So then what happened?'

'He put the plan he had agreed with the elders into action. He persuaded the Cananefates to rise up and attack the westernmost border forts, which were only manned by a single cohort of frightened auxiliaries, then petitioned the Romans to be allowed to put our militia into the field against the rebels.'

Scar nodded knowingly.

'His plan actually being to combine with the Cananefates and roll up the border forts one at a time, right, to prevent their garrisons being pulled out?'

'Yes, but they didn't fall for it, since Labeo was clearly telling them our true intentions. They sent their fleet downriver and pulled most of the Frisii troops out of their forts and back to safety, while they sent more auxiliary cohorts west from further up the river to form a force they felt would be able to deal with us, under the command of some centurion called Aquillius.'

'And?'

Bairaz shrugged.

'I wouldn't have known very much more than that, because I was selected to come and give you this message the night before Kiv planned to give them battle, but we were overtaken by a messenger on the road. He made the mistake of stopping to water his horse where we were taking a midday breather, and the bigger mistake of not working out who we were before sharing the news he was carrying.'

'That explains the somewhat dour-looking rider your men were gathered around to keep him out of plain view.'

'Yes. We took his message, and it makes interesting reading.' He took a scroll from his belt, handing it to his brother. 'It's from the legatus augusti commanding the German legions, Hordeonius Flaccus, to his master Vitellius in Rome.'

Scar read the message aloud, smiling grimly at the twist of fate that had put a scroll intended for the emperor he had helped put onto the throne into his hands.

'"Unpleasant duty to report to the emperor . . . revolt of the Batavi and their allies . . . direct response to the conscription ordered by Rome . . . treachery of our allies . . ."' He looked up at his brother. 'This reads more like a list of excuses than a military despatch. Ah, here's the detail. "I sent forward two full-strength infantry cohorts and a cavalry wing to join the single cohort remaining in the frontier area after the earlier reallocation of the other three cohorts to join the emperor's own army, under the command of Centurion Aquillius, an officer previously recommended to me by the emperor's praetorian prefect." There's a lot of *you* and *your* in there for a man writing to tell his master bad news.' He returned his attention to the scroll. '"It was my intention to show the German tribes that Rome's legions would not be required in the suppression of this revolt, but it seems that the Batavi prince the emperor saw fit to release in January . . ."' he shook his head in amusement. 'There he goes again with the *you*. ". . . not only managed to subvert a cohort of Tungrians, but also persuaded the crews of the Rhenus fleet to mutiny against their officers, and turn their weapons on the rear of the loyal cohorts. The result seems to have been a total defeat."'

Scar looked at his brother with raised eyebrows.

'*Seems?* A defeat so complete that he doesn't even know how bad it was?'

The younger man pointed to the scroll.

'Read the rest of it.'

'"Under the circumstances I have immediately mobilised the remaining cohorts of the Fifth and Fifteenth Legions to move forward into Batavi territory, and I am bolstering their strength with the support of the remaining auxiliary cohorts and our allied Batavi cavalry . . ." That'll be Labeo, no doubt. "I have issued Quintus Munius Lupercus who commands these two legions with orders to eliminate this rebellion before it has the time to gather strength from the German tribes on the eastern bank of the Rhenus, and to act with both speed and decisiveness in attacking the Batavi capital, defeating the rebel army and bringing this man Civilis to justice. Under these circumstances I am obviously unable to offer any further support to the army the emperor is raising to confront Titus Flavius Vespasianus, as was doubtless the intention of the usurper's agents in fomenting this uprising. I will provide the emperor with regular dispatches detailing our progress in this critical matter as and when I have news worthy of relating." And the rest of it is the usual paying of empty respects.'

Scar looked up at his brother.

'Well, isn't that just perfect? Every other bastard in the four thousand men I command gets to follow the order *I'll* have to give on the back of this . . . this . . .'

He fell silent, looking up at the tent's ceiling for a moment before raising his voice in a bellow that made his brother start.

'Alcaeus!'

The tent's door flap opened and a uniformed centurion stepped through, his helmet topped not by a crest but instead by the snarling head of a wolf, the badge of a priest in the service of the cohort's god Hercules.

'Prefect.'

Scar looked at him with a jaundiced expression.

'I thought you'd be waiting somewhere nearby, close enough to hear me shout but suitably distant so as not to be seen to be eavesdropping.'

His deputy shrugged.

'I didn't need to eavesdrop. Your brother turns up at the head of a full century of cavalry with a Roman messenger as their prisoner and takes you off into a corner for a quiet chat? You can tell me the details later, but I don't have to be a genius to work out that there's something wrong with the state of affairs between us and Rome, given the not-so-subtle hints your brother's men are dropping. And if it's obvious to me, then I'd imagine it's pretty much clear to another man who'll have an opinion on the matter . . .'

'Tribune Verus?'

'I took the liberty of having a couple of my more subtle men follow him when he went off to find his tent, including young Achilles just in case the tribune fancied his chances with his blade—'

'Young *Achilles*?'

Scar shot Bairaz an amused glance.

'We have a new hero, brother, a young lad who only joined us at Saturnalia last year.' He turned back to Alcaeus.

'And?'

'And he walked straight to where his horse was tethered, as cool as you like, and was on the point of making a swift exit when my men persuaded him to stay a while longer.'

'Good. He can take a message back to Rome for us.'

The Island, August AD 69

''They're across the river.'

Hramn wearily placed his sword and helmet on a chair, picked up a cup and filled it with wine from the jug waiting on the broad wooden table, stretching his powerful frame with a grunt.

'Are you slowing down, Decurion? Starting to feel the toll of a day in the saddle in your back and thighs? The man who went to Rome three years ago could have ridden all day and still had the energy to spar with his best swordsmen for an hour, whereas it seems the man who came back might be happier going for a sleep.'

'Fuck you too, Kiv.' The cavalryman shot his royal uncle a disgusted glance and tossed the wine down his throat, reaching for the jug to refill it before sinking into the other chair. 'I'd like to see you after spending most of the day in the saddle, not to mention seeing to your beast's needs and getting your armour cleaned and back on its tree.'

Kivilaz raised his cup in salute.

'Just let me know when it gets too much for you and I'll find you a nice soft job on my staff. Draco could do with some help keeping the elders from panicking, now they've realised that we're properly at war with Rome, so perhaps your diplomatic skills would be well employed persuading them not to walk around proclaiming our doom?'

Hramn laughed darkly at the thought.

'My diplomatic skills would probably be nothing much more than an offer to put someone's teeth down their throat.'

The older man dipped his head in acceptance of his cavalry commander's sentiment.

'You've had a hard day, I take it?'

The second cup followed the first, and the younger man stared up at the roof beams for a moment before replying.

'If you consider a day spent scouting the path of an advancing legion in the teeth of Labeo's damned cavalry wing, operating under strict orders not to engage them in combat as *hard*, then yes, it was hard. Especially as I had to order whole centuries of my horsemen to run away from mere squadrons of his. If I'd slipped my boys from their collars just once out of the half-dozen times when your orders had us falling back rather than taking the fight to them, then we'd have given that treacherous bastard a bloody nose that he wouldn't have forgotten in a long time. But, as it is, his horsemen are roaming freely, and pretty much have the run of the eastern end of the Island. As *you* commanded.'

Kivilaz shrugged.

'And what have they done with that freedom? Have they stormed Batavodurum? Burned out any farms? Killed any defenceless families? Discerned our intentions by aggressively scouting forward to find our army?'

Hramn stared at him for a moment before shaking his head.

'No. They've been fairly unadventurous, as it happens, just scouting the ground around the point where it looks like the Romans will come across the river and otherwise pretty much keeping to themselves. There seems to have been no attempt to spread the sort of panic that I'd be looking to cause if I were the opposing general.'

The prince nodded.

'It's much as the Roman Flaccus hinted it would be, then, and we're all still playing nicely. After all, this is nothing much more than a local dispute at the moment. No Roman legionary has died yet, and our treatment of the auxiliaries we've captured has been suitably restrained. Their total casualties are no more than a few dozen, because their army fell to pieces too quickly at the battle by the river for any serious fighting. At this point in time, were we to come to our senses and sue for peace, there would be no need for mass executions or enslavements, just as long as we promised to be good boys in the future . . . if the ringleaders of this rebellion were handed over for punishment, of course.'

He grinned wryly at Hramn.

'You and I would face an uncertain future, me as the man who has led the tribe to revolt, and you as my senior military commander, at least until Scar and his cohorts find their way back here.'

'*If* they decide to join us.'

Kivil shook his head.

'What other choice can they have? Any emperor, whether it be Vitellius or Vespasianus, can see that eight cohorts with a third of their strength in horsemen is too strong a force to remain concentrated under one leader, especially if that leader is a man with sympathies towards the tribe from which they are drawn. Scar can either decide to fight his way back to join us or submit to having his cohorts separated, or even broken up and used as replacements for legion casualties. And besides, just like you, he's a family member. Blood is the key to a decision like that.'

Hramn nodded and drank again, leaning back in the chair and stretching, making the wooden joints creak under the strain.

'So let's say he decides to bring them north to join us. It won't be easy, because all that'll be needed to stop them in their tracks is for the legion based at Bonna to block the road past the fortress while the two legions from the Winter Camp advance north to take Scar and his cohorts from behind. If they can work that out, as I can, then I'm pretty sure it won't be beyond the Romans; they'll put our boys in all sorts of trouble.'

Kivilaz shrugged.

'A few understrength legion cohorts composed mainly of new recruits, against eight cohorts of the best fighting men in the empire, every one of them a combat veteran? I doubt Scar will have too much trouble working out how to deal with them.'

Hramn pursed his lips.

'But even if they do punch through the Romans blocking their way, what good will it do when they arrive here in a month's time to find that we've already been overrun? There's a full legion's strength advancing north to meet us, and we've got barely enough men to match them even before I count their auxiliaries in. Not to mention Labeo's cavalry wing.'

'Do you trust me, Hramn?'

The big man stared at his cousin in evident frustration.

'More secrets? This would all be a lot easier if you would just share whatever it is that you've got held behind your back, wouldn't it?'

Kivilaz shrugged.

'That's the problem with secrets, Prefect. If I tell you what it is that I know and you don't, then your current mystification will become tight-lipped insight. Which will mean that your centurions will start trying to get you to tell them what it is that you evidently know and they don't. Whereas as things stand now, you can tell them with the straightest of faces that you have no more idea than they do, and be sure that your aggrieved protestation that you are as much in the dark as they are carries the weight of truth. Can't you?'

Germania Superior, August AD 69

'You realise that this is treason, pure and simple, Prefect?'

Scar nodded equably at the tribune standing before him. Verus had been treated with cool politeness since his attempt to escape the previous evening, to the degree that he still wore the sword his father had given him on his gaining adulthood, although a pair of Batavi warriors drawn from Alcaeus's century stood within a few paces with their hands close to the hilt of their swords, ready to put him down should he show any sign of making a suicidal attack on the man standing before him.

'That much is obvious, Tribune, although I appreciate you making the effort to sway my loyalty back to Rome.'

'But you're not for turning.'

'No.' The Batavi prefect shook his head wistfully. 'I almost wish I could, if you can understand such a contradictory emotion? I've served Rome for more than twenty-five years. I swam the river Medui in Britannia as a youth, in the surprise attack that made the victory against the Britons possible. I was the first man behind Draco and Kivilaz, my prefect and my prince, when they led the tribe to victory, and I rescued a legatus and his eagle from defeat and disgrace the next day. I marched the hills and valleys of that island alongside the Fourteenth Gemina, putting the fear of Rome into any tribe that dared to oppose us, and I was a centurion at the battle that finished the revolt of the Iceni, when one legion and our own swords put ten times our number of barbarian rebels to flight. Fighting alongside Rome has been more than just my profession . . .' He smiled wanly. 'Fighting alongside Rome has been my *life*, Tribune. But when I hear the stories of the way that Rome has decided to treat her best and bravest allies, I cannot abandon my people to an uncertain and probably bloody fate. Could you, if our positions were reversed?'

Verus shook his head slowly.

'In truth, no.' He sighed. 'So what now? If you meant to kill me I suspect I would have died last night.'

'*Kill* you?' Scar smiled. 'No, Tribune, I do not plan to kill you. What I do intend is for you to take a message to the man commanding the legions of the German frontier. I'll release both yourself and the messenger my brother took under his wing on the road, but only on the understanding that you'll ride north, back to the Winter Camp, rather than south and over the mountains to Rome.'

Verus nodded.

'And the message?'

Scar thought for a moment.

'Tell the legatus augusti that we, Rome's loyal allies, have been driven to the point of defying the empire by recent actions and events that make it clear that Rome no longer sees us as friends. You have attempted to conscript our people, in contravention of the agreement we made with Julius Caesar, which has ruled our relationship since Rome's first dealings with the Batavi, and worse than that, your centurions have presided over physical assaults on our youth. All of this makes war inevitable, as I am sure even he would privately admit, were he free to do so, and it's clear to me that this war has already begun. I have no doubt that were we to obey our orders to march south and join Vitellius's army there is already a plan in place to break up our eight cohorts as replacements for battle losses, and to remove the threat that we too might mutiny at some later point. I also have little doubt that you're well aware of such a plan, and of the critical importance to the empire of your role in neutralising the threat we pose. So war it must be, and war it will be. Hopefully a war whose fire can be quenched before it destroys us all, but a war that neither the Batavi, nor Rome, it seems, has any ability to avert.'

Verus stared back at him wordlessly, and Scar inclined his head momentarily in acknowledgement of the younger man's confidence.

'However, there are options to be considered here. That we will return to our homeland at the best possible marching speed is inevitable. What we do once we reach it is the remaining question. Will we confine ourselves to the defence of the Island, in the expectation that by doing so we can bring about peace between our tribe and Rome? Or might we, as I expect my cousin Kivilaz, the man you Romans know as Civilis, will demand of us, engage in offensive operations against the Roman presence that threatens us from the Old Camp, and the legions it houses? We can either stand on the side of continued peace or outright war, if that is the course our leaders have chosen, and in doing so determine the way this quarrel among friends develops. That is a choice that Rome can still make, between reconciliation and hostility, if the Legatus Augustus who commands the legions of the Rhenus is prepared to be reasonable.'

He leaned forward and spoke softly, his words audible only to Verus and his own deputy Alcaeus who was standing close behind him.

'I am willing to place my personal honour behind the following offer to Rome, as a guarantee that the Batavi will stand by its terms should he choose to agree to them. After the battle at

Cremona we were made promises, rewards for the vigour with which we first saw off an attempt on the army's right wing by a force of gladiators recruited from Rome, and then broke both the First Classica, rescuing the Twenty-first Rapax's lost eagle from their hands, and then the Praetorian Guard themselves. We were promised, by Vitellius himself, three things: a donative to be paid in gold, double pay for life for every man of the cohorts who fought in the battle and, most importantly, that our entire strength would become cavalry, rather than the one man in three we currently boast. If all three of these promises are honoured, and promptly, then we will return to our homeland and there stand loyal to Rome as a formed military unit, rather than as separate cohorts or casualty replacements, unless and until Rome attacks our people.'

Verus shook his head with a knowing smile.

'You only make this offer because you know that Hordeonius Flaccus will never grant it. Your men might initially be delighted with such a reward, but on arriving home they are likely to come under severe pressure to fight alongside the rebel forces, pressure to which many or most of them will quickly bow.'

Scar shrugged.

'That supposition is beside the point, Tribune, because that's my only offer. I suggest that you take it to Legatus Flaccus with all possible despatch, because tomorrow morning I'm going to turn my men around and start marching north again.'

Verus shook his head in bafflement.

'But the legions of the Winter Camp and Fortress Bonna will crush you between their two forces. Why would you take such a risk?'

The older man smiled at him.

'With no disrespect intended to the composure and under-standing that you display, Tribune, which are admirable for a man of your age, you still have a lot to learn about war. If you have the chance to witness the likely clash of arms when we reach the Winter Camp, and the two half-legions that remain there are sent out to meet us – *if* their commanders are sufficiently unwise to send them out to meet us – then you will have the opportunity to discover what I mean.'

Verus looked at him uncomprehendingly, and Scar lowered his voice again.

'And if you end up on the other side of that fight, Tribune, make sure you march with men you think you can trust to handle themselves with discipline and dignity in the case of a defeat. It would be a shame to see a promising young officer such as yourself undone by the unreadiness of his own soldiers.'

The Winter Camp, Mogontiacum, Germania Superior, August AD 69

'Thank the gods for an hour's peace and quiet, and the chance to stretch my legs. I hear that the man who commands the Old Camp exercises with sword and shield for two hours every morning, without fail, but how he ever finds the time in between driving himself blind reading all manner of nonsense and being driven deaf by an endless stream of petitioners and punishment cases is beyond me.'

Legatus Vocula and his first spear had established a routine of walking the fortress's walls after the dawn recall and breakfast, the senior officer taking pleasure in the opportunity to escape from the usual routine of paperwork, letter writing and audiences with local dignitaries, all of whom seemed to regard the two legions under his command as the answer to their monetary needs.

'I get everything from ruined crops to murdered slaves brought to my audience chamber, with every man expecting me to happily drop a few aureii into his palm and wave him merrily on his way!'

Antonius nodded his understanding, setting his face into careful composure before replying.

'Every legion needs a man of letters and diplomacy, Legatus. Imagine if your petitioners were to be received by a legion centurion?'

The senior officer smiled at the thought.

'I can well imagine. "Your request for compensation is refused! Your punishment for making an unjustified complaint is ten lashes!" I can see how that would add excitement to military civilian relations! So you're trying to tell me in your own subtle way, First Spear Antonius, that endless paperwork and having to sit politely through the dreary whining of people determined to extract gold from the empire's apparently bottomless purse is the price I have to pay for this glorious military life we lead out here on the frontier?'

'With your permission, Legatus, I'll make an observation?'

Vocula raised an eyebrow.

'I didn't think you centurions allowed yourselves anything so risky as "an observation"? An incredulous glance when a man suggests something you think is less than optimal under the circumstances, we've all seen that, and respected it. Private unhappiness over wine in your mess when there's nobody that can be offended listening, I have no doubt. I once heard one very bright centurion tell a particularly stupid tribune that what the tribune in question was saying was something entirely different to what he actually did say, and to give the young man due credit he not only didn't bat an eyelid but went on to enthusiastically agree with the revised version. But an actual *opinion*, First Spear?'

Antonius shot him a swift glance, but the legatus was smiling.

'Come on man, let's hear it. There may well be legion commanders who wouldn't want to risk the embarrassment of hearing a subordinate's view of matters, but you can rest assured that I'm not one of them.'

'Well, Legatus, it seems to me that part of your role as our commander is to provide your officers with the freedom to train our men to be the best soldiers they can possibly be. And given our relative experience of soldiering, and where we came from, it also seems to me that I'm the best possible person to train my legion to the peak of readiness for war. And then, when the legion is as sharp as the best gladius you ever wielded, it's your job to use that weapon to destroy our enemies.'

'Ah.' Vocula was still smiling. 'So I am to use ninety-nine per cent of my time protecting you from the collected frustrations and meaningless detail of military life, so that you can forge me the glorious weapon of a legion, which I will then use to win battles for Rome by means of my superior intellect in the remaining one per cent. Is that your argument?'

'In a way, Legatus, yes.'

Vocula threw his head back in genuine amusement, the nearby sentries turning in surprise at his belly laugh. After a moment to compose himself, he shook his head at the first spear.

'All I can say to that, First Spear Antonius, is that I can only hope your theory throws us up some weak-minded enemies, because all this administrative nonsense has made the weapon of my intellect as blunt as a practice sword, good for little more than bludgeoning rapacious farmers away from Rome's gold! I—'

'First Spear!'

A shout from the southern gate interrupted his further thoughts on the subject.

'Riders! Two men approaching!'

Antonius followed the pointing hand of the sharpest eyed of his wall sentries as he strode back towards the gate with his superior at his shoulder, just about able to make out the figures of two horsemen over a mile away down the road that led to the south.

'Well spotted, legionary!' He turned to the centurion with responsibility for the watch on the southern section of the fortress's wall. 'We'll use this as an opportunity for a battle drill, I think. Call out the garrison!'

A swift blast on the officer's whistle had the gate's alarm bell sounding an instant later, a clanging alert that was taken up by a dozen others swiftly enough to have the senior centurion's head nodding in appreciation as the men of the fortress's two legions raced from their various duties and training to their appointed places on and beneath the stoutly built walls. Bolt thrower crews threw themselves at their engines, swiftly removing their covers and taking the thick bowstrings from their waxed wrappers to be fitted to the iron bow arms whose stored energy would spit missiles the length of a man's forearm out to a distance of four hundred paces. Looking around him, waiting for the last of the crew captains to raise a hand and indicate his weapon's readiness to shoot, the first spear nodded approvingly as the signal was given just as his count reached one hundred.

'Very good, First Spear! Perhaps the fastest ever stand to?' Vocula was nodding his approval as he looked around. 'All that vigorous encouragement seems to have borne fruit, wouldn't you say? So, I wonder who our pretext for turning out the entire fortress will prove to be?'

The two men turned to look out across the open countryside at the oncoming riders, whose steady canter had halved the distance between themselves and the fortress in the time it had taken for the legions to man their positions. Vocula put a hand up to shade his eyes, taking a moment before venturing an opinion.

'One of them is a military courier, to judge from his attire, but the other . . .' He frowned, seeing the second rider's sculpted bronze armour and taking a moment for the realisation to dawn upon him. 'Isn't that the young tribune who went south with the Batavians last week? What was his name?'

'Aelius Verus, Legatus?'

'That's it! But why?' The two men exchanged glances, Vocula turning for the stairs that led down into the fortress's interior. 'You'd better come with me, First Spear. I doubt that young man's out on his own with only a message courier for company from choice.'

Germania Superior, August AD 69

'It's obvious, isn't it? The time has come to take a side, and the only side we can take is our own!' Grimmaz looked around the tent party's camp fire challengingly, daring any one of them to have a conflicting opinion. 'What about you two?'

'No, we can't argue against that, can we?' Andreios glanced at his twin brother Andronicus, the two men so alike that their nicknames in the century were 'The First One' and 'The Other One', and his younger twin shook his head. 'If we don't take a side we'll end up with Rome occupying the Island, and we all know how that will end up.'

A moment of silence greeted his comment, as each man around the fire reflected on the misery they had seen visited on the local people by the army of the Rhenus under Caecina, as it had advanced south through their lands, the legions' rapacious appetites for gold, drink and female flesh brutalising entire towns in a single night.

'Beaky?'

The subject of his question leaned back, milking the moment in the way to which the tent party had quickly become accustomed. Blessed with a nose that was by far his most distinctive feature and which had the simple effect of making him quite spectacularly ugly, and, lacking either the stature or the temperament to prevent it from making him the butt of his comrades' humour, soldier Adalwin had swiftly learned to use harsher humour still as a means of reflecting their verbal barbs back onto them. His posting to their ranks, as a survivor from a tent party that had lost five of its eight men to a berserk marine with a boarding axe at the battle of Cremona, had given Grimmaz's men an element that had been sorely missing – a man who always had a joke of some nature to lighten their mood or take the sting from a moment of conflict.

'What do I think about the prefect's decision to take us home? I think the women of the tribe will be wetting themselves at the thought of *this* soldier's return. Many are the stories of my prowess in the hay, and—'

The leading man shook his head and turned to the man next to him, overriding the monologue with an effortless ease born of long practice.

'Ugly?'

Levonhard, a veteran of the Boudiccan revolt and thirty years of age, well into his second decade of service and nicknamed for being possessed of features so forbidding that even notoriously hardened fortress whores often jockeyed for position not to be his chosen purchase for the evening, shook his head briskly.

'Fuck them. They went too far.'

Grimmaz nodded and turned his attention to Lanzo, the best soldier among them until Egilhard's sudden and unexpected flare of brilliance had put even his effortless competence into the shadows of the younger man's incandescent talent.

'Dancer?'

The soldier shrugged.

'What do you expect me to say, Grimmaz? That I support what the prefect decided to do? Of course I do, what other opinion could I have? But it'll end badly.' The leading man stared back at him, and Lanzo raised both hands in protest. 'How can it *not* end badly? There are four thousand of us, and seven legions on the great river. And five thousand men to a legion. Even I can work out five thousand times seven.'

'Most of which legions are either in Italy or hollowed out to send men south to fight for Vitellius alongside them. All that's left is a shadow of their strength, and most of their men no better than fresh recruits. And we're the *Batavi*!'

The other man smiled sadly.

'You asked what I think, Grimmaz. So here it is. I think we'll win half a dozen battles without having to break a sweat, and then they'll either crush us under the boots of more legions than we've ever seen in one place, when this war for Rome's done with. That, or they'll just get lucky and catch us out in some way. And they only have to get lucky just the once, don't they?'

'Well, you're a fucking bundle of laughs.' The leading man shook his head in disgust. 'Anyone else share our brother's gloomy view? Tiny?'

Wigbrand shook his head.

'I want to see my mother and my sisters. Going home is the best thing that could have happened.'

Silence ruled the group for a moment, every man around the

fire acutely aware that the big man had never quite thrown off the dark mood that had gripped him so strongly in the wake of Cremona, a bloody fight in which the cohorts had played such a key role in taking the throne for Vitellius. He still woke sweating from evil dreams most nights, and both he and his tent mates were so accustomed to the nocturnal visits of the spirit that haunted him, an enemy soldier so young as to be no more than a boy, and whose throat he had cut in the collective blood lust that had possessed them all during the battle, that the routine nightly occurrences passed unremarked.

'Achilles?'

'What?'

The youngest of them, even if he was their new crowned cohort champion, Egilhard had been lost in a reverie of home, the memory that had faded to a distant blur for most of them still pin sharp given he had been away from the Island for less than a year.

'Wake up, lad! I was asking the boys what they think of us marching back home.'

He looked back at Grimmaz for a moment, then round at the circle of his friends, realising with a shock that they were literally hanging on his answer.

'I think we need to do what's best for the tribe.'

'There, see Dancer? Achilles knows—'

Egilhard spoke again without even meaning to override his leading man, his voice so soft that the men around him had to lean closer to hear the words.

'Although I have to admit that I don't really *know* what's best for the tribe. If we don't fight, then we lose. But if we do fight, do we lose even harder?'

He fell silent, and the tent party was quiet for a moment as they absorbed the apparent wisdom of their youngest member's uncertainty.

'But I do know one thing.'

Grimmaz, who had been on the verge of admonishing his soldier despite the reasonable nature of his musing, closed his mouth and waited, raising a clenched fist of approval as Egilhard tapped the hilt of his sword, reciting the words of the oath the cohorts barked out at the start of every formal parade.

'This is my father's sword. And his father's before him. I carry it with pride, and I will use it to bring honour to my family, my cohort and my tribe.'

The men around him nodded silent approval, and after a moment the leading man spoke, his eyes shining with pride.

'Achilles speaks for all of us. Because those words are more than words to us. They are the promise we live by. Which is why I know that if it comes to a war with Rome, Lightning there won't stay dry for long.'

Lanzo reached out a hand and patted the young soldier on the shoulder.

'I couldn't have put it better myself. You've got wisdom beyond your years, Egilhard.' He looked round the fire at the others, nodding slowly. 'He has the right of it. We may be starting a fight we can't lose, but we have no choice in the matter. Rome started this, and the Batavi don't back down. Not from anyone.'

His comrades nodded and muttered their approval, Grimmaz raising his cup with a hard grin.

'My tribe, right or wrong! Batavi!'

They stood, raising their cups.

'*Batavi!*'

Germania Inferior, August AD 69

'You expect them to allow us to cross the river unchallenged, Prefect?'

Legatus Lupercus shook his head in bafflement at Labeo, who bowed his head in respect for the Roman's opinion. Hordeonius Flaccus interjected swiftly, apparently well attuned to any hint of discord between his officers.

'And you clearly do not expect the Batavians to allow us such free license to roam, Legatus, despite their apparent timidity thus far. What exactly is it that you're not comfortable with?'

Lupercus turned to face his superior with an expression that Marius had come to recognise as the outrider to a rare but occasionally incandescent loss of temper.

'My discomfort, Legatus Augustus, is based on the fact that we're seriously considering conducting a legion-strength river crossing onto hostile ground, in the teeth of a rebel army that has already managed to defeat a well-trained force of auxiliaries with embarrassing ease. The only presence we have on the other side of the river is this man's cavalry wing, and the inconvenient but inescapable fact is that his men are from the very tribe whose territory we are about to invade. While Prefect Labeo may be the very essence of trustworthiness, it is clear to me that for us to regard his men's scouting reports as the absolute truth with regard to the enemy's deployments would be unwise, to say the least. And the idea that we can ship my legion across the river piecemeal, one century at a time, is to totally ignore the risk of the Batavians using their intimate familiarity with the ground on the other side of the river to make an unobserved approach, and then attacking at the moment of our maximum vulnerability. I could lose several cohorts under the wrong circumstances, men we have little chance of replacing given the tribes' indifference to our recruiting efforts.'

Legatus Augustus Flaccus nodded slowly.

'I cannot deny the logic of your concerns, Munius Lupercus. What course of action would you prefer in taking the war into the Batavian heartland?'

Lupercus glanced briefly at Marius and Aquillius before replying.

'My senior centurions and I are of the firm opinion that this situation, with certain loyalties potentially clouded by tribal ties, means that we must proceed on the basis that all intelligence gathered by the Batavian scouts on the far side of the river is . . . *questionable.* In which case, given that we do not in truth know exactly what it is that we'll be facing, centurions Marius and Aquillius have persuaded me that our force must have the ability to both enter and withdraw from action as quickly as possible, in the event that we find ourselves at risk of losing the only effective fighting force between here and Novaesium.'

Flaccus nodded solemnly.

'I concur, Legatus. But surely the same ships that take you across to the western bank could be used to extract you, were the need to arise?'

Lupercus smiled, shaking his head.

'The fleet has already failed us once, Legatus Augustus. Centurion Aquillius learned that lesson in the hardest possible way, and very nearly at the cost of his life. And such a retreat could only be conducted one century at a time even if the fleet were sufficiently strong-minded to carry it through, leaving an ever more vulnerable body of legionaries on the hostile side of the river. No, putting the legion ashore on the other side without any opposition will be hard enough, but extracting our men under concerted enemy attack could be a death sentence for both my legion and the fleet itself. What we need here is a bridge.'

Flaccus frowned.

'But surely a bridge will take weeks to build?'

'Centurion Aquillius has experience of bridge construction using naval vessels from his time with the Eighth Legion. He believes that we can use local timber to fashion enough planking to span the river in less than a day.'

'But surely that would require engineers?'

The legion commander smiled again.

'When it became clear that most of my legion would be removed from my command and sent south to fight for the empire, Legatus Augusti, I was very quick to make some personnel transfers out of the cohorts that I was expecting to lose. After all, what Legatus Augusti Valens clearly needed was soldiers, not carpenters and stonemasons. As a consequence of which, the Fifteenth Legion's remaining cohorts have a somewhat higher proportion of skilled men than is usually the case. Clerks and craftsmen in the main, and the latter have their tools waiting, under armed guard, in the legion supply train. I learned a very long time ago that the lack of such skilled men can leave a legion unnecessarily uncomfortable in time of peace and needlessly vulnerable in time of war. So my proposal is that we invest a day in building this bridge, under Centurion Aquillius's tuition, and then cross the river as a formed military unit rather than a rabble of centuries jumping out of boats in whatever order the fleet jumbles them into. And if the need to retreat arises then I'm far more likely to get a formed legion back over the river across a bridge – especially a bridge secured by a man who has very little reason to love the fleet, given previous events.'

Flaccus nodded, conceding the point, perhaps recognising his officer's iron determination not to be browbeaten into a course of action he considered overly risky, but before he had time to comment, his secretary stepped into the room with an apologetic expression.

'Your pardon, gentlemen, I have an urgent message for the Legatus Augusti.'

Flaccus raised an eyebrow.

'So urgent that it required the interruption of a command conference?'

His freedman lowered his head fractionally in recognition of his breach of protocol.

'Under the circumstances, Legatus Augusti, you might feel the interruption justified. It's news from the Winter Camp at Mogontiacum, and it doesn't sound good.'

3

Aquillius strode the length of his bridge one last time, his eyes roaming the ropes that the legionaries who had built the improvised structure had used to lash the twenty-six ships of the Rhine fleet into place, each one pointing upstream and further secured in place by their own anchors. The planks beneath his feet were steady, held in place by massive nails hammered through them and into the beams that ran the length of the bridge, the beams in turn nailed to the ship's timbers with swift and brutal practicality that had made more than one ship's trierarchus turn away in disgust at the wanton damage being inflicted on his command in the name of military expediency. Reaching the bridge's eastern end, he walked down the gently sloping ramp and onto solid ground, raising his voice to address the legion craftsmen and labourers who had sweated and bled to throw the structure across the river in less than a day.

'Outstanding work, soldiers! You are an inspiration to your legions! And now you are dismissed back to your cohorts!'

The exhausted workmen filed away, all glumly aware that, having laboured all night by the light of torches, with a screening force of Batavian cavalry on the river's far bank to protect them from the unwanted attentions of the locals, they would now be expected to equip themselves for war and march across their construction within the hour. Aquillius turned to face the trierarchs and centurions who had been ordered to leave their vessels and report for briefing, noting the looks of dissatisfaction that to his mind completely justified the suggestion he had made to Legatus Lupercus earlier that morning.

'My name is Gaius Aquillius Proculus, and I am the first spear of legio Fifteenth Primigenia. You men all now report to me, and are subordinated to me until such time as Legatus Lupercus decides to terminate my command. Your ships, your sailors, your marines, and you yourselves, are all now mine to direct to whatever I deem to be the most appropriate course of action.'

He waited to see if any of them would see fit to comment, calculating that at least one of the vessels' commanders would be unable to resist the urge to express frustration with such an unwelcome turn of events.

'We know who you are, Centurion. You're *that* Aquillius. The man who lost three cohorts and fifteen good ships not far from here.'

The trierarchus who had spoken out set his jaw pugnaciously, and Aquillius walked slowly towards him, allowing the naval officer, big man though he was, plenty of time to reflect on the legion centurion's hulking frame and brooding presence. Stopping a single pace from walking into the man, he stared dispassionately into his face for a moment before replying.

'As a statement of fact that is correct. But it is also incomplete. My army was undone both by an act of treachery and the incompetence of imperial officers who failed in their duty. One of my three cohorts turned traitor, and attacked the weakest of the three, breaking it instantly and beyond any hope of rallying, and from that moment the battle was probably already lost. But the death blow was a blade in my army's back, or to be more precise the bolt throwers of the fleet.'

They stared at him in sullen silence, uncomfortable in the face of his growing anger.

'Officers who an hour before had been all confidence and full of "you do your job and we'll do ours", not much different to you as it happens, managed to lose control of their vessels to their German oarsmen. Rebels who then turned their bolt throwers on my remaining cohort and broke it with three volleys. I have sworn to Nemesis to have my revenge on them for that act of treachery, and I will see every fucking one of them that I capture crucified at the site of that battle.'

He swept a cold gaze across them, shaking his head slowly in evident disdain.

'I look at you . . . *officers* . . . and all I can see is the same careless attitude to discipline. The same inefficiency. The same lack of readiness that made the marines of every one of those ships surrender to unarmed Batavian oarsmen. And you know it. You try to hide it behind the surface appearance of seasoned veterans, but I don't think there's one of you with the balls to stand up and fight, man-to-man.'

'You *fucking—*'

Aquillius's response was so fast that most of them didn't realise that he'd taken their colleague by the throat until the hapless man was dangling from his clenched hand, feet scrabbling at the ground just touching the toes of his boots, his other hand ready at the handle of his dagger.

'In case you misunderstand, Trierarch, I am now your commanding officer. Legatus Augusti Flaccus appointed me to command your ships before he left to sail south, despite my protests that I would prefer to be commanding real soldiers. Under the code of military law, I have the right and indeed the duty to punish any man who chooses to disregard my authority with death. To be executed as a field punishment without any legal process, if necessary, to make an example of the individual. So choose, Trierarchus. Will it be silent obedience, or will you provide me with a little satisfaction to brighten up an otherwise frustrating morning?'

He allowed the officer to sink back onto his boot soles, fixing him with an enquiring expression as the subject of his pitiless scrutiny fought for breath.

'*Silent* . . .' the naval officer coughed the word out, choking from the fierce grip on his throat, '. . . *obedience.*'

'A wise choice. The next man to be so unwise as to curse at me won't get the choice. So, let me explain how this is going to work. Legatus Lupercus shares my low opinion of your men's abilities. When I went to see him last night, and reminded him of the fact that it was a naval mutiny that sealed my army's defeat, he saw the sense in a proposal that I then made to him. Which means that when we've finished discussing my orders, which will be the moment I've finished issuing them as there will be *no* discussion, your marines will parade at this end of the bridge as a formed cohort of soldiers. In about an hour, when the final preparations have been made, the men of legio Fifth Alaudae and legio Fifteenth Primigenia will march across that bridge. And your marines will be going with them. They will be accompanied by Ubian and Treviran auxiliaries, and of course the valiant horsemen of the Batavian loyalists stand ready to join their force on the far bank. The plan is that all those soldiers will march forward into the Batavian homeland, find the enemy's main force and destroy it by the application of a good old-fashioned meat-grinding battle, killing the enemy until they decide that they've had enough. Or that, at least, is the plan. But, as I have recent and painful experience of the weaknesses in our strategy when this man Civilis starts picking at it with the points of his men's spears, I intend to ensure that we have a line of retreat kept open.'

He pointed at the bridge.

'And this crossing is the only possible line of retreat. If the worst happens, and the men of the legions – and your marines – find themselves on the back foot, the plan is for them to make a fighting retreat to the bridge, and then to withdraw one cohort at a time back to this side of the river. But for that to be possible the bridge needs to still be here, which means that your boats will need to remain in place until the last men are across.'

'Won't that mean that the Batavians can cross the river as well?'

Aquillius nodded, conceding the point to evident general consternation.

'True. Although I've read enough about disputed river crossings to know that if Civilis were to send his men across this span and into the teeth of our spears and scorpions . . .' he waved a hand at the ships' bolt throwers, dismounted from their platforms and arrayed along the river bank, 'then they will pay a heavy price. That's the thing with bridges, they funnel the attacker into a frontage so narrow that every bolt we loose into them at such close range will kill two or three men. But I also have little doubt that if this man Civilis sends his warriors at us across that strip of wood, despite the blood that will stain the river red, they will eventually manage to take it from us. At which point we will all be counting the hours we have left to live, rather than the decades we all hope for, because he will send them after us like a pack of wolves, inspiring them with stories of the huge wealth we Romans all carry and demanding vengeance for all the injustices we have heaped upon them over the years.'

He stared around at their sober faces.

'If we lose the bridge then we lose the legions. If we lose the legions, then we lose the Old Camp. And if we lose the Old Camp, this war is over until such time as Rome can spare more legions to come and deal with these upstart goat-fuckers, which they'll have to do without the benefit of a fortress from which to operate. Which is why we're going to be ready for an unhappy outcome, when our army marches out to face theirs. Your marines are marching to fight with the legions, but a cohort of my legionaries will be replacing them. Once the army has crossed then my men will accompany you back onto your boats in the place of your marines. In truth they'd be better employed in the battle that's going to happen over there very shortly.'

He pointed at the land beyond the far bank, and one of the naval centurions raised his voice to ask a question that had the men around him nodding their agreement.

'So why not send them over and leave us our lads? They're not used to fighting like you mules, they're trained for ship fighting!'

'Why do you think?' Aquillius allowed the retort to hang in the air for a moment, sweeping a disparaging stare across them. 'It's to ensure that you heroes don't attempt to cut yourselves loose from the bridge before the order to do so is given.'

The marine bridled.

'Are you trying to tell us th—'

Aquillius took a pace towards the man, and he instinctively flinched away from the big centurion's evident anger.

'No. I *am* telling you that as far as I'm concerned you're next to useless for anything other than putting those ships where I want them. I think that if I turn my back for a moment you'll have men with axes ready to cut away the bridgework just as soon as things start to look bad on the battlefield. I think you'd abandon two legions to their fate if it meant you could get yourselves out of danger. And I think that even if you did have enough balls to stand your ground, your crews can't be trusted not to rebel at the wrong moment and you can't be trusted to stop them. I watched ships just like those, commanded by men *just* like you, fail to control their oarsmen despite the presence of marines *just* like yours. They lost those ships because they didn't have the balls to put a few hairy-arsed oar pullers to the sword.' He leaned closer to the centurion. 'And if you're so bothered about your men, you'll be pleased to know that you centurions will be leading them out with the legions. The example of your leadership can be an inspiration to them.'

He held the other man's gaze for a moment until the white-faced centurion looked away, then stepped back and raised his voice to ensure he was heard.

'If this battle goes the wrong way my Legatus is depending on me to keep that bridge open for long enough that his legions . . . including *my* legion . . . escape to fight another day. So my legionaries are going to make sure that nobody gets nervous and starts trying to get their ship free. I'll be walking the bridge, and if I see any sign of panic I'll have my men deal with you so hard you'll wish you'd never been born. There'll be axes ready to use at the far end, once the legion's across, ready to sever the bridge so that we can pull the whole thing across the river in an arc to stop them using it, but if you or any other man attempt to cut them free before I deem that the time is right then it'll be an occasion not for axes, but for rope.'

The Island, August AD 69

'Are your men ready to fight, Prefect?'

The young Tungrian nobleman who had until a week before commanded one of his cohort's centuries and was now a newly promoted prefect nodded at Kivilaz's question.

'They are.'

'And they don't miss the officers who left us, after the battle by the river?'

'No, Prince Kivilaz. They are hungry for another victory over the Romans to avenge their fallen comrades.'

The Batavi nobleman nodded.

'I promised that we would have our revenge on Rome for attempting to bring about an eternal state of hostilities between my tribe and yours. As members of our people's ruling families we both see the danger that we have averted by joining our forces, rather than allowing them to set us against each other in their usual scheming way, forever turning every situation to their own advantage and inventing a reason for discord where none exists. But today, Prefect, will be a little different.'

He outlined what it was that he wanted from the Tungrians, and the newly promoted Prefect shook his head in puzzlement when his instructions were done.

'I understand your instructions, Prince Kivilaz. But I cannot pretend to see their purpose. Surely—'

'I know.' Kivilaz cut off his puzzled question. 'You wonder why I should command such a thing. As would I, were our places reversed. But they are not, Prefect, and sometimes an army's commander needs to do what his enemy least expects. Suffice to say that yours will not be the only formation on the battlefield today whose leader is finding his orders hard to comprehend. If you do as I have instructed, then you will be fulfilling my battle plan perfectly. Can you do that, Prefect?'

He left the unspoken corollary to the question hanging in the air, unstated but as plain as the order he had issued to the nonplussed Tungrian.

'Yes, Prince Kivilaz. I can do as you have instructed. I know my men will find it strange, difficult, even, but we will obey your command.'

He saluted and turned away, leaving Kivilaz and Hramn standing alone.

'I thought he'd be delighted.'

Hramn shook his head, his unhappiness evidently every bit as great as that the Tungrian had displayed.

'Delighted?'

'Why not? He'll take part in a victory over the Romans without any of his men suffering as much as a cut finger, if they can avoid falling on their own spears in the advance.'

His guard commander looked across the field at the legions advancing from their bridgehead, still a mile distant but already deploying into battle formation as they came on.

'If his view is the same as mine, he'll see Roman boots on our soil, Kivilaz. He'll see the traitors in their service guarding their left flank. And he'll see raw recruits, trained to march nicely enough but lacking even the bare minimum of battle experience, whereas even his cohort has a hard core of men who stood and faced the Iceni ten years ago.'

'And he'll want blood? I doubt it. His view is that of a Tungri nobleman. The Romans haven't invaded the Tungri's lands yet, only ours. He'll be happy enough not to fight today, and so will his officers, when the idea sinks in.'

The prince stared out at the advancing legions, nodding as they shuddered to a halt with their line fully extended, ready for battle.

'Whoever's commanding over there knows his trade, no matter how green his men are. A tidy formation, tactically sound, and close enough to the crossing point that they'll be able to retreat back to their side of the river if it all goes wrong.'

'Except—'

'I know. You don't like your orders either.' The prince turned to look at his guard commander with a wry smile. 'So, since you're going to have to trust me that they're the best thing we can do, under the circumstances, I suggest you get on with making them happen?'

'There they are.'

Legatus Lupercus followed Marius's pointing finger, failing to make out the enemy warriors for a moment before the rustling of a hedgerow gave him the visual clue he needed to discern what it was that his first spear had seen. The vantage point of a small rill allowed them a clear view over the heads of the ranks of legionaries waiting nervously for the enemy's first move, and the silhouettes of men's upper bodies and heads were appearing above the distant line of foliage in growing numbers, each one topped by the gleaming point of a long spear held perfectly upright.

'Civilis's mounted guard?'

The centurion nodded, scanning the ground before them with a critical eye.

'I'd say so. He has them anchoring his right flank just like he did at the battle by the river.'

The enemy army was emerging from the cover of the hedges that lined the fields across which the Roman army had been drawn up to wait for them, their equipment and demeanour a curious combination of barbarian and Roman. The Batavi Guard, five hundred horsemen who had until the previous year been the emperor's bodyguard, were equipped with armour and weapons to match the best quality available to the legions, while their evidently meticulous discipline bespoke both long hours of drill and total confidence in their ability to defeat any enemy.

'Nasty. I don't envy Prefect Labeo's men their task this morning, if Civilis chooses to send those monsters forward to test his loyalists' commitment to our cause.'

Marius nodded. His colleague Aquillius, left back at the river bridge despite his best efforts to persuade the legatus to delegate the task of keeping their escape route across the Vacalis's natural barrier intact to another man, had guessed that Civilis's elite horsemen would be placed at their line's far right end, as had been the case the last time he had faced them in battle. He had argued vehemently that the apparently loyal Batavian prefect, a man he still suspected of harbouring sympathies with his countrymen, was the last man who should be tasked to face them, but the absence of any other mounted forces had made his concerns of no more than academic interest to the senior legatus. On the Guard's left, and presenting a complete contrast to the crisp ranks of cavalrymen, a body of tribesmen that he estimated as four or five thousand strong was pushing their way through the hedgerow and into view, their leader striding out before them and raising a sword aloft in encouragement.

'The Cananefates?'

He stared at the mob of long-haired warriors for a moment before answering Lupercus's question.

'Aquillius estimated that they were about two thousand strong as I recall it, Legatus. I'd say that Civilis's victory at the river has resulted in the men of the tribes on the other side of the Rhenus flooding to his banner at the command of their kings, and what you see there is the result. Give them another month and they'll have three legions' strength. They'll provide our men of the Fifteenth Legion a decent test, I suspect, fired up by their previous victory and expecting the same again. Let us hope we can provide them with an unpleasant surprise.'

'And then there's their militia.'

Both men regarded the ordered ranks of spearmen who had taken their place on the enemy line's left, facing off against the Roman auxiliary cohorts that had been placed on the army's right, and after a moment the legatus shrugged fatalistically.

'That should be a straight enough fight. The Ubians and Trevirans are long established and well-trained cohorts, so even if the Batavians have a little more strength than they do there should still be a balance between them. And in any case, we're both deployed now, so the dice are in the cup and there's no going back.'

Marius nodded, envying the other man's obvious comfort with the idea of an impending battle.

'So the auxiliaries hold their militia, Labeo's horses counter the

Batavian Guard, and the Fifteenth take their iron to the barbarian horde and persuade them of the error of their ways in the time-honoured style. And once the barbarians have been dealt with, we'll be well placed to attack into the flanks of either their Guard cavalry or the militia. Or both. And with the three cohorts of the Fifth in reserve I think we have all possible eventualities covered. It seems that Civilis has held back his traitor auxiliaries of the Tungrians and the Ubians for just the same purpose.'

Lupercus looked up and down his army's line.

'Which means that we're matched, more or less. If the battle goes well then we could have these rebels put to flight by the end of the day, and if not then at least we have an escape route open to make sure we're not trapped on this side of the river with a blood-crazed army of Germans at our throats, if it all goes wrong. In truth, Marius, I'm not sure what more we can do, given the forces available.'

He looked at the first spear with a raised eyebrow, and the senior centurion shrugged, his face creased into a wry smile.

'I'm probably not the best person to be asking, given our respective experience of battle, but no, Legatus, I'm not sure what more we could have done either.'

Lupercus leaned a little closer, lowering his voice conspiratorially.

'There are more battles to come, Marius. This won't be the last of the Batavians we'll be seeing across a field, no matter how it goes today, unless of course both you and I end up dining with our ancestors this evening. And before each of the battles to come, inexperienced men are going to look to you for the courage and imperturbability that they expect to see in their leaders, especially when those officers have seen the ugly face of war and lived to tell the tale. And you will think back to this moment, and remember me telling you that the first battle is both the easiest and the hardest. The easiest because you simply do not know how you will react to the whole terrifying business, and the hardest for exactly the same reason. Whereas the next time you stand awaiting the enemy's charge, or for our trumpets to send us forward at them, you will know exactly how it feels to be the man to whom every soldier looks for orders, for bravery, for an example of courage when the blood's flying. And what happens when otherwise sane men are driven towards each other with orders to kill or be killed. I hate it, First Spear, I loathe its waste, the tiny errors that needlessly kill good men, its noise, its stink and its terror.' He sighed. 'And I love it, for the roar of the blood in my ears, the speed with which my mind works and for the intoxicating joy of victory.'

He looked at the Batavi line again.

'Most of those men fought at the river, and saw friends fall beside them, smelt the stink of their blood as it sprayed across flesh and armour. Some of them saw an enemy die at close quarters, gone in the blink of an eye or lingering for hours in agony until someone gave them the mercy stroke to stop their wailing. You might envy them their experience, knowing what is to come. And they might well envy you your innocence, believe me when I tell you that. You are about to exchange uncertainty for something even worse, I'm afraid, unless you're a single-minded killer like Aquillius.'

Trumpets sounded behind the Batavi army, and with a tidily precise movement forward the enemy militia were in motion, a roaring cheer from the mass of tribal warriors next to them announcing their own advance as they strode towards the Romans. Lupercus stood in his saddle, flexing his thighs to push himself up to look across the ranks of the enemy army with a perplexed frown.

'They advance with the centre and the left, but not with their strongest cohort on the right. Why?'

'It's Labeo! It has to be Labeo!'

The cohort commander standing next to Aquillius on their vantage point of a small hillock close to the bridge's western end frowned at the sudden outburst from his first spear.

'Labeo? What has to be Labeo?'

The big man pointed at the Batavian Guard, waiting motionless on their horses while the rest of the enemy army started their advance towards the Roman line.

'It's the battle at the river all over again! They didn't attack Labeo then and they're not attacking him now! It can only mean . . .'

He spun and faced the senior centurion, eyes alive with his realisation of impending disaster.

'I have to go and take command of the Fifth! You're in charge here, Dexter!'

The other man's mouth gaped in incredulity.

'But you're the—'

The big man raised a hand to silence him.

'That traitor Labeo's going to switch sides! And without someone who knows what they're doing in command of the reserve force, the Batavi Guard will have the Fifteenth at their mercy, with their left flank wide open and ripe for the picking! So just do what I would have done if I'd stayed here!'

He turned and started to run, his muscular thighs pounding as he powered away from the bridge.

'But what's that?'

The answer was shouted back over the big man's shoulder.

'Execute the first man who shows any sign of making a run for it!'

Aquillius watched the soldiers manoeuvring before him as he ran, staring intently at the Batavian cavalry anchoring the Fifteenth Legion's left flank. Abruptly, and seemingly confirming his worst fears, Labeo's command was in motion, peeling away from their position in a wheeling turn that sent the leading riders around to their left. Then, while the legionaries of the Fifth Legion waiting behind the main battle line stared at them in stunned disbelief, they reversed their direction, riding through the one hundred pace gap between the rear of the Fifteenth Legion and their own position, the Batavi riders silent as they cantered past the hapless cohorts on either side. Aquillius cursed and spat, maintaining his pace as the long tail of the cavalry wing's snake-like formation made the turn and vanished into the space between the two legions. Marius's deputy Gaius saw him coming and walked out to meet him with a look of bemusement that changed to alarm as the big man drew his sword and pointed breathlessly at the space the Batavian cavalry had deserted.

'Wheel your cohorts left . . . guard the Fifteenth's flank!' The other man dithered momentarily, then blanched as Aquillius raised his sword with an expression that brooked no argument. *'Do it!'*

Gaius stared at him for a moment and then turned back to the waiting cohorts, raising his voice to a parade ground bellow invested with every ounce of his authority.

'*Fifth Legion . . . at the double march . . . Left! Wheel!*'

Aquillius watched, still panting for breath, as the three cohorts lurched into motion, the men closest to him barely moving position despite the pounding of their feet as they anchored the manoeuvre, while the legionaries at the far end of their line were practically running as the depleted legion's centre and right wing cohorts advanced around to their left. Walking briskly out behind the legionaries, the centurion's heart fell as he gained a clear view of the army's right flank beyond the Fifth's pivoting line, shaking his head in disgust as Labeo's command, having traversed the entire rear of the Fifteenth Legion, executed a perfect battle turn to the left and fell upon the rear of the auxiliary cohorts that constituted the defensive line's right wing. The distant thunder of their mounts' hoofs was suddenly underpinned by the screaming and incoherent bellowing of men fighting and dying, as the Batavian cavalry ripped into their hapless victims with their long spears. With a convulsive shiver, the Ubian and Treviran cohorts broke, their cohesion shattered, men flying in all directions as they desperately sought refuge from the twin threats of the cavalry tearing into them from the rear while the Batavi militia advanced implacably on them from the front, their collective voice roaring out the tribe's paean.

Legatus Lupercus bowed his head, eyes closed in evident despair, as the nature of Labeo's treachery became horribly clear, his voice almost too quiet to be heard above the chaos playing out to their right. The two men had stared aghast at Labeo as he had ridden past them barely twenty paces distant, the Batavi nobleman giving them nothing more than a brief expressionless glance as he led his men along the rear of the legion and into the defenceless auxiliaries beyond their rightmost cohort.

'He's played us for the fools we are. We've lost.'

Marius looked swiftly along the line, shaking his head in denial of his superior's verdict.

'Not yet we haven't! Look!'

The legatus followed his pointing finger, his eyes narrowing as he realised that the Fifth Legion was already in motion, apparently unbidden, swinging out of their reserve position in a parade-ground-perfect wheel to the left that was rapidly closing the open door of the Fifteenth's unguarded flank.

'Gods below, Marius! Whoever it was you left in charge of the Fifth is going to earn his phalerae today!' Appraising the battlefield for a moment, he turned back to the waiting first spear with fresh determination. 'Our only hope is to make a fighting retreat back to the bridge, and pray that Aquillius can keep the damned navy from cutting themselves free and making their escape while the going's good! If you can get the right flank closed off in the same way then we might just have a chance of holding them off for long enough!'

Marius saluted, turning away in the direction of the Roman's pointing finger and sprinting pell-mell down the legion's rear with Lupercus's shouted commands for the front rank to prepare to receive the barbarian attack audible over the screaming melee to the legion's right. Reaching the first cohort he needed to manoeuvre backwards and to their right, he shouted a swift order down at their hard-faced senior centurion as the man walked out of his men's ranks.

'When you hear my whistle blow three times, wheel back to close off this flank. We're going to make a fighting retreat to the bridge!'

The veteran officer nodded and saluted, shouting back the only words Marius wanted to hear even as he ran for the next cohort in line.

'Yes, First Spear! We will do what is ordered and at every command we will be ready!'

Labeo's cavalrymen were in among the terror-stricken auxiliaries with their swords, and showing no sign of accepting the surrender that most of the routed infantrymen were attempting to offer, as if the period spent professing their loyalty to Rome were a crime that could only be expunged by drenching themselves in the blood of their hapless enemies. As he watched, spellbound by the wanton slaughter, one soldier, braver than most of his comrades, pulled a rider from his horse and set about him with his dagger, inflicting half a dozen bloody wounds to the Batavi's throat and face before being run through by another man's spear. Another auxiliary, hemmed in on all sides by cavalrymen leaning out of their saddles in their eagerness to spear him and managing only to impede each other's efforts, crawled under a horse for shelter from the probing blades only for the beast to react as it had been trained, stepping smartly forward and then snapping out its back legs in a two-hoofed kick that left the man's shattered jaw hanging loosely from the remains of a ruined face. Tearing his gaze from the scene of carnage, Marius realised that the rightmost cohort's senior centurion had stepped out to meet him with a crisp salute.

'First Spear Marius! Have you come to join the fun?'

Marius forced a grin onto his face as he fought for breath, knowing that what the men before him needed was more than just leadership but a swaggering example of arrogance in the face of disaster to buoy their spirits.

'I thought I'd come . . . for a look . . . at the bastard . . . who's betrayed us. I want to know him . . . when I have him . . . at the end of my sword!' He paused, taking several deep breaths before speaking again, as if he had all the time in the world. 'But that won't be today!' Raising his whistle, he looked up and down the line of men and shouted his command loud enough to be heard over the cacophony of slaughter. 'In just a moment I'm going to blow this! And we're going to do some drill, you men and I! We're going to wheel these three cohorts back to face this scum, so that they can't take our flank, and then we're going to take a stroll back to the river!'

The soldiers who had turned to look at him grinned, guessing what was coming and loving him for the offhand description of what was likely to be a bloody fight if they were to regain the safety of the river's far bank, one of them shouting a question over the battle's shouts and screams.

'What about them cunts, First Spear?'

He affected to follow the legionary's pointing hand, seeing the barbarians massing before the Fifteenth's line.

'Those barbarian cunts, legionary?' He grinned, putting on his best square-jawed centurion face. 'Trust me, they're the least of our worries! When we've killed enough of them then the wall of their dead will keep the rest from getting anywhere near us!'

He drew a deep breath, shouting the order that they were waiting for.

'On the whistle! Cohorts four, five and six will wheel to the rear!'

The trierarch leading the deputation of officers who had gathered around Centurion Dexter pointed back across the river at the embattled legions on the far side.

'Look at them! They're *fucked*! And if we stay here so are we! We should get out now, while we can! There's not one of them even going to reach the river,' he pointed to the bridge, 'never mind get back over this floating death trap!'

The centurion turned away to stare at the battle with both hands at his belt, apparently considering the naval officer's words, and another one of the half-dozen trierarchs gathered around him took up the argument.

'Nobody's going to thank you for throwing away a cohort of good men that could march back to the Old Camp intact, are they, Centurion? And if you allow twenty-six ships to be taken by the rebels, you'll probably find yourself being executed for dereliction of your duty to the empire, as the only man left alive to punish!'

Dexter stared bleakly across the river, nodding slowly, and the officers looked at each other in hope and calculation, ignoring the tent party of soldiers standing stolidly behind him.

'You're right.'

Triumphant expressions began to creep across their faces, the deputation's leader nodding at his comrades and signalling with a raised hand for them to tread softly.

'These legions probably won't make it back to the river, not with that many men attacking them, not now the Batavian cavalry have betrayed us. I'd say those poor bastards over there have been hung out to dry.'

The centurion turned back to face them, looking from one face to the next.

'And you're all of the same mind, right? You all want me to bring my men back over the bridge, and allow you to cut your ships loose before the Batavians get here?'

Eager nods greeted his question, and he shrugged, turning to the centurion leading the party of legionaries at his back, a precaution Aquillius had taken before he'd run out onto the battlefield.

'You heard them. Go and get it. Enough for all of them, mind you.'

His comrade nodded and walked away, and Dexter turned back to find that the naval officers' momentary delight had become uncertainty at best, hostility at worst. He looked at them for a moment, while they waited for him to explain.

'I know, you're confused. What does that mean, and what's he gone to fetch?'

'You'd better—'

Their leader, leaning forward to put a finger in Dexter's face, recoiled as the centurion's dagger leapt from its scabbard with a speed that left them blinking, the cold iron blade pale in the late morning sun.

'He's gone to get some rope, Trierarchus. Enough rope to hang you six as the cowards you are, and provide your men with six fucking good reasons to hold their nerve.'

They shrank away, only to find more soldiers behind them with swords drawn.

'But . . .'

He stared levelly at the deputation's leader.

'You looked across the river at our lads being dipped into the shit by a traitor, and you decided that you didn't want any part of it. Which makes you all traitors too. So you thought you'd come and throw your weight around with me, didn't you? Thought you'd see if I had the same sized stones as Centurion Aquillius? And when you thought I didn't, there you all were, congratulating yourselves that you could slide out from under this one and leave the army to die on the wrong side of the river. And do you know what? You were right. I don't have a pair of balls anywhere near as big as the ones Aquillius is carrying around. I'd give my back teeth to be anywhere but here, watching my mates face thousands of barbarian arseholes and knowing that it's my turn next. But if it comes down to a choice between facing down *you* traitors or having to face *him* when he gets back over the river, which I know he will no matter how many barbarians try to get in his way, I know which choice scares me more. Take them!'

The trierarch snarled as a pair of legionaries pinned his arms, struggling ineffectually in their iron grip.

'You bloody fool! You know we're all going to die?'

Dexter shrugged.

'Eventually. And the oath I took did make some mention of the possibility for it to be sooner rather than later, but perhaps *you* swore to a different set of words? Ah, here's my colleague with the rope now. Let's get to setting an example, shall we?'

'Fucking Kiv, eh?'

Hramn turned away from his bemused contemplation of Labeo's act of treachery and looked at the decurion who was deputising for his second-in-command Bairaz blankly.

'What?'

'Kiv. Have you ever known another man like him?'

'Have I ever known another man like him? As clever, as devious, as bloody minded? No. He's one of a kind. Just when you think you know what it is that he's got behind his back, that's the moment when he'll show you that you have no clue whatsoever.'

'All that time letting us think that Labeo and his men had abandoned us.'

Hramn shrugged.

'We should have known. The speed they made themselves scarce at the battle by the river. The way he wouldn't let us take them on when they crossed the river yesterday, just begging to have lumps kicked out of them. All the signs were there, if I'd had the eyes to see them.'

Kivilaz had told him as much, when he'd revealed the secret of Labeo's defection an hour before, fixing him with his one good eye and grinning at him with genuine pleasure as he pointed across the space that separated the two armies.

'Well if you couldn't see it coming then hopefully neither will they. Which means that when my co-conspirator Labeo and his men fall on the Ubii and Treveri auxiliaries, the shock of it will have his legionaries shitting down their legs. All that leaves is for you and your command to enact your orders to the letter. Do you think you can do that, Prefect?'

He'd nodded in silent acceptance, knowing all too well that his command was seething with the need to get at their enemies, burning with a frustration that had gnawed at them since the rebellion's first battle, a fight that had been over before they had been allowed to take any part, a glorious victory in which they were unable to take personal pride beyond the performance of the tribal militia they had trained.

A horn blew to the Guard's left, three swift blasts and one long, and Hramn grinned wolfishly.

'There's the signal!'

He turned in his saddle and raised a hand.

'Follow me!'

On the enemy's right flank the Batavian Guard were moving at last, walking their horses forward with the disciplined patience of men who understood the need to arrive at the point of contact with their mounts capable of fighting, rather than blown by a headlong charge across the battlefield. Some of Aquillius's men had already spotted the movement, legionaries pointing at the compact mass of riders as they gradually accelerated to a trot, still three hundred paces distant, the beating of the horses' hoofs now a faint ripple through the earth beneath their hobnailed boots. Centurions and chosen men were ranging up and down their centuries, talking, cajoling and haranguing their men, working to straighten the legion's line and ready them to receive the horsemen's inevitable attack. Aquillius could almost smell the fear permeating the new recruits who formed the bulk of the legion's three cohorts, knowing from grim experience that threats and physical violence could only keep such a fragile body of men in their places for so long, after which the urge to self-preservation would take over, no matter how illogically given the fact that their only chance of survival lay in standing together. Instinctively knowing what it was that they needed to bolster their courage, he walked out in front of them, shouting to be heard over the legionaries' mutterings of disquiet as his officers fell silent.

'*Soldiers of the Fifth Legion! You all know who I am! You know my reputation!*'

It was true enough. Everywhere he went in the camp men saw him coming and straightened their backs, saluting respectfully. He was already a legend among the soldiers of the Old Camp's legions, the only survivor of a defeat so catastrophic that not even the fleet had been spared from the ignominy of losing every ship sent to bolster an army that had apparently surrendered at the first sight of the enemy. The fact that he had walked back into the camp several days later with blood caked into the creases of his armour and ingrained under his fingernails had only served to strengthen his fearsome reputation, and the legend of the cold-blooded way he had infiltrated the enemy camp on the night of the defeat, killing at will and dragging away a prisoner for a swift and brutal field interrogation was already widely known and accepted by even the most cynical of men.

'*You believe that we are already defeated!*'

He allowed the words to hang in the air for a moment, allowing each of them to reflect on the truth of it, even those officers driving their men forward purely on instinct.

'Legionaries, we are only beaten if we allow it!' A momentary pause. *'And I will not allow it!'*

The Batavian cavalry were cantering steadily now, two hundred and fifty paces distant and coming towards the waiting legionaries in a formation tidy enough to grace a parade ground display.

'You have been trained for this! You know how to face cavalry! You know they cannot break our line if we stand fast!'

The leading riders were turning back in to face their intended victims, and Aquillius smiled fleetingly, his mouth a tight line of amusement at the thought of their dismay at finding three cohorts blocking their path.

'It's simple! If you run, you die! They will reap you like ripe wheat! But if you stand and face them with spears and shields, they will have no way to break our formation! So stand and fight with me, if you want to live!'

The Batavi horsemen were two hundred paces distant, and at the call of a horn they accelerated to the gallop, men leaning over their mounts' necks with spears thrust forward. Aquillius drew breath to shout the last command, bellowing the order over the growing tumult of the oncoming cavalry.

'Fifth Legion! Ready! Spears!'

'Bodyguard! On my command!'

Bellowing to be heard over the thunder of his command's advance, Hramn raised his sword hand, lifting the weapon's glinting silver bar high into the air in readiness to give the signal he had briefed to his decurions only moments before. The empty space where Labeo's cavalry had been a moment before was now filled with legion infantry, a line having formed out of the chaos of their hurried advance to guard their army's flank. A single officer was out in front of them, his voice lost in the cacophony of the Bodyguard's hoofs as they cantered towards the enemy line, but the veteran decurion knew from experience that he would be challenging his men to resist the thundering mass of horsemen bearing down on them. The fate of the battle hung in the balance, poised between his men's ability to break the Roman line, and reduce the legionaries from a formed body of men to a shattered and terrified mob, casting away weapons and armour as they fled for the illusory safety of the river's far bank, and the legion's training and discipline, their mental strength to remain in place in a line that would ultimately frustrate his horsemen's headlong charge if they proved themselves capable of standing in the face of his men's thundering charge. Tensing his thighs to rise in the saddle he lifted the sword's shining blade high.

'*Bodyguard, ready!*'

Aquillius stepped back into the Fifth's ranks, watching with hawk-like focus as the legionaries obeyed his command, each man hefting his pilum and drawing his arm back until the pointed and barbed iron tip of its long iron shank was level with his ear, the rear ranks stepping back to allow space for the step forward that would invest their throws with all the strength of their powerful thighs, conditioned by months of marching and incessant weapons drill. The legion's stand-in first spear joined him, staring in evident trepidation at the oncoming horsemen, and Aquillius laughed softly, inaudible to all but the man next to him.

'Do you want to know the secret to stopping them, Centurion Gaius?'

Knowing that he was gambling not only with their lives but with the very survival of both legions, he ignored the nervous glances of the centurion beside him, only too well aware that if he allowed the horsemen to ride up to the line unchallenged and use the elevation of their mounts to stab their long spears down into his men, there was every chance that they would find a weakness in the Fifth's defence. That, or simply panic the untested legionaries, and in doing so break through into the space behind them to wreak havoc in the two legions' rear by riding down the scattered legionaries in the grisly work of pursuit and slaughter at which cavalry were the masters. They were no more than one hundred paces distant, and still coming on fast, the man who had to be their leader at their head with his sword raised high, a warrior Aquillius had last seen standing out in front of his men at the battle by the river, denied the chance to fight by the speed of the Roman forces' collapse. He raised a hand to point at the man, raising his voice to be heard over the din of thundering hoofs.

'He knows! The secret is in timing the spears *just* right!'

Aquillius knew that he and the Batavi cavalryman were both frantically calculating, as the enemy horse rushed towards his line, knowing that for his part the timing of the legion's spear volley was of the utmost importance, to disrupt the enemy's front rank and hamper the onrushing mass of beasts behind them without leaving it so late that dead and dying horses crashed into his formation. For his opponent the question would be whether or not to subject his command, the finest horsemen in the rebel army, to the potential of a terrible slaughter, even if doing so might smash the Roman line apart simply by the violence of the impact of those men whose horses were not felled by the rain of iron that might well be the legion's last act of defiance.

'Fifth legion! Spears . . .'

'Bodyguard, now!'

Sweeping the sword out and down to his right, Hramn dragged his mount round into a tight turn, praying that his men could pull off the manoeuvre that he had been commanded to carry out.

Aquillius stared levelly at the enemy horsemen, the command to throw spears unvoiced as the oncoming cavalrymen split to either side at the bellowed order, their speeding horses passing within thirty paces of the legion's line, barely outside the range of the legionaries' spears. Centurion Gaius turned to him in amazement, grinning like a man spared from impending execution.

'They're running!'

He shook his head at Gaius's exclamation, then bellowed for

silence as men started to cheer along the legion's line, watching through narrowed eyes as the mounted guardsmen cantered away from his men and swiftly reformed their ranks at a hundred paces from the Roman position, still threatening the army's flank with their spears.

'*Silence!* They're not running! They were just never attacking!' He stared as the last of the Batavi riders trotted into place and settled back into their previous formation, horses snorting and pawing the ground, still eager to run. 'But why?'

'What game are you playing here, Civilis?'

Legatus Lupercus watched in disbelief as the entire Batavi army halted a hundred paces from his legions' line, looking to the right and left to reassure himself that both flanks had been made safe by his centurions' efforts, not realising that he'd spoken the question that was on his mind aloud until the men close to him turned to look at him. As if to answer him, a tall figure stepped out of the battle line and shouted a question into the sudden silence.

'Legatus Quintus Munius Lupercus, will you come and talk with me, man to man? Safety is guaranteed and I will come alone and unarmed!'

'Don't do it, Legatus.'

He turned to find Marius at his shoulder.

'I have to, First Spear. For one thing, there may yet be a way to extract ourselves from this disaster. And for another . . .'

He fell silent, contemplating the memory of a distant battlefield.

'Legatus?'

'When I was little older than the youngest of our recruits, Civilis put himself between me and a warrior, a hard-faced killer who would have beheaded me without his intervention. I still owe the man my life, Marius. The least I can do is go and talk to him.'

He climbed down from the horse and drew his sword, handing it to the senior centurion and meeting his subordinate's disapproving expression with a wry shrug.

'If he promises to come unarmed it would be churlish not to return the compliment, wouldn't it?'

The legionaries opened a path through their ranks without having to be bidden, watching in awestruck silence as their commander stepped out onto the battlefield's grassy space and strode out to the point equidistant between the two forces where his opponent waited.

'Prince Civilis. My apologies that the legatus augusti couldn't be present.'

Kivilaz nodded, accepting the clasp the Roman offered.

'I know. My spies tell me that he left for the south by river when news reached him that our cohorts have turned for home to join our army.' He smiled as Lupercus absorbed the blunt statement. 'Come now, Legatus, I'm sure you have men within the tribe, carefully placed to pass you whatever intelligence they can discern, so you can hardly have expected that we wouldn't have our own sources of information.' The legatus nodded acceptance of his point. 'And to formally return your greeting, welcome, Legatus Quintus Munius Lupercus, to the Batavi homeland. Not that you'll be enjoying its hospitality for very long, but I know you for a gentleman and will of course treat you as such. Civilis, I should point out, is not the name I'm known by now, but I can forgive you for preferring the version you became used to in Britannia.'

Lupercus regarded him for a moment before replying.

'It seems like a century ago. We've both earned our share of scars and grey hairs since then.'

The Batavi nobleman nodded his agreement.

'Time has taken its toll of us both, Legatus, but not entirely for the worst. When we fought together for the first time you were no better than a youth, but now you look every inch the Roman general. You have roamed the empire putting barbarians to the sword for the last twenty-five years, I presume?'

Lupercus smiled.

'I realised early in my career that the treacherously slippery pole of advancement in Rome wasn't for me, especially with a man like Nero on the throne. Much to my father's disgust. He came round in the end, before he went to meet our ancestors, but only after I'd been promoted to command a legion in Moesia. And yes, I've seen my share of fighting. As have you, I hear.'

The Batavi nodded.

'Battle upon battle, fighting for Rome so many times until they all seem to blur into each other. Although some things do tend to stick in the mind better than others. My first kill, for example . . .'

Lupercus raised an amused eyebrow at the Batavi's lack of subtlety.

'I remember you cutting away your plait while he was still heaving and shuddering. But then how could I forget the death of the man who would have been my own killer, had you not intervened? And that I still carry a debt to you? Was that your point?'

Kivilaz shrugged.

'In a way. Perhaps I'm simply seeking to remind you that we fought on the same side, the Batavi loyally making Rome's interests their own, back in the days when the empire knew how to reward service.' He tapped the leather patch that covered his right eye. 'And when the Batavi's scars were worn with pride in that service, rather than as the marks of exploitation.' He shrugged. 'And as to saving your life, there is no debt to pay. It was your intervention with Vitellius, pointing out that my death would needlessly provoke my people, that led him to spare me during my second incarceration by his legions.'

The legatus bowed his head momentarily in recognition of the point. He looked across the waiting ranks of Kivilaz's men, taking stock of their evident readiness to fight.

'My compliments on the army you've raised. You seem to have combined the very best traits of your countrymen with the ferocity of your neighbours, although how you persuaded your tribal warriors to stop short of attacking us is something I'd be curious to know.'

The Batavi prince returned his smile.

'Anything is possible, if you have the right lever. In the case of the Cananefates and our other allies I simply promised them first pick at the spoils of your defeat, if we ever meet you on the field of battle again. But I told them that today will not be the day of that defeat, and their king accepted that bargain with all the eagerness I expected.'

'Why?'

'Why not today?' Kivilaz stared at him levelly for a moment before replying. 'In all of my dealings with Rome, Munius Lupercus, I have always been careful to observe the empire's need to be respected. Your rulers have an obsession with your empire's dignity, as if an affront left unanswered will result in the loss of your ability to strike fear into your subjects and neighbours. Any number of crimes might be committed against your allies and happily be forgiven under the right terms, when the time for settlement of the argument comes, but woe betide the enemy who throws a single spear at the walls of a Roman fortress. I learned that first hand by watching the way the Iceni tribe was dismembered after their defeat. They had their moment in the sun, they burned out Roman cities and despoiled their populations, but when the reckoning came Rome was as cold and dispassionate in the tribe's destruction as could be imagined. I should know this, of all people, given the part my cohorts played in that massacre.'

Lupercus nodded, accepting the rationality of his opponent's calculation.

'And so in refusing to offer my legions battle, a battle you believe you would win in the absence of my auxiliaries and your comrade's cavalry, you avoid insulting Rome's dignity while making clear that we have no right to enforce imperial will on your land?'

The Batavi nodded.

'You have it. I will allow you to retreat from Batavi territory unharmed, as a gesture of my continuing respect for the empire despite all the wrongs that have been heaped on my family and my tribe. Although my forbearance will only last a certain amount of time.'

'Just long enough for me to get my legions off your soil?'

Kivilaz inclined his head in acknowledgement of the Roman's perception.

'This way honour is satisfied. I can tell my tribe's elders that I met your invasion of our land and repelled it, and yet did so without giving Rome a casus belli. There will be no impassioned speeches in the senate, no angry insistence that the Batavi must be subjugated no matter what the cost. And you can answer your critics with the simple truth that you were betrayed by Prefect Labeo, and your auxiliaries cut to pieces. Left with only raw troops, and with my army nipping at your heels, you managed to make a disciplined and orderly retreat to the river and thereby preserved your legions for another day. The northern frontier is not lost, Rome continues to rule the land up to the edge of our territory, and honour is satisfied for both parties. Vespasianus will take the throne and promptly grant the Batavi our independence, as promised by your legatus augusti, Hordeonius Flaccus.'

He grinned at the Roman's reaction.

'You didn't know that Flaccus and I were allies in this matter? I'd wager you suspected it though.'

Lupercus nodded slowly.

'It explains his somewhat ambivalent attitude towards your revolt over the last few weeks. So it's to be peace then, is it?'

Kivilaz shrugged.

'Who can say? But as long as Rome itself remains immune from insult, with the Batavi too intelligent to cast the first spear that would bring your legions down on us like crows on a corpse, then I have high expectations of a tidy end to this expression of our discontent.'

'If Vespasianus wins. What if he loses, and Vitellius stays on the throne?'

'Then word of that defeat will reach us long before your legions in Italy can make such a long march. And my people will have to decide whether to submit to the brutal treatment that will surely follow when your legions march north in victory, or take up their arms and show Rome the true terror of the Batavi at war. You'd best look to your defences, Legatus, for if we come south it will be with fire and sword, with no further thought of mercy.'

The legatus shook his head in puzzlement.

'The Old Camp is a new fortress, built to replace its predecessor no more than ten years ago. Its walls are thick and its artillery is powerful, strong enough to withstand a year of siege. And your people are hardly blessed with military engineering skills, or even an understanding of siege craft. What makes you think you can stroll through our gates with such ease, if it comes to a real fight?'

Kivilaz raised a wry eyebrow.

'Everywhere I go men want to know my secrets, friend and foe. And my answer is always the same. Wait and see, Legatus. Wait and see.'

4

'Shouldn't we be taking a more westerly road? Marching up the river's bank takes us past the camps of six legions. Surely they're not *all* going to just sit in their barracks while we stroll past?'

Scar shook his head, not shifting his gaze from the walls of Bingium, a fort twenty miles from the legion fortress of the Winter Camp by which his cohorts had paused in their march north. A number of auxiliary soldiers were watching them from their place above the gate, clearly nonplussed at the presence of men whose shields' green paint and distinctive decoration immediately identified them as the Batavi.

'I'd imagine whoever's left in command in there will be fairly shitting themselves at the thought of eight cohorts of us marching past, given most of them will have gone south with Vitellius.'

He turned back to Alcaeus.

'So go on then priest, enlighten me. What more westerly road? The roads from here to the Island nearly all converge at Colonia Agrippinensis, so there's not really much point marching twice as far to avoid Fortress Bonna when all the legion there has to do is march a few miles north to meet us. That or just lurk in our rear until someone gets up the nerve to try and stop us, in which case they'd have us with spears to front and back. I'll grant you that we could march west through the forests to Mosa Ford, and then down the Mosa to the Island, but I'm not inclined to take the extra time, or run the risk of our being ambushed in the trees where there's no room to manoeuvre. And in any case, it's of no matter what I think, is it? Kivilaz's orders were very clear on the subject. He expects this man Hordeonius Flaccus to offer us a negotiated passage north, and he intends that we should take full advantage of it. Apparently the man who commands the army of Germania harbours a secret allegiance to his friend Vespasianus, and will do whatever he can to weaken Vitellius's cause without openly being seen to do so, in this case colluding with Kiv to strengthen our cause and thereby ensure that there's no way they can send any more legionaries south to join the war, or ourselves for that matter. And if that keeps the Winter Camp's legions bottled up in their barracks rather than bringing them out here to dispute our right to the road, then it's all to the good, especially if the only price we have to pay is an hour's wait while he rides out to meet us. So if the man who commands every legionary and auxiliary in Germania asks me to pause on the road for a meeting then simple dignity compels me to at least listen to what it is that he has to say, don't you think? If there's a chance that an hour of talk will remove the need for us to fight every damned legion on the frontier then I'll spend that time, and as much more as needed, to see just how far this man Flaccus is prepared to go in support of his true allegiance.'

A small detachment of cavalrymen had ridden out to meet them that morning, their decurion conveying Flaccus's desire to meet with the Batavi prefect in lofty tones that spoke volumes for the poor regard in which the legions camped in the massive fortress that dominated the area held their one-time allies. Scar yawned and pushed a hand inside his armour to ease his evident discomfort with something trapped between the coat of layered iron scales and his skin.

'Whoever it was that decided centurions should wear scale armour should have been tied to a post and given a good beating twice a day until he saw the error of his ways. One of the wires that holds these damned scales on has come loose, and it's sticking right through my tunic and stabbing me like a miniature pugio.'

One of the men who had ridden out from the cohorts' camp to provide Scar with a bodyguard pointed at the road to the east.

'Horsemen, Prefect.'

They watched in silence as a carriage rolled into view with an escort of a dozen cavalrymen following it down the broad ribbon of road that led west from the Winter Camp to the fort outside which the Batavi were waiting.

'That must be the man himself. Kiv did say that he'd have to be hoisted into the saddle if he were to ride out to meet us, so presumably he's decided to exchange a little dignity to avoid the spectacle of having to be pushed back up onto his horse when our discussion is done with.'

The Romans stopped fifty paces short of the point where the Batavi stood waiting, and Scar gestured to Alcaeus.

'We'll walk forward to meet them. Perhaps that wolf's head on your helmet will help with the picture I intend to paint for this legatus.'

Strolling forward until they were halfway between their own men and the Roman emissaries, the two men watched in silence as the legatus augustus dismounted ponderously from the cart, waved away his mounted bodyguard and walked stiffly towards them accompanied by a single officer, a man clad in the bronze plate and magnificently plumed helmet of a senior tribune.

'Well now, look who's come to see us. It's our friend Tribune Verus.'

The two men stopped five paces from the Batavi officers, the younger man inclining his head in a gesture of respect with a faint smile as Scar saluted the two men with punctilious precision.

'Legatus Augusti. Tribune.'

Flaccus returned the salute with the look of a man still not entirely used to military formality.

'Prefect Scar. I see you and your men have made good time in your march north.'

'The road is well maintained, Legatus, and the weather has been particularly kind to us, neither too hot nor too cold and with hardly any rain at all. If this keeps up the Rhenus will become a difficult river for your ships to navigate, I expect, which will give you a new set of challenges keeping the legions supplied. Especially as I'm told that we now possess a good number of your ships?'

Flaccus smiled knowingly.

'Straight to the point, eh, Prefect?'

Scar nodded briskly.

'I think it best to waste as little time as possible, Legatus. I'm sure you're a busy man with everything that's happening both here and elsewhere, and I'm keen to get my men on the road north without losing too much more time.'

The Roman nodded, a hint of amusement creasing the skin around his eyes.

'Indeed. And your march north is obviously the subject I have asked you here to discuss.' Scar nodded in silence, waiting for the Roman to make the first move. 'You have been summoned back to your tribe's land by your kinsman Gaius Julius Civilis, I am told.'

'We call him Kivilaz, Legatus, but apart from that your information is correct. The elders of my tribe have delegated military command of our forces to him, and he has sent the order that we are to march back to Batavodurum to join the forces defending our independence from external assault.'

Flaccus shook his head with a gentle smile, as if pointing out the error of the statement to an erring child.

'Defending your independence, Prefect? Your people are bound to Rome by a treaty that dates back to Agrippa's conquest of Germania, so you are hardly in a position to declare any such *independence.*'

Scar raised a hand, gesturing aside the legatus's assertion.

'A treaty that Rome has torn up and thrown away. A treaty shamefully ignored in the conscription of our men, even those either too young or too old for service. A treaty shamefully sullied by physical assaults on our children. A treaty shamefully abrogated by Roman boots trampling the soil we hold so dear without any such invitation, boots worn by men with their swords and spears sharpened for war. Under these circumstances we can no longer be considered allies of Rome, but rather a disappointed neighbour who will defend our land and people as zealously as we once defended your empire's honour.'

The legatus nodded his understanding.

'And yet you offered terms to Tribune Verus, before releasing him to ride north with news of your change of allegiance, the news that brought me upriver to meet you? A donative, to be paid promptly, the guarantee of double pay for life for every one of you, and the expansion of your cavalry to encompass every man in your cohorts. All promises, the tribune assures me, that were made to you in the wake of the battle at Cremona, and by no less august a person than the emperor himself. Of these three demands the last is the most troubling, as I'm sure you know, so much so that I could almost suspect that you make it simply to have it refused.'

Scar looked at him in silence, and Flaccus shook his head in frustration.

'The donative is impossible, of course. Were I to make such a payment my legions would know of it within hours, and would be rightly incensed at such a use of gold when the empire is in ferment, not to mention their own expectations of such a payment. I believe that Vitellius's promise of such a gift, and that of double pay for every man who fought at Cremona, were both intended to be fulfilled at a happier time, when the empire is not at war with itself and the treasury is not empty. And I also believe that you know this very well. As to converting your entire strength to cavalry, do you really imagine that I can authorise the creation of eight new cavalry wings, with the huge change in your tribe's military power that would result, given these recent developments? Vitellius would order my execution the moment he heard of it. So it's out of the question. That's clear enough to both of us, I suspect.'

Scar nodded.

'In which case I believe we have nothing to discuss, Legatus. If you'll excuse me?'

The Roman raised a hand.

'Perhaps there is something more we might profitably consider between us?' He gestured to the ground beside the road. 'Will you walk with me?'

Alcaeus and Verus watched them stroll away with equal bemusement, and after a moment the centurion shrugged and unlaced
the cheek guards of his helmet with a bemused grin.

'It's too hot to stand here sweating myself stupid, unless you
think we should go at it for the honour of our respective causes?'

The tribune smiled back at him and took off his own helmet.

'You really think you can march north past Fortress Bonna, and
Colonial Agrippinensis, and Novaesium, and the Old Camp? Surely
you can see that the moment you leave this spot Flaccus has no
choice but to send word to Bonna to block your path and to lead
the legions waiting in the Winter Camp to put your cohorts into the
jaws of the nutcracker? How can you hope to reach your homeland
with four legions waiting for you and two more at your backs?'

Alcaeus grinned back at him.

'A year ago you'd have been right, Tribune. Back then the
legions you're talking about were at full strength, and recently
blooded against Vindex's revolt in Gaul. But now . . .'

Varus nodded, acknowledging the point.

'I know. You're going to tell me that they're shadows of their
previous strength. But you still can't expect to make the march
without taking casualties, and dealing them out threefold in return,
if your reputation is anything close to the truth. Men will die on
both sides. Attitudes will harden. Surely this must result in all-out
war?'

The centurion shrugged.

'One of the joys of being no more than a mere junior officer,
Tribune, is that I don't have to worry about such things. If my
prefect orders me to march, I order my men to march, and make
sure they march as fast as required. If my prefect orders me to
fight, I order my men to fight, make sure they fight well, and
fight alongside them to the best of my own abilities.'

'Really? You don't give even a moment's thought to the implications of what it is that might result from this insanity? You know
that the civil war must come to an end soon enough, and that
when that happens whoever has won will send legions north to
settle the score with your people?'

Alcaeus shrugged.

'Who can tell how this will end? I know I can't, and I'm pretty sure that you can't either, for all your obvious education. What I do know, Tribune, is that if we'd obeyed your orders to march south back over the mountains, we'd have been divided up among your legions, rather than still forming the cohorts you see behind me. Your orders would result in the certainty of disaster, against its mere possibility by the path we have chosen. There's not a man among us who wouldn't accept the risk of death in an honourable battle rather than the slow death of division and humiliation at the hands of your soldiers.' He grinned again. 'And besides, you're forgetting something.'

Varus raised a questioning eyebrow, and the Batavi leaned in close to speak softly.

'If the men of our cohorts were the half-trained and half-hearted recruits who populate the legions you expect to stop our march north, then I might share your pessimistic view of our chances. But we're not. We're the best soldiers in the empire, trained veterans who will fight to the death and to the last man if that is what is called for. Not for this.' He raised the vine stick in his right hand. 'And not even for this.' He tapped the wolf's head that topped his helmet, symbol of his priest's status. 'Although both of these things will routinely inspire them to do things that you Romans might consider heroic on the battlefield. No, they will commit themselves to either death or glory for one very simple reason.' He tapped his chest. 'Because of this. Because they have the blood of our people running through their veins, and because they know that every man in the tribe would change places with them in an instant given the chance. Because, Tribune, they are *Batavi*.'

He turned to look at Scar and Flaccus, who, having walked away together for fifty paces were pacing back, the Roman speaking animatedly to the Batavi prefect.

'And it seems from what I hear that your legatus augusti shares my view. As well he might. Send all the legions you have against us, but you won't enjoy the sight of what we send back to you.'

The tribune stared back at him for a moment, then laughed softly.

'Same old Batavians, eh? Full of piss and vinegar, and so . . . German.'

The priest bowed slightly with a wry grin.

'We're a mixture, Tribune, one part Roman discipline, one part German blood drinker, and one part . . . well, even I'm not sure.'

'One part Greek?'

'Pardon?'

'Your name, Centurion, is Greek, is it not? I made a point of looking it up once I had access to the fortress commander's library at the Winter Camp. Alcaeus was a Greek poet in the time when Rome was little more than a collection of towns ruled by an upstart king, a poet of wine, and war, who composed hymns to the gods. How does a German blood-drinker end up being named after a dead Greek?'

The older man smiled.

'My father's sister's son served with the German Bodyguard in Rome, back in the time of Claudius. His name was so barbaric, and so likely to be mangled by the Romans, that he decided to take a name from Greek history. All the good names, Achilles, Hector, Ajax and the like were all taken already, and the rule in those days was that a name could only be used once, not like these days when they all want to be called something heroic, and so he chose the name Alcaeus. Said he liked the idea of a man who sang songs to the gods. Although he told me it was really because he loved wine, one night when he was in his cups. And my father chose to name me after him, as a sign of respect and to link the two sides of the family.'

Varus gestured to the wolf's head.

'It seems appropriate.'

'It does, doesn't it? Although the abilities that put the wolf on my helmet can be both a blessing and a curse.'

'How so?'

'I see things in my dreams, Tribune. Things that often come to pass.'

'Really? How . . .'

'Interesting? Exciting? Sometimes. Awful? Sometimes, Tribune, that too.'

'Kivilaz.'

Prefect Labeo bowed his head in a gesture of respect for the Batavi prince's position within the tribe although, to Hramn's sharp eye from his place behind his cousin, the acknowledgement of his rival's superiority was almost curt enough to be deemed disrespectful. The council chamber was full, all of the chairs in the circle occupied bar one, that in which Labeo would normally have taken his seat. Hramn stood behind the prince's chair in a comfortable stance with his hands behind his back, not a member of the council but highly regarded both for his war record and his command of the imperial bodyguard before its disbandment, and a pair of his men stood guard at the hall's door. The Batavi Guard's commander was more than usually dour, his gaze fixed on Labeo as the prefect stood before Kivilaz to make his report. The prince looked up, acknowledging the other man's presence before him tersely.

'Prefect.'

The two men exchanged stares for a moment before Labeo spoke again.

'As you see, I have delivered you a victory over the Romans. Their legions have trodden our soil, tasted the bitter fruit of that invasion, and are now in full retreat.'

Kivilaz smiled up at him from his seated position.

'As you promised. You are, it seems, a loyal son of the tribe. Your men are following up on the Roman withdrawal?'

Labeo nodded.

'They dismantled their bridge and sailed the ships away up river, but of course that was no obstacle to us. My deputy took our horses across the river in the usual manner and is keeping a close watch on their retreat to ensure that they don't deviate from their march back to the Old Camp. The Island is safe from their depredations, thanks to us.'

The prince regarded his colleague levelly for long enough that the prefect shifted uneasily.

'Indeed. Thanks to *us*, our people are indeed safe once more from the threat of Rome's hunger for manpower. But I do find myself wondering, Prefect, whether you fulfilled your part of the agreement we made before the battle at the river quite as enthusiastically as your words imply.'

He sat in silence, watching as Labeo's self-assurance evaporated in an instant, the other man's face creasing into a frown at the first intimations that all was not quite as he had expected.

'I am . . . surprised . . . that you should even ask such a question, Kivilaz. Have I not just handed you a victory over the legions, the bloodless defeat that you stated was your aim, to run the Romans off our ground without granting them any meaningful justification for an all-out war? It was me who persuaded their legatus augusti that my men and I were still to be trusted, even in the face of our tribe's revolt. It was me who led my wing forward in their vanguard, both convincing them of our commitment to the empire and ensuring that there were no skirmishes with your guardsmen to cost us unnecessary lives. And it was me who led my men to attack their auxiliaries, making the legions' position on the battlefield untenable. I fail to see how you might have any grounds to suggest that I have done anything other than play a dangerous game that has ended in total success?'

Hramn flicked his eyes up at the hall's roof and shook his head minutely, and Labeo, nominally his superior as a member of the tribe's ruling council, frowned at him angrily.

'You shake your head, Hramn, as if my words are untrue. Perhaps—'

The guardsman shook his head in open defiance of his colleague's statement.

'Your advance, Labeo, was as inept as any I've ever seen. Half a dozen times I could have cut out one of your squadrons and put them to the spear before the rest of you could have ridden to their rescue. And every time I ignored the opportunities you presented me with, and ordered yet another retreat when I should have been on the attack to teach you a tactical lesson, I wondered just how blind the Romans had to be to miss such obvious lack of commitment on my part and equally clear incompetence on yours. Had they perceived that I was holding back from taking the golden opportunities you were serving up for me, then they could only have concluded either that I was as inept a commander as you or that we were playing out a game between us.'

His colleague's response was heated, both at the implied criticism of his abilities and the deeper implications.

'Not true! And even if it were, how does that diminish the role we played today? My men fell on the Ubians and Trevirans at the moment we agreed, and destroyed them, as we agreed, Kivilaz. What more proof do you—'

He fell silent as the prince raised a hand, looking to either side at the evidently supportive council members, to judge from the way they were regarding the cavalry prefect.

'You simply did what I ordered, Labeo. Your role in today's battle was to follow your instructions, not to enact some magnanimous agreement between the two of us. And even if you did as you were ordered, I am forced to observe that you did not carry out the order as it was given. Your instructions were to destroy the Ubians and Trevirans, to *eradicate* them, and thereby provide a lesson to those other tribes who might yet decide to side with Rome against us, and to punish them for renouncing their tribal name and taking on the title the Romans gave them when they conquered their homeland and relocated them across the river where they might be better controlled. Instead of which . . .'

He paused, waiting for the prefect to fill the silence, but Hramn beat him to it.

'My guardsmen tallied what was left of the auxiliary cohorts, while your men rode away to watch the Roman retreat. And I was disappointed, if hardly surprised, to find that your assault had only killed a third of their strength, while the rest of them had either managed to surrender or simply escaped. And given that we only have four hundred or so prisoners from two cohorts that mustered at least nine hundred men between them, with only three hundred and thirty corpses of dead soldiers, then at least two hundred more of them are still at large on our land. My cohort is sweeping the fields and farms at this very moment, completing the task that you were set to perform and failed to deliver before your failure can result in innocent deaths.'

Labeo's mouth gaped in astonishment and anger.

'I did what was ordered!'

'Indeed. But just not very well, it seems to me. So you stand accused either of incompetence or lack of interest in fulfilling the orders of this council.'

His gaze flicked back to Kivilaz, his head shaking in a furious attempt at rebuttal.

'You ordered me away to follow the legions east before the task could be completed!'

The prince leaned back in his chair, pondering the man before him.

'What to make of you, Labeo, still evades me. On the one hand you purport to be loyal to the tribe . . .'

His rival waved a dismissive hand, furious anger reddening his face.

'I know your game, Kivilaz, you and your nephew Hramn behind you! I hear your dismissive words, painting my actions in support of our uprising as being somewhere between incompetent and uncommitted! I see the way in which you are ready to pronounce upon my part in this victory in the manner of a ruler, rather than the equal you told me was the case when we agreed to this course of action!' Kivilaz sat back in his chair magisterially, listening intently to the increasingly irritated outburst with a faint but unmistakable smile that only served to further inflame Labeo's anger. 'You see me as a rival for the throne, don't you? You intend to—'

'A rival? And for the *throne*?' Even in the middle of his tirade Labeo was instantly silenced by the note in the other man's voice, and in that moment of insight his anger evaporated, replaced by a sense of impending disaster as he realised how fully he had played into Kivilaz's hands. 'I don't seek a *throne*, Labeo, even if such a thing seems to be your own ambition. My only desire is to see my tribe liberated from Rome's control, granted the same status as the Frisii, allied to the empire but not subject to the whims and uncertainties of their rule as so clearly displayed by this current war for *their* throne. But neither will I submit my people to a similar power struggle, as you seek to take the throne with which you are so obsessed, in defiance of the men the tribe has empowered to exercise that authority. And I am not minded to watch my back for your blade, distracting me from my sworn duty of delivering the will of the council through my *temporary* leadership of the tribe's spears.'

He fell silent and stared at Labeo with a questioning expression, while the prefect shook his head in disgust at both the trap he had walked into and his own lack of guile. When he spoke again his voice was dull, laden with the realisation of his defeat at a moment when he had least expected to face any such threat.

'You have me, it seems. I am apparently condemned of plotting to make myself king, and out of my own mouth, no less.' He flicked a glance at Hramn, still brooding behind Kivilaz's chair. 'Presumably that thug, your nephew, will be the man to take my life?'

The prince shook his head, looking up at the other man with an expression of perplexity tinged with sadness.

'Take your life, brother? Again, you seem to judge me by a different set of standards to those to which I aspire. I don't plan to take your life, Labeo, but rather to ensure that my own is not under constant threat from your ambitions.' Hramn gestured to the guardsmen who had moved from their positions at the hall's door to wait behind Labeo, and the two soldiers briskly disarmed the prefect by pulling his sword and dagger from their scabbards, leaving them hanging forlornly empty while Kivilaz continued pronouncing his fate. 'I have discussed your case with the other members of our council, and we are agreed that your ambitions are too powerful to be allowed to run out of control. You will therefore be exiled from the tribe, and sent to live among our allies the Frisii. This temporary confinement will provide you with an opportunity to gain a deeper understanding of how a tribe can co-exist with the empire while remaining apart from Rome, proudly independent while retaining their status as allies. They will accord you the respect you are due as a prefect of the Batavi, and provide you with food and shelter. While you are with them perhaps you will have adequate time to reflect upon the true nature of service to our people, and to contrast it to your own urge to seize power? Take him away.'

Labeo raised his open hands, turning to look at the council members seated around him and holding the guardsmen momentarily at bay with a stare invested with all that remained of his authority.

'I am unjustly accused in this, my brothers. I am traduced by a man who will at some point not very far away assume the powers of a king, if not the title! He will soon hold you all in his hand, with the same regal power he has used to discredit and exile me, and you will come to regret falling prey to his scheming all too soon. On the day that your new king insults the empire's dignity one time too many, the day when the tribe stop being allies of a pretender and become enemies of *any* emperor, you will come to see how deep is the hole you will have dug for yourselves.'

Hramn gestured angrily to the guardsmen, but Labeo's raised hand bought him time for one more brief statement before the big man stepped around Kivilaz's chair and hustled him away.

'Under Kivilaz's rule you will discover soon enough what it means to be enemies of Rome!'

The Old Camp, Germania Inferior, August AD 69

'Civilis actually told you to fortify the camp, Legatus?'

Lupercus shook his head with a slight smile at Marius.

'No, Centurion, not in quite such a direct manner. In point of fact he made no reference to our fortress's defences at all, other than an oblique reference to some means of undermining them that he wouldn't detail. It was more what he didn't say that leads me to the conclusion that we need to be ready for a siege.'

The two senior centurions stared at him expectantly. The legatus had remained tight-lipped on the subject of his conversation with his former comrade throughout the forty-mile march back south from their defeat by the Batavi, but both men had known that something the Batavi prince said had left him in a state of intro-spection.

'Our enemy is clearly a man more deeply steeped in calculation then the hot-headed warrior I knew in Britannia. He could have turned his dogs on us back there, and slaughtered the entire army. The destruction of two legions, however understrength they might have been, would have gifted him the reputation of a latter-day Arminius, victor over the best soldiers Rome has to offer. And let's be honest with ourselves, his cavalry could have prevented us from making a run for the bridge, they made that abundantly plain by their mock attack on us, and his tribesmen and soldiers would have overrun us soon enough. But his losses would have been significant. A pitched battle against five thousand legionaries, even men as partially trained and raw as ours, could only have resulted in the loss of a major part of his own army. So imagine this scenario, gentlemen: imagine that Civilis had attacked with his full force instead of pulling his punch to maintain the poten-tial of a way to row back from this uprising. Imagine our legions destroyed, and no Roman force between here and Novaesium, but Civilis's own army badly mauled in achieving that result. Imagine that Civilis were to find himself with a Batavi army weakened by serious battle losses, while at the same time thou-sands more barbarians flock to his banner from the surrounding tribes, drawn by tales of slaughter and captured legion standards. In this scenario Civilis finds himself the leader of an army composed mainly of tribesmen, barbarian warriors who greatly outnumber his own force, which is not only reduced in size but also a burden on the Batavi people, due to their large numbers of wounded. Worse, he now has thousands of men with no tribal loyalty to the Batavi on his land, their obedience to his orders uncertain and their presence a constant threat, were they to turn on his weakened forces in hopes of claiming the most productive farmland in the whole lower course of the river for themselves. I for one would not envy him that balancing act.'

'Whereas . . . ?'

The legatus shrugged at Aquillius.

'It's obvious. He's run us off his tribe's land with our tails between our legs. Our auxiliary forces have deserted or been destroyed, our army is incapable of threatening his people's independence without reinforcement in legion strength and more than one legion for that matter. He, on the other hand, retains his full military capability, with his militia, his guardsmen, his cavalry and the Batavi's traditional allies the Cananefates all intact, nicely balancing the barbarians flocking to his standards across the Rhenus. But there's more strength to be had, much more, and not long from now if his plan succeeds.'

Marius nodded, understanding Lupercus's argument all too well.

'The cohorts?'

'Exactly, First Spear. The cohorts. Four thousand men, one third mounted, able to cross rivers at will and borne into battle at the speed of a cantering horse, every man trained from childhood by fathers and uncles who formerly stood in their ranks, and know the exacting standards expected of their sons. These are no mere auxiliaries, they are professional soldiers whose martial skills match the best men in our own army. Imagine, gentlemen, a legion's strength of superbly trained soldiers, experts with spear, sword and shield, and freshly blooded in the civil war only a few months ago. Men who fought at Cremona with distinction, and earned the praise of the emperor for their part in the destruction of the Othonians' left wing. Now consider that strength from Civilis's perspective.'

'If the cohorts reach the Island then his army will be powerful enough to hold off several legions, as long as the tribes stay on his side.'

'Yes. Except there's no "if" to it. I think we can be quite sure that they'll reach the Island, because it seems that my superior officer is colluding with Civilis in the matter.'

The two centurions stared at him in amazement, Aquillius nodding slowly.

'Flaccus?'

'Yes, Flaccus. If what Civilis told me was the truth, then the legatus augusti has been playing both the black and white counters on the soldiers board at the same time. On the one hand he declares loyalty for Vitellius, while on the other he quietly does all he can to aid the cause of his rival Vespasianus. And if he ever shows his face here again then you'll be joining a queue if you want to exact some degree of revenge for such treachery, because everything he's done until now seems to have been calculated to maintain some sort of balance between ourselves and the Batavi, rather than to deal with them decisively.'

Marius shook his head grimly.

'The Batavi don't do balance, Legatus. They do total, overwhelming brutal victory and not very much else, not on the harpastum field and not on the battlefield.'

'I know. I've fought alongside them, and seen just how ruthless they can be.' Lupercus leaned back in his chair. 'Civilis will be keeping the tribes happy by promising them further conquest, and the establishment of a German empire that will be strong enough to face down any force that the emperor can send north. Which means that he'll need to come south and seek to remove the Old Camp's threat, and soon, if he is to avoid the tribesmen growing bored of waiting and becoming restive. He's put a saddle on a savage beast that needs to be fed meat if it is to be kept from turning on its rider.'

Marius frowned.

'But he told you that he has revolted at the request of Vespasianus. Surely he'll wait to see the result of the civil war before making the decision whether to attack Rome directly? The moment he attempts to defeat our walls he signs his own death sentence.'

The legatus nodded.

'True enough. No matter who the emperor is, Vespasianus or Vitellius, they will have no alternative but to make an example of him in order to prevent a dozen other such rebellions from springing up.'

'So why?'

'Why take that momentous step, and cast the fatal spear at our walls that will have the same effect as attacking Rome itself? There are two potential reasons why he would do such a thing. He will see the prize to be won, when his forces reach their full strength, nothing less than leadership of a confederation of tribes that might make him so strong that he could negotiate terms with whoever wins the war for the throne from a position of impregnable strength.'

He sipped his wine again.

'That's the first possibility. The second is that Civilis is simply overreaching himself, driven by pride, and hate, and the urge to revenge. He may just have overestimated his ability to face Rome in open war, or decided that the empire is too riven by this civil war to deal with him. You and I know that Rome will crush this uprising with all the ruthlessness that we always use with errant subject nations, but Civilis may believe that this will never happen. Which would make him a fool – but a fool with a knife at our throats. So, gentlemen, we need to prepare for a siege in the little time that we've been granted. Your thoughts?'

The two senior centurions looked at each other, and Aquillius spoke first at Marius's silent invitation.

'We need to stop drilling the troops, for one thing.'

Marius nodded at his colleague's statement.

'Absolutely. If we've got no chance of beating the Batavians in open battle, then there's no point spending even a moment longer preparing them to a straight fight. Or conditioning them for a campaign either. Being able to march twenty miles in full equip-ment isn't going to be much use either.'

Aquillius turned to the office's planning table, using a hand to smooth over the sand with which they had planned the abortive mission across the Rhenus.

'Our only priority now must be making this place and our men ready to hold off a determined attempt to break in. If I may, Legatus?'

Lupercus nodded, and the big man quickly sketched a diagram with a fingertip, drawing the camp's rectangular shape before adding the circle of its arena to the south and a jumble of smaller buildings between the two.

'Whoever built this fortress picked a decent position, given how flat the land around here is. The northern wall is positioned on a slope that's steep enough to make an attack from that direction difficult to say the least, although the other three sides are easy enough to approach. The walls are tall enough and stout enough, although there aren't enough bolt throwers or catapults and I'd prefer a higher parapet to protect us from arrows and thrown spears, but that's nothing that can't be solved with enough time and plenty of wood to build it up. Nor is it really clear to me how long the walls themselves would stand up if thousands of barbarians get any time to go at them with axes and hammers, so we'll need some means of punishing anyone who gets close enough to try that approach. Add to that the fact that the vicus would allow them a covered approach to the southern side, and as it stands I'd expect a determined attack to succeed within a day.'

Marius nodded.

'I agree. We need to put some of the men to felling trees and hauling them into the camp for timber, to reinforce the defences while the rest strengthen the walls and double the number of bolt artillery positions, with some form of protection to prevent the Germans from showering them with spears and arrows and killing their crews. And we'll need to dig out the ditch to a proper depth, and put in plenty of lilies as well, to make their approach harder. The main problem is that this place was designed to house two full-strength legions, but we only have the equivalent of one legion to hold it. If I were this man Civilis, I'd move his men around under cover of darkness, and attack a different point every day.'

Lupercus stood up, leaning over the sand table.

'Problems only exist to be solved, gentlemen. The problem of the vicus is simple enough, I'd say. We have a good number of axes in the stores?'

Marius nodded slowly.

'Yes, Legatus. What do you want to do with the townspeople?'

The older man shrugged.

'We'll bring them all into the fortress. The men will have to be conscripted to assist with the re-fortification work, and if Civilis does as I expect, they can join the defence. Having their families inside the walls will serve to sharpen their appetite to resist, I'd imagine, and the women and older children can act as fire watchers when the barbarians start lofting burning arrows over the walls. Oh, and with that in mind, if we only have a single legion's strength in a camp built for two, perhaps we might consider demolishing some of the buildings *inside* the walls as well as outside?'

The two centurions stared at him for a moment before Aquillius spoke.

'My apologies, Legatus, I've misjudged you. I thought I was the most single-minded man in this fortress.'

The legatus turned to face his subordinate, his face an emotionless mask.

'Don't imagine that I'm happy with the idea of condemning hundreds of innocent woman and children to the very likely prospect of being subject to the attentions of the Germans if they break through these walls. The very thought of it will trouble me for the rest of my life, if we manage to live through what's coming. But if we have a choice here, between an honourable defeat and a victory sullied by the decisions that only I can make, then I'll carry the burden of that dishonour with the knowledge that I made the survival of two legions possible. And since you are one of the *three* most warlike men within these walls, you and your colleague here can decide between you who will be the man to provide the discontented men of the vicus with the smack of firm leadership that they'll need, if they are to have any chance of surviving the horrors of a siege.'

The Winter Camp, Mogontiacum, Germania Superior,
August AD 69

'We must *fight*! Our honour as Roman gentlemen *demands* it! To
do anything else will simply bring shame upon our reputations,
and those of the legions camped here!'

Antonius watched impassively as legatus Vocula walked to the
window of his legion's principia to stare north over the Winter
Camp's high wall, the direction in which the rebellious Batavi
cohorts had marched away the previous day. Hordeonius Flaccus
raised a questioning eyebrow from his place behind his desk,
leaning back in his chair and spreading his hands in an expression
of apparent confusion.

'I'm somewhat surprised at your change of heart, Dillius Vocula.'
Flaccus's tone was light enough, as behoved the superiority of his
position as the man who commanded the entire army of Germania,
but there was no mistaking his underlying nervousness at his
subordinate's display of irritation. 'Only yesterday you agreed that
with your legions so badly stripped of their fighting power, and
with such a high proportion of new recruits, and with the temper
of our auxiliary forces so uncertain, we might best fulfil the
emperor's orders by remaining in place and allowing the Batavians
to march north to their homeland. Where, it is to be hoped, they
will be satisfied to camp on their native soil and glower at us
across the river?'

Vocula shook his head as he turned back to face his superior.

'That was the feeling of the meeting *you* called, Hordeonius
Flaccus. That was the sum total of the concerns felt by my tribunes, men who for the most part, like you, are quiet supporters
of Vespasianus. That was not my view, but one you decided to
adopt as your own for whatever reasons.'

His unblinking gaze disconcerted his superior, who was well
aware that there was a body of men within their senatorial class
whose patience with the niceties of rank often ran a poor second
to their pride in their own abilities and their regard for their
familial honour, and that Vocula, the first of his line to enjoy

senatorial rank and thereby beholden to nobody in particular, was just such a man.

'Are you trying to say that—'

Vocula raised a hand, palm out.

'Legatus Augusti, let's not attempt to pretend that I'm not aware of your feelings on the matter of who would make a better emperor. You are a known friend of Titus Flavius Vespasianus. When other men were calling him *mulio* for the way in which he restored his fortunes by dealing in pack animals, you were one of the few senators in Rome who chose not to join in the general merriment at his expense. And now that he's roused the east against the emperor, you naturally feel sympathy for his cause. I understand that.' Flaccus waited in silence for his subordinate to continue, his expression imperturbable. 'You were therefore open to the arguments made by our junior officers who, I note, are not the best that were to be found among the men of the Fourth and Twenty-second Legions, but rather those who it was felt could safely be left behind while their more able colleagues went south with the bulk of my legion and the rump of the Fourth. I may feel some sympathy towards Vespasianus, if not as strong as your own, but I know my sworn duty to the empire. I did not agree at the time, and I do not agree now, and a night of unhappy reflection has only hardened my feelings on the subject. We should march north after these Batavians, catch them in the jaws of the vice with the men of Fortress Bonna and Novaesium, and put their rebellion to the sword, before it has the chance to be fanned from a local uprising to a full-blooded war. They'll be laying siege to the Old Camp within the month if we don't act decisively!'

The older man nodded slowly.

'I can see the value of what you counsel, Dillius Vocula. But are your men really ready for war?'

His subordinate smiled grimly.

'They're a damned sight better than they were six months ago. A touch of the vine stick can do wonders for the most disaffected of men, and my First Spear is a most determined and capable man.'

Flaccus inclined his head in respect of the truth behind the other man's point, shooting a glance at Antonius that the senior centurion carefully avoided meeting directly. After a moment's thought the legatus augusti nodded decisively.

'Very well, Legatus, I can see the truth in what you say. I'll write to Herennius Gallus at Bonna and warn him to have his men of the First Germanica ready to block the rebels' path, while we march north in their wake at the campaign pace and reach the point where he has to stop them at the same time they arrive. Will that satisfy our honour, do you think?'

Vocula pursed his lips.

'Our four thousand legionaries attacking from the south, while Herennius Gallus's men stand firm across the road to their north? I'd say that should be enough to make them think twice, and surrender rather than face the prospect of being enveloped. A full-scale war in Germany will be averted, and you will be able to send good news to our imperial master in Rome. I would have thought that everyone could be satisfied with such a conclusion.'

'Except, perhaps . . .'

The legatus stared at his superior expectantly, and when the older man failed to enlarge upon his opinion he raised a sardonic eyebrow.

'Except perhaps that it doesn't fit with your personal aspirations, Legatus Augusti.'

Flaccus looked back at him with such a knowing expression that Vocula was momentarily nonplussed.

'My personal aspirations matter little when compared to the fate of the empire, Dillius Vocula. As do your own, which are of course to see battle and triumph over these barbarians so as to earn the approbation of your peers. No, my musing was to do with an altogether different aspect of the matter.'

'Which is?'

He smiled into his subordinate's irritation.

'You thought that everyone could be satisfied with such an outcome. Except, perhaps these Batavians. And my experience to date, Legatus, has taught me that they don't deal with disappointment all that well.'

The Old Camp, Germania Inferior, September AD 69

'You want what?'

Marius stood his ground, staring at the man facing him with an impassivity he was far from feeling.

'It's not a question of what I want. A decision has already been made to demolish these buildings, to prevent the barbarians from using them as cover to get close to the south gate. You'll have to choose whether to come inside and join us until this war's done with or take your chances somewhere else. I'd recommend the former, but it's your choice.'

The smith looked away for a moment, gauging his support from the men gathered behind him, then turned back and raised a broad, scarred palm in rejection of the centurion's argument.

'You can fuck off! This is our town and these are our homes! Our businesses! If you legion bastards think you can just tear them down, then you can think again! I've lived here fifteen years, I've got a wife and two children and a business to run, so there's no way I'm going to let you destroy everything I've worked for.' He looked at the men behind him. 'And neither will they!'

Marius shrugged.

'I understand. My father was a tavern keeper, after he retired from the service. Everything he had was in that tavern. Under these circumstances his response would probably have been the same, at least until he realised the depth of the shit he was about to step into if he ignored the realities of the situation. Which is what you're doing.'

Lupercus had raised an eyebrow when the centurion had informed him of his intended approach to the issue of the vicus and its population.

'You're sure, First Spear? Shouldn't you take some men with you? What if they decide to argue, or even to resist? I'd imagine that feelings will run high on the matter.'

Marius had nodded agreement.

'Undoubtedly they will. And yes, they'll argue, and yes, they might even try to make a fight of it. We could just march a century down there and force them in through the gate at spearpoint, but what would that achieve? They'd be sullen, ready to knife us in the back at the first opportunity, untrustworthy, dangerous, even. I might as well just have them all killed if that's the way we approach the matter, because that's the way it'll end up.'

Aquillius had spoken up, nodding sagely at his colleague's opinion.

'He's right. If these people don't join us of their own free will then they'll either have to be forced to work in chains or sent south. And sending them south would mean diverting men we can't spare from the preparations we're making.'

Lupercus had looked at them both in turn.

'Accepting that for a moment, there's still the matter of one of my two senior officers proposing to go into the vicus single handed to confront two hundred men with the suggestion that they need to abandon their homes and livelihoods, a suggestion that's really an order, which is something I doubt will escape their notice. What if they just turn on you?'

Marius had smiled tightly at his superior.

'I'm a legion centurion, Legatus. Civilians don't worry me.'

The smith raised a big hand, stabbing a finger at his scale-armoured chest.

'What realities? So you lot have picked a fight with the Batavi. So fucking what? Go and have your fight with them, just leave us out of it!'

The men gathered behind him muttered their agreement, and Marius shook his head.

'It's not that simple, even if we both wish it were. You've lived off the legions camped here for years, and become part of the camp yourselves. So when the barbarian army arrives to lay siege to these walls they're going to see you as nothing more than easy meat! If you want to be outside these walls when they arrive, you be my guest, if, that is, you want your women at their mercy, once they've finished cutting you fools to pieces? And your children? Do you think they'll spare a girl of ten years from their indignities? What about eight years? Six?'

The men behind the smith stared at him in dawning realisation of their predicament.

'We can leave! Take our families south to the legions up the river, or west into Gaul!'

The centurion shook his head.

'And leave your businesses behind? How are you going to make any money without your furnace and anvil? And how will you feed your family when you get to wherever it is you think you'll be safe? The men of wherever you end up will work you like slaves, rob you blind of whatever money you have and prey on your families at every opportunity. And that's *if* you manage to avoid the bandits and enemy scouts between here and wherever it is you decide to go to. Whereas if you stay, and work with us to prevent the fortress falling, I personally guarantee you'll get assistance to set up your businesses again, once the danger has passed. You can bring your stock and your tools into the fortress, we have plenty of spare space for their storage and to accommodate your families, then work with us to make sure that these walls protect them from the barbarians.' The men of the vicus were looking at each other, some nodding reluctantly, others clearly unconvinced. 'We'll pay you all as legionaries for the duration of your service, and provide you and your dependants with the same rations our men receive. Either that, or you can take whatever you can carry and try to make it to somewhere the barbarians won't catch up with you, in the hope of being allowed to make a fresh start by the men who already make money doing what you do, wherever it is that you end up.'

'What about our homes?'

Marius turned to face the man who had shouted the question.

'All buildings outside of these walls will be dismantled, and the materials used to make the fortress walls we're all going to be dependent on stronger. When the threat has been dealt with the legion will assist you with the rebuilding of your property.' He shrugged. 'Take your time and talk it through. Decide what's best for you, to stay here with the certainty that as long as the fortress stands you and your families will be safe, or to leave for who knows where, and who knows what. Come to the gate and ask for First Spear Marius once you've decided.'

'How long will you give us?'

'A day. After that these buildings are coming down, whether you've removed what you need from them or not.'

He turned away, only to pause as a big hand took his arm. Turning, and restraining the strong urge to grasp the hand and break its owner's wrist for having the temerity to touch him, he found the man's face riven with uncertainty.

'I have your word that you'll find room for my family in there?'

Marius nodded.

'We have plenty of empty barracks, you already know that. So many empty buildings that we're going to have to knock some of them down to stop them burning in the event of a siege.'

'And I can bring my anvil and tools in with me?'

'We'll help you. The one thing we're not short on is muscle.'

'And you'll feed us?'

'The same food we eat. We've enough for months, and there's more on the way from the south.'

The smith nodded decisively, waving a hand at the men behind him.

'This lot can do whatever they want. I'll come in there, and set my forge up in one of your empty buildings. You'll be needing smiths, won't you?'

The centurion nodded.

'Oh yes. There are one or two little surprises we have in mind for them that will make very good use of your skills.'

The Winter Camp, Mogontiacum, Germania Superior, September AD 69

'This is madness! Have you taken leave of your senses, Hordeonius Flaccus? I've got almost the entire garrison ready to march out on the parade ground, eight cohorts of legionaries just waiting for the order to go, and then just as I'm about to have the trumpeters sound the advance, you think you can just call me back into the fortress and casually tell me that I'm not going north after all?'

Vocula was practically snarling his disgust with the sudden turn of events, but if his insubordination bothered Hordeonius Flaccus the older man evidently wasn't inclined to let it show. He handed a scroll to the younger man, waiting with his face carefully composed while the legatus unrolled the message and read it with a stony face.

'It's from Vitellius.'

Vocula looked up at his superior momentarily, his expression stony.

'I can see that. I thought you were going to ask me to sully my honour with the message from Vespasianus's legatus augusti Antonius Primus that rumour has it arrived this morning!'

Flaccus's lips twitched in a slight smile.

'I suggest that you pass over the first paragraph where he makes it very clear that our previous defeats by the Batavians are entirely my own fault, based on my total failure to replace the twelve cohorts he removed from my army to march south and win him the throne.'

Vocula nodded with a hint of sympathy, having himself been downcast by the manifest failure of his recruiting officers to bring new legionaries to his standard.

'"*Given your utter failure to crush this rebellion at its source, you are hereby ordered to concentrate all efforts to the defence of Mogontiacum . . .*"'

He looked at Flaccus with an expression of utter disbelief.

'Gods below! He's ordering us to abandon the Old Camp legions to their fate! "*All of your legions are to focus on the defence of their fortresses and the control of their local populations in order to prevent the rebellion spreading any further from the Batavian home-land. The defence of the Mogontiacum fortress, and the prevention of any barbarian incursion into either the upper part of Germania or Gaul is to be prevented at all costs.*" Gods below, the man's forbidding us to do the one thing that might enable us to choke this fucking revolt off at its source! If those damned cohorts reach the Island, this man Civilis will have them besieging the Old Camp in no time!'

He shook his head at Flaccus in amazement.

'You intend obeying this idiot order, I presume?'

The older man raised his hands in question.

'Of course I do! What else would you suggest? I'm already clearly being blamed for the situation, I'm not about to defy a direct order from Rome and risk having some blank-eyed frumentarius sent to cut my throat! Your legions are to return to barracks, and I'll send a message to Herennius Gallus to stand his men down and allow the Batavians to pass unhindered.'

Vocula nodded morosely, the anger having boiled out of him with the sickening realisation that the imperial edict made it impossible for him to carry through the planned envelopment of the Batavi cohorts.

'Which is inevitable, I suppose. There's no way the man will have any chance of stopping four thousand battle-hardened barbarian maniacs with what's left of the original First Germanica and a few half-trained conscripts, and I very much doubt he'd be foolish enough to try with or without this most recent decision.'

5

'It looks like they might just have a go at stopping us after all, the poor bastards. I mean, look at them, I don't think they could wipe their own arses with both hands and a sponge the size of my head . . .'

Grimmaz's pronouncement on the scene before them elicited reluctant chuckles from the men of his tent party despite the evident gravity of the situation. Half a mile to the north of the spot where the Batavi cohorts stood, afforded a vantage point to the north by a rise in the road that ran parallel with the Rhenus, a straggling stream of soldiers was hurrying from the gates of the Bonna fortress to take up a position across the route past its high walls. Lanzo's opinion was stated in his usual soft tones, but where Grimmaz was all bombast and bravado, the Dancer's views were as always somewhat more understated.

'If that's the best that Rome has to put in our path, then the northern frontier might as well be declared open to all comers.'

The cohorts had halted half a mile from the fortress in march formation, Scar clearly retaining enough caution to provide his men with sufficient room to manoeuvre in the event that the garrison decided to put up a fight rather than allowing the Batavi soldiers to pass unhindered. Grimmaz spat on the ground at his feet, shaking his head in amusement.

'From the look of them it's been a quiet year, with little by way of making themselves ready for war. Their good officers probably all went south, and all that's left is the lazy bastards and idiots.'

'Lazy bastards and idiots, indeed? I'm sure there's a good

number of both, Leading Man Grimmaz, due to their policy of promoting men who might better have been left running tent parties!'

Banon had walked briskly down the century's column and halted by the tent party, gesturing to the head of the formation with his hastile, the brass-knobbed staff that was his badge of office.

'The centurion has been ordered to go forward and give the good news to whoever's in command of that rabble, and he's asked me to find him a tent party of unsurpassed ugliness and unpleasantness to escort him in the appropriate manner, gurn at the enemy and generally make sure that he's protected from nasty men with sharp iron. So fall out and follow me.'

He led them up the column to where Scar and Alcaeus were waiting, and the former smiled grimly at the sight of their serious expressions.

'Here you are, priest, your escort awaits. And you men had better keep your wits about you, because if you manage to lose me my right-hand man, then Hercules himself will have to be content with taking his ire out on whatever there is left of you all once I'm finished.'

Alcaeus saluted him and led them away down the hillock's slope and along the paved surface that ran arrow-straight past Bonna's fortified walls, looking around him with a professional eye and shaking his head at what he saw.

'Given they've had the best part of two weeks to get ready for us I can't say I'm all that impressed. I'd have had them out every day digging lily pits and putting up some sort of barrier to fight behind, but this ground's as smooth as a newborn's arse. My sort of battlefield.'

Banon grunted agreement.

'They don't look like they're up to much either.'

'No, they don't, do they? And they seem to have brought some friends with them just to make it even more amusing.'

The legionaries, whose formation now spanned the path past the fortress, were drawn up in a line four men deep from Bonna's thick, brick-faced walls to the forest three hundred paces to the west, their cohorts interspersed with the green shields of their auxiliaries, while behind their line a large group of armed civilians clamoured to be allowed through at their new enemy. A cohort of Hamian archers were readying themselves at the right-hand end of the line in a businesslike manner, stringing their bows and pushing arrows into the turf in front of them, ready to shoot. The party stopped thirty paces from the legion's line, and Alcaeus stepped forward to shout a greeting while the men around him tensed themselves to raise their shields against a spear throw from the Roman ranks.

'Good morning, soldiers of the First Legion! I am Alcaeus, wolf-priest of the First Batavi cohort, and I have come in peace to speak with your legatus in the hope of averting any unnecessary bloodshed! We are weary of war, and only seek to return to our homes and live in peace!'

He waited, and after a moment's pause the bronze-armoured figure of a senior officer stepped out of his men's ranks.

'I am Publius Herennius Gallus, legatus commanding the First Legion Germanica! I have orders from Legatus Augusti Hordeonius Flaccus to bar your path to the north! He is close behind you with the Fourth and Twenty-second Legions, marching from the Winter Camp to cut off any possibility of your retreat! You Batavians will soon find yourselves caught between the hammer and the anvil! Better to abandon this fruitless attempt to re-join your countrymen, and take your rightful place in Rome's service, than to suffer the indignity of defeat and all that accompanies that shameful outcome!'

Alcaeus grinned at the men standing alongside him.

'So, it's to be shit rather than sugar is it?' He raised his voice again, his tone still reasonable but just as firm. 'Our service to Rome, long and honourable, is at an end! We have given everything we have to your empire, and in return have found the outcome to be little more than empty promises mixed with threats of dire retribution if we renounce our oaths of loyalty! Oaths violated by Rome long before we came to our decision to end our association with you! Allow us free passage and we will travel north in the spirit of peace and co-existence! Bar our way and we will have no choice but to raise our shields and lower our spears! And you know how that will end as well as I do, Legatus Gallus!'

He raised the scroll which Scar had given him.

'And in the spirit of peace I offer you this! It is a message from your Legatus Augusti to you, Legatus, countermanding a previous order to block our path while he attacks us from the south! Doubtless you received a similar message by river courier, but the rider despatched to bring this copy to you fell victim to our patrols two days ago! There are no reinforcements from the south, Legatus, only yourselves! Do you really believe that this rabble can prevent the Batavi from forcing our way past you? They might believe such a fantasy, but you are an educated man. You know the reality of this situation.'

'Let's fucking have them!'

The angry shout from the legion's ranks was instantly joined by a dozen other raised voices.

'There's more of us than them!'

'We'll rip their guts out!'

'Stop fucking about and get into them!'

The legatus waited until the outburst had died away under the hard stares and raised vine sticks of his officers before replying, his voice tight with the tension.

'The First Legion stands ready to do its duty, Priest. I suggest you return to your comrades and prepare them to meet their ancestors!'

Alcaeus shrugged, then saluted and turned away.

'Well, that's that then. Let's be away from here before some bright boy takes a fancy to my wolf's head.'

He turned and walked away, the men of his tent party walking backwards with their shields raised until they were out of bow shot.

'They're advancing!'

Alcaeus grinned at the disbelief in Banon's voice.

'It's a sound manoeuvre, given the circumstances. If they try to block the road they can only bring half their spears to bear on us, whereas this way they can spread out and attack us from the flanks, I suppose. Come on, I think we've walked long enough for the sake of our dignity.'

Scar was waiting for them at the top of the rise with an amused expression as they trotted back to join him.

'Don't tell me, they declined our generous offer to go on our way in peace. What reaction did you get to the message from Flaccus?'

'It seemed to put a bit of a dent in their legatus's threat to put us between "the hammer and the anvil", but it also looked to me as if he was barely in control of his men, if at all. They'll fight.'

The prefect gestured at the oncoming legionaries and auxiliaries.

'Oh they'll fight, look at them. All bursting with the urge to prove their loyalty to Vitellius and be the men who showed the Batavi the error of their ways. Not to mention the opportunity to get at our purses and pay chests. Poor fools.' He looked out at the enemy force, which was thinning out and dividing to either side of the road. 'Mind you, I have to admire their ambition. I wouldn't fancy attempting an envelopment against disciplined troops, not unless I knew my men were steady enough to pull it off, never mind with a half-trained rabble like that. But you can only fight what the enemy lays out before you, I suppose . . .'

Turning to the trumpeter at his side he nodded decisively.

'Sound the signal to move three abreast.'

The signaller blew the note that would catch his officers' attention then a long drawn-out tone followed by three short notes. Even as he drew breath to repeat the signal the cohorts were in motion, hurrying to make the adjustment to their formation from the march formation to that ordered by Scar's signal. By the time the horn had sounded for a third time the rearmost men were moving into their places in a formation that put three of the eight cohorts side by side with another three close behind them, and the last two tucked in at their rear, while the mounted soldiers cantered their mounts back down the road to the south and took up a position a quarter-mile distant in battle formation.

'I'll show him the meaning of the hammer and the anvil. Trumpeter, give the signal to form square by cohort!'

At the horn's command each cohort transformed itself from a column of five hundred men marching four abreast to a hollow square with fifteen files of eight men on each side. The legion and their auxiliaries were closing in on all three sides of the Batavi force, but seemed to pause as their enemy's battle formation shifted from the familiar to something they had never seen before, and in the moment of their hesitation Scar roared out his last command before the battle joined.

'*Batavi! We salute Magusanus!*'

With a roar his waiting soldiers began slapping the backs of their shields with their spear shafts, the rhythmic pulse of their martial prowess stirring those men for whom the cohorts' manoeuvres had been no more than simple obedience to the horn commands and the urgings of their officers, raising hairs and narrowing eyes as the legionaries and auxiliaries advanced on them.

'I'll take my place, with your permission, Prefect?'

Scar nodded at his deputy, and Alcaeus stepped into the rear of his century with a shout to the men around him.

'You know the drill, boys, so don't let me down! The only dead men I want to see when we're done are those poor bastards! Second century, ready!'

'We'll have you in the front rank I think, Achilles. Come on.'

Egilhard blinked in confusion as Grimmaz pushed him forward to the front of their tent party's file, suddenly finding himself at the first cohort's front rather than buried deep in the comforting ranks of armoured men. Around him soldiers with years of experience were nodding and mouthing encouragement, and with a mouth suddenly dry he croaked a feeble protest.

'But there are men with much more—'

'None of that. You're good enough, so you're old enough. Just do the rest of us proud, eh?'

Resigning himself to the apparent inevitability of having honour thrust upon him, the recruit checked that his shield was aligned with those to either side, then looked up at the auxiliary soldiers advancing towards the cohort's waiting square of men. They were close enough for individual faces to be visible, some set hard with clenched jaws, some blank of any apparent emotion, some evidently terrified and only still advancing because of the press of men behind them.

'Second Century! Ready!'

Egilhard's voice joined the collective roar of assent that greeted their centurion's challenge, so loud that he barely heard the voice close behind him, as Grimmaz leaned in to mutter in his ear. The usually irascible leading man's voice was pitched low, as soft as a man whispering to a sleepy child.

'Nice and steady, Achilles. Shield first and spear second, no playing the hero. But take the chances they'll give you, eh? Nobody's better at that than you.'

A horn sounded behind the enemy ranks, and the soldiers facing them lurched forward, some eager, some stumbling, white-faced, a few having to be physically pushed forward by the men behind them, encouraged by the roared imprecations and threats of their centurions and chosen men, audible over the jingle of their equipment and individual shouts of encouragement as men within the advancing ranks sought to reassure both each other and themselves that they were ready for the fight. A volley of arrows from the Hamians on the enemy right sleeted down onto the square, soldiers crouching into the protection of their shields as shafts sprouted from the wooden boards and clattered off helmets, a chorus of curses greeting the iron rain as a man to Egilhard's right staggered out of the line with an arrow through his calf.

'Set!'

The Batavi front rank raised their shields ready to fight at the command, spears sliding in and out of the gaps between them as men experimented with the thrusts that they would be making in earnest once battle was joined. Egilhard drew his own weapon back slightly, ready to strike, and moved his feet minutely to test that his footing was sound, watching and waiting as the enemy line drew closer. A soldier in the opposing front rank defecated explosively, seemingly without even realising it, liquid faeces running down his legs and filling the air with an unmistakable sharp tang that drew a fierce chuckle from the men around the recruit, one wag shouting a jibe at the humiliated auxiliary.

'Looks like you should have gone earlier, don't it!'

The hapless victim of his wit shouted an incoherent reply, his face a hate-filled mask, then broke ranks and rushed forward with his spear raised as if seeking revenge for such cruelty. Egilhard reacted with the unconscious skills gifted to him by long days of training at the hands of his father and uncle, lunging forward a pace and thrusting his spear's bright iron head upwards in an unerring strike that lanced the weapon's long blade deep into the oncoming soldier's throat. Recoiling, the auxiliary staggered to a halt, staring disbelievingly down the shaft's length at his killer, tottered for a moment and then, as the Batavi pulled his weapon free and stepped back into the line, crumpled to the grass with blood gushing from his torn flesh. The two men closest to Egilhard vaulted their dying comrade as the enemy fell onto the cohort's shields, throwing themselves at the young soldier with the eagerness of men not thinking beyond their immediate urge to take revenge on the man who had slaughtered their tent mate. Intercepting one spear blade with his shield, punching the wooden board's iron boss into the attack to throw the enemy soldier off balance, he ducked away from the other man's attack as the auxiliary lunged his spear's shining iron head in over the shield's curved wall. Untroubled by the risk of becoming a target himself, Grimmaz stepped close in behind the young soldier and slightly to his left, to avoid any risk of being caught by his spear's butt spike, snapping out a hand and gripping the ash shaft just behind its leaf-shaped blade, pulling at it in a bid to drag the weapon away from its wielder, or simply pull him closer to the line of shields and open him up for the waiting Batavi spears. Struggling for control of the weapon, the auxiliary gasped in shocked agony as Egilhard lowered his own spear and put the blade through his right thigh, twisting the weapon's shaft and then tearing it loose in a stream of blood that instantly confirmed that he had inflicted a fatal wound.

The mortally wounded soldier staggered backwards, dropping his weapons and trying futilely to stop the flow of blood with his hand, and the Batavi used the room he had won to step forward, shield boss to shield boss, a violent punch slamming his new opponent back on his heels and then, while the other man was still off balance, hammering the sharp point of his spear's butt spike down though the thin leather of the auxiliary's boot and into the delicate bones beneath. With a screech of agony that cut through the battle's angry tumult, his victim reeled backwards into the men behind him, who, still eager to get at the Batavi line, showed little concern for his injury and thrust him forward again, move and countermove dragging the embedded spear from Egilhard's hand with a fresh scream of pain from the hapless auxiliary as the spike moved inside his foot, and in a flash of memory he was back on the Island with his father and uncle standing before him behind their shields.

'You're in battle, right boy? Some arsehole's just cut the blade off your spear. What do you do?' Even as he'd reached for his sword's hilt, his uncle had jabbed him with the wooden head of his own spear, a sudden point of heat and pain beneath his breastbone, then rapped the practice weapon's shaft against his shield's metal rim. 'Too fucking slow! Try it again, but this time make some use of this!'

Ducking momentarily behind his shield he swept out Lightning's long, deadly blade, then lowered the board and stared bleakly at the stricken soldier as the auxiliary tore the spear from his foot with another scream of pain and then fell to his knees in front of Egilhard, his own shield and spear lost in his agonised contortions. He looked up for a moment, silently entreating the man who had maimed him for life to show mercy while the auxiliaries behind him paused involuntarily, realising that they had delivered a man to his death unless the iron-eyed Batavi facing him spared his life.

'*Do it!*'

Acting without conscious thought, already in motion even as Grimmaz issued the command, Egilhard swung the blade in a low arc and decapitated the kneeling man, spittle flying as he screamed out a challenge to the aghast auxiliaries.

'*Batavi!*'

He stepped forward, sword raised, eyes flickering across the disordered ranks of the enemy in search of his next victim, but a firm grip on the collar of his mail prevented his advance while the men in front of him quailed at the savagery in his face and the bright edge of his blade, flicking horrified glances at the headless corpse of their comrade as it slumped heavily to the blood-soaked turf. Along the cohort's leading edge the auxiliaries were backing away from the Batavi's shields, the scattered corpses of their dead and dying littering the ground before them as grim evidence of the degree to which their enemy outmatched them.

'Can you control it?'

Recovering his composure, Egilhard nodded, his voice still thick with anger when he replied to the leading man's question.

'Yes.'

He shrugged free, sheathing the blade and taking up his spear, watching as the auxiliaries backed nervously away from the increasingly vocal Batavi line, the soldiers clamouring to be unleashed on their increasingly trepidatious enemy. Looking to his right the young recruit could see that the legion troops were still fighting where they had engaged the cohort squares in the centre and to the right, but the auxiliary force facing the first cohort was already starting to unravel, individuals turning tail and sprinting for the safety of Bonna's walls as they realised that they had rushed headlong into a fight with a pack of wild dogs, while the civilians who had been so loud in their urging for battle were already nowhere to be seen. Behind him a voice was shouting, and Egilhard was in motion even as he realised what it was that Alcaeus was roaring, reacting to the tone and urgency of his command as much as to the order itself.

'*Form line! Battle drill!*'

The cohort was scrambling into position to turn defence into attack, exchanging a fleeting moment of vulnerability for an eight deep line of men ready to go forward, the front rankers staring impassively over their shields at their tremulous opponents, clearly too terrified to advance but not quite brave enough to risk the anger of their officers by running. The last men hurried into their places, and Scar's voice rose over the din of battle, his bellowed order ringing out to unleash death on the enemy.

'Batavi! With spears! *Advance!*'

As the cohort's line lurched into motion he roared out the first line of the tribe's paean, and in an instant every man within earshot joined the song.

'Batavi! Swim the seas!
Worship mighty Hercules!
Swords and spears!
Take your ears!
Never showing mercy!'

Faced with a line of advancing spearmen, their every step accompanied by out-thrust blades whose points were already scoring and pitting the faces of the shields behind which the auxiliaries were cowering, the enemy cohort broke asunder, hundreds of men turning to follow the dozens who had already fled and leaving a handful of centurions and their chosen men facing the oncoming Batavi soldiers.

'First cohort! Right . . . *wheel!*'

Contemptuously ignoring the remaining auxiliaries, the line began to swing through a quarter-turn, changing its facing from their defeated and fleeing foes to the legionaries still desperately flailing at the cohorts to their right. With a thunder of hoofs the mounted troops who had been sent back into reserve streamed past, lowering their spears to harry the retreating auxiliaries and scattering the few remaining officers before beginning the grisly task of riding down the slowest of the runners, spearing them as they ran and then tearing their long iron blades free to strike again. Just as the cohort's line completed its turn to face the increasingly harried legion, whose ranks were struggling to contain the incensed

Batavi as the rearmost cohorts moved to support their comrades, the untrained legionaries reaching their collective breaking point. A single running man was joined by two more, then a dozen, a trickle that became a flood in the blink of an eye. As Egilhard watched open mouthed in amazement, the legion unravelled from a formed body of men into a mass of terrified individuals running for their lives. The Hamian archers were still lofting speculative shots into the mass of the cohorts, but increasingly they were running too, pausing only to shoot ineffectually into the line of shields that was all they had to aim at.

'*Reform!*'

Scar's voice rose over his men's triumphant shouts and taunts.

'*Let them run! Reform line of march! Panic will do the rest of the work for us.*'

Alcaeus strode down the line of his men, his gaze searching the ranks of soldiers for any sign of battle fatigue but finding only hard stares and an evident readiness to fight on.

'Looks like that's it for the day, boys! They came, they saw, they ran like frightened children!'

While his men guffawed at the old and tested joke, he nodded to Banon.

'Keep an eye on them, they're still itching to fight and I don't want any silliness breaking out to spoil the victory.'

The chosen man hefted his staff.

'I know just the thing to calm down a man whose blood is still fizzing with the urge to spill blood. Off you go.'

The wolf-priest grinned as he turned away, waiting for the first clang of the staff's brass-bound head on an errant soldier's helmet and nodding as the sound reached him before he'd covered a dozen paces towards the front of the formation.

'That's for being an arsehole! If you'd like a proper beating for all your other obvious faults, then step out and take your lumps!'

He found Scar at the column's head in conversation with his own chosen man, the prefect turning to greet him with a grin of triumph.

'Just as we expected, no more resistance in them than—'

The wolf-priest flinched as blood sprayed across his face, blinking furiously to clear his eyes, opening them to find his friend on his knees with the shaft of an arrow protruding from his throat. Staring up at Alcaeus, his eyes were pinned wide with the realisation that his death was upon him, coughing and spluttering blood in a hopeless effort to draw breath. Mastering the reflex to breathe, he mouthed a word at the priest, and Alcaeus bent to put his ear next to the dying man's mouth, the whispered words just audible in the shocked silence that had fallen across the first century's ranks as they watched their prefect's last moments.

'Carry me home.'

'I will.' He took his superior's hands and held them tightly, staring into the other man's eyes as his body convulsed with its need for air. 'I'll carry you to the Island and tell your family that you fell at the moment of victory. You'll be burned in the temple of Hercules and your ashes scattered on your farm. And I'll tell your sons just what sort of a man I served under, so they have the pride to carry your name in their hearts.'

He fell silent as Scar's eyes rolled upwards, and his body's shuddering fight to breathe against the blood running down into his lungs was lost. Lowering the corpse to the ground he stood, looking around him in shock while he regathered his scattered wits. The men of Scar's first century were utterly silent, while the jokes and jibes of the succeeding centuries were distantly audible over the shouts and cries of the retreating enemy. Snapping back into the moment he turned and looked across the ground between the cohorts' column and the fortress, taking the measure of the men who had faced them only moments before as they streamed back towards the safety of its walls, no longer running in the face of an apparent lack of pursuit. Pushing his vine stick into the straps of his phalerae harness, wrenching the sword from its scabbard and raising the blade high, stepping back to be seen by the officers standing by their centuries down the column's length and roaring an order at them that was more incitement to murder than call to arms.

'Scar is dead! Kill! Them! All!'

Turning back to the enemy, snarling at their uncomprehending backs, he started running across the weapon and shield-littered ground that separated the Batavi from their prey, and with a collective roar the men of Scar's century broke ranks and charged at his heels, turning from a disciplined military formation to a pack of ravening animals in the blink of an eye. Men at the rear of the retreating legion turned, took a moment to absorb what was happening and then routed afresh, their panicked shouts and sudden flight communicating the fact of the Batavi's blood lust across the scattered legionaries in an instant as they realised their deadly peril. Turning to run, their attempts at flight were swiftly frustrated by the mass of men between them and the fortress's gates, the twin narrow openings' deliberate restriction of access to make their defence easier suddenly and horribly evident as a death trap for the terrified soldiers. The relative order of their unharried retreat descended abruptly into a swirling chaos, soldiers fighting each other to get to the gate, some drawing their daggers and taking the weapons to their comrades in their desperation to escape the thousands of enraged Batavi warriors baying for their blood.

Alcaeus reached the legion's rearmost rank and took down the first man in his path with a lunging stab, staring into the legionary's eyes with visceral hatred as the soldier died on his blade, then kicked him off its three-foot length and lunged into the men behind him with a snarl. The enemy rear was suddenly a slaughter house, hundreds of furious warriors rampaging into the mass of terrified soldiers with spears and swords darting and flickering as they started their brutally grim harvest of the defeated enemy, the screams and entreaties for mercy of the men they were tearing into galvanising those closer to the fortress gate to fresh heights of desperate struggle to get through the twin doorways and into the relative safety of the camp. Hacking another man down, leaving his jerking corpse in the trail of dead that he had carved through the panicking enemy ranks, Alcaeus stopped to breathe, panting with his hands on his knees and momentarily defenceless if there had been any sort of threat from the routing legionaries, then straightened his back to look up at the walls looming over them. The First Germanica's legatus was recognisable even at a hundred paces, staring down aghast at his command's shameful surrender to their massacre even as the crews of a pair of bolt throwers worked their engines on either side of the gate, clearly making ready to start shooting. Looking to left and right, he realised the full horror that he had inflicted on the legion, a sea of dead and dying men whose breaking wave was a ravening pack of Batavi warriors still hewing furiously at what little defence the terrified enemy could raise. Banon staggered up to him, his armour blasted with the blood of the men he had killed, panting for breath from his furious exertions.

'Enough. This won't . . . bring him . . . back. Call them . . . off.'

The bolt throwers thumped and a warrior only paces from the two men convulsed as a missile buried itself in his spine, killing him instantly. The centurion nodded, raising a weary hand.

'Help me.'

Gradually, losing men to the artillery's pitiless lash who were still maddened for the blood of the men responsible for their prefect's death, Alcaeus and his centurions pulled their men away, until they were safely outside the range of the bolt throwers and could slump exhaustedly to the turf, faces turned introspectively to the grass for the most part. The ground between where they had come to rest and the walls of the fortress were littered with dead, too many to count, while the Batavi losses were carried to one of the supply waggons, hastily sewn into shrouds improvised from the cloaks of dead legionaries and loaded with as much reverence as could be achieved by their weary comrades. Other men scoured the ground over which they had fought, going as close to the fortress as they dared in search of Roman weapons and equipment, stripping corpses of their armour where it remained usable and collecting spears, swords and shields by the hundreds to be loaded onto other transports for distribution to the revolt's fighters.

'You're right.'

Banon looked up at his centurion, who had returned from a

swift conference with the commanders of the other seven cohorts with the look of a man not relishing his new responsibilities. His armour and weapons were still painted with dried blood, its iron stench permeating the battlefield along with that of other more noisome bodily fluids.

'What am I right about?'

'What you said under their walls. That it wouldn't bring him back.'

'But?'

'But it's a fitting farewell to the man. If this revolt of Kiv's goes the way we fear, then you and I may have far less glorious lines in the song of the dead.'

The chosen man nodded slowly.

'Put like that, I see your point. Even if I don't especially like it.'

'Put like that I can't say I like it either. But it's what fate's doled out to us so we'd better make the most of it. How are our men?'

Banon shrugged.

'Just like everyone else. Tired. Sick to their stomachs of the stink of dead men. So, do you think they've got ten miles in them?'

The chosen man nodded.

'They don't have a choice, do they? We need to get out into open country and put some space between us and *this* . . .' He gestured to the sprawling field of dead and dying men. 'Besides, we've tidied away our dead, it's time we left the party and allowed our hosts the chance to clear up the mess.'

'You'll live.' The century's bandage carrier snipped off the loose ends of the thread that bound Egilhard's wound, stepping back to admire his handiwork. 'Not bad, even if it's me saying it. You'll scar though.'

The young soldier had never seen the spear blade that opened his face from the base of his chin to the point of his jaw, just sensed a flash of silver and felt the sharp iron's cold bite as the weapon's blade, aimed, he guessed, at his throat, had missed its mark by a matter of inches.

'Perhaps we ought to change his nickname?'

Banon was doing the rounds of his tent parties, taking stock of casualties and weariness now that the cohorts had bedded down for the night and the less urgent injuries could be dealt with in the late evening's warm light.

'Change his nickname? Why?'

The chosen man looked at Grimmaz with a sardonic smile.

'Those of us who have actually read our Homer are aware that Achilles was famous for being invulnerable, all bar that tiny spot on his heel where his mother Thetis held him as she dipped him in the Styx to make him immortal. Our man hardly looks invulnerable now, with a scar the length of his jaw, does he?'

The leading man shrugged.

'Doesn't bother me. Doubt it bothers anyone else that matters either?'

He looked around the tent party, who were for the most part too tired to do anything other than shake their heads or wave the suggestion wearily away. There was no one among their number without a reminder of the massacre beneath the fortress walls, cuts and bruises, skinned knuckles and flesh wounds that would heal as small but honourable reminders of the day's events. Levonhard was sporting a huge black eye, courtesy of a monstrously tall and strong legionary who had held out against four of them for what had seemed like an eternity, an island of blazing anger in a sea of cowardice, armed with nothing more than shield and gladius and yet, in his rage, driven to fight off men on all sides with a singular skill until, tiring of the fight, Lanzo had hamstringed him from behind and left him waiting, arms spread wide and defiant to the last, for the mercy stroke. The leading man shook his head at his superior.

'No, Achilles he was and Achilles he stays.' Banon shrugged, clearly bone weary, and went to carry on with his rounds, only for Grimmaz to raise a questioning hand. 'What now? Now we've smashed a legion and fought our way past the last fortress before the Old Camp?'

Banon turned back to face him with a tired smile.

'If I had a woman waiting for me in my tent for every time I've been asked that question in the last hour, then I'd be considering a change of profession. So here's the answer I've given every other swinging dick that's asked me to second guess what Alcaeus and the other centurions will decide to do. I don't know. Happy now?'

Lanzo spoke up, his voice as soft and authoritative as ever.

'I think what our leading man was asking, Chosen, was whether we'll have to fight again before we see home?'

Banon chuckled wearily.

'And what I was trying to tell you, Dancer, was that I don't have any idea whatsoever. Alcaeus called for the other senior centurions the moment we stopped marching and they've been huddled round their fire ever since. Drinking a jar of Scar's wine and chewing the fat as to what to do now, from the look of it. I'm sure we'll all know what it is they decide we should do well enough in due course, and in the meantime I suggest you all get some rest because I don't think tomorrow's going to be much easier than today. Because if you want my opinion . . .' He smiled at their sudden attentiveness, even the exhausted Adalwin sitting up to listen. 'I'd say that we'll do what we always do, and bull our way through them. March north at our best pace and push past the Old Camp to get back to the Island as fast as we can.'

'Won't the Old Camp legions try to stop us?'

The chosen man shook his head at Wigbrand's tentative question.

'I wouldn't. They'll know about what happened today before we get that far north, you can be sure of that, and it's the sort of story that only grows with the telling. And look at the facts. A legion came out to face us with all their auxiliaries, and we had them running so quickly that neither side really took all that much damage. They broke like chaff on the wind. And then we must have killed one in every three men on that battlefield, when they did for Scar in defiance of our truce and sent us wild. Now look at that from the viewpoint of the man who's in command at the Old Camp. His legions are no better off than the First was before they came out to fight, in fact given they've been shown to the door by Kiv's army once already, to judge from what Bairaz told Scar, then they're probably even worse than that. And a slaughter like that one we inflicted today has the tendency to grow into legend pretty quickly. No, his men will be shitting in their boots at the thought of facing us, so I don't think they'll come out to play when we march past. If they have any sense they'll be working like slaves to make the fortress stronger, because if there's one thing our glorious leader is going to want to do quickly, it'll be evicting those legions and burning the place to the ground.'

Lanzo tipped his head to one side and frowned.

'I thought the revenge of Rome was the one thing we didn't want to risk? Isn't that why the prince kept his battle with the Old Camp legions bloodless?'

Banon shrugged.

'We've just butchered a thousand men and more, Dancer. As declarations of war go that's pretty strong stuff, intended or not. I suspect we've just taken the decision out of the grown-ups' hands.'

6

'Today, legionaries, you are going to learn how to plant lilies!'

Marius smiled thinly at the puzzled expressions that spread across his men's faces as Aquillius's words sank in, tapping his vine stick meaningfully into a cupped palm to ensure that nobody in the six centuries gathered before them mistook his colleague's words for an opportunity for levity. Aquillius looked up and down the ranks with his customary scowl, pointing at the ground between them and the Old Camp's walls.

'A field of beautiful lilies that might one day save your miserable lives! Lilies perfumed with the delicate scent you'll all recognise the moment you smell it! Leading men, if you're not at the front of your tent parties then move so that you are, now. I'll be holding you responsible for this job being done right, and if it isn't done right then you'll be doing it again. And trust me, once you've seen what I've got for you, you're only going to want to do this once!'

He held out a hand and took a standard-issue spade from one of the cohort's centurions, holding it up for them all to see.

'First you dig a pit, three feet deep and five feet across!'

Passing his helmet to the same man he set to with the spade, swiftly digging a hole of the requisite size and depth while the men around him watched in fascination, taken aback at the sight of a senior centurion undertaking physical labour.

'There. Three feet deep and five feet across! If your pit is the wrong size you'll have to fill it in and then dig it out again, so get it right the first time! Now for the fun part! Bucket!'

At his command another centurion walked forward with a bucket whose contents were painfully evident, both from their appearance and aroma.

'This, is you'll already have guessed, is shit! There's a bucket like this for every tent party, full to the brim with yesterday's dinner! And this is what you're going to do with it! Stakes!'

The centurion handed him a bundle of five wooden stakes, each one cut from a forked branch and with one half of the fork removed to leave a flat end, while the other half was whittled to a point and fire hardened, reducing the risk that time or mishandling would dull their penetrative ability.

'You have stakes, a hammer and a bucket of shit. And what you do with them is this!'

Plunging the stake into the bucket of excrement and stirring vigorously to ensure that its upper third was liberally coated, he bent over the freshly dug pit and pushed the clean end into the mud, holding out his hand out without turning from his task.

'Hammer!'

Placing the hammer's iron head against the stake's wooden stump he swiftly pounded it deeper into the ground, until only the portion coated with faeces protruded. Another four stakes followed, the resulting ring of wooden points pointing inwards to form a deadly trap for an unwary foot. Standing, he wiped his excrement-smeared fingers in the grass until they were moderately clean, then shrugged and turned back to his men.

'And that is what I expect from you! Starting ten paces from the wall you will dig me a lily every three paces, out to a distance of fifty paces! If you get any of them wrong, you'll be filling them in and starting again! If you get the spacing wrong, you'll be filling them in and starting again! If the stakes aren't covered in sufficient shit, you'll be filling them in and starting again! And trust me, I've dug enough lily pits to know there's no way to do it without getting covered in the stuff, so we'll have no mincing about, just get on with it, get dirty and sweat it out in the baths later! You've all got a pass to the calderium once your section of the defences is completed to my satisfaction! Which means that you don't want to be the tent party having to re-dig your pits while everyone else watches and the baths fill up with men who don't stink of excrement! Carry on!'

He turned away and Marius inclined his head in genuine respect.

'Kudos, brother. I've never seen that done before, but the way you set out your expectations was masterful. Will these things really make a difference?'

Aquillius nodded.

'I find that clear expectations combined with an incentive not to fuck up usually produce effective results. And will they work?' He pondered the question for a moment. 'We've been digging lily pits since the time of the Divine Julius and long before, or so my old first spear told me. And if they worked in the time of Caesar then they'll probably work now. Knowing they're there won't help a man avoid them, not when he's charging at the walls in the dark. As long as those mules put them in right then they'll do the job they were invented for.'

His brother officer chuckled.

'They'll all be supervising each other's work, that's for sure. Shall we go and have a look at the vicus?'

The small town that huddled under the fortress's south wall was already half-demolished, working parties that were two-thirds legionaries and one-third civilian methodically tearing the wooden structures down, careful to avoid breaking the timbers that were then being carried away into the fortress through the nearest gate.

'Given a week we'll have the wall fit to defend. If the First Germanica manage to deliver the supplies we need then we might just have a fighting chance of holding out long enough for the civil war to be settled and reinforcements to arrive. If only they could provide us with some more manpower we'd be even better placed.'

Aquillius shook his head dismissively, turning away and following the line of labouring porters along the road that led to the fortress gate.

'You seriously think Legatus Gallus will send any of his men to join us after the beating the Batavians gave his legion? The best we can hope for is that he gets some more food and bolt throwers down the river before they close it. We're a sacrifice, Marius, a goat staked out for the wolves to keep them from roaming further south and rousing the German tribes who aren't already involved. Not forgetting the Gauls. If we hold out for three months that'll be three months in which the fortresses upriver can prepare for attack, and concentrate on keeping their local tribes in their place.'

They walked into the fortress past saluting sentries, and into a scene greatly changed from that which would have greeted them only a few days before.

'This is going to take some getting used to.'

Aquillius nodded with a smile of satisfaction.

'Perhaps our only saving grace is that we're not having to deal with one of those idiots who sometimes end up commanding legions. I can think of more than one legatus of my recent experience who would have choked on the very idea of destroying half the barracks in the camp, but your man Lupercus didn't blink an eyelid.'

The permanent structures closest to the Old Camp's walls were being unceremoniously torn down, reduced to materials for the work on the wall's improvement, leaving a significant gap between the rampart and the remaining barracks buildings into which, it was hoped, enemy fire arrows could fall harmlessly, and leaving only enough accommodation for the garrison's actual strength.

'They'll know about all this from their spies, of course, but knowing about it won't make the changes any less effective. We just need another week or two to be—'

A shout from the wall above them cut across his musings.

'First Spear! Soldiers approaching!'

They hurried up the steps to the rampart's walkway, dodging around a work gang labouring on the construction of a wooden bolt thrower platform, then stared out over the parapet at the road to the east. A long column was visible a mile distant, marching towards the Old Camp along the road that lead back to the south and east, and Marius stared at them for a moment before speaking.

'It's the Batavians. It can't be anyone else.'

The news of the massacre at Bonna had reached them the previous day, to the disappointment of the legions' officers and the amusement of the Fifteenth legion's new first spear, who had expressed his opinion in a typically forthright manner.

'What did any of you expect? A legion's strength of battle-proven veterans against half-trained children and the idiots who were too slow to outwit the recruiting officers? The only thing I don't understand is why the legions from the Winter Camp weren't on hand to ram their spears up the Batavians' arses.'

The enemy column was marching fast, clearly intent on getting past the fortress without pausing, and Aquillius's expression hardened to a broad grin.

'Shall we go for a look?'

Marius turned to look at him with an expression of near incredulity.

'What do you mean, shall we go for a look? What if they turn their spears on us?'

His brother officer shook his head.

'They won't. Not if we don't offer them a fight. And this might be the best chance to get the measure of them before the next time we see them, which will be when they come to storm our walls. Come on, let's go and see what we think of them, and trust that professional courtesy will keep them from anything unpleasant. Or were you thinking of living forever?'

They walked briskly across the fortress's parade ground, and past the amphitheatre in which the soldiers were entertained by gladiator shows and boxing matches between the cohort champions, reaching the main road that ran past the fortress and away to the north and west just as the leading elements of the Batavi force were approaching. A pair of mounted infantrymen rode up to within spear throw, considered the two men for a moment and then turned about and galloped away. The first cohort was within bow shot now, and Marius watched with jealous eyes as the hard-faced auxiliaries swept towards the spot where he and Aquillius stood, their faces impassively fixed to the front.

'Look at them. No sign of weariness, no curiosity, no other interest than the next mile of road and what they might find at the end of it.'

His comrade nodded.

'Roman discipline and tribal ferocity. With four thousand men like that I could hold the Old Camp for a year and more. Ah, this should be interesting.'

A man had detached himself from the marching column and was walking towards them with a half-dozen soldiers at his back, the head of a white wolf with its lips drawn back in a permanent snarl fixed to the top of his helmet. He stopped within speaking distance, but sufficiently distant to be safe from a sword, looking first at the two centurions and then at the camp behind them.

'You're not going to try to stop us?'

Marius shook his head and held out a hand, moving slowly so as not to alarm the other man's escort.

'There'd be no point. You've already severely embarrassed the First Germanica from what we hear, and our men aren't any more ready to meet you in open battle than they were. We'll concentrate on defending ourselves, while hoping that a fight between our legions and your cohorts can be avoided. I'm Marius.'

The wolf-headed officer stepped forward and took his hand, then turned to consider Aquillius, who was appraising him with a direct stare that put Marius in mind of a predator sizing up potential prey.

'I'm Alcaeus, wolf-priest and centurion. Your comrade here is considering whether my life is worth his.'

After a long moment of silence the big man shook his head.

'You're not worth my life, not even for the satisfaction of seeing that wolf's head freed from your helmet.' He reached out a hand. 'Aquillius, Centurion, Eighth Augustan Legion and temporarily detached to lead the Fifteenth Legion in this coming battle.'

The Batavi nodded, a faint smile creasing his lips.

'An accurate summary of my importance to the tribe. Life

would indeed continue untroubled without me. You think there will be more fighting? Our reports from the Island say that your legions were allowed to withdraw from our soil without a fight, in the hope that peace can be achieved between Roman and Batavi. Our leader Prince Kivilaz has declared his support for Emperor Vespasianus, that much is true.'

'And we stand behind the Emperor Vitellius.'

'But still, some compromise must be possible? After all, once the war between these two men is settled we still all have to live together.' A waggon rumbled past, its flat wooden bed loaded with tightly wrapped corpses, each one covered by the dead man's shield, and Alcaeus gestured to its grisly cargo. 'After all, both of our respective sides have already paid a price in blood. Every one of those men was a son, a brother, a father, and every one will be mourned by his family.'

Aquillius shrugged.

'And that, Centurion, is the price of war. A price you will find Rome all too willing to pay with the lives of its legionaries.' He laughed softly. 'And its centurions. You know we will fight, because you know that we have no choice. But given that we are too weak to attack you, our next best choice must be to prepare to defend ourselves in case a compromise proves not to be what your Prince Kivilaz has in his mind. And soldiers who might not offer you much resistance on a battlefield, where men can turn and run with some hope of escape, will fight like cornered rats when their only choice is to resist or die. Tell your prince that Aquillius and Marius will take a grievous toll of your men, if you are sufficiently unwise to send them against those walls.'

Rome, September AD 69

'Caesar.'

Having entered the emperor's inner sanctum, acknowledged the crisp salutes of his guardsmen with a nod and bowed his head in obeisance to the man who ruled most of the known world, the immaculately uniformed praetorian waited, silently counting to judge the amount of time that the emperor would leave him hanging before acknowledging his presence. After a long pause Vitellius looked up at him with a wintry smile, which was all that was needed to confirm that at least one of the other men around the table had been in his master's ear on the subject of his guard prefect's loyalty during his absence. As he'd expected, of course. Perhaps, he mused, it was time for his restraint with regard to their individual weaknesses to be relaxed a little.

'Alfenius Varus. Don't stand on ceremony, prefect, join us.'

Varus looked around the conference table at the men Vitellius had gathered in council, finding it hard to see them as anything better than the dregs of Rome's senatorial class which had, for the most part, decided to keep its head well down until the war for the throne was settled one way or another. The senate still professed eternal loyalty to their emperor, of course, and donations still flowed to keep the legions fed and shod, but the men who sat alongside Vitellius when he made the decisions that would define his imperium were, as Varus saw them, the same ill-made rabble that had somehow, by a combination of unthinking audacity and blind luck, managed to defeat Otho's army at Cremona months before. The emperor's idiot hothead brother Lucius, the consuls Celsius, Simplex and Atticus and, of course, the two legati augusti who had delivered the throne to their master at Cremona, the fanatical Valens and his utterly corrupt colleague Caecina, were all in their usual places. Varus nodded to each in turn as he took his own seat.

'Your inspection tour of the army is complete?'

'Yes, Caesar. I have reviewed every legion in Italy and spoken at length with their legates and tribunes.'

'And?'

'And I am happy to relate that every legion in your army is ready for battle, fit, well equipped and in good spirits. If Vespasianus comes over the mountains this side of Saturnalia, he'll get a warmer welcome than he might expect.'

The emperor nodded distractedly.

'Good. Although Vespasianus, our spies tell us, has remained in Egypt like the coward he is, sending Marcus Antonius Primus to lead his legions west.'

Varus digested the news in silence. Vespasianus was clearly no fool, knowing that control of Egypt gave him the power to tighten his fist about Rome's grain supply and effectively starve Vitellius from the throne once the hunger riots began. The emperor continued, his tone morose.

'Nor is the news from the north especially favourable. Your tribune clearly failed to persuade the Batavian cohorts of their duty.' Varus nodded, already well aware of the events north of the Alps. 'And now they have fought their way past Fortress Bonna, grievously insulted the First Germanica, and marched away to the north leaving Herennius Gallus with well over a thousand men dead and nothing better to be said of the matter than the fact that their leader seems to have been killed by a lucky arrow.'

Varus said a silent prayer for the Batavian prefect, a man he had fought with at Cremona and who he had found to be a man of both courage and honour.

'I'm surprised that the legions from the Winter Camp didn't intervene. An envelopment, if properly managed, would have taught these tribesmen a powerful lesson.'

He already knew the reason why such a tactic had failed to be enacted, but kept his face appropriately bland as the two generals scowled across the table at him, reacting with nothing more than a raised eyebrow when the hard-eyed Valens slammed a bunched fist down onto the table's polished wooden surface for emphasis.

'We ordered the Fourth Macedonica and the Twenty-second Primigenia to hold position, Prefect. Our strategy is to allow these Batavians to caper and prance to their hearts' content within the confines of their own dungheap, and for our legions to ensure the security of their areas of responsibility. Once Vespasianus has been defeated we'll have the resources to invade their Island and tear them limb from limb, but in the meantime the safety of the Rhenus frontier must be our priority. What we have, we hold!'

Varus nodded, inclining his head in respect.

'A pragmatic strategy, and one which might even work—'

'*Might* work? Are you questioning the emperor's decision, Alfenius Varus?'

The praetorian locked gazes with his colleague, leaning forward and allowing his ire to show through his usual urbane facade.

'No, Fabius Valens, I'm questioning the logic that resulted in that decision being presented to the emperor as this council's recommendation. Our master can only succeed in his struggles with these upstart barbarians, who have doubtless revolted at the behest of Vespasianus himself as the emperor has already astutely discerned, if his council is properly informed. And I do not believe that this decision has been made with consideration of all the relevant facts.'

'Such as?'

Valens was bristling now, personally affronted in exactly the way Varus was hoping to provoke, cutting the emperor out of the argument and thereby enabling him to expose the manifest flaws with the course of action that Vitellius had authorised at the council's request without offending his master sufficiently to put his own position at risk.

'The Batavians, Legatus, are the most warlike and competent soldiers I have encountered in twenty-five years of service to the empire. Once they have their cohorts back on friendly soil they are unlikely to confine themselves to celebrating the temporary independence of their homeland from Rome. I believe that they will swiftly organise themselves, then march east to attack the Old Camp. They will outnumber the legions based there significantly when their tribal allies are taken into account, and it will only be a matter of time before the fortress falls.'

Valens shook his head in amused rejection of the argument.

'Attack the Old Camp? Are you mad, Alfenius Varus? What sort of lunatic would cast a spear at Roman walls after the example Vespasianus made of the Jews only a few years ago? We'd have no option but to go after them with every man we could spare and to utterly destroy them as a people!'

Varus smiled back at him.

'And yet not a moment ago you said that once Vespasian was defeated we'd have the resources to tear them limb from limb. Your mind is already made up on the subject, which this man Civilis will know only too well given that he's been accused of treason twice already.' He avoided the emperor's eye momentarily, knowing that Vitellius had released the Batavi prince from captivity in an attempt to keep the tribe compliant after his unexpected elevation to the purple by the German legions. 'As far as Civilis is concerned he's got nothing to lose from destroying the Old Camp, and everything to gain. He'll challenge the garrison to swear loyalty to Vespasianus, and when they refuse to do so he'll have his pretext for an attack. Because he knows that we'll destroy the tribe whether he does so or not, and in the expectation that he can throw himself on Vespasianus's mercy in the unlikely event that the would-be usurper manages to overcome your loyal legions, Caesar. And if he manages to break down the walls of the Old Camp, destroying our ability to easily project our power into the lower reaches of the Rhenus, it won't stop there, I can assure you of that. If the fortress falls then every tribe along the length of the river will rise up and join the men fighting under his banner, and that won't be all.'

He paused for a moment, and Valens stared back at him with all the previous certainty washed out of him.

'So far we've only been discussing the Germans, gentlemen, most of whom reside on the far side of the Rhenus. But what about the Gauls?'

'What about the bloody Gauls? They'll do whatever—'

Varus slammed his palm down on the table with a furious bang that made every man around it jump despite themselves.

'The *bloody* Gauls, Consul Valens, are a subject people, nothing more and nothing less! Since the Divine Julius subjugated them, they have been willing to subordinate themselves to us, a dominant military power whose rule of Gaul and Germany west of the Rhenus has been unchallenged for a hundred years. Yes, the Germans taught us a bitter lesson in the Teutoberg Forest, but we held them at arm's length and kicked their arses until they wanted nothing more than to be left to lick their wounds. The Gauls aren't fools, and they've always lived with the reality that any sign of dissent would result in a dozen legions descending on them from every direction. But if the Old Camp falls that spell is broken! They will be forced to consider the reality that Civilis represents more of a threat to them than we do. And they'll rise, Valens, they'll cast us off and form their own empire under some previously compliant nobleman officer or other, a Gallic Civilis with an eye to the big prize – an empire of his own!'

Silence fell around the table, broken after a moment's consideration by the emperor himself.

'So in summary, it is your considered opinion that the decision taken by this council . . .' he paused momentarily to allow the words that placed the blame on the men around the table to hang in the air, and Varus knew his argument had succeeded, 'whilst made with the best intentions, has in fact brought about the conditions under which both the Germans *and* the Gauls may rise against us?'

Varus inclined his head.

'As perceptive and to the point as ever, Caesar. I fear we will find our entire northern frontier in flames, and of course the Britons have never been slow to revolt if they see the opportunity to do so, and with a good portion of Britannia's legions absent to fight Vespasianus they might well make that judgement too.'

'And I risk being the emperor who lost three or four provinces, rather than the man who rescued Rome from the grip of a usurper and who will yet defeat Vespasianus's opportunistic challenge. What would you recommend we do?'

All eyes turned from emperor to prefect, and Varus thought for a moment before answering.

'We can only act with the forces we have, Caesar, since to weaken the legions awaiting Vespasianus's army would be tantamount to suicide. Depleted they may be, but the legions on the Rhenus are still the *emperor's* legions, sworn to your service. Fourth Macedonica and Twenty-second Primigenia at Mogontiacum, First Germanica at Bonna and Sixteenth Gallica at Novaesium.

But we must act swiftly, and with all the force we can muster, or the Old Camp will fall and the current order on the northern frontier may very well fall with it.'

Batavodurum, September AD 69

'Greetings, Centurion!'

The perfect silence that had followed the abrupt and meticulously timed halting of the cohorts' column at the gates of Batavodurum seemed to magnify the strength of Draco's voice, even the usually noisy flock of crows that fed on the city's refuse pits having taken flight at the thunder of four thousand pairs of hobnailed boots on the road from the east. The previous evening had been spent cleaning and polishing leather and iron, and the crisply presented ranks of soldiers remained impassive despite their eagerness to see their families, waiting in perfectly disciplined silence as the tribe's senior veteran stepped forward to welcome them home. His grave expression creased into a wintry smile as the officer at the column's head snapped to attention and saluted crisply, and he paced forward to embrace the younger man warmly, his voice pitched to carry to the closest men of the leading cohort.

'The Roman ways of doing things are no longer to our taste. Salutes are all very well for men lacking fire, but we are the Batavi.'

The two men slapped each other's backs and then Draco beckoned the man waiting behind him to come forward.

'My happy duty of greeting our cohorts back to the Island is done. And it is Kivilaz who commands here now.'

The one-eyed prince embraced the newcomer, then turned to present him to the assembled members of the tribal council.

'I told you that our brothers of the cohorts would not disappoint us in our time of need!' He half turned to point at the long column of armoured men stretching away down the road. 'See, a legion's strength of the finest warriors in the world! With these men in our army we are truly free from Rome's empire! Our own people, with our own lands, and our own future!'

The cohorts' leader bowed formally.

'Greetings, Prince Kivilaz. The men of the Batavi cohorts have returned at your summons, scattering all forces placed in our way in our haste to obey your call. We stand ready to fight for the tribe, and only ask you to direct us at our enemy. I bring you the battle standards of three cohorts of the First Germanica, shamefully abandoned by their bearers during their failed attempt to stopping our progress north. I would have delivered their eagle to you as well, but they were too swift to spirit it away when the fact of their defeat became apparent to them.'

The older man nodded, his good eye fixed on the centurion before him.

'My joy at your return is tempered only by the losses you took in breaking through the Roman resistance to your return, brother. You reported that thirty-two men were lost in the fight outside Bonna.'

Alcaeus nodded gravely.

'Your cousin Scar among them, lost to a chance arrow. We killed many times that number, and their panic will have cost them as many again as they trampled each other in their haste to escape to the safety of the fortress.'

He looked up at the clouds scudding through the sky above them, then addressed Kivilaz with eyes misty at the memory.

'Scar died as he would have wished, leading his men forward against an enemy who could no more stand in the face of our righteous anger than hold back the great river's water.'

'You have his body?'

The priest bowed his wolf-headed helmet.

'And all those of the men we lost breaking through the First Germanica and their followers.'

Kivilaz bowed his head solemnly.

'Their kinsmen will praise your name for allowing them the chance to bid the tribe's sons farewell. And I thank you. Get your men into camp and then come to the meeting hall. There's a lot to discuss.'

Washed and dressed in his off-duty uniform of an ornately

decorated tunic and his uniform belt with its dagger riding on his right hip, Alcaeus reported as commanded to find the tribal council waiting for him, and a chair positioned to face the men who ruled the tribe. Kivilaz walked forward to meet him, embracing him again in a deliberate show of his power within the tribe.

'Relax, Centurion, you're among friends for the first time in a very long time. Take a seat, and tell us in your own words what has happened since you received our order to turn north.'

The centurion sat, looking about him for a moment before speaking, gauging the council's mood.

'Respected men of the tribe, my report is simple, for the most part. Having received Prince Kivilaz's message when we were two hundred miles south of the Winter Camp, we turned around and marched first north, to the great river, then followed its course along the roads the Romans use to control and supply their frontier. We expected to have to face the legions housed in the Winter Camp itself, but they did not come out to meet us. This may have been the result of a discussion that Scar shared with their legatus augusti, Hordeonius Flaccus.'

Kivilaz leaned forward.

'Flaccus? What did Scar tell you of their meeting?'

'As was customary between us, knowing that informed leadership would be essential if he were to fall in battle, he recounted it to me word for word. The gist of it was that while Flaccus has to be seen to obey the emperor, in truth he is a supporter of Vitellius's rival Vespasianus. He told Scar that, while news of their discussion could go no further for fear of Vitellius discovering his true allegiance and removing him from his position, he would do everything in his power to ease our passage north.'

'Why?' Draco leaned forward in his chair, his attentive gaze fixed on Alcaeus. 'Why should this Roman betray his own men and allow you to reach the Island unhindered with enough strength to utterly change our fortunes in this war?'

'I'll answer that question.' Kivilaz turned to face the man. 'I met with Flaccus a few weeks ago, well before the battle where we put their legions to flight without spilling a single drop of Roman blood. He told me that his instructions from Vespasianus were to do everything within his power to turn Vitellius's attention away from the coming fight for the throne, and to prevent any further reinforcement of the emperor's legions. He told me that he would do everything he could to enable our men to return home and put the legions in the Old Camp under such pressure that any idea of sending men south would be deemed impossible. The idea that we might defeat them without killing any legionaries was his.'

'So we have entered into a pact with this Roman?'

Kivilaz shook his head.

'No. We take what he offers, and we give nothing in return. We act in the interests of the tribe, not Flaccus, not Vespasianus and *not* Rome.' He turned back to Alcaeus. 'So tell us, Centurion, what happened during your march north?'

'The legions from the Winter Camp did not come to challenge us. It seems that Flaccus found some pretext for keeping them in their barracks, and sent orders for the legion based at Bonna to let us pass. We captured one of his messengers and read his new orders to the First Germanica's legatus.'

He handed Kivilaz a message container, and the prince opened it, taking out the scroll of parchment. He read for a moment before turning to the council members and reading aloud.

'"The decision has been made by Rome not to jeopardise the frontier by risking a defeat that might result in the loss of one or more legions. The integrity of the empire's northern provinces must be prioritised, and the loss of your legion would be a disaster at this time. You are therefore ordered to allow the Batavian cohorts free passage to the north, and we will deal with the question of their attempt at rebellion at the right time, when sufficient forces can be spared to snuff it out with minimal risk." You see, my brothers? This man Flaccus plays a dangerous game, professing loyalty to one man while secretly doing everything he can to undermine him. And in doing so he has played into our hands by giving us the most dangerous body of men on the entire

German frontier, and at a cost so low that I would have reluctantly accepted ten times as many losses to have the cohorts returned to us. Although I mourn the loss of my cousin Scar almost as deeply as that of my brother, both taken from us before their appointed time at the whim of Rome. Tell me, Alcaeus, how did he die?'

The priest shook his head.

'Needlessly . . .' He smiled wanly at the memory. 'Gloriously. And yet by the cruellest chance. Once the First Germanica and their auxiliaries were on the run, we reformed to march on but a few of their archers were still shooting into us from the flanks, and by mischance one of them loosed the perfect arrow, through the line, between the heads of a dozen men and straight into your cousin's throat.' He paused momentarily, looking at his feet as the memory bit into him again. 'He died in my arms, coughing and choking as the blood filled his lungs.'

'And then?'

Alcaeus looked up at him, his face hard.

'I doubt the man who killed your cousin lived to celebrate the feat, if he ever knew of his success. Our horsemen cut down every archer they could find, when his fate became known, and I took my cohort forward and took the bloodiest revenge I could on them.' He swept the council's members with a gaze turned cold by the memory of the slaughter that had been inflicted on the terrified enemy soldiers. 'The gates weren't large enough to let many men through, especially given they were fighting and climbing over each other to get away from us.' He paused, shaking his head at the memory. 'They probably lost as many men in the crush as we killed. Eventually the only men left outside the fortress walls were the dead and those few who managed to take shelter under the gate where we couldn't come at them for fear of their bolt throwers, and spears thrown down from above. So we left them to count their dead and made our way here.'

'The legions at the Old Camp didn't try to stop you?'

'No. A pair of their senior centurions came out to meet us, but all they did was watch as we passed. They told us their names, one of them in particular wanting you, Kivilaz, to know that he will be waiting for you. A man by the name of Aquillius?'

The prince nodded dourly.

'Then this man Aquillius will burn with the Old Camp, when we break through their defences and take our spears to them. And you, Centurion, you have my thanks for the safe return of both the living and the dead. Consider your duty as the cohorts' temporary prefect to have been discharged faultlessly, as do I, and return to your priestly duties in the knowledge that you have fulfilled your responsibility to the tribe exactly as Scar would have wished.'

'Who will lead us, my Prince?'

'The best qualified man for the task. A man who carries sufficient hatred of Rome and its people to inspire your men to even greater feats of bloody vengeance on our enemies.'

The Old Camp, Germania Inferior, September AD 69

'These are all the archers I have left, I'm afraid. I could have marched the best part of a cohort in through your gates before the Batavians went through them like a pack of wolves.'

Lupercus looked at the remaining Hamians with an expert eye, swiftly tallying their remaining strength.

'Gods below, Herennius Gallus, we heard that you'd been roughly handled, but there can't be more than two centuries of them?'

His fellow legatus nodded grimly.

'And doubtless Rome will want to pass judgement on the matter at some point, when all the excitement's done with.'

'What happened? Really happened, not the version that goes in the dispatches.'

Gallus grimaced, staring at the horizon with eyes whose blank gaze betrayed his inability to come to terms with the disaster for which he had been responsible.

'I received orders to lead the First Legion out when the rebels approached Bonna, and to establish a blocking position across the road. The Fourth and Twenty-second would march north behind the Batavians and we'd have them in a trap. It seems that our colleague Dillius Vocula had managed to convince Flaccus to send him north to stop them before they could rejoin the rebel army. And of course I had the order read to the legion, which got them all eager for battle, legionaries and auxiliaries both. The rumour started circulating that the Batavians had their pay chests with them, and before you know it the fools had not only worked out what their share of the spoils would be but were busy making plans to spend it. Word gets around in legion fortresses, and before a day had passed half of the civilians in the vicus had decided that they wanted a part in what everyone had decided was going to be little more than a formality of a battle followed by a quick pillage, before heading back to their favourite taverns and brothels to spend their new-found wealth. Idiots.'

He shook his head in grim, exasperated amusement.

'Then the second order arrived from Flaccus. A total change of strategy, with the Winter Camp legions no longer marching north to support us and the First ordered to allow the Germans to pass unhindered, on the direct orders of the emperor.'

'Vitellius ordered you to let them through? Why in the names of all the gods would he do that?'

Gallus shrugged.

'Who knows? Bad advice? A failure to appreciate just what it is we face here? Whatever the reason, my legion wasn't having any of it, and nor were the auxiliaries. The civilians were the worst, full of piss and vinegar when most of them had never seen anything worse than a tavern fight. So when the Batavians marched into sight they opened the gates and marched out to block the road, all deluding themselves that they could still defeat four thousand of the best men in the empire, rebels or not. All I could do was preserve some shred of my dignity by being seen to have led them out, but I tell you truthfully, Munius Lupercus, the whole thing was no better than a bloody mutiny. The rot set in when Vitellius accepted their demands that he declare himself emperor, and gave them the idea that their opinions are more important than those of the men who command them. Anyway, they opposed the Batavians in the field and paid a heavy price, all except for the civilians of course, they ran for safety at the first sight of blood. I had the ringleaders of that little mutiny executed, since they hadn't had the decency to die on the battlefield.'

He shook his head, watching as the last of the supply waggons rolled in through the gate.

'That's all the food I can spare. I'd like to have marched some legionaries up here to bolster your garrison as well, but not only have I barely enough to defend Bonna, they're not in very good condition after the beating they took. I don't think you'd find them of much use.'

Lupercus inclined his head in thanks.

'Your additional rations should enable us to hold out for a good few weeks longer than what we had left, and the archers will doubtless have a chance to redeem their honour. One of my senior centurions has some ideas about fire arrows.'

Batavodurum, September AD 69

Hramn stared at Kivilaz questioningly when the older man told him of his promotion to prefect.

'Surely this requires the agreement of the elders? You'll have Draco on your back if you ignore them in making such a decision. And who will command the Bodyguard?'

'Bairaz can take command of the Guard, now that he's returned from fetching the cohorts back to us. You know he's more than ready for the responsibility, and his brother's death at Bonna will give an edge to his eagerness to get at the Romans next time we meet them in battle. And as to the elders, they've already been consulted. Draco was first among the men clamouring for you to be made prefect, so your position in command of the cohorts is a decision that's been sealed and stamped by all those men with

the right to have a view on the matter. That was the easy decision
. . . Prefect.'

Hramn inclined his head in thanks.

'I might have wished to have received such an honour in better
times, but I am nonetheless proud to have been chosen. I will
strain every sinew to provide the tribe with the leadership expected
of me, and you with the steadfast support that I know you will
need over the coming months. I presume the difficult decision
was to do with the Old Camp?'

Kivilaz nodded soberly.

'Yes. The debate raged long into the night once that subject
came up for discussion.'

'And your position on the matter was . . . ?'

The prince raised a fist, his expression dark.

'A simple one. The Old Camp is the greatest threat to our
independence, Hramn, and must be destroyed.'

'But surely that will spell our doom? I thought you were set
on avoiding an all-out war with Rome?'

'I was following the dictate of our elders. They are . . . *were*
. . . convinced that one spear thrown at the Old Camp's walls will
result in the full weight of Roman vengeance descending on us.
That as many legions as it takes to subdue us will come marching
north, once the war for the throne is done with and the bastards
have settled their differences and closed ranks.'

Hramn nodded.

'It's what they do. No rebellion against Rome goes unpunished,
you said so yourself when you chose not to annihilate their legions.
Insult a legion and you have insulted Rome herself. And that ugly
old bitch doesn't take an insult well.'

The older man nodded.

'I know. But the massacre at Bonna has changed everything.
If Vitellius wins, then the men of the legions who marched south
to fight for him will return to the north with revenge for their
comrades' defeat in their hearts, battle hardened and ready to
come at us with spears and shields. And when they eventually
beat us, as they inevitably will, they'll do all the things the Romans

always do to defeated tribes. Slaughter. Rape. Enslavement. Resettlement. And they'll do this whether we've attacked the Old Camp or not, in revenge for the humiliation we have heaped upon their proud reputations.'

Hramn nodded.

'Which means that if the Old Camp is still standing when they return victorious then we'll have left them a secure base of oper-ation to fight us from. Whereas if we destroy it, they'll be on the back foot, vulnerable to our attacks in the absence of walls to hide behind. But what if Vespasianus wins? Surely he'll have to avenge the insult to Rome's pride, and even if *he's* not feeling vindictive, you show me a legion that'll go easy on a defeated tribe and I'll show you my foot-long-cock.'

Kivilaz shrugged.

'In that case we can claim that our actions were purely intended in support of him. We'll swear our loyalty to the man, and I'll make it clear to their legatus that my only objective is the fortress itself, not its occupants, and that his legions have the opportunity to march away if they won't declare for Vespasianus – and that if they won't leave voluntarily then we'll just have to show them the error of their ways. If we're merciful when the time comes to take their surrender, then I don't believe the new emperor will have undue cause to repudiate our agreement. Not with Flaccus to bear witness to the bargain we struck in his support. So tell me, Prefect, what's your view of our situation? What do you think we should do?'

The younger man thought for a moment.

'The legions bottled up in the Old Camp are in a difficult position. They're too weak to bring the fight to us, and they should by rights already have evacuated the place and marched south to join up with the forces at Novaesium and Bonna, but no doubt Roman pride stands in the way of such a logical course of action. Even if the reports of our spies are accurate, and they're readying the fortress for a siege, they have the strength of a single legion to defend walls intended to be manned by twice as many men. I say we attack now, quickly, and remove the threat those walls represent. And given that their northern rampart is raised up on a ridge and therefore impossible to storm, my plan would be to send the tribes in strength against the west wall to divert their attention, then use the cohorts to break open the southern gate and finish it quickly.'

Kivilaz smiled.

'An excellent plan. I want that camp burned to the ground before Vespasianus has the chance to either win or lose the empire, so that we can profess our loyalty to the man and credibly beg his forgiveness for attacking Rome herself in his name. Give your new command a few days' rest, then we'll march south to show these people that they're not the only ones who can lay siege to a fortress. I have a small surprise for them that ought to work well as part of your scheme.'

Batavodurum, September AD 69

'Come here you little bastard!'

Frijaz wrapped his nephew in a bear hug so tight that Egilhard was starting to worry about whether he would be allowed to breathe before he passed out, but at length his father's brother released him, holding the young soldier out at arm's length and looking him up and down with a satisfied smile. Around them in the great hall's torch-lit vast space hundreds of families were conducting equally heartfelt reunions.

'Less than a year and here you are, a real soldier and with a tent name to be proud of! And champion of your cohort too, from what I hear! All Lataz and I ever managed was to be the best men in our cohort at drinking and wh—'

Lataz coughed loudly, casting a jaundiced look at his older brother to remind him of the presence of the young soldier's mother, then looked his son up and down, putting out a hand to touch the angry red wound that was still healing on his chin.

'So, my son, you return without your plait, freshly scarred, and with Lightning newly honoured by the blood of the tribe's enemies.'

Egilhard bowed to both men, as custom demanded.

'Father. Uncle. Your long years readying me for my service have been generously rewarded by the gods' favour.'

The two veterans regarded him for a moment, his uncle Frijaz still grinning like an idiot while his father's mood was harder to discern. At length he stepped forward and took his son in an embrace which, if not as stifling as his brother's, lasted a good deal longer.

'Well done, Egilhard. Very well done. Your uncle sought a moment of your centurion's time this morning and asked the boy what he saw in your future, what with him being a priest. Not the same as the priests we had in our day, of course, but still a holy man with the vision.'

His son smiled at the description of his centurion as 'the boy'.

'And what did he tell you, Uncle?'

The older brother's grin faded to an expression that combined pride with an edge of sadness.

'He said that you're a hero, brother-son. He told me about your first battle, where you killed two men in the space of a single breath. And about that fight at Cremona, and the axe man you put down when he was running wild in our ranks. And about this recent fight, where poor old Scar took his arrow. Said you'd conduct yourself with dignity when you're not in a fight, but run wild like Achilles himself when the iron is flying. Said . . .'

Frijaz hesitated, and Lataz addressed his son with a solemn face.

'He said you hadn't made the mistakes the heroes usually make. Not yet, at least. But when Frijaz asked him what he saw in your future he wouldn't answer. Any idea why that might be, eh, boy? Planning to go to meet your grandfather and his forefathers before my time comes, are you?'

Egilhard had no idea how to answer the question, but was saved from having to do so by his mother who, having waited with the appropriate degree of respect for her husband and his brother to complete their greeting of the returning warrior, decided that enough was enough.

'That's quite enough of your nonsense, Lataz, and as for you . . .'
She fixed her husband's brother with the hard stare that she reserved
for those moments when he showed signs of tempting her husband
away from the obvious path of reason. 'That's more than enough
talk about my son being a hero. He's just my Egilhard, and he
doesn't need you two filling his head with ideas that will get him
killed. And there are some more practical matters to be considered,
given he'll be away south with the prince before you know it.'

Taking her son by the arm, she led him away to show off to
half a dozen of her friends, all of whom happened to have daughters of around the marrying age, leaving the two brothers looking
at each other.

'Alcaeus did tell me one thing, before he closed up tighter than
a duck's arse.' Lataz waited, knowing full well that his brother
would give up whatever it was that he had coaxed out of their
former comrade in his own time. 'But I'm not sure what to make
of it. He said . . .'

Frijaz paused again, and this time his brother found his patience
crumbling.

'Come on, you old b—'

'He said that he's dreamed the same dream several times. Wood
over water, and our boy with a great man's life at the end of his
sword.'

'That's it?'

'That's what he said.'

'Wood over water, and Egilhard with a great man's life at the
end of his sword. Does the boy know?'

His brother scoffed.

'Of course not. I might be *your* brother, but I'm no fool.'

'Good. That sort of omen might be just be enough to distract
him at some point. And if his destiny's to be a hero despite all
our efforts to make him see sense then he doesn't need to be
distracted by the dreams of a man who used to clean our boots
when he was a recruit the boy's age, does he? And now we'd
better go and rescue the boy from the women, before my wife
gets him into even deeper trouble with one of those girl children.'

The Old Camp, Germania Inferior, August AD 69

'Here they come!'

The two first spears stood by the side of one of the new bolt throwers that had been built in the previous few days, their metal components copied from spare parts by the civilian smiths who had moved inside the Old Camp's walls and set up their forges in empty barracks blocks, the weapons' wooden bodies and firing platforms built by the legion's carpenters. Marius turned and looked down into the fortress, surveying the open space between the walls and the buildings that remained, now that the legion work gangs had finished tearing down everything within fifty paces of the rampart. The walls were studded with artillery on all four sides of the camp, each one of the heavy bolt throwers double-crewed to ensure that men tired by the effort of rewinding the weapons could be rotated to maintain the best possible rate of shooting. Baskets of iron- tipped and finned bolts were stacked neatly behind the wooden shields that would be dragged into place by waiting legionaries, designed to protect the men working the big weapons from enemy archery as the bolt throwers traversed to left and right in search of targets. Smaller man-portable scorpions, weapons taken from the fleet's vessels before they had retreated back up the river, stood ready with crews and their own shield bearers alongside the ranks of soldiers waiting in the empty spaces on all sides of the fortress, ready to hurry to whichever point of the wall was the first to come under attack.

'If it's not ready by now then it never will be. Better to concentrate on the enemy and start working out what their first move might be.'

Marius nodded at Aquillius's dour statement, turning back to stare out over the expanse of mantraps and jutting stakes that now surrounded the fortress at the enemy force approaching them from the west.

'They won't attack immediately. They'll want to know what it is that they have to overcome. But when they do . . .' He scanned the Batavi column for a moment. 'I don't see any siege equipment, do you?'

The other man shrugged.

'No. And nor did I expect to. These tribesmen might have served with the legions, but that doesn't make them engineers. And there's a big difference between watching a siege engine at work and building your own. They'll know all about the use of catapults and towers, but the odds of them being able to build them are probably about the same as my being able to jump off this wall and avoid hitting the ground below us. A battering ram will probably be the limit of their abilities. And any men sent to swing that ram will be dead long before they get the chance to test our gates with all this artillery at our disposal.'

They watched in impassive silence as the enemy column turned off the road, splitting to either side as the various parts of the Batavi army set up camp according to their usual practices.

'So, what do we have here?'

They turned to find the legatus approaching down the wall's length, fully arrayed and ready for battle in his bronze armour and magnificently plumed helmet.

'You'll make an easy target wearing that headgear, Legatus, once the barbarians start throwing arrows around.'

Lupercus smiled knowingly at Aquillius.

'And I'd like to be able to tell you that I won't be wearing it, once the barbarians start throwing arrows around. When battle is joined, if I had any sense, you'd find me wearing an issue legionary's helmet, just as several men of your rank have suggested to me over the years. Unfortunately that's not what's expected of a Roman gentleman, I'm afraid, so I'll be just as enticing a target as I am now.'

The centurion nodded, his grim expression unchanged by his superior's attempt at humour.

'In which case, Legatus, I'll be careful not to stand too close to you. It would be irritating to say the least to stop an arrow that was actually intended for another man, no matter how honourable his presence might make my death. And as to what we have here . . .' He waved a hand out at the enemy force. 'A thousand cavalry, not that they'll be much use in a siege, four thousand of the best soldiers in the empire, another thousand militia who'll be solid enough, a thousand or so traitor auxiliaries.'

'And Jupiter only knows how many barbarians.'

Marius chuckled quietly.

'They're *all* barbarians, Legatus, trust me in that. Playing harpastum with men soon reveals their true nature, and when we met their guardsmen on the pitch it was all too quickly apparent that they were going to do whatever it took to rip the ball away from us and take it back over the line. This isn't just an uprising for them, it's a fight to the death. And I'd say there are ten thousand tribesmen out there, give or take, warriors from all over free Germania.'

Lupercus looked out over the rampart at the straggling host of warriors.

'Our spy in the Batavian camp managed to get word to us of the promises Civilis has received from the tribes across the Rhenus, before communications became impossible, and his estimate was that they would soon have another ten thousand men from the Bructeri, the Tencteri and half a dozen lesser tribes. Which means they could soon have twenty thousand men against barely four thousand of us, plus a handful of disgruntled civilians and their children. Is that enough for them to defeat us?'

Aquillius shrugged.

'More than enough, if they know what they're doing. If they pick one point along our walls and attack it in strength, and keep attacking it with everything they've got, then eventually they'll break the wall, or a gate, and get in. And if they get in then make no mistake, we'll be meat for the crows within an hour, all of us. All our advantages are lost the moment they get inside the fortress.'

'Legatus sir! There's a man approaching!'

They turned their attention back to the rebel army, and followed the bolt thrower captain's pointing hand to see a lone figure walking forward between the rows of lily pits that awaited the unwary among his followers. In his wake came a party of men apparently drawn from each of the bodies of men commanded by the Batavi leader, each man carrying aloft a standard captured in the three battles that they had already fought against Rome, the badges of pride and honour that had belonged to cohorts and centuries defeated and incorporated into the rebel army.

'It's Kivilaz. I can't fault the man's sense of the niceties of warfare, or his skill in the arts of seeking to demoralise an enemy. He must have thirty captured standards behind him. And no, before you ask, I can't order this weapon's captain to put a bolt through him. For one thing my honour would be forever tarnished in the eyes of my family and peers, and for another there may still be some way to negotiate a way out of this desperate mess.'

'Will you be going out to meet with him?'

Lupercus smiled bleakly at Marius.

'I think not, First Spear. Today feels like a day to be speaking from a height and from behind a palisade, not for gambling that my enemy shares my sense of honour.'

The Batavi leader halted ten paces from the wall and stared up at them in silence for a moment before calling out a greeting, a spear held in his right hand.

'Munius Lupercus! Well met once more! And my congratulations to you for the changes that have been made to the defences of this fortress in the days since your inauspicious retreat from the Island! The Old Camp almost looks capable of resisting an attack by my army!' He chuckled. 'Almost capable . . .'

Lupercus looked down at him in silence for a moment before replying, allowing the tension to build.

'Gaius Julius Civilis!' The enemy leader smiled at the use of his Romanised name, knowing that Lupercus was looking for a way to get under his skin. 'I presume from your followers' warlike appearance that you've not come here to surrender?'

The Batavi warlord shook his head, a tone of equal levity in his voice when he replied.

'You presume correctly, Legatus. We have come on the behalf of our sworn ally, Titus Flavius Vespasianus, to demand that you swear an oath of allegiance to the one true emperor of Rome just as we have already done. Join with us, and there will be no need for unnecessary bloodshed. Join with us against the usurper's legions, forcing him to divert his attention to both east and north, and when Vespasianus is victorious both you and I will be able to hold our heads high in his presence, and reap the rewards that he will surely bestow on us!'

The Roman smiled down at his former comrade.

'If only I could do as you suggest! The problem is that I have already sworn an oath, witnessed by Mars, to obey the one true emperor! His name, in case you have forgotten, is Vitellius! To change sides now would not only bring the retribution of the gods, but my fellows would consider me a traitor to my class in breaking such an oath! And besides . . .' his smile hardened, 'I hardly need to be given lessons in loyalty by a man who has already attacked his allies not once but three times, four if I count your cohorts' routing and massacre of the First Germanica at Bonna! My fortress is ready to resist your assault, my legion's pay chests have been sent south in exchange for bolt thrower ammunition, and my senior officers and I will make sure you squander more men than you can afford to lose, if you attack these walls! And in the simple act of casting the first spear at a legion fortress you cast your dice irrevocably, you know that much!' Lupercus pitched his voice to a softer, more sympathetic tone. 'This can only end badly, old friend, for you personally and for your people too. You may have them convinced that Vespasianus will pardon the Batavi, if he takes the throne, but you know that Rome will punish your tribe for this in ways that will ensure you can never rise up again. Do you remember what they did to the Jews for attacking Twelfth Fulminata's fortress only a few years ago? Do you wish for such a horrific outcome to be visited upon your people?' He paused, shaking his head in affected sadness. 'It's in Rome's nature, I'm afraid, to brook no insult. So are you sure that old comrades like you and I can't agree some compromise that leaves this fortress intact, and your people safe from the inevitable retribution that must descend on them no matter who wins this civil war, if you take such a momentous step?'

Kivilaz nodded in his turn.

'Your reply is all very much as I expected, Munius Lupercus, but the offer had to be extended! And now that you have rejected it, I am left with only one choice.'

He stepped forward, hurling the spear high over their heads, the missile arcing down into the camp behind them to land within inches of a startled legionary, much to the amusement of his tent mates. The Batavi leader stared up at Lupercus for a moment longer.

'The first spear is cast! For now, I will return to my camp and consider my next steps! But the next time you see me, you will know me by the colour of my hair, I promise you that! You're not the only man who will draw the attention of his enemies by the nature of his appearance once battle is joined!'

He turned and walked away, seemingly untroubled by the fact that the crews of several bolt throwers were following his steps, their captains waiting for the order to kill him.

'Well said, Legatus. But what did he mean by the comment about his hair?'

Lupercus watched the receding figure for a moment, as his one-time comrade walked away between the lines of lily pits, then turned to Marius with a sombre face.

'That was another piece of information from our man in their camp. Our noble enemy plans to apply an old tribal custom to this siege as a sign of his commitment to seeing us defeated. Batavi warriors still follow an ancient tribal tradition, when they reach manhood and become soldiers, of dying their hair bright red and growing it long, plaiting it to avoid it becoming an encumbrance in battle. They cannot cut the dyed hair away until they have taken a man's life for the tribe which, I suppose, makes their young warriors terrifying in battle, as their only thought is to kill one of the enemy and remove the hated symbol of their youth to enter the warrior caste as men. Kivilaz cut his away on a battlefield in Britannia having just saved my life, at the battle of the Medui river. I was young, rash with it, and immortal, of course, and in my foolishness found myself sword to sword with a tribal champion who was easily my match and more. He had me at his mercy when that man down there took him down, with a little help from a prefect by the name of Draco. And while the poor bastard was still bleeding out, Kivilaz took his bloody sword, cut away his plait and dropped it onto the dying man's face.'

'So if he plans to dye it red again, that must mean . . . ?' Lupercus turned to Marius.

'Exactly what you think it means. He'll swear an oath not to cut his plait away until he's captured this fortress, at a guess, and has our standards to add to the array of battle prizes he already boasts. And quite possibly my head too.'

The Winter Camp, Germania Superior, September AD 69

'What? Now we're marching north again? You reckon they'll actually let us get our fucking boots off the parade ground this time?'

Antonius stood in silence in front of his legion while his officers made their last pre-march inspections, each of them ready to visit his ire on any man whose equipment failed to meet his sharp-eyed expectations as they ranged up and down the lines of legionaries, listening to the opinions being voiced behind him with the alertness of a man who knew just how disaffected his men were. Not that he could entirely fault their logic after they had paraded ready to march a few days before, only for their orders to be cancelled at the last moment and his grumbling centuries returned to barracks.

'Nah, they'll find another reason not to let us go out to play. Another made-up order from the emperor.'

'What, again?'

Antonius frowned, but kept his back turned and his vine stick grasped firmly in both hands behind him. In point of fact he had, like every other senior officer in the legion, been shown Vitellius's order for the Winter Camp's occupants to remain in their fortress rather than go after the Batavians, and was therefore perfectly satisfied that the decision had been made in Rome, but his men clearly had a different opinion.

'No, it's an order from an emperor that held us back alright . . .' Antonius raised an expectant eyebrow as the new speaker paused for a moment to give the already tired joke what he clearly hoped would be comic timing. 'Just not from *our* emperor!'

It had become an article of faith, in the days since their abortive preparations to pursue the rebellious Batavians, that the last minute order for their march north to be cancelled had been issued in the interests not of Vitellius, former legatus augusti of the German legions and the man they considered their own, but by officers whose sympathies they believed firmly lay with Vespasianus, the emperor's eastern challenger. As men who saw themselves as having put their own man on the throne, and who expected to be richly rewarded for their loyalty to his rule once the usurper from Syria was defeated, they were deeply and openly distrustful of their leaders' apparently treacherous intentions. Rumours were rife that the army's commander was in league with Vespasian's leading general, who was even now marching the eastern legions towards Rome with the intention of unseating the man who, they firmly expected, would one day make them all rich.

'That's right! Fatty Flaccus commands what Antonius Primus demands!'

A ripple of laughter spread across the cohort at the shout, and Antonius decided that he'd heard enough for one day, turning to face them with a look of anger that abashed some but not all of the legionaries paraded before him.

'Stop your fucking moaning and get ready to march, you mouthy cunts!' His hard gaze swept across the ranks of his men, and the vine stick held across his thighs bent slightly as he flexed the muscles in his forearms reflexively with the urge to strike out. 'I saw the order from Vitellius! I saw the emperor's signature! I saw his seal! I spoke with the messenger who'd ridden with it from Rome! The fucking order . . .' He paused, waiting until he had them all hanging off his next words, then spat them out with violent emphasis. 'Was! From! Rome! And any man that wants to call me a liar can come out here and take his lumps, here and now!'

Nobody moved, none of them willing to risk the ire of a man who had boxed successfully for his century for several years and whose right hook was capable of cracking a man's jaw, but nor did any of the men paraded before him look convinced.

'Permission to speak, First Spear!'

He nodded graciously, recognising the legion's long tradition that senior legionaries who had earned the right to have an opinion were allowed, if they asked with sufficient respect and took enough care in framing their comments, to express the views of their comrades. The legionary in question, a fifteen-year man known and respected throughout the cohort, stepped forward and snapped into the brace position.

'The feeling of the men, sir, is that our officers don't care much for the emperor, as he's not got the right reputation with the nobs!'

Fighting the urge to agree with the sentiment, Antonius shook his head curtly, raising his voice to be heard by the men of his cohort.

'I spend a good deal of time with the gentlemen who command this legion, and nothing could be further from the truth! Every one of them stood here with us back in January and swore the same oath of allegiance that we did, didn't they? Legatus Vocula is a proper officer, hard but fair, and he tells me that he'll do whatever he's commanded by the emperor. You all saw him that morning we were stopped from marching, his face was like thunder when he got the order to stand the legion down, but he did what he was told! And he'll do just the same thing this time, now that Vitellius has decided to let us off the rope! Back in the ranks, soldier.'

'A good reply.' One of his cohort commanders had strolled out to join him, and turned to look at the paraded legion with a tight smile. 'Do you think it's true?'

Antonius pursed his lips.

'The legatus is a true Roman gentleman. He'd march the legion into the Underworld if Vitellius told him to. But as for the rest of them . . .' He paused for a moment, recalling the unguarded moments he'd spent in the presence of the Fourth's tribunes. 'The thing is, they sometimes say things in front of me that they shouldn't. Perhaps they see me as one of them, or perhaps I'm like a servant in their eyes, just part of the furniture.'

'What do they say?'

'Between us?' The other man nodded, meeting his stare with the candour of an old comrade. 'They say things that you wouldn't believe. They look down their noses at Vitellius, say he was a friend of Caligula when he was young which is how he got the limp, in a chariot accident. They say that he was favoured by Nero, and that he took part in all the revolting things that Nero did which resulted in the senate declaring him an enemy of the people.' They shared a moment of dark humour. 'Which of course really meant that he was an enemy of the senate. Some of the things they say Nero did would make your eyes water, women raped and their husbands and fathers murdered if they tried to stop it, and they blame Vitellius for having been there and done nothing to stop it. And they talk about this man Vespasianus too. They say he's a simple man, a soldier "like us", as if any of them are really soldiers. They say he's an old-fashioned man at heart, straight as a mile of road, and so poor that he had to buy and sell mules to feed his family for a while. They respect him, Julius, and most of them seem to believe he'd make a better emperor than our own man.'

'Whereas the *dives miles* here . . .'

Both men chuckled at the memory of their men chanting the term after swearing allegiance to Vitellius, the words 'rich soldier' echoing back and forth across the parade ground as they had celebrated having taken the throne for the army of Germany, with all the benefits they expected to accrue for their seizure of power. Antonius nodded in agreement.

'And there you have it. Our officers want the man they see as best for the empire, or at least the best as seen from the big houses in the nicer parts of Rome. Loyal they may be, but they know what will serve their own interests best. And that's not Vitellius, not from what I hear them telling each other.'

'And the legion wants the man they put on the throne, the man who'll reward them richly once Vespasianus is nothing more than six feet of freshly turned earth and a fading memory. Question is, who do we want? The man who's supposed to be the one who's apparently going to make us rich, or the man our betters secretly think is the best man to rule the world?'

Antonius nodded slowly.

'Not the best of choices, is it?' He stiffened as a familiar figure walked briskly onto the parade ground. 'And here's the one man whose opinion really matters. Best put any thoughts of who rules to the back of your mind, Centurion, because if I know Legatus Vocula, it's going to be a bit more than a brisk stroll this morning. He's got the look of a man who wants to go a very long way in a very short amount of time.'

7

'Fuck me . . . look at the size of him!'

Grimmaz stared with unashamed amazement at the biggest of the tribesmen who had walked down the paved road to the spot where the massive wooden carriage waited, a long-haired, hard-faced giant of a man a head taller than the biggest of the Batavi soldiers. His gaze flicked over them dismissively before he crawled under the vehicle's wooden side wall and inside the contraption to join the thirty or so of his fellows, the biggest and strongest men of all the thousands who had flocked to the tribe's banner, who were already inside its protection. It had been built under conditions of total secrecy, in a grove five miles distant from Batavodurum, the location closely guarded by Bairaz's guardsmen, who turned away anyone with no reason to come within sight of the wheeled edifice, but the rumours as to its purpose had run wild in the hours since it had been pulled forward to the battle line by a team of a dozen horses, speculation that had built to a fever pitch when word got out as to the other secret that lurked inside its thick oak timbers. Built, it was said, under the guidance of a skilled craftsman who had deserted from the Fifth Legion, the structure had an open rear, ten-foot-high walls of stout wooden planking, and was topped by a pitched roof of the same thickness to fend off heavy stones thrown down from the fortress walls. Its frontal protection was a double thickness of the same sturdy oak, arrayed around a hole through which peeped the iron head of a heavy ram, cast to resemble a goat's head complete with horns that curved back on themselves, and the whole construction was covered in the hides of freshly skinned beasts to render it fireproof. As the Batavi soldiers watched the ram's crew preparing themselves to heave it forward into battle, a crow flapped down to perch on its peaked roof and peck hungrily at the covering, cawing at the men gathered around it. Egilhard's tent mate Lanzo stared up at it gloomily, pulling his sword up a few inches to make sure it would come free of its scabbard when required, tersely stating what every man present was thinking, given their recent experience of battle and its grisly aftermath.

'That bird knows that this many men in one place can only result in a meal the likes of which he'll never see again.'

Alcaeus grinned at his leading man's awestruck face as the last of the big tribesmen disappeared into the ram's protective carriage.

'I'm not sure what impresses me more, the size of them or the fact that Kiv actually managed to get a testudo built to house that ram. Not to mention having the ram cast in perfect secrecy. And those boys need to be big, because first of all they've got to push that thing five hundred paces to reach the gate, then they've got to swing the ram long enough and hard enough to stove the gate in. If they can drag it away after that then so much the better, but we'll be going in through the hole they leave whether they're in the way or not.'

Grimmaz nodded slowly, his face creasing into a hard grin.

'So it's definitely an assault then. I just hope the prince is ready to acclaim me as the "wall breaker", 'cause I'm going to be the first man through the gate once Muscles there and his mates have torn us a gap.'

'And then you'll be the first to die.' They turned to find their new prefect standing behind them contemplating the distant fortress, his voice dry with knowing humour. 'The award of the title "wall breaker", I'm reliably informed, usually goes to the cleverest of the men in the leading wave, the one who knows to rush in at the back of the others and then take whatever cover he can find and keep himself alive for long enough that the rest of his cohort turn up and save his bacon. And now, if you'd like to hear our orders?'

'Silence! Silence for the prefect!'

The cohort fell silent at Alcaeus's shouted command, their speculation as to the likely battle plan dying away and more than a few men suddenly looking pale at the prospect of imminent action as Hramn raised his voice.

'Men of the First cohort! We have been given the honour of being the men who break Roman power in Germany forever! Our prince has tasked me with leading you forward in a direct assault on the Old Camp! The men of the German tribes are going to attack on the western side of the fortress as a diversion, giving us the chance to kick the southern door in and put the Romans to the sword before they even know the battle's begun! That carriage is built of timbers thick enough to stop a heavy bolt at close range, and fireproofed as well, which means that the big lads inside will be able to push it all the way to the fortress, then knock the gates in, and then back it away again! While they're doing that we'll go forward alongside them in two columns of four cohorts, one column on either side of the road, ready to exploit the breach the moment it happens! The leading cohorts will attack through the gate while the men behind attack the wall with the ladders that have been made for that purpose, to keep the defenders busy. We'll have some tribal archers and slingers with us to keep the Romans' heads down and stop them getting brave enough to try and stop us, but once the gates open there'll be nothing for it but a straightforward charge and hack at anyone that gets in our way. They'll throw everything they have at us once we're inside, and they'll have the advantage of fighting from the walls, so keep moving and don't give them any easy targets! They'll want to pin us down around the gate and use their bolt throwers to thin out our numbers, so don't stop to fight because you'll only slow down the men behind you! If a Roman comes at you then you put him down and move on, and leave the men behind you to finish him off! Advance as far into the fortress as you can, and as fast as you can, to make room for another man to get through the gates behind you!'

He paused for a moment, looking about him to encompass all of his men with his gaze.

'The gods are watching what you do today! Be quick, be ruthless, and write a new line in the tribe's history to bring glory to our people!'

He turned to Alcaeus, gesturing for him to perform the sacrifice that had been agreed, and the centurion held a hand out for the goat that was struggling against the rope tied around its neck, leading it to the ram's iron head, drew his dagger and expertly slit its throat, waiting as the animal sank to its knees in a puddle of its own blood, bleated fitfully and then stopped moving. Opening its belly, he crouched over the steaming entrails, feeling the still-warm liver with fingers long accustomed to finding the slightest imperfection that might be a portent of ill fortune, then swiftly cut it loose and got to his feet with the bloody organ raised high, roaring out his verdict to be heard by every man in the cohorts.

'Perfect and unblemished! A victory omen!'

Hramn stared at his deputy for a moment and then turned away, calling for his men to take up their battle formation.

'Form line of battle by cohort!'

Striding to the head of his men as they hurriedly dressed the columns on either side of the massive structure, he rapped his shield against the carriage's massive timbers in the signal for the men inside to advance, waving a hand at the leader of the tribal archers waiting grim-faced on its shallow pitched roof.

'Forward! Tonight we'll dine on meat cooked over the burning remnants of a Roman fortress!'

'This will be it, I'd imagine.'

The legatus looked out over the Old Camp's western wall at the warriors of the German tribes, watching with his two first spears as the barbarians readied themselves at a point just outside effective bolt-thrower range, the voices of their leaders faintly audible as they harangued their men with fierce encouragements to do their utmost in the coming fight. Marius nodded agreement.

'They'll have been pounding their chests and telling each other how they're going to smash their way in and tear us to pieces like a pack of wild dogs since before the sun came up. Getting pissed up as well, I'd imagine.'

Whatever it was that their chieftains were telling the warriors elicited a wild roar of approval, and as the echoes died away those men with shields raised them to their mouths and began their barritus, the rolling, booming murmur that would swell to a roar and sink back to a whisper as many times as the men leading them decided would kindle the fire of rage in their hearts to send them at the Roman defences without fear. Behind them were gathered their camp followers, the women already raising their voices in shrill imprecations, pointing to the captured standards and banners that were gathered at their heart and commanding their men to repeat the feats of bravery that had resulted in the booty. The first spear looked down at the ordered rows of man traps, their excrement-smeared stakes almost invisible against the dark earth of the pits into which they had been sunk.

'Now we'll get to see how effective all those lilies are.'

Aquillius shrugged next to him.

'The lilies will take their share of them, and make them waste their effort trying to fill them in, but the main point of them is that they restrict the enemy to lanes of approach positioned to allow our bolt throwers to shoot straight into them as they come forward. And the good thing is that I can't see any sign of siege equip—'

A trumpet sounded from the southern wall, and a centurion waved urgently at them in the prearranged signal that the legatus's presence was requested. The three men hurried down the length of the wall to its corner with the southern rampart to be met by a senior centurion of Aquillius's Fifteenth Legion.

'I thought you gentlemen would want to see this.'

He pointed out over the trampled earth where the fortress vicus had stood only days before, and the three officers stared at the massive shape of a wooden structure on wheels that was making ponderous but unmistakable progress towards the wall's gate. Slow-moving ranks of soldiers were advancing alongside the carriage, their precisely ordered ranks a stark contrast to the chaos of the tribal war bands facing the fortress's western defences. After a moment, Lupercus spoke, his voice hard-edged with a sudden understanding of the threat they faced.

'This may very well be the moment that Rome comes to bitterly regret making an enemy of a people who have fought alongside us for a hundred years. That, gentlemen, is a testudo, a covered siege waggon, which, given that it's being driven towards our southern gate it would seem reasonable to speculate that it contains a ram.'

Aquillius nodded his agreement.

'Why go to the trouble of building a testudo if they don't have something special to protect? Those men marching alongside it are their recently returned cohorts, and I don't think that's a coincidence. They'll look to break the gate in and then spend men like water to get a toehold inside the wall and push us away from the breach. We know they're brave enough, and we know they're nasty enough, so I reckon that's the most dangerous thing they have on their side. They'll come in through any gap in the wall like a pack of wild animals, so if they break the gate then we lose the fortress. It's as simple as that. And I've been on the losing side in too many battles of late to have any enthusiasm for repeating the experience.'

The legatus looked back at the oncoming Batavi for a moment.

'Very well, gentlemen, I think their intentions are clear enough.'

Lupercus looked down into the fortress below them, pointing at the open ground that had been created by the removal of the barracks block that had previously crammed the space to within a dozen paces of the fortress wall.

'First Spear Aquillius, we'll have three of your cohorts arrayed around the gate, please, and the other three to man the wall above it.'

The big man turned and was gone at the run, bellowing for his cohort commanders in a voice that raised the hairs on the back of Marius's neck despite his having already grown familiar with the man. Lupercus smiled at him, nodding slightly.

'I know, he has the same effect on me and I'm supposed to be his superior. And as for you, First Spear Marius, I'd be grateful if your three cohorts could defend the western wall against the tribesmen. That ram might be the biggest problem we have this afternoon, but ten thousand screaming barbarians determined to break in and commit a range of unpleasantness from arson, to buggery, looting and murder at no matter what the cost in lives must run it a fairly close second.'

He turned away, raising his voice to bellow an order the length of the southern wall.

'Bolt thrower captains! Concentrate all shooting on the ram! *Shoot!*'

'Are we there yet? We've been marching for *hours!*'

Grimmaz answered the plaintively voiced question without looking back at the men behind him.

'If you couldn't take a joke then you shouldn't have joined, should you, Beaky?'

The soldier continued his line of complaint without acknowledging the jibe.

'It's not the fact that we're about to storm a double legion fortress. It's not the bolt throwers and catapults that will shortly be trying to put holes in me or squash me flat. It's not even the fact that Wigbrand's farts smell so bad that it's a wonder I haven't thrown up down his back—'

A chorus of muffled titters greeted the last comment, and even Wigbrand himself smiled faintly at the baseless jibe.

'Get on with it, Beaky, before I have Achilles hamstring you and leave you here for the crows to make an early start on!'

'It's just, do we *really* have to march this slowly?'

Alcaeus's voice sounded from the century's head, the centurion walking in front of his men with an apparent total disregard for the danger posed by the fortress's defences.

'I find it ironic that a soldier who spends most of his time on the march complaining about the pace, now that we're practically marking time to stay beside the prince's secret weapon, is complaining about the fucking pace? Do you have anything other than complaint to share with us? Something to make us all laugh, perhaps?'

'Now you mention it, Centurion, I did hear one the other day that made me smile. What do you call two soldiers fighting over a woman on pay day? Anyone? No? Two soldiers fighting over a woman on pay day is a tug of w—'

'Fuck!'

Grimmaz flinched at the column's head as a speculatively launched bolt bounced off the turf twenty paces ahead of the front rank and slammed into his shield, rebounding from its iron boss with a loud clang and leaving a dent the size of half an apple in the metal. Before anyone could react, Hramn's voice snapped out in an instant rebuke from his place in front of the first century.

'Silence in the ranks! We're the Batavi, not some legion scum to start squealing the moment nasty men start throwing sharp sticks at us! And if you insist on dying despite my orders strictly forbidding it,' the men around Egilhard tittered at their new prefect's growled reproach, 'die quietly!'

The leading man shook his head in disgust, staring at the walls before them over the rim of a shield he already knew would present no more obstacle to a clean bolt shot than a sheet of tunic wool.

'Well, they know we're coming, that's pretty certain given the fact we're walking beside a carriage the size of a legion shithouse! Let's just hope they concentrate their attention on the ram, and not on knocking us over like so many fucking skittles!'

'Jupiter, look at them!'

With a collective roar the German tribesmen were on the move, hurrying forward with the screams and yells of their women in their ears, a wave of men the length of the fortress's western side washing forward up the slight slope, instinctively clumping into tight knots as they reached the first line of lily pits, carefully laid out at the bolt throwers' maximum range. Briefed to begin shooting without waiting for an order, the weapons' commanders bellowed an almost simultaneous order to their crews, half a dozen of the deadly missiles soaring up into the clear blue sky before plunging into the oncoming barbarians, vanishing into the mass of warriors like pebbles tossed into a stormy sea. Muscular legionaries raged at the winding mechanisms of their engines in a fury of effort under the critical eyes and bawled encouragement of their captains, stripped down to loin cloths in the sure knowledge that they would be dripping sweat within minutes, while replacements waited close by to replace them when they staggered away from the mechanisms to gasp for breath and rub their aching muscles.

'Six of them dead. Perhaps a dozen. It'll take a lot of bolts to make them think better of the idea.'

Marius smiled at his deputy Gaius, standing beside him and watching the oncoming tide of enraged barbarians with an expression that combined fascination with horror.

'I voiced the same concern to my colleague Aquillius the other day. I asked him how we could expect a few bolt throwers and some mantraps to stop ten thousand mad-eyed tribesmen from swarming over these walls and tearing us all a new arsehole in no time flat, once their blood's up.' The other man looked at him expectantly. In the short time that he had been in command of the Fifteenth Legion, the grim-faced Aquillius had won the respect of both his own officers and those of the Fifth by his uncompromising attitude and apparent fearlessness, born of a fatalism that seemed to verge on a total disinterest in whether he lived or died. 'He told me that it's not the bolt throwers, or the lilies, or the wall, or anything else that matters.'

The big man had stared levelly at him when the subject first came up, shrugging at the question as to how they could hope to stop a determined attempt to overwhelm the defences, then tapped his head with his usual deadpan expression.

'It's this, brother. What's in your men's heads is really all that matters. If they believe they can send half a dozen tribes away with their arses caved in, then they will. And if they expect to be overrun, then they will be. All we can really do, when all the toys are in play and it still isn't enough to stop them rushing the walls, is convince our men that fighting to the death will keep them alive, whereas holding back for fear of death will only result in death, and a lot worse before that.'

'He told you that? We fight to the death to stay alive?'

Marius grinned at the apparent absurdity of the sentiment.

'He did. And you know what?'

The centurion shook his head.

'He's right. So go and tell your lads that we're not fighting for Rome today. Just for the right to see the sun rise tomorrow.'

Another salvo of heavy bolts whipped in from the fortress walls, the howl of their iron tail fins making more than one man duck his head reflexively as they hammered into the ram carriage's thick wooden side, one impacting at such a narrow angle that it skated down the structure's flank, its sharp-edged iron fins scoring a long line in the hide covering and leaving a ten-foot section of the wooden planking naked as the protective cow skin peeled away and hung uselessly, scraping along the ground as the carriage advanced. Another shot went high, whether by deliberate aim or accident unclear, catapulting one of the archers crouched atop the structure down into the soldiers marching on its far side in a spray of dark red blood. Hramn's voice rose over the squealing of the testudo's wooden wheels, a note of warning in his shouted command.

'Lilies! Pick your way through them but stay low! If the man commanding those bolt throwers has any sense he'll shift targets to us any time about now, because he's not going to stop the ram with them!'

Three men back in the Second Century's ranks, Egilhard looked down at the ground beneath their feet, following Levonhard's lead as he stepped to the right fractionally to avoid the first of the mantraps laid out in rows around the fortress. Five sharpened stakes smeared with something noisome protruded up in a circle, angled inwards to ensure that any man unlucky enough to step into the pit would have his leg pierced in several places. Around him men were doing the same thing, altering the direction of their advance to left and right to avoid the deadly traps, and the young soldier found himself cheek by jowl with the man to his right, their footing perilous as five men were crowded together into a space large enough for three.

'Keep moving!' Hramn was urging his men forward, stepping out in front of them despite the risk of becoming an obvious target for any bolt-thrower captain alert to the opportunity. 'Move as fast as you can, we need to get too close for them to shoot at us!'

Something hot and wet sprinkled across Egilhard's face, and the man to his right staggered against him, almost pushing him into the pit to his left. The wooden shaft and iron flights of a bolt were protruding from his chest, blood running down his armour in a thick rivulet, but even as he staggered under the dying man's weight, the warrior in front of the stricken soldier folded bonelessly to the grass, a bloody rent in the mail across his back where the bolt had torn through the thick iron rings with the brutal force that had propelled it straight through his body. Along the Batavi line shouts of horror and anger erupted as more bolts flickered out from the fortress walls and arrowed down into their defence-less ranks, and Hramn's voice was raised again in a bellow of command.

'Forward, as fast as you can! We need to get into the shadow of the walls!'

The tribesmen assaulting the western wall were still coming forward, slower than before but still with the same deadly intent, barking and screaming blood oaths as they fought their way through the sea of lily pits, a seething mass of infuriated warriors washing towards the Old Camp's walls intent on destruction. Marius looked up and down the wall's length, nodding to himself as more and more hands were raised by the men who had manhan-dled their scorpions up the flights of stairs and onto the wall, signals indicating that they were ready to shoot. Judging that the mass of the enemy was within their range, he blew a shrill blast on his whistle and raised his own hand, keeping it aloft for a moment before sweeping it down. At his signal a score of bolts flicked out from the wall into the tribesmen's front rank, while a continual stream of shots from the heavier artillery continued to pummel the Germans, inflicting losses that, while minor in the face of the enemy's overwhelming numbers, still meant that every missile that smashed into their ranks sprayed the men around its hapless victim with blood and bone fragments.

'Ladders! They've got ladders!'

The first spear stepped forward alongside the soldier who was pointing down at the advancing horde, seeing the long siege ladders that were being carried on the backs of a dozen tribesmen apiece with the obvious intention of their being thrown up against the Old Camp's wall to allow their bearers to attack the men on the rampart.

'Of course they've got fucking ladders!' His note of scorn was almost pitch perfect, he judged, for all that he was almost as taken aback by the sight of their potential doom as the man beside him. 'What were you expecting, a flagon of wine and an invitation to marry their daughters?' The men around him laughed, and he clapped the soldier on the shoulder before he could become the butt of his comrades' humour. 'But well spotted for all that. There's a round of drinks for this man's tent party, on me, if we all get through this!'

Marius walked away as the soldier's mates cheered, shouting comments that they fully intended to survive and take their first spear up on the promise, watching as the artillery crews laboured to send bolt after bolt down into the heaving barbarian mass. Drawing in a lungful of breath, he blew three sharp blasts of the whistle, the signal for the centuries along the wall's length to deploy the next layer of their defence, a trick that had been suggested by a recruit in his eleventh cohort who he had promptly promoted to the rank of watch officer as a reward not just for the idea but for having the courage to take it to his centurion. The two legions' smiths had been labouring non-stop for days producing the weapons that the man had proposed as their final means of thinning out the German ranks before they reached the wall, and the first spear smiled grimly as every man along the wall's length stepped forward to deliver the small but horribly efficient devices that had been distributed among them that morning.

'It's not working, Legatus! That thing's too well protected!'

The ram was still rolling forwards, driven by men hidden within the heavy wooden structure, which was proving just as impervious to the bolt throwers' powerful attacks even now it was less than fifty paces from the wall, close enough for the section on its left side where a ricocheting bolt had cut away a section of its cow-skin covering to stand out, the hide flapping loosely to dangle on the road surface. Lupercus nodded at the man who had expressed his frustration, the captain of the engine alongside which he was standing. The barbarian archers crouching on the carriage's roof were getting bolder, lofting arrows at the men on the wall that had already found one target, a legionary sprawled full length on the internal road beneath the parapet where he had fallen with the fletching of an arrow protruding from his throat. Judging that the soldiers of the Batavi cohorts had advanced so close to the walls that they were no longer effective targets, he shouted a command at his artillery crews, pointing at the men atop the ram.

'Switch targets! Clear away those blasted archers!'

The order was passed down the line in a succession of roared commands that were received by each bolt thrower captain and passed on in a stentorian roar, and a flurry of bolts flicked out to pluck the tribal bowmen from their perches. One German, bolder than his companions, stood his ground rather than flinching from the sudden barrage, picking a target and loosing his shaft with an unnerved deliberation that was rewarded by a scream somewhere to the legatus's left, but in doing so made too good a target for the eager engine crews to miss. A single heavy bolt punched through him with such power that he stood stock-still for a moment, the bow dangling from fingers abruptly robbed of feeling, then fell full length to lie face down across the carriage's slight pitched roof. More tribesmen climbed up the structure from where they had followed in the protection of its massive shadow and took their places, but as fast as they replaced their fallen comrades they became fresh targets for the scorpion crews who had turned their attention away from the advancing enemy column at the legatus's command. Lupercus barely flinched as an arrow hissed past his head, missing by no more than a hand span, lost in concentration as he stared at the fortress's potential nemesis.

'Is it time for the Hamians, I wonder? There's a gap in that thing's fireproofing that might just be our opportunity.'

The Legatus turned back to the hulking first spear who, having arrayed his men in a tight formation around the gateway beneath them, had returned to the rampart's vantage point. Heedless of his previous avowed intention not to become a target in Lupercus's stead, he was standing next to his superior, apparently untroubled by the archers' close attentions.

'Yes, First Spear. I think it's time to make that roll of the dice.'

Aquillius turned away and shouted for the Arab archers to come on to the rampart, then raised his voice to be heard by the soldiers waiting for them along the wall on both sides of the gate. The Hamians hurried up the steps and spread out along the wall to the right of the gate as directed, each of them selecting a soldier and ducking down into the rampart's protection next to him, each of them carefully placing the lighted lamp he carried at his feet and stringing his bow in readiness for the archery duel to come.

'Shield men, you know your part here! Each of these archers is worth twenty of you! Any one of you who fails to put your board, and if need be your body, between these men and the enemy shooting back at them will have me so far up his arse he'll think he's sat on a tree trunk! Bring up the tallow!'

A dozen men hurried up onto the fighting surface, each carrying several jars of tallow that had been warmed through to make it liquid, depositing them alongside each of the archers who solemnly pulled the first of their arrows from the quivers hanging at their sides and dipped the strips of cloth tied behind the arrowhead into the oily fluid. Waiting until every one of them had allowed the excess to run back into the jar and stood ready to shoot, the grim-faced first spear pointed at the oncoming ram.

'Archers, aiming for the bare wood . . . *shoot!*'

Lowering their bows momentarily to allow the tallow-soaked cloth strips to touch the tiny lamp flames at their feet, the archers waited for fire to take hold of the flammable material and greedily feast on the oils soaked into the material, then raised their weapons and swiftly loosed the burning arrows in expertly judged shallow arcs. A radiant golden rain of missiles flicked out from the wall trailing tails of thick black smoke, their sharply pointed heads penetrating deep into the solid wooden planks that protected the structure's occupants and draping the burning strips across the testudo's surface. Aquillius raised his voice to roar another order over the whirring sound of the winders labouring at their tasks.

'Continue shooting! Bolt throwers, target anyone fighting the fires! Either that thing burns or we'll all pay a high price!'

The tumbling caltrops fell like silver rain, their freshly sharpened points glittering in the sunlight as they arced to the ground close to the wall. Clearing the last row of lily pits, the Germans ran full pelt for the protection of the rampart's shadow, where they knew the bolt throwers would be unable to reach them, but as they covered the last twenty paces in a lunging sprint men began falling in sudden screaming agony, bellowing helplessly in pain and clutching at their feet to find hard iron spikes protruding from the torn leather of their boots. Ripping the evil little devices free they tossed them away in their agony, heedless of the risk to their fellow warriors, the waves of men following them so tightly packed that it was impossible for the caltrops, twin sections of thin iron rod welded together in such a way that three of the four spikes would always land on the ground with the fourth standing upright, not to wound another man in turn.

'*Gods below . . .*'

Marius nodded at Gaius's horrified whisper.

'Whoever invented that nasty little trick must surely have been one of the most evil-minded men ever to fall out of a woman. But if it takes another few hundred of them out of the fight I'm willing to have it on my conscience. Besides, there's worse in store for the men who get to the ditch.'

They watched, waiting for the moment that the Germans began their assault on the walls, peeping through the gaps in the rampart's protection with a careful eye for the enemy archers, even though, Marius suspected, an arrow's impact would probably be the first and only indication any of them got that they had become a target. The barbarian warriors cast throwing spears as they came on, most rebounding uselessly from the wall's facing of mud bricks and only a very few clearing the rampart. A legionary less cautious than his fellows staggered back from the rampart in silent agony, the sinews standing out in his neck with the pain of a spear blade that had punched through his thigh to protrude from the back of his leg. He tottered on the wall's edge and fell to the hard road surface twenty feet below, the crunching impact silencing his wail of pain. Marius and the centurion looked at each other for a moment, then the first spear peered over the wall's edge at the increasingly large concentration of men gathered in the freshly re-excavated ditch along the rampart's length.

'*Water, ready!*'

Dozens of legionaries turned to the fire pits that had been dug behind the wall, each one filled with a carefully tended pile of blazing logs and over which were suspended the heavy iron pots that the tent parties used for cooking in the field, now turned to a darker purpose. With hands heavily wrapped in woollen windings, two men took each pot and lifted them off their cradles, straining at the weight of the bubbling cauldrons as they climbed the steps and stepped forward to the wall's edge under the direction of their leading men, who had carefully peered out to find the best place for their burdens to be delivered. Grunting with the effort, cursing as the pots' heat began to burn through their woollen protection, they upended the iron pots over the wall and onto the men, boiling water falling in cascading torrents of scalding rain onto the men below. In an instant the air was rended by the hysterical, crazed bellows of the hapless warriors who had taken the attack's brunt. Unable to move in the crush of their fellow tribesmen, they screamed in agony, their howls and roars of pain only ceasing as they passed out or were gifted the mercy stroke by the men around them.

'They sound like spirits in torment. I'm almost tempted to pity the poor bastards.'

Marius nodded at his friend's grim musing.

'You'd better spend the time praying that they don't manage to get over this wall in numbers, Gaius. Because after everything we've inflicted on them, this won't end well for any of us.'

Another shower of fire arrows dragged their black trails from the rampart to their target, studding the ram's exposed woodwork with pinpricks of flame. As each missile struck, the impact sprayed drops of burning fluid across the planking, and while some sputtered out almost as soon as they hit the carriage, others burned on, the strength of their flames growing as the wood smouldered and then caught fire, heated by the flames licking out from the burning tallow-soaked strips of linen.

'Put those fires out!'

A dozen men responded to Hramn's shout, rushing to the ram and beating at the flames, knocking away the burning arrows with the rims of their shields and reaching up to pull out those that had extinguished themselves by the force of their impact. A soldier from another of the Second Century's tent parties, known to Egilhard by no more than the occasional nod of mutual respect, stretched to pluck out an arrow that was almost out of his reach and then, by the cruellest of chances, was spitted through his reaching hand by a bolt, instantly pinning him on tiptoe to the carriage's wooden side. His outraged bellows of pain and fear had the young recruit on his feet in an instant, only to find himself being pulled back into the cover of his shield by a strong grip on his belt.

'His time has come, Achilles. Yours has not.' Alcaeus was crouching behind him, shaking his head forbiddingly. 'Any man who goes to his rescue will only die with him. Watch and see if I'm right.'

A pair of soldiers from the trapped man's tent party ran forward, intent on rescuing their comrade, the first of them falling with a bolt through his spine to lie motionless on the cobbles before he even reached his friend, while the second was hit by a fire arrow as he tried to climb the structure to wrench out the bolt that had pinned the struggling soldier. For a moment he did no more than stagger back to the ground with the missile's impact, but even as the shaft dropped away from his mail, having failed to penetrate the iron rings, the oil that had sprayed across his back at the moment of impact took fire, feeding on the padding of the filthy subarmalis underneath his armour. Burning fiercely, flames fed by a combination of the hot tallow and the grease that had soaked into the garment over years of use, the padded arming jacket was suddenly ablaze, turning the man's frenzied efforts to pull off the mail into a jerky parody of a dance as the fire consumed his clothing and tortured his body. Flames licking up his back took hold of his hair, and with a piercing scream of agony he tore away his helmet, staggering back against the ram as his body became a spasmodically jerking human torch. Another bolt struck him, smashing him into the wooden planking alongside his trapped comrade and forcing the helpless soldier to contort his body away from the blazing remains of his friend, still screaming his lungs out at the horror being inflicted upon them, the howls of desperation taking on a more frenzied, animal note as his own clothing took fire with the same awful speed. His agonised bellows spelled doom for the men inside the ram carriage whose timbers took light properly, the fire becoming a blaze as the horrified Egilhard watched his comrades being consumed alive by the flames.

'Now they're pissed off!'

Marius nodded at the statement, keeping his head down behind the parapet as a shower of darts and spears flew at the defenders from the mass of men raging at the western wall. Thousands of barbarians had gathered at the foot of the rampart, flailing at the stout timber's brick protection with hammers and axes in a fury of frustrated rage. Two soldiers staggered to the parapet carrying a heavy stone the size of a cow's head between them, grunting with the effort as they tossed it blindly over the edge to fall into the mob below. Turning away, one of them jerked as a lucky shot put an arrow between his plate armour and his helmet's neck guard, the feathered shaft protruding stiffly as he toppled onto the wall's fighting platform and convulsed in choking death throes.

'Keep your fucking heads *down*!'

A dull thud on the other side of the parapet made Marius risk a swift peep over the brickwork to find the wooden legs of a scaling ladder against the wall's top.

'Spear!' He held out a hand to the man next to him, beckoning urgently as the ladder bounced against the wall with the effort of the men climbing its rungs. '*Quickly!* Get ready to push!'

Getting to his feet he pushed the spear's sharp iron head into the topmost rung, feeling the iron pierce the wood as he leaned forward into the weapon's shaft, pushing harder until he knew he was on the verge of lifting the ladder's feet from the wall despite the weight of the men whose frantic climbing was shaking the wooden structure perceptibly. Feeling hands gripping his back, he thrust the spear forward with a twist of his powerful shoulders, forcing the weight of the ladder and its as yet unseen occupants to start to move out from the wall. Voices were raised over the battle's roaring hubbub as the Germans below realised what was happening, and Marius shouted a command to the men behind him.

'*Push!*'

A pair of legionaries threw themselves onto his body, their added power giving him the necessary strength to lever the ladder away from the wall. As their effort's momentum pushed him forward against the parapet, the ground below the wall came into view, and Marius found himself staring down onto a scene whose horror would stay with him for the rest of his life. As the ladder teetered on the brink of falling backwards into the war band's chaotic, swirling mass, a long-haired warrior with a sword in one hand came into view, so close to the Roman that they could have exchanged pleasantries had the situation been different, but while the man's face would be etched into his memory forever in the moment of perfect balance before his fall, it was the backdrop that assaulted the first spear's senses, widening his eyes in amazement. Below the wall, where the ditch had been dug out at Aquillius's command to make scaling the palisade that much more difficult, a baying mob of warriors was seething beneath him, the sprawled, broken and maimed bodies of men with horrific wounds and the stench of sweat, blood, urine and faeces assaulting his senses. Dead, dying and wounded men were everywhere, some horrifically injured by boiling water or falling stones, but the majority of the tribesmen were snarling up at the defenders or hammering at the wall with their weapons, seeking in vain to force an entry. The ladder hung in mid-air for an instant, the topmost warrior drawing back his sword to strike out at the Roman who was trying to kill him and then, seemingly unbalanced by the weapon's weight, he fell away with an expression of hatred and frustration as the ladder toppled back into the war band, vanishing into the mob's frenzy. A spear thrown from below hit Marius's helmet with a clang, shaking his wits momentarily, and he staggered backwards into the arms of the legionaries behind him.

'Careful now, First Spear! We don't want you dropping off the back edge of the wall now, do we?'

Drawing breath to thank them, his attention was instantly drawn away by movement to his right, a flurry of action on the wall at whose centre stood a tribal warrior with two short spears. As Marius watched he turned, ducked a sword thrust, then pivoted and lunged with the right-hand weapon, moving with a lithe speed that would have drawn an appreciative nod from the senior centurion were it not for the fact that the twitching bodies of two legionaries lay at his feet while a third jerked spasmodically with the spear's long blade deep in his right eye. The remainder of the tent party on either side of him were backing away in a manner that suggested they were on the verge of running. Behind the enemy warrior another man was climbing over the parapet with a drawn sword, and the first spear knew that their numbers would rapidly swell to a dozen and more, enough men to hold their section of the wall and start advancing out in both directions. Without conscious thought he was first running towards the scene, then sprinting, the spear still in his hands, bursting through a knot of legionaries fighting to push another ladder off the parapet, bellowing the war cry that was so familiar in his mouth from his time on the harpastum pitch.

'*Alaudae!*'

The soldiers backing away from the German shrank aside as he hurtled through them, their bodies masking the enemy warrior's view of his oncoming threat until the very last moment. Raising a spear in instinctive self-defence, he shuddered with the impact of Marius's pilum, the needle-pointed iron shank punching cleanly through him as the Roman snarled triumphantly, stepping back and kicking the dying man off the weapon's shaft. The swordsman who had been second over the wall raised his weapon to attack, but Marius saw the movement in his peripheral vision and stepped into the blow, raising the spear across his body to take the blade's impact. As the pilum's shaft broke in two under the blow's force, he took another step, close enough to smell the tribesman's rank breath, ramming the broken weapon's pointed iron shank up into the German's throat with such force that the tip snapped through the top of his skull, leaving the swordsman staggering for a moment with his eyes upturned to show the whites before tripping backwards over the parapet onto the men climbing the ladder behind him.

'*Get that fucking ladder off my fucking wall!*'

Momentarily taken aback at the sight of their usually imperturbable first spear wild-eyed and spattered with the blood of his victims, the legionaries dithered fractionally, then instinctively obeyed the lash of his bellowed order, spearing the tribesman at the top of the ladder and then thrusting it away from the wall to fall back into the war band's heaving mass. Marius turned away and stalked back towards his previous vantage point, stopping as he realised that the tent party's leading man was staring at him.

'First Spear! Your face . . .'

★

'This is a lost cause! We need to pull back!'

Hramn stared bleakly at the blazing ram carriage for a moment before turning back to Alcaeus. The tribal warriors who had been pushing the massive structure had fled, half of them lying dead or dying on the road where the Roman archers had shot them down as they ran, while his cohorts were huddled behind their shields on either side of the burning siege engine, still exposed to the deadly power of the enemy bolt throwers.

'Yes. There's nothing to be gained from the price we're paying to stay here and stare at the walls of that fortress. And I'm not prepared to send men up against those walls without the distraction of a breach to split the defenders' attention.' Alcaeus nodded, but as he turned away to start issuing orders the big man stopped him with two words. 'You knew, didn't you?'

The priest looked up at him in silence.

'I knew what, Prefect?'

Hramn snorted.

'Don't play the fool with me, Priest! There was something wrong with that sacrifice, you knew it and I could see it from the look on your face as you performed the ceremony! I witnessed enough ceremonies in Rome to know whether a priest is genuinely content or just putting on an act, and I saw you pause for a moment when you touched that liver! It was cursed, wasn't it?'

The other man shrugged.

'And what would you have had me do? Shout at the top of my voice that the omens were poor? Scare the living shit out of our men when they had no choice but to attack at Kivilaz's command? Or should I have called on you to cancel the attack?'

Hramn shook his head.

'This is not a discussion for now. Get this column pulled back and I'll get the other one moving! We've lost enough men to a lost cause for one day!'

Marius could sense a growing frustration in the mob of warriors baying at the wall beneath him, a pent-up fury that demanded release, and as he watched over the parapet's edge, having pulled off his crested helmet to avoid drawing attention to himself, he realised that the war band was concentrating on a point beneath him. The bolt throwers continued to spit their deadly missiles into the mass of men, but it was as if the tribe's warriors had meta-morphosed into a collective organism, impervious to the pin-prick wounds inflicted by the fortress's defenders as they surged forward in one last titanic effort.

'Fuck me, they're forming a testudo!'

He looked round at Gaius, shaking his head at his opinion of the Germans' purpose in emulating the Roman formation, which used raised shields to shelter the men within from hostile missiles.

'It's more than just a testudo, if I'm right.'

As they watched, tribesmen began to clamber onto their comrades' raised shields, hurrying forward across the uncertain surface raised into place by the men below them, locking their own shields in turn to provide a further level of height to the impromptu human formation.

'They're trying to build a fucking great big siege ladder out of bodies!'

A third level was forming, the wooden surfaces of the warriors' shields only feet below the top of the wall, tribesmen flooding into the space beneath the lowest level to add their strength to that of the men who were the formation's foundation.

'They just might succeed as well.' Marius stood, ignoring the risk of a thrown spear finding him as he called down to the men waiting beneath the wall. 'Stones! Bring as many stones as you can, as fast as you can! *Move!*'

The Germans were in a hurry, warriors throwing themselves onto the structure with the haste of men who knew that it could only be a matter of time before the defenders realised their desperate plan and set about nullifying it. As their tower of bodies grew taller the artillery teams to either side began to shoot directly into them, bolts skipping away off the flat surfaces of the shields or plucking away individual tribesmen as they climbed onto their uncertain surface, but it was evident that they were fighting a losing battle as the enemy warriors poured into the attack. A soldier stepped onto the wall carrying a heavy piece of masonry taken from the piles of rubble that Aquillius had ordered to be placed next to every stairway, and Marius pointed at the rampart.

'Throw it over!' The legionary grunted with the effort, heaving the chunk of stone over the edge to land with a thump on a shield below. 'More stones! You!' He pointed at the men huddled along the parapet, sheltering from the scattered arrows that were still flicking past intermittently. 'All of you! Fetch more stones! *Now!*'

He snatched a lump of rock from the next man, raising it over his head and hurling it onto the shields below him, grinning savagely as the boards parted under the impact and allowed it to fall into the structure. A fresh tent party of soldiers appeared at his back with a centurion at their head, hurrying up the wall from his left with the rest of his men at their heels.

'First Spear Aquillius sent us sir! There are more men behind us!'

He looked over at the southern wall, a thick black tongue of smoke rising over the gates, presumably from whatever it was that the Batavi had attempted to bring against the fortress.

'Your century can get ready to fight off anyone coming over the wall.'

'*Over* the wall?'

'You'll know it when you see it! You!'

The next officer in the stream of men hurrying up the wall from the south snapped to attention.

'First Spear!'

'Take your men down into the fortress and bring up the heaviest stones they can carry! *Quickly!*'

Within minutes the trickle of masonry being thrown onto the human tower had become a continual cascade of stone and brickwork, the last layer of shields trembling as the stones that fell through the top layer wrought unseen havoc below, while the sheer weight of that which remained supported by the tower tested the limits of the tribesmen's strength.

'First Spear!' He turned to find a soot-smeared chosen man at his shoulder. 'The water's boiling again, sir!'

'Bring it here! Get it all here!'

He waited, hard-eyed, while the men set to tend the boiling vessels manhandled them to the wall's edge.

'One at a time, and all in the same place!'

The first of the heavy iron pots disgorged its contents onto the layered shields that were butted up against the wall, and for a moment Marius wondered if there would be any effect. Then, in a sudden cacophony of bellowed pain they parted as the men holding them up forgot everything but the searing pain where the boiling water had scalded them.

'Next!'

Another cauldron was emptied into the structure, and this time the reaction was even more violent as the steaming liquid poured into the lower levels, packed with men unable to avoid its burning touch.

'Next!'

The third vessel's contents were the final straw for men already scalded, some twice, and with a sudden convulsive heave the entire structure collapsed in a heap of writhing bodies. Seeing the moment of maximum opportunity, he ordered the fresh centuries forward, pointing down at the disordered Germans below.

'Spears!'

Lining the rampart, the legionaries drew their spears back and then hurled them down into the enemy, a fresh chorus of agonised screams assaulting their ears as dozens of tribesman were transfixed by the evil metal-shanked weapons, sharp-pointed heads intended to pierce armour penetrating skulls and rib cages with the ease of darning needles lancing through tunic wool. Those men who remained unwounded retreated away from the wall across the sea of bodies that littered the field, no longer afraid of the lily pits as most of them were filled by the corpses of their comrades, those still alive raising their hands in supplication as their brother warriors trod them down onto the pits' agonising stakes. Marius leaned against the wall, suddenly weak with reaction to the battle's intensity, watching the enemy flood back towards the disapproving ranks of their women and children.

'It won't be a happy evening in their camp.'

The centurion next to him nodded.

'Unless they come back for another try?'

His superior shook his head.

'I don't think so. Most of those warriors will have travelled to join the Batavi in family groups, and it's my guess that the older men have probably lost enough sons for one day. The ground wouldn't favour another attack today in any case, not now it's churned to destruction and carpeted with corpses. No, I reckon they'll lick their wounds for a few days while they try to work out what they do next.'

'What would you do?'

Marius turned to find Aquillius at his side.

'Glad you could join us.'

His brother officer grinned humourlessly at the jibe.

'We were lucky. The archers managed to set their ram afire, and without it their soldiers retreated quickly enough.' He peered over the rampart's parapet at the scene of devastation. 'They're quicker to recognise a lost cause than those fools. The legatus suggested I bring you some reinforcements, although it seems to me that you have the situation under control well enough. We're reinforcing the gate with earth and stonework, so they won't be able to try that trick again.'

Marius nodded tiredly.

'We were lucky too. There was a moment there I thought they might get enough men onto the wall to force us off our ground.'

Aquillius shrugged, staring dispassionately out across the sea of corpses.

'An old centurion of mine used to use the same line whenever anyone complained about his luck in winning the prize for best century yet again. "A funny thing, luck," he'd say. "The harder I drive my boys the luckier I get." We make our own luck in this world, brother.'

Marius nodded exhaustedly, the battle's abrupt end leaching the energy from his body and leaving him weak-legged with fatigue and a sudden ravening appetite.

'And now?'

Aquillius smiled faintly.

'Now? That was the start, nothing more. They came to break our door down and we sent them away battered, but hardly defeated. With their ram burned out, and thousands of dead and dying men strewn around the fortress for the crows to dine on for the next week, they'll take their time to mourn their losses and come up with a better plan. And then come at us again just as hard as they did today.'

'And you? What would you do in their place?'

Aquillius shrugged dispassionately.

'What would I do? I'd sit back and starve us out. But that's not their way. They want us at the end of their spears and they know they only have to get lucky once, whereas we, Marius, we have to be lucky *every* time.'

8

The Old Camp, Germania Inferior, October AD 69

'In all the years . . .' Adalwin pushed his spade into the turf, flicking a glance at the fortress's walls to their left '. . . that my father spent training me for the cohorts . . .' He lifted the tool and its cleanly cut chunk of turf, allowing Wigbrand to take it off the metal surface and pass it to Egilhard for placing on the slowly growing wall of mud that abutted the ditch in which he was standing. '. . . there was one weapon he never took the trouble to teach me the use of.' He cut another turf and passed it up to the big soldier, who seemed totally uninterested in his story. 'And it's this fucking thing! There, that's my hundred!' Holding the spade up he made to climb out of the ditch, only to find the young soldier blocking his way. 'Oi, I said—'

'Not even ninety. I can count, Beaky.'

Opening his mouth to argue he was cut off by Grimmaz, who was labouring with his own spade behind him.

'So can I. And I make you fifteen short of your share of the digging, which under the usual rules of the punishment of lazy bastards means that you need to cut another thirty turfs before you can take a turn at laying the wall.'

Adalwin stared at him for a moment before deciding not to push his luck and turning back to his task.

'So tell me again why it is that I'm working my arse off building a wall that's never going to be needed? I just can't see the point of digging a camp around them when they're already very happy behind their walls?'

The leading man spat on the damp soil of the trench he was

busily excavating, shaking his head with a look of bemusement.

'Does anybody want to tell him? I'd do it but I'm too busy cutting my share of mud.'

Lanzo walked over from his place watching the Roman fortress and lowered his shield's metal rim to the ground.

'We're digging a siege line, Beaky, to keep the relieving force out. Because as sure as the unavoidable facts that apples are green, blood is red and you've got a tiny manhood, at some point the Romans are going to rediscover their pride and come looking to break through us and rescue their mates. Give it a week and we'll have two walls, one facing each way, with stakes so thick and ditches so deep that there'll be no way through, not with us on the other side to punish anyone that's stupid enough to try.'

Adalwin shrugged, cutting another turf and passing it up to Egilhard.

'So why are we doing the digging? Wouldn't it go a lot quicker if the tribes were doing their part?'

Alcaeus had strolled up during the course of their conversation, and he smiled beneficently down at the labouring soldier with the goodwill of a man whose digging days were behind him.

'Military discipline, Soldier Adalwin.'

'Yes, Centurion!'

The wolf-priest shook his head at Adalwin's uncomprehending stare with an expression that combined both disappointment and disdain.

'And there it is, right on cue. There's that look that tells me you have no idea what it is that I'm talking about.' Alcaeus shook his head in apparent bafflement. 'I might be biased, but I swear we weren't as simple in our day. What it is that I mean by those two words, Soldier Adalwin, is that while you have spent most of your life preparing for service, what with your father's tuition when you were a snotty-nosed little bastard, and then the exhaustive training that we put you through when you join the cohorts, the average tribesman has no more idea of being a warrior than charging into battle as part of a mob and relying on the fortune of his gods to keep him alive. And part of that extensive training, although I know you didn't appreciate it at the time, was the digging of a marching camp wherever we went, no matter what the weather or the conditions underfoot, and the expansion of that camp into a veritable fortress when we stayed anywhere for any length of time.'

He looked down at the evidently baffled soldier, adopting the kind tone of voice a man might use with a confused elderly relative.

'We dig fortifications at every overnight camp, Soldier Adalwin, to prevent the risk of rough men with bad intentions from creeping up on us in the dark and surprising us while we're asleep. It's what the Romans do and therefore, since they are the masters of field craft if not actually of fighting battles, we do the same. Which makes us very good at it. Whereas the tribes' idea of field craft extends little further than lighting fires and finding somewhere to open their bowels that's not already been used by someone else.'

He raised a hand to forestall the comment he could tell was on the tip of Beaky's tongue.

'And, before you ask, yes, perhaps you should transfer to one of the tribes . . .' He winked at Grimmaz, who had looked up from his digging. 'What do you think, Leading Man?'

'A perfect solution, Centurion! I get rid of a work-shy slug whose sense of humour seems mainly to consist of references to his frankly disappointing manhood, and whichever tribe you choose get a man with one skill that will serve them very well.'

Alcaeus nodded.

'I see what you mean. I'm willing to bet some of those big hairy monsters haven't had a fuck for weeks. Fancy that, Soldier Adalwin?'

The soldier stared at him for a moment before bending back to his task.

'No, Centurion. Thank you.'

'Good! The sooner we finish this the sooner we can get back to some proper soldiering, eh? So get your back into it and let's see those turfs fly, shall we?'

Fortress Bonna, Germania Inferior, October AD 69

'Well, this *is* a novel situation.'

Antonius stared grimly at the tribunal from which the army of Germania's legatus augusti was playing a nervous gaze upon the two legions paraded before them. His Twenty-Second Primigenia had marched out from their temporary barracks first, followed closely by the fortress's resident legion, the First Germanica. And it was evident to a career soldier like Antonius that the men of the First were not at all happy with the situation as they understood it.

'That's one way of putting it.' His deputy Julius had paced up the legion's line with the tense expression of a man who sensed that violence was a distinct possibility even if he wasn't quite sure why. 'The First look like they've had the bottom cut out of their purse and are getting ready to give whoever they can put the blame on an almighty kicking.'

As a description of the other legion's mood it was apposite. The men of the First Legion, their ranks thinned somewhat by the disaster that had befallen them when they had rashly sought to prevent the Batavi cohorts from passing Bonna on their way north, were clearly not in the mood to be charitable to the man they deemed to have been responsible for the failure of the Winter Camp legions to back them up. It hadn't helped Flaccus's credibility that he'd been forced to travel downriver from the Winter Camp in a naval vessel, due both to his inability to keep up the forced march pace that Dillius Vocula had insisted on setting for his men from the very first mile of their progress north and the legatus's refusal to countenance the indignity of their commander travelling by cart.

'The way I hear it they were ordered not to try to block the road north but came out to fight anyway. Apparently some idiot got it into his head that the Batavians would have their pay chests with them, and decided that there was an opportunity for everyone to get rich.' Antonius paused for a moment, playing an expert, appraising stare along the First's line. 'Bastards. Look at them. Improperly turned out, grubby, slovenly useless bastards to a man.

They've got all the discipline of a pay-day piss-up. That's not a legion, that's a gang of whore-mongers, thieves and candidates for the scourge. Whoever commands that lot should have his vine stick shoved right up his—'

'Men of the First and Twenty-second Legions!' Legatus Augusti Flaccus had stepped to the front of the tribunal, his voice ringing out clearly across the parade ground. 'I am informed that you are not content with your lot! While I understand that you men of the First Legion are still mourning the loss of your comrades from the battle with the Batavians, I have no alternative but to proceed with the execution of the orders our emperor has given me! I therefore—'

'He's *our* emperor, not yours!'

As was often the case when thousands of men paraded, it was impossible to say from where in the First's ranks the shout had originated, but none of the legion's officers appeared to be showing any sign of interest as to who the culprit might have been. Another voice took up where the first had left the subject.

'You don't even support Vitellius, do you, Fatty?'

Even as the echoes of the accusation died away, a third man shouted an accusation so damning that Antonius found himself staring at the men on the tribunal in amazement.

'You've received a message from the usurper, haven't you?'

Total silence fell, and Flaccus took a moment to stare directly at Herennius Gallus, the First Legion's bemused legatus, before turning his attention back to the men before him.

'As it happens, I have received a message from Flavius Vespasianus. It was delivered, as I'm sure you're already well aware, by a party of emissaries from the east, who, you will be gratified to hear, are already under arrest pending their despatch to Rome!'

'Read us the message!'

Silence fell again, and Antonius shook his head slowly at the temerity of the anonymous soldier's demand, muttering through his clenched teeth loudly enough to be heard by the men of the front rank standing behind him.

'If any of you ever dare to make that sort of demand, I'll see that man die slowly with my gladius sheathed in his guts.'

To his horror, Flaccus shrugged equably.

'Why not?'

The legatus augusti held out a hand to his secretary, who was standing at the tribunal with a tablet and stylus, busily scribbling notes into the wax, and the senior centurion's lips creased into a lopsided grin.

'He knew. He *knew* they were going to challenge him with it. But he's playing a dangerous game.'

Taking the scroll that was ostentatiously handed to him, the legatus augusti cleared his throat.

'"To Legatus Augusti Marcus Hordeonius Flaccus, commander of the armies of Germania Superior and Inferior, greetings from Titus Flavius Caesar Vespasianus Augustus!"' A dark muttering broke out across the First Legion's ranks, and Flaccus stopped speaking until some degree of silence had been restored. '"My long-standing belief that an emperor will arise who will rescue Rome from a difficult situation has been proven justified! The armies of Egypt, Judaea and Syria have unanimously acclaimed me as emperor, and to their ranks have since been added Moesia, Pannonia and Illyricum! All of the auspices have been favourable, and the blessings of the gods are clearly bestowed upon my claim! I am confident that my generals will shortly demonstrate to the misguided legions who are still declaring their support for Vitellius the depth of their error, and it is in the hope of avoiding needless bloodshed that I write to you now! I entreat you to reason with the men of the valiant legions you command, seven of the most renowned military formations in the empire, and beg them to see the reason behind my legitimate claim to represent the best opportunity to restore the empire to its full glory, and end this war."'

He stopped reading and looked out over the First Legion's disapproving sea of faces.

'There is more, but it's in much the same vein. Vespasianus has requested that I bring the support of my legions to his cause. And I . . .' Total silence fell, with none of the fidgeting and muttered comments that had greeted his reading of Vespasianus's letter. 'I have written back to him denying any possibility of such an accommodation on the part of legions that have sworn loyalty to the emperor, and telling him that his emissaries have been taken into custody and—'

'That's all very well, but are *you* loyal to the emperor?'

A chorus of shouts followed the initial outburst.

'And *which* emperor?'

'*Our* emperor?'

'Why did you leave us to face the Batavians alone?'

Flaccus drew himself up to speak again, but as he did so Antonius's eye was caught by Dillius Vocula's brooding presence alongside the older man. He was staring down at the First's ranks, and something in his face put the senior centurion in mind of a particularly fierce dog that had frequented the streets around his childhood home, a beast that, when challenged for primacy within the pack, had always preceded the inevitable fight and its inevitable victory with a prolonged staring match intended to cow the other animal into submission. Then, as he watched his legatus he realised with a shock that the stare was less intimidation than the simple fixed attention of a predator preparing to strike.

'I was ordered by the emperor – by *Vitellius* – to keep the Fourth and Twenty-second Legions in the Winter Camp, with strict instructions to safeguard the security of the empire's borders against invasion by the tribes across the river. As a loyal servant of the throne I—'

Stifled merriment erupted throughout the First's ranks, and Legatus Vocula's patience snapped. Stepping forward to the tribunal's edge, he fixed the First's senior centurion with a flinty gaze.

'Get a *fucking* grip of your men, First Spear, either that or I'll do it for you! You're supposed to be soldiers of the empire, not a squabbling set of halfwits! This is my one and only warning . . .' He paused to play his stare across the legion's ranks. 'One more word from any of you and the legatus augusti here will order the ringleaders of this pathetic mutiny to be led away in irons!'

Turning back to the astonished Flaccus he gestured for him to continue.

'As a loyal servant of the throne, Legatus Augusti . . . ?'

'Yes . . .' The senior officer regathered his thoughts. 'As a loyal servant of the throne I was bound to do as I was commanded, although I did send a fast messenger to Rome entreating the emperor to allow me to send a legion in support of both yourselves and the legions at the Old Camp. Permission that was duly granted to me five days ago in this order.' He raised a second scroll. 'An order that references my previous instructions not to send any men north, and—'

'Leave us hung out to dry!'

Vocula turned to Flaccus, his face a study in barely retrained anger.

'I expect you'll want to have the man who shouted that last comment imprisoned, Legatus Augusti? With your permission I'll lead your lictors to him?'

Flaccus blinked, as taken aback by his ire as with the suggestion.

'I . . . yes.'

The legatus was in motion before the half-hearted assent was complete.

'Lictors, you heard the command! Follow me!'

Catching Antonius's eye, he gestured for the first spear to follow him as he stepped down from the tribunal and made for the First Legion, a group of bemused lictors following in his wake bearing the ceremonial bundled rods and axes that were their badge of office. Hurrying to his legatus's side, the senior centurion fell into step with his superior, muttering quietly as they hurried down the ranks of the cohort Vocula had been taking such a close interest in.

'You do realise that this could be a very quick way to get us both killed, Legatus?'

The other man snorted derisively.

'These pathetic excuses for soldiers don't have it in them!'

He stopped in front of the century for which he'd been heading, pointing at its horrified centurion and barking a command at the men behind him.

'This man has chosen to defame the commander of our army with the false charge of loyalty to a man who is not our sworn emperor! Arrest him and punish any further attempt to speak ill of the legatus augusti with the appropriate severity.'

The leader of the lictors, a former legion first spear who had been selected to join the legatus augusti's staff well before Hordeonius Flaccus had been appointed to the position, not only understood exactly what was expected of him but clearly took great pleasure in receiving orders that allowed him some measure of his previous role's godlike power, clearly had no intention of disappointing the hard-eyed legatus who had decided to make common cause with his master. Stepping forward he put a massive hand on the culprit's arm, his sausage-like fingers closing in a grip that had been the fear and envy of soldiers and centurions for the two decades of his service.

'Come along with me, sonny, and keep your mouth shut if you don't want a good beating once we have you in the cells, eh?'

Coming to his senses, as he realised that his career was teetering on the brink of disaster, the centurion shouted desperately over his shoulder at the ranks of men behind him.

'This isn't right! He's been colluding with—'

Whatever it was that he had intended to blurt out was lost in a grunt of shock and pain as the chief lictor swung his bundle of rods at his prisoner's knee, staggering him with the abrupt searing pain as the joint gave under the blow's casually delivered but brutal power. As he was dragged away, any further protests were silenced by the pain in his leg and the threat of the chief lictor's cudgel, the other lictors moved to stand either side of Vocula and Antonius, playing hard stares on the ranks of legionaries while the legatus barked a challenge at the First's stunned ranks.

'Any other man who wishes to join him in the fortress cells has only to repeat that baseless slur and I will be happy to oblige him! There will be *no* further sedition in this legion! You men will follow the orders you are given as quickly and completely as if it were the emperor himself issuing them! We are going to march north and liberate the garrison of the Old Camp from the rebels who have encircled their fortress, and you men of the First Germanica are going to win battle honours that will make you a respected legion, able to hold your heads up in any company, rather than the men who rushed to confront the Batavians and paid a high price for their mistake!' He waited for a moment to see if any of them would try to dispute a version of events that clearly angered them, but the legion stood in glowering silence. 'Good! Fight well and the legatus augusti and I will petition our emperor on your behalf for a donative that reflects your bravery and achievements! I know you won't disappoint me!'

He turned away, and Antonius swept one last stare across the men in front of him before following, muttering a comment as the two men stalked away from the silent legion.

'I'd say you've subdued them for the time being, Legatus. Right now they fear you more than they hate you, which is enough to keep them under control for the time being. I just hope you can stay that angry, because if they see a hint of weakness from you they'll turn on us like the dogs they are.'

Batavodurum, October AD 69

'So what now?'

Kivilaz leaned back in his chair mulling over his prefect's question, unconsciously toying with the end of his dirty red plait, dyed before the attempt on the Old Camp's walls in a symbol of his determination to take the fortress. Hramn and Alcaeus stood before him, the latter with his attention on the wall behind his prince while Hramn had fixed a questioning stare on his uncle.

'The Old Camp still stands.' Kivilaz stood, pacing away to stare at a Roman map of the river's length, the Winter Camp and Mogontiacum at its south-eastern end, his gaze following the stream as it flowed past Bonna, Colonia Agrippinensis and Novaesium before reaching the Old Camp and continuing north and west to the Island. 'Our assault was brave, but undone by the smallest of details. If your men had managed to prevent the ram from burning we'd have broken in, and put every man in that fortress to the sword.' He pointed to the words "Germania Inferior", positioned by the cartographer with Rome's usual casual assumption of superiority so that the first word overspilled onto Batavi territory. 'Roman power in "Germania Inferior", as they still consider it, would now be broken. Instead of which we have provided them with the opportunity to relieve the garrison and re-establish their control over us, if they can move swiftly enough.'

Hramn shrugged at his uncle, apparently untroubled by the barely veiled criticism.

'If your carpenters had double-layered the cow skins perhaps the ram wouldn't have been left unprotected against their fire arrows. And besides, the day was inauspicious.'

'Inauspicious?'

'Yes. My priest here performed the sacrifice and was not happy with the result.'

Kivilaz turned to Alcaeus.

'What did you find?'

The warrior-priest shrugged.

'The liver was blemished, my Prince. Barely so, just detectable with my fingertips. But blemished nonetheless. I said nothing, of course.'

The prince nodded.

'Of course. To have postponed the attack would have been disastrous, given the rage that the tribes had worked themselves into. And your augury was a fair one. We failed by the smallest margin.'

Hramn shook his head.

'We failed because of the smallest oversight. The sacrifice was a warning we chose to ignore, and we paid the price.' He shrugged. 'But the milk's on the floor now. So, Kivilaz, what are your orders?'

The older man turned back to the map.

'The Fifth and Fifteenth Legions still occupy the Old Camp. Our attack probably only cost them a fraction of their strength, which means that they can almost certainly hold us off at arm's length for as long as their food lasts, and we know that the First

Germanica's legatus brought them supplies by river last week. Whereas the attack cost us at least a quarter of our tribal warriors and what, two hundred of your men?'

'One hundred and twenty-three dead, and another seventy who won't fight with the cohorts again this year. Perhaps thirty of them will recover from their wounds. The losses are bearable, but they're not used to losing, Kivilaz, and they were walked into the killing zone of a dozen bolt throwers and then asked to endure a hail of iron while watching friends being burned alive by those godless eastern archers.'

Kivilaz nodded.

'I understand. It was a sacrifice I was willing to make, given that I expected the ram to tear a hole in their defences for you to exploit. And I have already told the elders that I stand by that decision as having been the right choice at the time. But it failed, and as you say, we need to get over the disappointment and decide what we should do now. The tribes will need more time to mourn their dead, most of whom still lie beneath the walls of the Old Camp, may Magusanus curse the Romans for the bastards they are.'

Alcaeus had walked back down the road to the fortress's southern gate late in the evening of the day of the battle, alone and unarmed. The same two senior centurions he had met on the road a week before had come to stand on the wall over the gates, looking down at him dispassionately as he laid out the terms he had been sent to offer them. At length Aquillius had shaken his head dispassionately.

'No, Centurion. We don't accept the possibility of surrender, no matter how honourable and "assured" it might be. Even if we were minded to surrender I wouldn't be advising my legatus to put the lives of two legions in the hands of a ragtag army of barbarians whose arses we kicked so hard this afternoon that they'll be walking bow-legged for a month. But you can send parties of men to collect your dead once we've retrieved our own. You will be allowed fifty men, and no more, in groups of two, and no more, collecting your dead individually and taking them to be burned somewhere sufficiently far away that we don't get any of the smoke across these walls. If any of the smoke does come our way, we'll assume it's the prelude for an attack and start shooting anyone within bolt thrower range. And the men collecting the bodies are to be unarmed. Any man bearing anything more dangerous than a knife will be shot without any warning being given. Those are our terms.'

'You realise these terms mean that their task will be painfully slow? That the dead will be rotting by the time that we recover the last of them?'

'That's hardly my first concern, Centurion.'

Alcaeus had looked up with an expression of genuine sorrow.

'I pity you, First Spear. The gods will not take kindly to a man who denies his fellow warriors a timely and decent burial, with their comrades and families unable to mourn over them before their bodies begin to spoil and crows feast upon them.'

The man on the wall above him had snorted his derision.

'The gods? Spare me your pity. The gods have already shown me enough disfavour in this life to convince me that they're playing a cruel game with me. So I'll take whatever I have coming on the day someone manages to stop my wind, but in the meantime I'll fight this war the only way I know. To the death.'

Grimacing at the memory of the Romans' implacable refusal to allow a swifter removal of the dead, the wolf-priest stepped forward, bowing his head respectfully to Kivilaz before speaking.

'The tribes are not my concern, my Prince, but the cohorts are. And our men are mourning their dead in a different way to that I usually see, not as fallen heroes but as needlessly killed.'

Kivilaz raised an eyebrow.

'You're still as outspoken as ever then, Alcaeus?'

The centurion returned his gaze unblinkingly.

'I am.'

The older man smiled, nodding his head.

'Good. At times like these we should always keep in mind that those men are our greatest weapon, and that we need to consider their needs just as carefully as those of the tribe they have sworn to protect. So, brothers, what do you have in mind?'

Hramn and his deputy exchanged glances, and Kivilaz laughed out loud.

'Did you think I couldn't see what was in your mind when you asked to see me? Come on, spit out whatever idea it is that you've cooked up between you.'

Hramn walked over to the map.

'We expect that by now the Romans will have concentrated their force here . . .' He pointed to the fortress at Bonna. 'They'll move forward to Novaesium to collect the Sixteenth Gallica and then work out how best to use the three or four legions they have in a way that doesn't expose their raw recruits too badly. So I don't think they'll rush forward to offer us battle. For one thing half their strength must be auxiliaries, and every time they've offered us a fight their auxiliaries have either betrayed them or turned tail. And since their legatus augusti favours the challenger Vespasianus, rather than the emperor his men appointed, I'd expect him to hold off fighting a battle on behalf of Vitellius when his rival might be emperor before Saturnalia. And if our men have to sit around moping for as much as a week they'll start to lose their edge. What they need is someone to fight.'

'And you have someone in mind?'

Hramn nodded, pointing to the northernmost part of the province of Gallia Belgian to the Island's south.

'The Menapii and the Morini. A brief march away, and likely to offer us little resistance. I propose to raid both tribes, burn out their towns and put down any resistance from the local auxiliaries. Not only will it restore the spirits of our men, but the Gauls will be sent a very clear message that Rome cannot protect them. And we'll be close at hand in case the Romans do decide to advance north more quickly than expected.'

Kivilaz nodded thoughtfully, walking across to look at the map again.

'If we send the cohorts south to attack the tribes of northern Gaul, as you suggest, then perhaps our German allies on the eastern bank of the river might take a hand as well.' He pondered for a moment. 'The Ubii and the Treveri are both tribes that have embraced Roman rule without any reservations, and which are likely to provide them with a good deal of the army who will be sent north to relieve the Old Camp. They would make an excellent target for a diversionary attack, and not only slow up the Roman advance but give their people time to consider whether their unstinting support of Rome is really the best course of action as the empire's rule in these parts begins to unravel.'

He slapped a finger down on the Ubian city of Colonia Agrippinensis.

'Yes. There. We'll send a message to our brothers across the river and ask that they mount a raid on the city that the Ubii dedicated to Claudius's wife. They won't break in, of course, the Ubii are too wary of their neighbours to let their guard down, and with good reason given their long association with the Romans, but they'll create their own special kind of havoc in the farmland around the city, and that might be enough to slow down any attempts to relieve the Old Camp. Go and prepare your men to march south. Give them back their pride and send a message to the Gauls that there's a new power in this part of the world – and it isn't Rome!'

Novaesium, Germania Inferior, October AD 69

'At last it's starting to look a bit more like an army.' Legatus Vocula looked out over the paraded troops, swollen in numbers by the arrival of three more cohorts of Gallic auxiliaries since the legions had marched from Bonna. 'And a little less like a ragbag collection of recruits, malingerers and those men no centurion in their right mind would ever have selected for the service.'

Antonius nodded in silence, knowing how frustrated his superior was with the state of the legions based along the Rhenus. Vitellius's decision to send much of their strength south to fight for the throne had resulted in the removal of most of their competent soldiers for that mission, leaving the remaining legates with legions that were military formations in name only for the greater part.

'Too many new recruits, not enough good men to train them, and this overbearing expectation that just because they made Vitellius an emperor he's going to make them all rich in return.'

'You don't believe he'll deliver on his promise of a donative, Legatus?'

Vocula shrugged.

'I have no idea what he'll do, First Spear. But I do know that matters which look simple enough when seen from here on the frontier are a good deal more complicated when considered from the perspective of the big chair in Rome. This civil war will have emptied the treasury, and I doubt there was all that much gold in it to start with given the heroism that Nero brought to the art of profligacy. And to make it worse, the men we sent south will come back full of piss and vinegar at their part in defeating Otho, and possibly Vespasianus, and with whatever they've managed to loot or been granted as a donative for their part in Vitellius's victory. This isn't going to be a happy collection of legions for years to come, I suspect. Tell me . . .' he turned to Antonius and lowered his voice to ensure there was no chance of their being overheard. 'Do you think these men will fight if it comes to a battle with the Batavians?'

Antonius pursed his lips in unconscious equivocation.

'It's hard to say, Legatus. The First Legion didn't exactly cover themselves with glory against their cohorts. But it's not just about the legions, is it?'

Both men looked out over the Novaesium parade ground at the three understrength legions drawn up in front of the tribunal on which Hordeonius Flaccus would shortly be making his appearance. Herennius Gallus's First Germanica and Vocula's Twenty-second Primigenia had been joined both by the Sixteenth Gallica, the Novaesium garrison's legion, and the five auxiliary cohorts that had responded to Flaccus's messages requesting reinforcement for his campaign to relieve the Old Camp.

'No. As you imply, the auxiliary forces will be critical too.'

'And in every battle to date the auxiliaries have either betrayed us or turned and run at the first sign of a fight.'

Vocula nodded.

'On the other hand, those cowards and traitors were for the most part locally raised. They either sympathised with the Batavi or were terrified of them from long association. The men who Hordeonius Flaccus has recruited from Gaul and beyond will be a different proposition, I'd say. They certainly look the part, and there are probably twice as many cohorts yet to join us from further afield. We even have men marching from as far afield as Hispania.'

A flurry of movement on the tribunal caught their attention, the customary escort of lictors preceding Flaccus's entrance. With a painful gait that betrayed just how much pressure his obesity placed upon his ageing joints, the legatus augusti climbed onto the tribunal and walked forward to address the thousands of men gathered before him. That he was uncertain as to his reception was evident to Antonius in the way he stared out across the sea of faces, remembering the senior officer's response to being told that justice had to be seen to be done in the case of the man who had been arrested in Bonna, before the army had decamped to the north down the river.

'But surely we can simply leave the man in question to rot in a cell? Do we have to remind everyone of the matter by dragging him out for trial?'

Vocula had shaken his head, but before he had a chance to speak Herennius Gallus, the centurion in question's legatus, had interjected in a tone that implied considerable nervousness on the subject.

'I have to say that I find myself in total agreement with Hordeonius Flaccus. My men are restive enough without further inflaming their sense of grievance.'

His first spear had nodded solemnly, but Vocula was having none of it.

'Your men are restive, Legatus, because they're not getting enough discipline. They complain constantly, the centurions no less than their legionaries. They complain that they've not been paid because of the civil war that Vespasianus has drawn out, that their rations aren't plentiful enough, that the German tribes are raiding across the Rhenus because the gods have turned against us and sent a drought to lower the river's waters. They complain about anything and everything, rather than doing what we should expect of them, which is to shut their mouths and soldier.'

Vocula had put his knuckles on the table and leaned forward.

'They lack discipline, Herennius Gallus, because you're not imposing it on them. They weren't properly under control when the Batavi marched past your fortress, as a consequence of which they were taught a painful lesson on military preparedness, and they're not under control now. They're seeking to blame someone or something else for their stupidity in defying the legatus augusti's orders to allow the enemy cohorts to pass by unhindered, and now that it's been pointed out to them that he did so on the orders of their emperor, they're desperate for some other reason to be up in arms. Holding that centurion without trying him will imply to them that you've got something to hide, legatus augusti, and that will only get worse the longer you do so. Better to try him, execute him and then we can all concentrate on the job that we're supposed to be doing which, I will remind you, is to advance north, defeat the Batavi by whatever means are required, and then relieve the two legions they have bottled up in the Old Camp.'

Flaccus had nodded reluctantly.

'I see your argument, Dillius Vocula. My nervousness is simply the result of the men's restiveness.'

The legatus's implacable response as he had turned for the door had left his colleagues in no doubt as to his intentions.

'Better that we deal with it quickly then.'

Flaccus and Gallus had yielded to their colleague's uncompromising approach, and as a result all three legions had been ordered to parade and hear the judgement that was to be delivered on the insubordinate centurion. The legatus augusti looked across their ranks with evident uncertainty, but just as Antonius was sure that his own legatus would start forward to take control of the announcement, the army's commander addressed the legions, albeit in a

voice that the senior centurion suspected was not strong enough
to reach all the men on the parade ground.

'Men of the First, Sixteenth and Twenty-second Legions, and
of the various allied cohorts that have marched to join our army!
Today it is my sad but necessary duty to pronounce sentence
upon this man . . .' He gestured to the prisoner. 'A previously
loyal centurion who stands accused and convicted by his own
words and deeds, committed in Fortress Bonna in front of many
of you, of sedition of the most ignoble and damaging kind.
Specifically, he has accused the commander of the army of not
sharing the legions' eagerness to advance north, and fulfil our
emperor's instructions to defeat the Batavi and end their miserable
rebellion. This is an accusation that is both baseless and damaging
to the army's reputation and morale. I have therefore decided to
pronounce the sentence that military law requires for this crime,
which is—'

'He's colluding with Civilis!' Vocula and Antonius started at the
prisoner's sudden frantic interruption. 'He asked me to take
messages to the Batavi! He met with Civilis and—'

The chief lictor swung his bundle of rods at the prisoner's head
with all the expertise of his twenty years of military experience,
dropping the man to his knees with his senses reeling and blood
pouring down his neck from a scalp wound inflicted by the sharp
bladed axe bundled in with the rods, and Vocula strode towards
the tribunal with a look of pure fury that Antonius suspected
wasn't just directed at the hapless captive.

'The prisoner is sentenced to death! The sentence will be
executed now!'

Drawing his sword, he mounted the platform, gesturing for the
centurion to bend forward. The chief lictor took a handful of the
stunned officer's hair and pulled his head forward, the dazed
prisoner incapable of either resisting or complaining. Raising the
sword above his head for every man on parade to see, the irate
legatus swung it down in a flashing arc, his blade snapping through
his victim's spine and severing the veins in his neck in a spray of
blood that spattered the lictors' grey togas. Their leader knew

what was expected of him, raising the severed head to cast its glassy stare across the horrified men of the legions, as the centurion's decapitated corpse sagged slowly onto the tribunal's wooden surface and into the slowly spreading pool of blood still pumping from the opened veins in its neck.

'He has lived!' The customary words used to announce an execution and ward off any evil spirits were greeted with a shocked silence, as the men of three legions stared at the centurion's lifeless body in amazement. 'Let no other man repeat these falsehoods, because military justice will be equally swift and merciless in any other case that is brought before the officers of these legions! Parade is dismissed!'

An awestruck silence reigned for a moment, before the legions' first spears, Antonius among them, recovered their wits and roared orders for their centurions to take the shocked legionaries back to their barracks.

'Legatus . . .'

Vocula turned to face Flaccus, his sword blade dripping blood onto the polished leather of his boots.

'No! Not a word! Turn around, leave the tribunal and go back to your office, Legatus Augusti! When I'm happy that I've managed to avert a full-scale mutiny by murdering that man, *then* you and I can discuss *exactly* what it was that he was trying to tell his comrades!'

The Old Camp, Germania Inferior, October AD 69

'They've settled in for a siege, it seems.'

Munius Lupercus stared out from the Old Camp's southern wall at the charred shell of the ram where it lay collapsed on the surface of the road thirty paces from the heavily reinforced gates that had been its target. The defenders had watched in horror, even men who had lost friends to the Batavi attack shook their heads at the scene, as men of the enemy's cohorts had come forward under the watchful eyes of the fortress's bolt thrower crews and literally scraped what was left of the two men who had burned with the siege engine from its charred wooden frame. With the grisly task of recovering their dead complete, the highly trained soldiers had swiftly and efficiently excavated an earthwork that ran all the way around the fortress, four hundred paces distant from the walls and just outside bolt-thrower range. Initially limiting themselves to a turf wall and ditch facing outwards, the Batavi soldiers had swiftly elaborated their defences, and as the days had stretched out another ditch facing in towards the defenders had been added, along with sharpened wooden stakes designed to make the task of crossing the barrier in either direction a matter of the greatest possible difficulty.

'They want to make sure that we can't easily break out, or a relieving force break in, while they starve us out. And I'd like to think that's because they've decided we're too tough a nut to crack with their teeth.' Aquillius shook his head dubiously. 'But that's not their modus operandi, is it, Marius?'

His colleague nodded grimly, the wound that bisected his right eye from temple to cheekbone a raw red line of healing scar tissue.

'No. If they were still focused on taking the fortress they would have regrouped, changed their tactics and come at us again by now, given they've cleared away the corpses of their brother warriors, because they're as uncompromising on the field of battle as they are on the harpastum pitch. The fact that they've not come back for another attempt means that they've decided to do something else.'

Lupercus nodded slowly.

'Walk with me, gentlemen.' He strolled away towards the wall's junction with the western rampart, exchanging salutes with a bolt thrower crew's captain as he passed. 'We have enough food for another six weeks, eight at best, if we start restricting the ration even more than we already are.' Both men nodded their agreement. 'And Civilis probably knows this, his spies will have known the state of our supplies well enough even before he besieged the fortress. He's tried for a swift break-in and failed, but lost nothing much that he can't replace easily enough with reinforcement from across the river. So as you say, now he's decided to play a longer game, and starve us into submission. But I'm guessing that's not all he's doing.'

The two men looked at him expectantly.

'We see plenty of smoke from the barbarian camp, and their warriors too, coming to stare at us and plot their revenge. But how much smoke do you see from their cohorts? Not much, by comparison. They've dug the ditch to keep us in here, counting on it to dismay us sufficiently that we'll just sit here and wait to be rescued, rather than try to break out. Not that I'd be surrendering this fortress in any case. But they're not there anymore, for the most part, not if my hunch is correct. Just enough men remain to give a show of strength, that's all.'

He stared bleakly down at the ground in front of the western wall, the previously flawlessly neat layout of ditch and lily pits utterly obliterated in a churned and blood-blackened sea of mud. Even with the corpses of the dead removed the scene still stank of putrefaction and faeces, and the hardier-minded among the defenders had passed the long hours watching over the men set to retrieve the bodies, gambling as to which of each pair of tribesmen would be the first to vomit. One long haired-warrior had found the whole thing too much and, snatching up a sword from where it lay half buried in the mud, had charged through the wasteland of corpses, bellowing his defiance at the men on the wall above him. A pair of scorpions had discharged their deadly missiles at the same moment, their impact from left and right almost tearing him in two to loud cheers from the watching legionaries.

'No, the tribes are still here, mourning their losses and regaining their strength with more warriors from the other side of the river, but not the cohorts.' Aquillius looked out over the scene of devastation as he spoke, his voice cold and authoritative. 'They've gone elsewhere, perhaps to face down any attempt at rescue, perhaps to spread chaos and distract the Germans or the Gauls to our south from assisting the Romans.'

Marius looked out across the sea of churned mud.

'But they'll be back. And when they return we can expect another assault, better thought through than the last, I expect.'

Lupercus nodded slowly, looking back at the testudo's charred remains.

'They will. And since they seem to have some source of expertise with regard to siege craft, I find myself wondering what surprise they might have for us the next time they come at these walls.'

'How many of your men do you think you could count on to match the men of the cohorts in a straight fight, brother?'

Marius pondered Aquillius's question.

'Of my three cohorts? Three, perhaps four centuries in total, half of them veterans who are steady enough to face those animals without fouling themselves, and the other half that small portion of my more recent recruits who have the stones to go toe to toe with an enemy of that ferocity. Why?'

The big man thought for a moment.

'I have another six centuries at best. So between us we can muster a cohort and a half of legionaries who might stand their own against the Batavians.'

'For a short time, perhaps.'

Aquillius grinned.

'A short time is all I have in mind.'

Novaesium, Germania Inferior, October AD 69

'Have you taken leave of your senses, Legatus Augusti?'

Dillius Vocula stared at his superior incredulously while the older man busied himself pouring two cups of wine. He turned to answer the question, holding out one of the cups to the legatus. The legatus's expectation had been that Flaccus would be appropriately abashed by the exposure of his apparent collusion with the Batavi leader, but if anything the army commander was even more relaxed than usual, and his blithe statement that he intended relinquishing command of the army to Vocula had shocked the younger man to his core.

'Not entirely, Legatus, although it's kind of you to be concerned.'

The satirical note in his voice caused Vocula's frown to deepen into a scowl.

'I don't find this funny, Hordeonius Flaccus! A man accused of sedition has accused you of being in league with the commander of enemy forces that have already defeated us on the battlefield twice! By rights I should be ordering your lictors to imprison *you!*'

Flaccus shrugged.

'Drink your wine, Dillius Vocula, and allow me to explain some of the more arcane of the facts of life to you.' Vocula took the cup and drank the wine in a single gulp. 'That's better. There's little that can't be softened by the application of good wine. Now, to answer your first question, have I been talking to Civilis? Yes, I have.'

Vocula put the palm of his right hand to his face.

'In the name of all the gods, why? What can have inspired you to such an act of . . .'

'Treason? One man's treason, Legatus, is another man's principled resistance.'

'But to conspire with the enemy?'

'I think the word "conspire" is a little heavier than the description I'd have chosen. Mediated, perhaps. Negotiated. Indeed, my actions may well have resulted in a good deal fewer Roman casualties than would have been the case if Civilis had proceeded with his original plan, which, as he told me frankly only a few weeks ago, was to lure the Fifth and Fifteenth Legions onto a battlefield of his choosing and then slaughter them to a man. I pointed out to him, in my role as Vespasianus's unofficial messenger, that—'

'You're *what?*'

'Come now, Dillius Vocula, you can hardly be surprised. There isn't a man of senatorial rank in Rome who could deny the truth of the matter, which is that compared with Titus Flavius Vespasianus, our very own emperor, Aulus Vitellius is a midget of a man. He was poorly suited to the command of an army, but putting him on the throne was like asking a donkey to put shoes on. Vespasianus is exactly the man Rome needs to rebuild the institutions of the state and stabilise the ship – steady, confident, well connected. I have no doubt whatsoever that he'll make an excellent ruler once he's supplanted our own dear leader.'

Vocula stared at him in horrified amazement.

'You're actually *betraying* Vitellius?'

'Yes. And history will judge me as a principled man who did the right thing to help restrain an unsuitable emperor while preserving the lives of thousands of Roman soldiers. It was my idea that Civilis command his men to repel the Fifth and Fifteenth Legions blood-lessly, other than the inevitable loss of some auxiliaries.'

'And now he's laying siege to their fortress!'

Flaccus shrugged again.

'The Old Camp will hold, I'm confident of that. And when the time comes for us to advance to their relief, I'm also confident that he'll retreat before us.'

'You've taken leave of your senses! The last messenger out of the Old Camp was sent to tell us that he'd thrown a spear at the fortress, before they closed their ring around the legions trapped inside its walls! The man fought alongside us for twenty-five years, he knows what Rome does to men who challenge the empire directly! He's going to fight tooth and nail to keep us at arm's length while he starves those legions into surrender!'

Flaccus shook his head.

'I don't think so. When news of Vespasianus's triumph reaches us we'll have the army swear loyalty to him, which will put us and the Batavians on the same side. I firmly expect that Civilis will come seeking forgiveness for overstepping his mark somewhat, and that the new emperor will be able to afford a little magna-nimity in his case. Honour will be satisfied on all sides.'

Vocula refilled his cup, his face a study in intense thought.

'Perhaps. If we manage to keep our legions from mutinying in the meantime.'

'But you're not going to allow that to happen, are you, Legatus? Not now that I've appointed you as the commander of the army in my place.'

The younger man shook his head in renewed disbelief, no more able to comprehend his superior's delegation of his responsibilities than he had been when Flaccus had insouciantly informed him that he was relinquishing command moments before.

'You have to be joking. You seriously want me to lead the army tasked with the relief of the Old Camp?'

Flaccus nodded earnestly.

'Of course I do. Isn't it obvious? The First Legion hate me with a passion, and your Twenty-second aren't all that far behind them in that matter. The Sixteenth will be ambivalent at best, which means that two-thirds of the army will remain likely to mutiny. How well do you think that's going to work? If one legion's in near open revolt and the other stands in sullen silence before they've even left camp, what do you think will be going through their tiny brains once we're out in the field with the Batavi dogging our steps? No, my mind's made up, Legatus! I'm delegating command of the army to you as of today.'

Vocula held out his cup for a refill.

'This isn't going to go down well in Rome, you do realise that? You know my father was an equestrian, which makes me barely acceptable as a legion commander, never mind as an army commander.'

The older man smiled, shaking his head slightly.

'Colleague, the emperor sits in a room a thousand miles away and makes decisions based on information that's at least a week old at the very best. He makes his mind up based on the advice of a close circle of men who are largely inadequate to the task and in some cases variously disloyal behind his back, motivated by their own ends and in one or two cases insufficiently mentally stable. His orders then take at least a week to reach us. So we're being directed to fulfil the commands of a man two weeks away whose advisors are frankly not competent, and whose agenda is mainly oriented to the retention of his throne, with the defence of Germania as a second priority and the restoration of our dominion over the Batavians no better than a distant third. Do you really think I'm at all troubled by his opinion of what I'm doing here, given that his interference has taken us to the brink of disaster?'

Vocula nodded slowly.

'Put like that . . .'

'Exactly.' Flaccus poured himself another cup of wine. 'Our only concern must be to ensure that this army remains intact, ready to resume total control of Germania once Vespasianus has triumphed and Civilis has come to his senses and made peace. Not with some minor point of senatorial "Whose turn is it today?" etiquette. You are the right man to take command of the army simply because you're the only man with the ability to grab them by the scruff of their necks and put them back in their place. Herennius Gallus is a broken reed since his legion ignored him and pranced out to attack the Batavian cohorts, both because his command ignored him and because they now blame him for not stopping them rushing into the worst fight of their lives, and I doubt that Numisius Rufus is in any happier a position at Novaesium, knowing the man as well as I do. No, Legatus, it's either you or it's effectively no one. So it's you. Isn't it?'

Gallia Belgica, October AD 69

'And you believe that this was worthy of us? A suitable offering to Hercules? At least at the Old Camp we earned the pride of having endured under the iron lash of their artillery.'

Hramn shook his head in dismissal of Alcaeus's complaint, looking about him in satisfaction at the scene of devastation that his men had visited upon the Morini town his men had fallen on an hour before.

'What's your problem, Priest? Strict orders have been given for the women and children to be spared, and for no man to be killed unless he comes at us with a weapon. The buildings we burn can be replaced in the space of a summer, and they've had enough time to run away with their valuables and their dignity intact. This is a lesson in knowing their place, not a conquest.'

The buildings clustered inside the oppidum, the fortified core of the settlement huddled behind an earth bank wall, were the only dwellings not yet burning. Forewarned by the wrath that had been unleashed on their neighbours the Menapii the previous week, their militia scattered and several settlements put to the torch, the Morini had chosen to fall back in the face of the cohorts' advance rather than to fight, leaving their settlement open to the whim of the invaders.

'My complaint, Hramn, is that this is not fit work for men of our quality. You might as well take a racehorse and put it in front of a plough. No good will come of this.'

Alcaeus fell quiet as a pair of soldiers marched towards the two men with one of the tribal elders between them, the white-haired ancient hurrying where their tread was deliberate. Seeing Hramn he fell to his knees in supplication, wringing his hands as the prefect looked down at him.

'Get up.' Seeing no sign that his command had been under-stood, he reached out and lifted the old man to his feet. 'We come to punish your people, not to subjugate you. There is no need for this disagreement between neighbours to be anything more than a temporary upset in our long relationship.'

'But *why?*'

The Batavi smiled cruelly down at the stooped figure before him, clearly selected for his advanced age and consequential expandability.

'Why? I'll tell you what I told the Menapii elders. The reason for this punishment is the fact that despite the Batavi's stand against an overbearing Rome, a Rome that chooses to abuse children and illegally and forcibly recruit our men to their army, neither the Menapii nor the Morini have raised a finger to provide any assistance.'

'But . . .' The old man's face creased in disbelief. 'But we are *Gauls*. We do not have any treaties of friendship and fealty with the Batavi, unlike your allies the Cananefates. Surely your people did not expect us to rise in support of your cause when we are part of another province? And after all, it was your cohorts who put down the revolt of our neighbours the Lingones last year.'

Hramn smiled and nodded.

'All true. But, and here's the thing, everything has changed. *Everything.* We know it. The Romans know it, given that we have two of their legions penned up in the Old Camp like lambs ready for the priest's knife. The tribes across the river know it, which is why they're sending tens of thousands of their men to fight alongside us, their historical allies. The only people who don't seem to realise it are you Gauls. But you'll see the sense of it soon enough, when the Romans' failure to protect you from the anger of your neighbours at your failure to rise up with us sinks in. When the Ubii and the Treveri have been punished in just the same way, their cities burned to the ground, their people spared from slavery only by the command of Prince Kivilaz, perhaps Gaul will realise that if Rome is still the answer then you're prob-ably asking a question that no longer matters. Take *that* back to your people.'

Hramn looked down at the elder pityingly for a moment before speaking again.

'Rome is no longer relevant to your people. What you should be considering now is what will replace it.'

9

'Not much to look at, is it, First Spear?'

Antonius made a show of staring out across the new camp's grassy expanse.

'No, Legatus, it isn't. Of all the legion fortresses I've served in, this one has to be at the bottom of the list when it comes to facilities.'

Vocula smiled at his sardonic tone. With Flaccus's abdication of his responsibilities, the two men's working relationship had become even closer than before, perhaps because the legatus, not being from an old senatorial family, found it easier to mix with the army's professional officers than his colleagues. Unwilling to trust his tribunes on the subject of his uncertainties with regard to the mission to relieve the Old Camp, he had tentatively approached his senior centurion with his thoughts on the campaign's planning, and had been delighted to find Antonius both helpful and frank in his responses. The centurion, for his part, while initially flattered to be asked to contribute by such an august personage, had swiftly discerned that his legatus had a genuine talent for military command that came as some relief after the concerns he had harboured as to Flaccus's capabilities.

'Walk with me, Antonius. I ought to show an interest in the work that the construction gangs are doing, and I thought we might discuss our progress so far.'

The first spear nodded respectfully, falling in alongside his superior as he strode out across the camp's sea of tents, along roadways laid out in the time-honoured cruciform pattern. Around the camp's perimeter, work parties were labouring hard to build a four-foot-high turf rampart to protect the three legions from an unexpected attack. Vocula gestured to the rapidly strengthening defences with an approving expression.

'I know that even the Batavians ought to think carefully before taking on this many legionaries, but their reputation for scorning odds that would deter rational men does somewhat go before them. So every section of the wall that goes up raises my spirits just a little.'

Antonius nodded.

'The work's doing a power of good for the men of all the legions too. They're too busy to complain about the delay in advancing to lift the siege during the day, and by the time they've built another section of the wall they're too busy to do anything but eat and sleep.'

'With that and all the training you're putting them through, they're also swiftly becoming as fit as racehorses. It just goes to show that soldiers can be taken on campaign outside of the summer months.'

Antonius looked at him for a moment with pursed lips.

'Legatus, forgive me for speaking freely . . .'

Vocula smiled.

'Perhaps a little more freely than might be appropriate between men in our respective positions?'

The centurion nodded.

'Yes.'

'Very well, First Spear. I owe you more than a moment of forthrightness. What's on your mind, as if I can't guess?'

Antonius looked at him for a moment before replying.

'This camp, Legatus? The punitive raids on the Cugerni? All the training you're having us carry out?' Vocula nodded but remained silent. 'Surely we have enough strength that the Batavians will be forced to retreat when we advance to liberate the Old Camp, which means that we'll be able to use the fortress as a forward base rather than build one afresh? Trying to pin the Cugerni down to teach them a lesson for siding with the rebels is like trying to nail piss to a wall, so that's a waste of time as well, and another three months of training wouldn't make these men any more proficient with their weapons. Only battle can do that, and yet battle seems to be the last thing on our minds. And all this while we're not much more than a day's march from the Old Camp. Are we deliberately leaving the Fifth and the Fifteenth Legions to dangle in the breeze?'

'Is that what the men are saying?'

The senior centurion shook his head.

'Not yet. But they will. Given enough time they'll jump to the inevitable conclusion that Legatus Flaccus and yourself are waiting to see which way the war in Italy goes.'

Vocula nodded grimly.

'And they'd be right.'

Antonius stared at him in surprise for a moment, his mouth opening wordlessly as he struggled for an appropriate response.

'But—'

'But we're sworn to the service of Vitellius? True. But there are two legions waiting for us to come to their rescue only thirty miles from here? Again, true. If our three legions attack the enemy together at the same time that the Fifth and Fifteenth counter-attack from the Old Camp, then even the Batavians and their allies will probably be forced to withdraw. So why haven't we advanced, now that all three legions are in place and effectively ready to go?' Vocula sighed. 'Because, as you have already so astutely deduced, my colleagues are collectively dithering as to what to do. If we attack now, and defeat a rebel tribe that has sworn allegiance to Vespasianus, then we make ourselves vulnerable to the charge of loyalty to Vitellius if Vespasianus wins. His army has invaded Italy, we hear, and is advancing to do battle with Vitellius's legions, so it could all be settled within weeks, which is only making Flaccus and my other two colleagues evermore determined to wait and discover who turns out to be the victor. We're perched on top of a very uncomfortable fence, First Spear, because if Vitellius triumphs he'll want to know what we've been doing all these weeks. And

I might be the army commander, but even I can't force the officers of three legions to go against their instincts.' He stopped walking and turned to face his first spear. 'Gods below, Antonius, even I'm not convinced that we've got anything to gain from pushing through to relieve the garrison. Herennius Gallus shipped them enough food and bolt-thrower ammunition to see them through to the end of November at the very least, and our cavalry patrols are reporting that the siege of the fortress continues, with an earthwork raised around the Old Camp to keep us out and the garrison inside, which wouldn't be the case if they'd been defeated. So . . .' He sighed again, shaking his head in disbelief at his own words. 'Here we are and here we stay, with just enough activity to make the men feel as if they're doing something positive.'

'Hence the fortress building?'

'And the raids on the Cugerni, and the training. Yes. We'll—'

A horn sounded, and both men turned to look for whatever it was that had caught the attention of the sentries posted to watch the road to the north and west down which a Batavi attack could be expected to come. Antonius made for the guard century whose trumpeter had raised the alarm at a run, the legatus following at a steadier pace in keeping with the senatorial dignity expected of him.

'What is it?'

The centurion pointed at the western horizon.

'A horseman, First Spear.'

'One horseman?'

The officer nodded.

'Yes sir. Your orders—'

'Said to raise the alarm if so much as a badger put its nose above ground. Don't worry, Centurion, I'm not about to censure you for doing as you were told, I'm just curious as to why a single man would be riding so close to the camp, and how he managed to get through the cavalry patrols. He doesn't even seem to be armoured, so I think you can stand your men down.'

They watched as the lone horseman approached at a leisurely

trot, Vocula strolling up to join them and looking at the oncoming rider with a sardonic smile.

'Well now, who's this with the balls to ride up to a legion encampment with no more concern than a man out for a pleasant ride in the country? You'd better challenge him, First Spear, or he might just ride through without stopping!'

Antonius nodded, but as he stepped forward to issue an order for the rider to dismount, he reined the beast in and dismounted with the agility and precision of a trained cavalryman, drawing his sword and pushing the blade into the grass just out of reach, then standing by the beast's head and waiting for the soldiers to come to him.

'Someone knows what he's doing, it seems. Coming, First Spear? This promises to be interesting.'

Waving the guard centurion away, Antonius followed his legatus to where the newcomer stood.

'Greetings . . .'

'And greetings to you too, Legatus.' The horseman inclined his head in a gesture of respect. 'I was just admiring the quality of your men's wall-building.'

Vocula inclined his head, his eyes narrowing as he stared at the newcomer.

'I know you . . .' He stiffened as the realisation hit him. 'You're a Batavian officer!'

Antonius swept his sword out, but the rider merely shook his head with a sad smile and raised both hands.

'I *was*. And yet here I am, stripped of my uniform and position.'

Vocula shook his head in amazement.

'You're *that* prefect . . .' He snapped his fingers together as the name came to him. 'Claudius Labeo! You're the prefect of the Batavi Horse!'

The newcomer nodded.

'Yes. I was. Another man commands my cohort now, and I am no more than an exile reduced to turning to my tribe's enemies for justice.'

Vocula stared at him in silence for a moment before turning to Antonius.

'I think this discussion would be better conducted in the head-quarters, don't you, First Spear?'

Labeo allowed his hands to be tied behind his back and his eyes blindfolded before the Romans led him into the camp, the soldiers labouring at the construction of the rampart staring curiously at the captive before turning back to their work under the verbal lash of their officers. In the headquarters building, a wooden structure that had been the first building to be constructed once Gelduba had been designated as the campaign's forward base, the Batavi noble was freed from his bonds under the wary gaze and drawn sword of a distinctly unnerved first spear. Hordeonius Flaccus had been summoned at Vocula's command, and stood to one side studying the traitor with open curiosity while his erstwhile subordinate turned to Antonius with a shake of his head.

'I don't think you're going to need the blade, First Spear Antonius. If I thought Claudius Labeo here represented a threat, I'd have put him in the ground the moment I realised who he was.'

Acknowledging the truth of his legatus's words the centurion sheathed his weapon, crossing his arms to emphasise the threat of his vine stick while never taking his gaze off the Batavi. Labeo rubbed at the marks on his wrists with a rueful smile, nodding his gratitude to Vocula.

'Your man could probably kill me with a single strike of that vitis, Legatus. I'd say you're safe.'

Vocula smiled wryly.

'I'm sure I am. Whereas you . . .'

'Have been sentenced to death in my absence, I'd imagine? The trusted barbarian auxiliary officer who turns on Rome is something you people understand all too well, isn't it? I'm the example that has to be made, not just for the purpose of imperial revenge but to demonstrate what happens to those men who choose to bite the hand that has fed them. The sentence will be crucifixion, I'd imagine, after the application of enough lashes with the scourge to break me, but not quite enough to kill me and thereby deprive the empire of the satisfaction to be had from my last tortured hours, writhing helplessly on a cross while your legions watch.'

He looked around as if to confirm his assertion, and Flaccus nodded equably.

'You know your history, like any well-educated tribal noble would. If Rome had ever managed to lay hands on Arminius after the disaster of the Teutoberg Forest, then you can be assured that his exit from this life would have been a good deal more protracted than his murder by his own people when the war turned against them. And frankly, Labeo, given your shameless imposture as an ally of the empire when all the time you were colluding with Civilis to turn your lances against us at the very worst possible moment, I'd say you've earned every lash, every nail and every last desperate gasping breath as you die. Wouldn't you? My only curiosity is why you were rash enough to ride in here knowing what your ultimate fate must surely be?'

The Batavi looked around at their hard faces, a small smile creasing his own.

'A fair question, Legatus Augusti. And the truth is, I'm not entirely sure myself. It would have been easy enough for me to slip away and change my name. After all, by the time Rome's done with the Batavi there'll be no one left alive to recognise some anonymous farmer hidden away deep in the channels of the land to the west of the Island. I considered it, of course I did . . .'

'But it wasn't to your taste?'

Labeo nodded.

'Exactly. A lifetime of hiding away from the world, when the alternative was to come and take my punishment? I'd like to think I'm better than that. But I might have one small chance of evading the scourge and the centurion's nails.'

'And what's that, traitor?' Vocula stepped forward and put his face close to Labeo's, staring at him intently. 'What *possible* reason could we have for pardoning you for an act of the grossest treachery possible?'

Batavodurum, October AD 69

'Ten days ago we took our rage against their fortress, at your command, Prince Kivilaz, and we *failed!* We men of the German tribes lost thousands of men in that attack. I myself lost a son and a brother. And now you ask us to attack those walls again?'

King Brinno of the Cananefates turned away from the half circle of chairs in which the Batavi elders sat in council, looking at the gathered leaders of the tribal contingents from across the Rhenus, a dozen hard-faced men who had appointed him to speak for them in recognition of the close relationship between his tribe and the Batavi, who had been allies of the Cananefates for as long as the men who tended the spoken histories of their two tribes could vouch. His voice had remained calm since he had stepped forward from their ranks and begun speaking, but there was clearly a deep well of anger in him, Alcaeus discerned, seeing the way his eyes glittered as he looked at each of the Batavi elders in turn. The cohorts had returned from their punitive mission into Gaul the previous evening, and Hramn had been summoned to the gathering of elders that had been called to decide on the tribes' strategy now that their most potent force had returned.

'Their arrow machines killed my son, pierced through with such force that his body was almost torn into two pieces. Their foot spikes crippled my brother, and then he was trampled underfoot into one of their lily pits until the wooden stakes were driven deep into him and took his life. Their machines, and their toys, and their traps, and their falling rocks, and their boiling water killed so many of my people, and those of the tribes from across the river, that it took days for us to burn their bodies, and that was after the Romans had committed one last indignity and refused us permission to remove their corpses with enough haste to prevent them from spoiling and becoming a feast for carrion birds.'

The wolf-priest cast a swift glance at his prince, noting that Kivilaz remained seated in the chair that was traditionally reserved for the tribe's war leader, his entire demeanour relaxed, that of a king listening to the representations of a neighbouring people rather than a general being subjected to an impassioned protest by an ally.

'I have lost men of my blood, and in ways which I would not have wished upon a dog.' He paused, and it seemed that every man in the room held his breath while he looked around at them, turning in a slow circle. *'And I demand my revenge!'* Brinno's enraged bellow hung in the air for a moment, his raised fist white-knuckled from the force of clenching it. 'We must attack again! Now! Now, while the anger still burns in my people's hearts, and those of the other tribes who have joined us in this fight to throw off Rome! And *they* must fight alongside us!'

With a start Alcaeus realised that the tribesman had raised his hand to point at the place where he and Hramn sat.

'These are your best men, so alike to the Romans that they wear the same clothing and carry the same weapons. These are the men who have fought alongside the Romans since the days of your grandfathers' grandfathers, you boast, as good as the Romans, *better* than the Romans. We must attack again, soon, and these warriors *must* join our attack against the walls of this fortress you so badly want to destroy. Let us all see the magnificence of the Batavi's favourite sons in battle!'

Kivilaz nodded equably and stood, straightening his tunic as he stepped forward to within a pace of the German.

'You speak the truth, Brinno, and I respect you all the more for it. Yes, our battle to take their fortress and destroy it, to send a message to Rome that we are independent of their rule now and forever, failed.' He looked down at his feet with the last word, allowing his voice to trail off in a dispirited manner. 'I walked the battlefield that same night, with my cousin Hramn here, and his wolf-priest Alcaeus who sits alongside him, and we mourned the loss of both our people and yours.'

In reality, Alcaeus mused, Kivilaz had stood at the edge of the sea of fallen tribesmen for a moment before turning away without a word, his thoughts unguessable behind a mask of what could either have been stoic acceptance or simple indifference, but he had allowed no trace of either to show upon his face.

'Such loss of life is enough to sadden the hardest hearted of men, and yet I knew at that moment that we would have to make another attempt at some point very soon. As I stared across that blighted field of dead heroes I knew that we will have to destroy the fortress, to gain a victory over the Romans that will make them shy away from the very idea of reconquering our lands, or sending their legions across the river to punish the tribes who have stood beside us. We must burn the Old Camp to the ground, as much to show Rome that we are not to be denied our freedom as to deny them the use of its walls in any such potential campaign of retribution. For to fail to do so will give them both the encouragement and the ability to commit such indignities again and again. And as to using the Batavi cohorts to storm those walls, cohorts which I will remind you contain not just our own people, Batavi, Cananefates, Marsaci and Frisiavones, but a fair few men from across the river as well, I can see your argument. Who better to storm an enemy fortress than men who understand the enemy's weapons and methods?'

Hramn leaned back in his seat, speaking quietly out of the corner of his mouth.

'Have no fear, Priest, we won't be joining them in their enraged charge at the walls, Kiv has another plan for us. Smile and nod wisely like the seer of truth you so clearly are.'

Kivilaz waited for a moment before resuming his reply, looking theatrically up at the hall's roof timbers.

'But then, my brothers, as I stood with the spirits of a host of warriors exhorting me to take revenge for their death at the hands of Rome, I realised that we must achieve more than simply burning out one fortress. For even when we have achieved that victory, and left them with nothing more of the Old Camp than scorched earth and a blackened, crumbling rampart fit for nothing better than penning sheep, they will still have more legions ready to attack us. And yes, surely no force of men would stand a better chance of defeating those walls than warriors who are in effect our own Romans?' Kivilaz smiled slightly as he turned to point at Hramn and Alcaeus, nodding his head knowingly. 'See, these men yearn for the joy of taking their iron to the enemy who until recently were our allies, and who have of late so deeply spurned that friendship in favour of small-minded revenge for imagined slights. But I have a plan, Brinno, a plan that came to me on the field of our fallen warriors, a plan that will make better use of our cohorts' skills than simply throwing them at the walls of the Old Camp.'

He walked across to the map that had been painstakingly painted onto one wall of the council chamber, pointing to the Old Camp's square outline.

'We have two whole legions bottled up in that trap of their own making. Two eagles caged, their talons still sharp, but steadily chewing through what remains of their rations, every day bringing them closer to the hour when they are forced to open their gates and march out and surrender for the simple lack of food. The Old Camp will fall. The only question is when?' His hand moved, following the river south and east to a point twenty-five miles distant from the embattled fortress. 'And here is their new fortress, still being constructed, our scouts tell us, and home to three more legions, one relatively steadfast, another of little quality, while the third is weakened and riven by the beating that these men and their warriors . . .' he pointed to Hramn and Alcaeus again, 'handed out to them on their way north to join us. They fight with each other, they distrust their leaders and they fear us in equal parts, and most importantly they sit tremulously behind their walls rather than advancing in the aggressive manner required to win a war, because their leaders fear being seen to be loyal to either of the men who is contesting the imperial throne. They invent reasons not to advance, but instead sit in their camp waiting for a winner to emerge, which makes them ripe for the taking. They *beg* to be defeated, brothers. And so what, I found myself wondering, if rather than simply storming the Old Camp once more, we struck an even deadlier blow against Rome? A hammer blow, strong enough to break the empire's grip not just upon the

Batavi but enough to destroy their control of Germania and Gaul too. Until now we have been fighting to destroy the little that is left of Rome's grip on our own lands, but what if we were free to take our spears against the collaborator tribes of Germania as well? What if the Gauls were freed to establish their own kingdoms, each hostile to Rome? In little more than a month we might well undo Caesar's conquest of Gaul and present the emperor, whichever one of them wins the fight for the throne, with a military reality that no number of legions could threaten. We would be freed from their yoke for ever.'

Brinno stared at the map for a moment.

'You propose to assault the legions that have been sent to free those we have trapped in the Old Camp?'

Kivilaz nodded slowly.

'I plan to place a wager on both sides of the coin while it spins in the air. On the one hand there is the chance that we might break into the Old Camp if we attack again, and remove its enticement for Rome to strike at us. On the other is an opportunity whose beauty you see as clearly as I do, the chance to smash the army sent to relieve Rome's trapped legions, spreading dismay among the men of the Old Camp's legions and resulting in their surrender from despair and hunger, for they will know that there can be no rescue for them before their rations run out and they starve. And so my decision is this . . .' A complete hush fell over the room. 'We will indeed attack again, and see if we can force an entry to the fortress that will spell their doom. The tribes will attack in the way that best suits them, and the Batavi cohorts will employ a new weapon that I have had built in the forest, using the knowledge of Romans who have seen the justice of our cause. Not a ram this time, but something quicker and less vulnerable. If that attack succeeds then we will have achieved what we wanted, but if not then their legions to the south will still be sitting waiting for us, vulnerable to attack. Either way we will destroy their hold on the lower reaches of the river, and whoever comes to the throne, Vitellius or Vespasianus, will have no choice but to recognise the kingdoms of the German and Gaulish tribes, and the loss of Rome's grasp on us. And we, my brothers, will have won our freedom. *For ever.*'

Gelduba, October AD 69

'What the *fuck* happened here?'

Vocula was beyond angry, having achieved a state of rage so incandescent that Antonius was both in awe and more than a little worried that his superior might draw his sword at any moment and lay about him. Having returned from repelling a raid from across the river on the Ubii tribe's capital, Colonia Agrippinensis, only an hour before, the legatus had been first amazed and then infuriated by the situation to which he had returned.

'I leave you on your own for less than a week to go and chase off the Germans attacking the Ubians, and what do I find on my return?' He stared at Herennius Gallus with undisguised contempt, shaking his head at his unkempt appearance. 'Look at the fucking *state* of you!'

His colleague was sporting a magnificent pair of black eyes, his nose had been broken and his lips were split and bloody, the obvious results of a thorough beating, while his wrists still bore the marks of the iron manacles that had been removed only moments before, and he was pale-faced from the terror that had been visited upon him before Vocula's return. Mastering his anger, the legatus pulled off his helmet, placing it on a table close to hand.

'I return to find you manacled and under armed guard, having clearly had the shit beaten out of you. So tell me, illustrious colleague, what it is that occurred here that was so terrible your own men felt they were entitled to abuse and imprison you?'

Gallus winced at the pain of his blood-crusted lips cracking, speaking slowly and barely audibly.

'A grain ship . . .' He gathered his wits and started again. 'The supply vessel carrying the camp's grain ration got stuck in the shallows a mile or so upstream. The river's so low that even skilled pilots can't avoid going aground these days. The Germans came out onto the mud and started dragging the vessel over to their own side of the river with ropes, so I sent a cohort to see them off.'

Vocula nodded grimly.

'Let me guess. Your men engaged the barbarians only to find themselves outnumbered?'

'Yes. So I sent in more men.'

'Of course you did. One cohort at a time, as quickly as they could be armed and marched out. And as each cohort arrived they found that the Germans had raised the stakes on them with yet more tribesmen. Did it occur to you at any point that they might have seen the grain ship getting into difficulty and hurried men to the bank, ready to engage once we tried to stop them? You lost the ship, I presume? And suffered how many casualties?'

'Two hundred or so.'

'Two *hundred*! You lost almost half a cohort's strength fighting an unplanned battle against an unknown strength of enemy warriors with potentially unlimited reinforcements and on ground they understand far better than we do?' Vocula rubbed his face tiredly. 'Presumably once the First Legion realised that they were only going to lose the fight they thought better of it and decided not to contest the ship? Which explains the general mood in the camp, but not your injuries or your imprisonment.'

'The legion revolted.'

Vocula laughed out loud.

'I'd guessed that much, you prize idiot! But what made them revolt, other than your display of military incompetence?'

Gallus looked up at him in silent protest, but found his colleague's face set hard against him.

'They mobbed back into camp carrying the bodies of the dead. And they called me a traitor! *Me!*'

Vocula nodded slowly.

'They ran true to form and retreated in the face of the enemy, which must have stung. And to be fair they were badly used. But to accuse their legatus of treachery . . .' He turned to Antonius. 'We're going to have to execute some men for this, First Spear, so start thinking about who you want to put together as a bodyguard. I want a century of your best and nastiest men at my back when we exact the appropriate punishment for this fiasco. And we need some names. See what you can do.'

Antonius nodded and stepped out of the room, leaving Vocula to ponder the state of his colleague's battered face. Outside the headquarters building he found the two legionaries who had been apprehended guarding the captive officer waiting under the spears of a tent party from his own first century, whose chosen man had appointed them as his unofficial bodyguard once the state of affairs in the camp had become clear.

'Call out our first cohort! I want every man armed and armoured and in this street!'

Turning to the prisoners, he took stock of their sullen expressions and the way they were refusing to make eye contact.

'You nasty little shits think you'll walk out from under this falling tree, don't you? You think your fellow soldiers will come to rescue you, once they realise we have you? And you might be right. But I'll have five hundred men in this street very shortly, and five hundred of my best men will go through you shower of useless cunts like shit through a goose.' Both men shrank from his sudden and apparently uncontrollable rage. 'So . . .' He drew his ornately decorated dagger, putting a fingertip to the point. 'Either one of you can tell me who I need to be looking for in addition to you two, or we can see just how good I am with this little beauty.'

Both men looked at him in silence, neither willing to risk the accusations and intimidation that would surely follow were they to inform on their comrades. Antonius shrugged.

'I've been on the road for most of a week, I'm tired, I'm hungry and my feet hurt. But instead of a bowl of hot water and a cup of wine, I find myself faced with the depressing prospect of having to screw what I want to know out of a pair of idiots who probably don't know anything worth telling.' He sighed, examining the dagger's wickedly sharp blade. 'So let's get this over with quickly.' The two legionaries exchanged uncertain glances. 'Do you know what it takes to get a centurion selected to be a legion first spear? What marks him out from the other fifty-nine men who perform perfectly well commanding their centuries and cohorts?'

Both men looked at him in puzzlement, as much at his conversational tone as the way he had turned the discussion away from the information they were withholding.

'No? It's simple . . .' He pivoted at the waist, swinging the dagger low and then thrusting it up into the closer legionary's jaw until only the handle was visible, snapping out his other hand to hold the twitching corpse erect as blood ran down his arm from the horrific wound, smiling at his comrade. 'A centurion only gets promoted to first spear if the man whose job he'll be taking believes him to be sufficiently ruthless. As your tent mate here just discovered the hard way.' He released his grip on the dead man and pulled the weapon free of the gory wound, allowing the lifeless body to crumple to the ground. 'But not as hard as you, because one of you was always going to die quickly as a demonstration that you mean no more to me than the shit clinging to my hobnails. He went quickly, so you're going to have to die slowly, suffering as much pain as I can inflict on you. Unless you'd like to start naming names?'

When Vocula stepped out into the street moments later his face was set in uncompromising lines.

'There's going to be blood, First Spear, they beat . . .' He looked down at the legionary's body without a change of expression. 'I see you've started without me. The First Legion's men beat the sense out of Herennius Gallus, not that there was much there to start with, and in return he actually told them that Legatus Augusti Flaccus is secretly in contact with Vespasianus, the fool. It seems they had him at knifepoint, although they clearly didn't have quite your degree of resolve in the matter.' He looked at the hundreds of legionaries who were paraded in cohort strength down the Via Principalis's length. 'We're going to deal with this matter in strength, it seems?'

Antonius dipped his head in acknowledgement of the implied compliment.

'I called out our entire first cohort, Legatus. It felt proportionate to the matter we have to deal with.'

'Thank you, First Spear.' Vocula pointed at the sprawled corpse of one of the men who they had found guarding Gallus. 'I assume from the fact that your arm is liberally painted in that man's blood that you decided to make an example of him?'

'It's an old field interrogation method, Legatus, one that I witnessed in Britannia after the revolt of the Iceni. And it seems to have lost none of its effectiveness.'

'I see. You made a swift example of the man to encourage his fellows, I presume. And?'

The first spear handed him a tablet whose wax surfaces were covered with the names of twenty or so men.

'These were the ringleaders, Legatus.'

Vocula looked at his senior centurion with new respect.

'Well done. Very well done. And if you were me, First Spear, what would you do with these names?'

Antonius answered without hesitation.

'I'd parade the First Legion, Legatus. I'd parade them in tunic order, no armour, no weapons. I'd have any man who comes on parade bearing either plate or blade pulled out by half a dozen of our men at spear point, to prevent any resistance, and executed. When they're paraded, I'd order them to untie their belts and place them at their feet. I'd tell them they're not fit to wear the military belt, and give that a moment to sink in. Then I'd tell them that any man who protests will be executed, there and then. I'd make it clear to them that the entire legion is guilty of breaking the sacramentum in their treatment of Legatus Gallus; you'll need him on parade to emphasise the fact that he's still their commander, unless of course you want to replace him. And I'd tell them that the crime of laying hands on an officer is punishable by death, read out those names and order them to step forward for punishment. I'd point to the cross that my carpenters will be erecting on the parade ground and tell them that any man refusing to step forward promptly will forfeit his right to a dignified and swift execution, and will instead be crucified. As each man came forward I'd have four of my own take him, two to control him and two with their swords out and ready for trouble, bring him out in front of the legion and put him on his knees. And then I'd have them killed, all together in as much time as it takes to say it.'

Vocula stared at him.

'And I thought I was ruthless.'

The centurion nodded.

'When they write the histories of these events, Legatus, you will be. In twenty years' time you'll be remembered as the man who restored discipline to the First Gallica and led the army to victory over Civilis.'

The legatus looked at him for a moment.

'I also believed you to be a perfectly competent first spear. It seems I underestimated you.'

Antonius nodded, his face perfectly immobile.

'It's usually best to display what you're capable of when you need to, Legatus, rather than giving the men you're about to deal with time to prepare themselves.' He gestured to the parade ground. 'Shall we go and make some history together?'

The Old Camp, Germania Inferior, November AD 69

'Surely they don't plan to attack now?'

Aquillius shook his head at Marius's question.

'No, why would they come at us when last light is less than an hour away? I think they have something else in mind. See? There . . .'

He pointed into the gathering gloom at the glowing spark of a fire that had been lit outside bolt-thrower range, and Marius stared at it for a moment before replying.

'That's a new one, if they're planning on camping in their siege lines?'

His comrade answered without taking his eyes off the fire, shaking his head as more points of light flickered into life.

'I don't think they're planning on sleeping. It'll be as dark as a money changer's heart tonight with all these clouds, perfect conditions to let them get close in without our being able to pick them off as they approach.'

The two men watched as dozens of fires blossomed in a wide circle around the fortress, and the evening's grey overcast faded out to black with the setting of an unseen sun, until the fires were the only light in the great black bowl of night that had settled over the fortress. The tribesmen were shouting and howling in the darkness, each call answered by a chorus of replies that grew steadily louder and more raucous as time progressed.

'I'd say they're getting ready to attack, stiffening their courage with that foul brew they drink and barking in the night to encourage each other. I'm going to walk the walls and make sure we're ready for them.'

Marius nodded as Aquillius walked away, smiling to himself as the big man stopped barely ten paces into his perambulation and barked a terse reprimand at a legionary leaning against the wall.

'Get off your fucking elbows and onto your feet, you worthless excuse for a soldier! If I catch you even *thinking* about sleeping on duty I'll have your armour off you and throw you down there for the Germans to have their fun with you! That'll keep your fucking eyes open!'

He stamped away leaving the alleged miscreant bolt upright and visibly shaking, such was his reputation for swift and brutal punishment, and Marius laughed softly.

'It's all very well for you. You're the only man in the entire fortress that's not shit scared of him. I've even seen the legatus give him that look, the one that says, "I'm going to do exactly what you tell me to, Centurion".'

He turned to find Gaius standing next to him, his sparsely illuminated features creased in a rueful smile as he stared out across the dark ground between the wall and the besiegers' fires.

'What makes you think *I'm* not afraid of him? He's a force of nature, and men like that don't brook any argument in my experience. He's cut from the same stone as Decimus, I'd say.'

His deputy shook his head briskly at the mention of their former first spear, long since gone south with the bulk of the Fifth Legion to fight for Vitellius, leaving Marius as the senior centurion until his return.

'Nah. Decimus is a different beast altogether. He can shout and scream alright, but at heart he's doing it because he knows that's what it takes to put a legion into the field ready to fight. Whereas your mate Aquillius doesn't give what he's going to say any thought at all, he just opens his mouth and lets fly with whatever crosses his mind. He's a natural. And so, First Spear, are *you.*'

Marius turned to face him.

'*Really?* You've known me for as long as I've followed this legion's eagle. You know how nervous I felt the first time I put on a cross-crested helmet.'

Gaius nodded, still staring out at the ring of fires.

'Yes. For a long time you weren't really quite sure what you were doing with a vine stick in your hands. You knew what it was for, and you put your mark on your fair share of men with it, but your heart wasn't quite in it. You could command men, but you didn't *need* to command them, if you know what I mean. With Aquillius it comes as naturally as breathing, whereas you considered the matter each and every time you raised that stick. But now—'

A great shout went up from the men gathered around the fires, a response to a faint but discernible exhortation. The two men waited for any sign of an attack, but after a moment it became apparent that the Germans were not ready to start whatever it was they planned.

'Not yet. They'll get themselves well pissed up on that rough-arsed beer they swill before they come to cut our cocks off. Now where was I . . .' Gaius pondered for a moment before continuing. 'Ah yes. In peacetime you were a perfectly capable centurion, good enough to be chosen to deputise for Decimus when he buggered off with eight cohorts to fight for Vitellius. But in wartime, Marius, you're a different animal. Remember the day of their first attack? Remember how you saw off those tribesmen who'd managed to get onto the wall?'

Marius's lips twitched in an involuntary smile, and he raised a finger to point at the angry line of scar tissue that bisected his right eye, cut through the eyebrow and down as far as his cheekbone.

'I'll always have this to remind me.'

'Some of the men who were there told me you were lucky that was all the damage you took. They said you fought like an animal, never giving the Germans any chance. But the leading man who was watching told me the most important point about the whole thing. He said—'

Another roar from the besiegers interrupted him, the Germans roared imprecations clearly rising to a crescendo.

'Not long now, they sound like they're getting ready to have another go. Anyway, old Caludius, you know, the one with the hook nose, he said that you speared the first of them, used the shaft of your pilum to fend off the other one's sword, stuck the sharp end up into his jaw, and then, and this is the important bit, you turned to the men watching you do all the hard work, with blood streaming down your face from that nasty little cut, and told them to "get that *fucking* ladder off my *fucking* wall". Caludius has known you as long as I have, and he told me, with a smile mind you, that the men have always known you were a bit diffident with the vine stick. They loved you for it, the fact that you weren't one of those blood and thunder officers but more like one of their own, but he also told me that war's made you a different man. That order you shouted on the wall? There was none of this in it . . .' he tapped his head, 'but plenty of this . . .' he tapped his chest. 'They were doing what you'd ordered before they even had a chance to think about it, he reckoned. You might have been a thinker in peacetime, my old friend, but you're a wild beast when the time comes to fight. And you know what? Those men that loved you for being one of them and not swinging your stick around like a maniac when you didn't need to? Now they know what a monster you can be when your blood's properly up, they love you all the more. You'll give Decimus a run for his money in the "who's the hardest bastard?" betting when he comes back from Italy and that's a—'

Another roar sounded from the Germans, no louder than before but imbued with an additional bestial ferocity, and with a sudden hiss of steam the fires were doused almost simultaneously, plunging the ground around the fortress into darkness. Marius bellowed an order, pulling his sword from the scabbard at his waist.

'Bolt throwers! Shoot at will! Legionaries, stand to!'

In the gloom beneath the wall there was a growing tumult, the tribesmen charging towards the fortress regardless of the threat posed by what remained of the lily pits. With a thump the bolt thrower next to the two centurions spat its deadly missile blindly down into the oncoming warriors, a pair of legionaries throwing themselves at the winding handles to renew the energy stored in the iron bow arms for the next shot.

'You'd better get back to your men, Centurion. They'll be putting ladders up against the wall any minute now.'

Gaius saluted and disappeared off down the wall, and Marius drew breath to shout another command that he knew the centurions along the wall's thousand-pace length would be repeating at the tops of their voices to be heard over the tumult of the oncoming tribesmen.

'Prepare to repel the enemy!'

The Germans were under the wall in the freshly dug six-foot-deep ditch now, and he nodded to the men waiting at the rear of the fighting platform with a steaming cauldron of boiling water. They carried it to the parapet, stiff-legged with the weight of the iron pot and its contents, tipping it unceremoniously down into the darkness and eliciting a chorus of agonised screams from the men below. A ladder slapped against the breastwork a dozen paces to Marius's left, and he watched with grim satisfaction as the tent party whose section of wall it was followed the drill they had been practising every day since the first attack, one man placing a shield against the ladder's legs while two more took positions to either side and gripped the shield's wooden frame. As the first of the tribesmen reached the top of the ladder, finding his way onto the wall blocked by the shield's curved surface and hacking at it ineffectually with his sword, the three men gave the shield a violent push, propelling warrior and ladder backwards to the point that gravity took over, toppling it down into the mob of men below.

'Stakes!'

The other men in the tent party were equally well drilled, hurling short wooden stakes fitted with conical iron tips down into the seething crowd of men and following up with heavy stones thrown upwards and out to fall randomly into the milling warriors.

'There are more of them than last time!'

Marius glanced round to find Aquillius beside him, his eyes alive with the joy of battle.

'Yes, and their blood's up. This is going to be the goat-fuck to end all goat-fucks.'

The big man nodded, hefting his sword.

'Then let's go and find some goats to fuck, shall we?'

The Old Camp, Germania Inferior, November AD 69

'You think this one will burn too?'

The craftsmen who manned Kivilaz's hidden forest workshop had worked day and night on a replacement siege structure to replace the ruined testudo whose burned-out frame still sat beneath the Old Camp's high wooden walls.

Grimmaz shook his head at Levonhard's question, leaning on his shield and squinting up at the tower's massive timbers, bathed in a gentle pink light as the sun's glow started to suffuse the eastern horizon and swathed in fresh-skinned hides whose pungent stench was wrinkling more than a few noses in the first century.

'Not this time. There's three layers of hides on that thing, so most arrows will just bounce off, and there's no way you can get hide to burn in a hurry without drying it out first. I reckon that thing will roll all the way to the gate no matter what they throw at it. And when it gets to the fortress we'll climb the ladders inside it and jump out onto the Old Camp's wall, ready to fight. This time we're not going through the walls, but over them!'

'We've still got to get to the walls though.'

'Yes you have.' Alcaeus had walked up behind them while they contemplated the tower, and now he stood next to Grimmaz radiating confidence in the massive wooden construction. 'But this time we're not going to stroll into the beaten zone of half a dozen bolt throwers and allow the Romans to hammer the shit out of us while we smile and take it. This time we wait at the edge of their range until the tower's nearly in place and then we'll advance at the run to be ready to attack when it reaches the walls. See, here come the big lads.'

A gang of powerfully built tribesmen were being led towards the tower by Kivilaz himself, and Beaky winked at his tent mates.

'Think we should tell them what happened to the last lot?'

The wolf-priest looked at him levelly for a moment.

'Only if you're ready to replace them in the tower when they take fright at your stories. Now go and join the rest of the century, I have work to do here and I don't need you cackling away in the background like a badly house-trained crow.'

He waited for Kivilaz to finish seeing the tribesmen into the tower, sharing a quiet word or a pat on the shoulder with each of them, then went to meet the prince and his own prefect.

'Today is the day. I feel it in my blood.' Kivilaz turned to his cousin. 'Our cohorts are ready?'

'Ready and eager.' Hramn tugged his sword loose of its scabbard's grip to ensure that it would slide into his hand easily when the time came. 'Your plan to keep our men away from the enemy artillery until the tower is in position will give us the maximum possible impact once its ladders give us access to their walls.'

'And the sacrifices were favourable?'

Alcaeus inclined his head.

'As far as my skills could discern, my prince, the sacrifices were impeccable.'

He had crouched over the still-warm bodies of three lambs at dawn with Hramn standing impatiently over him, pondering the entrails and blood flow of each in turn, eventually satisfied that there were no omens of disaster before him but still painfully aware that his abilities were those of a man who had trained under augurs of the highest quality and had been able to absorb some of their skills, rather than a truly gifted seer.

'Good. Then let us proceed. The Romans will be tired after the night of terror they've endured.'

The three men had watched the battle of the fortress's walls unfold from the west, as close to the walls as they dared, and had seen attack after attack hover briefly on the edge of victory, tribal warriors swarming up dozens of ladders to assault the Old Camp's walls, only for each attempt to be thwarted by the defenders' missiles and desperate last-ditch fighting. More than once their allies had managed to scale the Old Camp's walls and gain control of sections of the parapet, only to be dislodged by desperate shield charges mounted against their incursions that sent them tumbling from the wall and snuffed out their attempts to end the battle ignominiously. In the grey dawn Kivilaz had ordered them to pull back, before the enemy artillery had had the chance to go to work on visible targets. and take revenge for the night's casualties. A gruesomely familiar scene had greeted the sun's first light, the lifeless corpses of hundreds of men and the feebly gesticulating, helpless bodies of those too badly wounded to make their way off the battlefield. The prince's face was set hard as he ordered his cohorts into the fight.

'The sacrifice of our brothers from the tribes across the river must not be in vain! Make this count, cousin.'

The Old Camp, Germania Inferior, November AD 69

'What a horrible sight. It'll take them at least another week to burn all those corpses.'

Marius and Aquillius were walking the walls of the fortress alongside legatus Lupercus, all three men exhausted after a night of continual fighting whose intensity had redoubled in the last desperate hour before dawn. The legatus had removed his helmet to allow his sweat-soaked hair to dry in the cool morning air, and was staring out across the corpses that were scattered liberally around the fortress walls, their concentration greatest in the ditch where the majority of their deaths had been inflicted by defenders who had been unable to miss. The Germans had managed to gain a foothold on the wall in two places at almost the same time on different sides of the fortress, small parties of warriors creeping close in the darkness from the west while their brothers stormed the eastern rampart, and while Marius had run for the closer incursion his colleague had sprinted across the fortress to the other. The fighting had reached a new and terrifying level of bestial horror in those final moments, tribesmen pouring over the parapet as fast as they could climb their ladders while the men facing them, knowing that to lose the wall was to lose their lives, had rushed at them with the reckless abandon of the truly desperate, stabbing, punching with their shields, and kicking out with hobnailed boots in a desperate battle to take back their lost ground.

Aquillius nodded at Lupercus's awed statement.

'We were lucky to see them off this time.'

In the melee that had followed, fifty paces of wall had been transformed into nothing better than a deadly brawl, a struggle to the death where men died in the dark without ever seeing their killers, the fighting surface quickly slick and stinking with blood. Marius had watched a legionary fight his way into the enemy with the berserk rage of a man who had lost his mind to the battle's madness, killing half a dozen men in short succession, each frenzied combat taking him deeper into the press of the enemy, only to die with a bolt in his back as a panicking scorpion crew loosed their missile blindly into the struggling throng. Attackers and defenders had become intermixed in the darkness, using their hands to find and identify the men beside them before striking as fast and as hard as they could with whatever weapon came to hand in the confusion. The corpses of two legionaries had been found locked in what had proven to be a fatal error for both, each of them still clutching their bloody bladed daggers and rent by the appalling wounds that even the least of a soldier's weapons could inflict at close quarters. The centurions calculated that the desperate fight, which had ended with the last of the attackers thrown bodily from the parapet into the mass of Germans below, had cost them two hundred dead and half as many wounded.

'But they lost. Again. And we must have killed thousands. Again.' Lupercus nodded.

'They'll replace those losses in days with men from across the river and have another roll of the dice soon enough.'

'First Spear! On the road!'

All three men turned to the look at the southern wall where a centurion was waving at them urgently.

'Well that didn't take long. It looks as if they've decided to roll the dice again without waiting for reinforcements.' Lupercus pulled his helmet back on. 'Let's hope that your guess as to what they might attempt next is correct, First Spear Aquillius. Because if it is we might just have the beating of them!'

The Old Camp, Germania Inferior, November AD 69

Hramn nodded briskly at Kivilaz's command, saluted and turned away, and Alcaeus followed him back to their place at the head of the first cohort. They watched as the massively heavy siege tower started moving, already pre-positioned on the road that led arrow-straight to the south gate, the only one of the four entrances to the fortress with a flat and level approach. Dozens of tribesmen were providing initial momentum by pulling on stout ropes attached to the tower's thick frontal timbers, and the massive construction quickly reached a brisk walking pace as they leaned forward against its weight and pulled with all their strength. With the tower moving they unhooked the ropes and cleared its path, the biggest among them taking up the role of pushing at its rear to keep its huge weight moving at the best pace, while the cohorts fell in behind. Bolts plunged down into the tower's thick timbers, launched high into the air for maximum range, and Hramn raised a fist in the prearranged signal for the first cohort to halt, the soldiers watching eagerly as the structure trundled imperiously along the road towards the fortress wall, apparently indestructible as bolt after bolt hammered into the wooden beams that lined its frontal surface, completely unable to penetrate their thick layered protection as it rolled past the remnants of the testudo that had been dragged aside with hooked ropes during the night. As the range from wall to tower shortened, fire arrows arced out to kiss the siege engine with their deadly flaming touch, but the triple layer of freshly skinned animal hide was impervious to the flying droplets of tallow that hissed against the protective layer, sputtering into quiescence on the damp, noisome flesh.

'Just a bit further . . .'

Grimmaz was muttering to himself, his sword hand unconsciously tapping out a rhythm against the weapon's pommel as he watched the tower closing with the walls, the thudding of heavy bolts into its timbers a stark and uneven drum beat, each impact signalling another failure to defeat its thick protection.

'Just a bit further . . .'

Alcaeus knelt on one knee, bowing his wolf-headed helmet and muttering a prayer to the gods to protect his men in the battle to come, while the soldiers nodded and pointed as archers climbed out onto the shooting platforms on either side of the tower and commenced shooting at the defenders, aiming for any man foolish enough to show himself now that they were within one hundred paces of the walls. The structure was still moving, slower now with the slight gradient that approached the fortress's southern gate. The initial brave showing by the archers was swiftly reduced to nothing as the Roman scorpion crews took a bloody revenge for those men the tribesmen had manage to fell with their initial volleys. The shooting platforms were swept clean by a withering hail of bolts, leaving the tower defenceless as it came within fifty paces of the walls.

'*Now! We go!*'

Hramn led them forward at a trot, each man knowing that they were running towards the deadly Roman artillery and raising their shields to maximise their protection, feeble though it would be if a bolt found them. The defenders, ready and waiting for the attack to begin in earnest, switched targets with commendable speed, and their missiles fell into the cohorts' ranks with impersonal, random power, smashing men back onto the road's surface dead or dying. Something hissed past Egilhard's head and thudded into a man in the next tent party, scattering the soldiers around him as he sprawled across the cobbles with blood spraying from his deep chest wound.

'Keep running! Another two hundred paces and we'll be on their wall!'

Hramn upped the pace as he bellowed the command, and the tower loomed over them as they overhauled it, running into the shadow of its timbers. The first century climbed in through the open rear and threw themselves at the ladders with the prefect at their head, racing to reach the second storey where the machine's boarding ramp awaited them. A hinged section of the tower's frontal surface, it was heavy enough to crush a man and utterly smash his body, and a massive hook protruded from its underside to catch and hold whatever surface it fell on to, needing only a push from several strong men to drop the combination of anchor and ramp onto the fortress wall and provide a six-foot-wide bridge across which the first century would charge into the waiting defenders in numbers too great to repel.

'It's stopped moving, so we must be in position! What are we waiting for?' Grimmaz put his head around the tower's corner, risking the flights of arrows that were now raking the column of men queued behind the tower, then ducking back into the structure's protection with a curse. 'They've got some sort of arrangement of beams holding us away from the wall! We're a dozen feet short!'

The Germans inside the tower were straining with all their might, but the wooden construction's wheels had stopped turning completely. Back down the cohort's column of men soldiers were dying under the lash of the Roman archers and the less frequent but terrifyingly powerful impacts of carefully aimed bolts. A man a dozen paces behind Egilhard jerked, then stood for a moment with a heavy missile stuck through his helmet to protrude from the iron bowl's rear, his eyes rolling up to display only the whites as a thin drool of blood hung from his open mouth, then sank from view onto the cobbles. Alcaeus pushed his way into the tower past the ranks of his men, shouting up into the structure.

'We're being slaughtered here! Can you get onto the walls?'

After a moment's pause Hramn dropped down the ladder from the first level, his face grim.

'They must have guessed we'd try this, or else they had intelligence of it! We're stuck too far from the wall to drop the ramp, and too far to jump it! We'll have to retreat!'

Alcaeus nodded, turning back to the men waiting under the Roman artillery's unrelenting scourge.

'Back to the siege works! *Run!*'

As one man the waiting centuries turned and fled, the bodies of the dead and wounded carried between several men apiece.

'Run! Those bastards will be showering us with arrows all the way back! Run and keep—'

Grimmaz went down hard, lying prone on the cobbles with the fletched shaft of an arrow protruding from the back of his neck, the missile having flown through the impossibly small gap between his neck guard and the collar of his mail.

'*Pick him up!*'

The order came to Egilhard unbidden, but his tent mates leapt to obey with the same alacrity as if it has been issued by the leading man himself, carrying his dead weight away between them with his head lolling down, bouncing with every step they took. A hundred paces from the spot where the siege engine had become stuck, the young soldier stopped to look back, an arrow rebounding from his armoured shoulder with a force that knocked him backwards a pace, but the impact failed to register as anything more than a peripheral event as he stared at the fortress. The southern gates were open, and armoured legionaries were flooding out in force, several centuries strong, stabbing down at the wounded as they swarmed the tower and killed the helpless tribesmen trapped in its bowels. As he watched, more soldiers flooded from the fortress, their armour bright with the flames from the torches they carried.

'Egilhard! Get moving before you stop a bolt! There's nothing we can do to stop them burning it!'

Alcaeus was beside him, turning him away from the scene and pushing him forward, both men flinching involuntarily as another bolt flicked into the mass of running men twenty paces back towards the siege lines, taking down one of the men carrying Grimmaz's body in a spray of blood that decorated his tent mates' armour with a grotesque pattern of gore.

10

Gelduba, Germania Inferior, November AD 69

'I'm unconvinced that this is the wisest thing we could be doing, Legatus Augusti!'

Hordeonius Flaccus nodded brusquely as he reached for his intricately decorated helmet, an object of such magnificence that Antonius was reasonably sure its cost would have equipped an entire legion century and still left enough gold for those eighty men to enjoy a substantial night of drinking and whoring. He had returned from Colonia Agrippina the previous day, expressed his thanks to Vocula for his harsh suppression of the First Legion's revolt and then, in a move that the legatus hadn't expected given his previous reluctance to remain the army's commander, bluntly told the legatus that he was issuing a formal order for the legions to swear allegiance to Vespasianus in the light of news received from Italy.

'You retain responsibility for the conduct of our campaign against Civilis and his allies, of course, but in the matter of such a crucial decision, with ramifications for us that will last for the rest of our lives, I feel entirely justified in issuing this instruction.'

Despite Vocula's vigorous protests as to the legions' likely response, Flaccus had proven immovable on the subject, and the men of three legions were gathering as commanded on the make-shift parade ground outside the sprawling camp while their senior officers readied themselves to do what was their duty to the empire, with only two significant dissenters.

'I'm well aware of your sensitivities on the matter, Legatus, and while I believe them to be genuinely motivated, the option of not declaring our loyalty to the new emperor is one that has been rejected not only by myself but by your fellow legates, their tribunes and indeed their senior centurions to a man.' Flaccus regarded Vocula and Antonius levelly, evidently impervious to their concerns. 'The only two men of substance in this entire command who are not in favour of immediately swearing the army to the service of Vespasianus are yourself and your ever loyal first spear. Who doubtless, were he not required by convention to support you to the hilt, would be siding with the rest of us! Wouldn't you, Antonius? Don't answer that, man, one should never come between a legatus and his senior centurion and I ought to know better, I suppose! I—'

Vocula shook his head angrily, casting aside any restraint of their relative ranks in the face of the other man's insouciant disregard for the reality of their situation.

'Far from it, Legatus *Augusti*, as you're happy enough to term yourself once more now that you think your man has his backside on the throne! Antonius here is of a like mind to myself in seeing the enormous risk that you're intending to take.' He cast a jaundiced eye around the room at his fellow officers. 'All of you were born to rich fathers and educated in Rome. You all know Titus Flavius Vespasianus personally or by reputation, and you all have a good opinion of the man. And as a matter of fact I know him too, a little, and what I saw of him was overwhelmingly positive. But the men to whom you plan to administer the oath of allegiance aren't like you!'

He clenched a fist in frustration.

'Gods below, how is it that the truth eludes you in this matter? Let me spell it out in the simplest of terms for you! The men you're going to order to swear allegiance to Vespasianus do not share your connection to the man. Nor do they believe that Vitellius is beaten yet! The captured officers that Vespasianus's general Primus has sent north to bring us these tidings carry news of a single defeat for Vitellius's army, not his complete defeat or his death, and for as long as that is the case those men are not going to relinquish him easily, because they still believe that he will make them all rich! He is the proverbial pot of gold, quite literally, to the soldiers of these legions, and they know all too well that Vespasianus isn't going to owe them any loyalty when they've contributed vexillations to the army that tried to stop him taking the throne! If you are foolish enough to force this issue now, rather than allowing them to come to their own conclusions in a few weeks' time when the news will doubtless arrive that Vitellius has eventually been deposed, then you will be attempting to put a collar on a large and very angry dog.'

Flaccus turned to face him with an expression that spoke volumes as to the degree of self-control he was exercising.

'While I understand your feelings, Legatus, I cannot allow you to hinder this essential step in what I expect will shortly lead to the conclusion of this civil war and indeed the revolt of our northern neighbours. Once these legions are sworn to obey the new emperor then I have no doubt whatsoever that Civilis will call a halt to his offensive against the Old Camp and present himself for admonishment and forgiveness. But for that to happen we must take this essential step, and so I expect that you will conduct yourself with the utmost professionalism while we conduct what I expect will be a relatively painless ceremony to renew our legionaries' sacramentum to the new emperor, and keep your views on the matter to yourself. That applies to you too, First Spear Antonius.'

Antonius snapped to attention, his gaze fixed on a point to one side of Flaccus's head, fighting hard not to express the contempt he was feeling.

'I'm amazed that you have the gall to say such a thing to a man who is the model of a professional military officer.' Vocula shook his head grimly. 'My senior centurion has watched in silent disgust while you and my other colleagues have dissimulated and delayed doing anything to relieve the siege of the Old Camp for fear of what such an action might mean to your careers in the event of a victory for Vespasianus, never once expressing his horror at such self-interest, and now you have the nerve to even hint that you suspect his disloyalty.'

Flaccus turned away, busying himself with the leather tie that secured his helmet.

'Your comments have been noted, Legatus. Come, gentlemen, let us go and administer the sacramentum to our legionaries and put an end to this damned civil war for good.'

Out on the parade ground Antonius walked out to his place in front of the Twenty-second in silence, but if he was still fuming at Flaccus's implied slur he soon enough forgot the matter as the legion's mood became apparent.

'They're not happy. And trust me when I tell you that they're *really* not happy.' His deputy relinquished the spot and turned to march back to his own century with a swift shake of his head. 'If what the rumours are saying is true, and they expect us to swear loyalty to Vespasianus, it might not end well.'

Flaccus spoke up from the tribunal, and for once there was none of the usual coughing and muttering that had accompanied so many of his pronouncements over the preceding months, the men of three legions listening intently to what he had to say.

'Legionaries of the First Gallica, Sixteenth Germanica and Twenty-second Primigenia! Soldiers of the allied auxiliary cohorts! I bring you news from Italy! These men . . .' he raised a hand to indicate the two officers standing close behind him, 'have ridden from Italy at the behest of Legatus Augusti Antonius Primus . . .'

He paused, but the silence hanging over the parade ground was profound, every man present hanging on his words.

'Tribune Varro and Prefect Montanus bear news of a battle that has been fought close to the town of Cremona, the same field where our legions triumphed over Otho's men in the spring. Soldiers, the sad news is that our army has been defeated, and that the legions that fought on our side have been taken prisoner. Eleven legions and their auxiliary cohorts loyal to the former emperor were defeated by the forces of Titus Flavius Vespasianus, and the army of Vitellius is no more. By the time of this announcement his grip on the throne will have been broken forever. And so . . .'

The first buzz of muttered comments reached Antonius's ears, and he turned to find his men staring intently at Flaccus with expressions that did not imply any degree of reconciliation with what they had just heard.

'And so, it is the decision of your senior officers that we must collectively swear allegiance to the new emperor, an action that will be communicated to his general in Italy, Antonius Primus, by the fastest means possible. There will be none of the usual imperial imagery that is usually present for such a ceremony, but nevertheless we will all now swear the sacramentum to our new emperor.'

He cleared his throat.

'I swear that I shall faithfully execute all that the senate and the people of Rome require!'

The stunned legionaries repeated the words after him, although to Antonius their declaration of loyalty sounded half-hearted at best.

'I swear that I will never desert the service of the empire!'

The strength of the legionaries' assertion of loyalty to the empire was louder than that of their promise to obey its rulers, but Antonius knew only too well what was coming next.

'And I swear that I will defend, to the last drop of my blood, the rightful emperor Titus Flavius Caesar Vespasianus Augustus!'

At the name Vespasianus the men behind him simply fell silent, muttered something inaudible or even simply spoke the name Vitellius, and all three legions stared back at Flaccus as if daring him to take any action to punish their evident lack of commitment. Looking at Vocula in his place behind the legatus augusti, he saw his senior officer looking up into the sky above them, and found himself nodding agreement with the man's evident sentiment.

'I think you've got that more or less right, Legatus. That fool's got himself into this mess, so now he can get himself out of it.'

Batavodurum, Germania Inferior, November AD 69

'He died quickly?'

Egilhard nodded mutely, unable to speak for the fear that whatever he said would trigger the uncontrollable grief that he knew was waiting just beneath the surface of his apparently imperturbable mask. Alcaeus stepped forward to stand beside the young soldier.

'He felt no pain. I saw it happen, and I've never seen a man taken so cleanly. You can be proud of his service to the tribe, and take comfort from the fact that his death was an easy one.'

'Thank you, Centurion.'

Grimmaz's father was stooped, a man in the last few years of his life, and as Egilhard reflected on the injustice of his being required to consign a son to the Underworld before his time, the old man accepted the flaming brand that the wolf-priest handed to him, and put it to the pyre's kindling with a hand shaking with both age and grief.

'Farewell, son. You did your duty.'

He turned away with halting, hesitant steps that betrayed his infirmity, the dead soldier's sword, which had once been his own, in one hand, not showing any sign of reaction as the kindling on which Grimmaz's tightly wrapped corpse lay took fire with a soft cough of ignition.

'Few men want to stand and watch a son's body burn. Whereas we are bound by both duty and love to watch until there's nothing to be seen of him.'

Egilhard nodded miserably at his officer's words, marvelling at the man's composure in the face of such a keenly felt loss. Standing before the pyre, his eyes barely focused on the roaring fire that was engulfing his friend's body, he realised that his vision was blurring with tears and that no amount of blinking was going to stem their flow.

'Don't wipe them away. Let them flow. His family will see how dearly his brothers miss him and there's not one of us is going to think any less of you for being a leading man who mourns his losses.'

A kind of anger at the priest's composure flared in the young soldier's mind.

'You're not mourning.'

'Yes I am.' Alcaeus's voice was soft and sad, ignoring the younger man's failure to address him by his rank. 'But I have no tears to shed. I never have them when the time comes to burn a comrade. And I burned a good few, on that island of savages and rain across the Oceanus Britannicus ten years ago. We were the Iceni tribe's nemesis, Rome's best and bravest, the wild dogs that were sent in first to savage them into submission, but being the bravest means taking losses whichever way you look at it, and they made us pay for that reputation in blood. All the way through that summer we lost men, in ones and twos, and once by the dozen, when the time came to fight them properly. I lost comrades and I lost close friends, but I never found it in me to weep once, no matter what indignities they visited on our dead when they were allowed the time to do so. I wish I could have cried.'

'Why?'

Turning his head slightly Egilhard saw that his centurion was smiling sadly.

'Because, Leading Man, it's my observation that men who do shed tears for their dead brothers tend to get over their loss more quickly than those capable only of brooding. And stop pulling faces every time I mention your rank, will you? It's starting to irritate me, and when you consider that I take a lot of irritating you're obviously doing it too often.'

Egilhard shifted his gaze back to the pyre, his mind wandering to the evening of the battle in which Grimmaz had been killed. The mood in the Batavi camp had been sombre, despite the relatively light casualties they had suffered, a mood more to do with the attack's failure than the losses sustained, although the death of a vigorous and popular leading man had hit the men of the Second Century hard, and a sullen silence hung over their section of the first cohort's camp. So bound up in his mourning for a man he had come to regard as a close friend that he had stopped listening to the conversations around him, the young soldier had been dragged from his reverie by the sound of his name being called out by an evidently irritated Banon.

'Egilhard!'

'Chosen Man!'

He had leapt to his feet, unsure what he'd done to have earned the tone of Banon's voice and surprised to see Alcaeus standing behind his deputy.

'Sit down, man, and listen this time. Lanzo should be leading man in Grimmaz's place by rights.' He had nodded, seeing the right of it immediately, and opened his mouth to agree only to have it closed by the chosen man's next statement. 'But he won't take the position.' Banon had thrown a disgusted glance at the soldier, who had ostentatiously ignored it, focusing his attention on polishing the last specks of blood from his helmet. 'Says he doesn't want to get in the way of the obvious candidate.'

'Who . . .' Egilhard's eyes had snapped wide as he realised that every man in the tent party was staring at him. '*What?* No . . .'

'Yes.' Lanzo had put the helmet down and looked across their fire at him with a small smile. 'It's obvious. And the only man who can't see it is you.'

'But—'

'But nothing, Achilles. You're the best man with a sword in the cohort. There isn't one of us you couldn't best in less than a dozen breaths, and you're good with your fists too, when we spar. There's not one of us will take the job when you're obviously the right person. So just agree to do it and we'll all get on with mourning Grimmaz, shall we?'

The young soldier had sat in amazed silence for so long that Lanzo had picked his helmet again with a shake of his head and a meaningful stare at the centurion and chosen man.

'Egilhard.' He had looked up to find Alcaeus standing before him, gesturing for him to stand up. 'Look around you. Every one of your tent mates wants you to take Grimmaz's place. Not one of them is willing to take it, which means that if you won't fill his shoes then I'll have to bring another man in from another tent party.'

'Which means, you young idiot . . .' Banon had stepped alongside his centurion. 'That you'll end up with a leading man who knows nothing about any of you, or cares all that much either. A man who'll feel he has to establish his right to the position, looking for the slightest indication of disrespect and punishing it without mercy. All that easy humour you men enjoy will be a thing of the past. Are you happy to let that happen? I doubt they are . . .'

He had waved a hand at the circle of men around the fire, and Egilhard once again finding himself the centre of their attention had shaken his head in bemusement.

'You *all* . . . ?'

'For fuck's sake, boy, do I have to tattoo it on my cock and slap you round the face with it?'

Egilhard stared at Adalwin for a moment, the unexpected humour slowly cracking his face into a smile as the perfect response came to him, knowing that the tent party's comedian had deliberately presented him with the perfect opportunity to stamp some sort of authority on his comrades. 'Do you know an artist who can work that small?'

And with that the decision had been made, as much for him as by him, his comrades treating him with an edge of deference that was still troubling him days later.

The tent party stood and watched as their comrade's pyre burned down to a pile of ash, each man alone with his thoughts, until, with a final twist of smoke, the flames guttered and died. Working quickly, while the ashes were still warm, they scooped as much of the fire's dust as would fit into a blue jar that Grimmaz's family had provided, each man touching the container and whispering a few words of farewell before Alcaeus presented it to the dead soldier's father with appropriate formality.

'And now there's nothing more that Grimmaz would have wanted than for us to go and raise a cup to his memory.' The centurion raised his purse. 'It's on me. And you can bring Lataz and Frijaz along as well if you like, they've been watching from behind that wall for the best part of two hours. Want to go and get them?'

He nodded and walked across to where his father and uncle were lurking, raising his voice to be heard.

'The centurion says there's a drink waiting for you both, but only if you stop pissing around.'

Frijaz popped out of hiding with commendable speed, his brother emerging behind him with a disgusted expression.

'One mention of free drink, eh? Is that still all it takes?' He nodded to his son, his eyes still bright with emotion. 'We wanted to show our respect for your leading man's father, we both soldiered with him when we were new boys, but we didn't want to embarrass you. And we wanted to see how you conducted yourself, given we hear that you're a leading man now.'

They decamped to a tavern, where Frijaz proceeded to take Alcaeus at his word and put his nose into a beaker of beer with impressive speed.

'He was a good comrade, I presume?'

'Best leading man I ever served under, no disrespect meant, Achilles.' Egilhard nodded his understanding at Lanzo. 'You could rip the piss out of him when it didn't matter, but when it did he was all business and no mistake. He'd have made a good chosen man.'

Banon nodded his agreement.

'I was going to recommend we promote him to replace that nasty old sod Hludovig as watch officer, when he reached his retirement. Doesn't look as if any of us will be leaving for reasons of age any time soon though, does it?'

Lataz fixed a serious gaze on Alcaeus.

'Are you men going to keep on risking my boy's life to no purpose, or is there a proper fight anywhere in his future? The bolt that took your friend could just as easily have left me without a son, and I wouldn't mind if there'd been any point to the attack but I'm fucked if I can see what it was you were trying to achieve.'

The centurion nodded easily, happy enough to talk on equal terms with a pair of retired soldiers whose questions were understandable under the circumstances and who could be trusted to keep his views to themselves.

'That's the last time we'll be going anywhere near the Old Camp, from the rumours I've heard.'

'Which can only mean one thing.'

Alcaeus frowned at the veteran.

'What?'

'Come on, Centurion, we hear the rumours just as much as you do. Probably better. There's a legion marching camp twenty-five miles south of the Old Camp, and three eagles have been camped there for so long now that they've probably taken root. Good old Kiv must have itchy fingers just thinking about parading those eagles through these streets, because if he does then never mind the Old Camp, there'll be nothing between here and the Winter Camp that can resist us.'

His brother put down his beer and nodded vigorously.

'And the Gauls must be starting to think the time for them to rise up is here. If he knocks over those legions there'll be nothing stopping a revolt all the way to the mountains. It almost makes me want to be back in armour.'

'Yes, I'm sure . . . *almost*. Another beer?'

Lataz waved the centurion back into his chair.

'We'll get these.' He put a hand out in front of his brother, palm upward. 'Coin.'

Grumbling dealt with and beer purchased, he fixed Alcaeus with a hard stare and hooked a thumb at his brother.

'Let's not forget, Centurion, that Ugly Features here and I remember you from when you were as young as my boy there. Which means that we know when you're telling the truth. So, still having that dream you told him about, are you?'

Alcaeus nodded.

'Yes. Not often, but often enough for me to know that it will come to pass exactly as I have dreamed it.'

Lataz lowered his voice further still.

'What was it you told my idiot brother here? "Wood over water, and our boy with a great man's life at the end of his sword"?'

Alcaeus nodded gravely.

'Yes. But don't ask me who the man in question is. The dream never reveals that to me, it's just a feeling I have as I dream it.'

Lataz shrugged.

'Best not to know. You've not told him, I presume?'

The centurion shook his head.

'Of course not. Why put that on the boy with everything else that he's having to deal with?'

'Right. I knew you were a good 'un from the first day I set

eyes on you. If you were of the right blood you could have commanded the cohorts instead of that hothead Hramn. I remember his father when he served, all bad temper and no thinking before he opened his mouth, and while the son might have a little more about him he wouldn't be commanding the cohorts if his uncle wasn't the tribe's war leader.'

Alcaeus shrugged, affecting to ignore such trenchant criticism of his superior.

'Command? Who wants that responsibility? Having to work out what Kiv's going to want next is difficult enough without all the pressure that goes with being the man everyone's looking at for whatever it is they want. Scar used to hate the job, all he wanted was to be an ordinary centurion again, and he was never happier than when he was out on the parade ground making us practise our spear work for the twentieth time in a morning. No, I'm happy with my lot, thank you, Lataz. And now I suggest that you and your uglier and less intelligent brother drink your beer and bugger off. The leading man here and I have a tent party to get drunk in honour of a man you never knew, so a little privacy is called for. And you can take away one thing from my dream that ought to give you confidence in your son's ability to survive the next few months.'

'What's that?'

'In my dream there are trees on the far side of the water. Close enough to see them clearly. And they're in summer leaf. So whatever it is this all means, it won't come to pass until much later in the year. Unless of course the gods are playing me false.'

Batavian field headquarters, Germania Inferior, November AD 69

'This is indeed the very best of news, Prefect Montanus. And we thank you for bringing it to us despite the risk you took in doing so.'

The Nervian officer bowed deeply to Draco in his place as the tribal council's leader, then half turned to either side and essayed swift bows to the elders. He then turned away and walked from the council chamber with the proud bearing of a man who combined tribal nobility and command of a Roman auxiliary cohort. At the door he found Kivilaz waiting for him and the Batavi noble beckoned him into a side room where two other men were waiting.

'Alpinus Montanus, these men are Prefect Hramn and Wolf-Priest Alcaeus, the commander of my cohorts and his deputy and chief-priest.'

Montanus nodded to the waiting officers.

'I recognise you, Prefect, from your presence at Nero's shoulder the last time I was in Rome, although you were known by the name Julius Victor in the emperor's service. And you, Centurion, I know by your exploits on the battlefield as related to me by Alfenius Varus, now praetorian prefect but at the time your prefect, I believe?'

Both men nodded, remaining silent and allowing Kivilaz to speak.

'Alpinus Montanus brings news of a victory for Vespasianus. Not a quite death blow for Vitellius but the next best thing. His eleven legions have been defeated, it seems, and Rome is effectively open for the taking. It can only be a matter of time before Vespasianus is on the throne and those legions that marched south from here to fight for his predecessor come marching back, bowed under the shame of their defeat and looking to unload that heavy burden onto someone else. Specifically, us. Prefect Montanus tells us that Hordeonius Flaccus has already sworn his men to Vespasianus's service, and that he carries a message from the legatus augusti himself, encouraging us to consider our revolt to have served its purpose and now to be at an end.'

'Put your spears down and all will be forgiven? That seems unlikely to me.'

Kivilaz nodded at his nephew's response.

'And to me. Vespasianus might just be able to ignore the repeated assaults on the Old Camp, even if the returning legions feel less charitable on the subject, but surely our attacks on the Ubii and the Treveri, and the prefect's own people the Nervii, and the Gallic tribes to our south, must surely mean that we'll be marked for retribution? The Batavi will be crushed, but we won't suffer that fate alone. The tribes that provide much of the strength of the army of Germania have failed Rome at every battle we have fought with them to date, auxiliaries either taking to their heels or defecting to our ranks. I expect that your own people's treatment is likely to be harsh, Prefect, as a consequence of the legions being unable to work out – or even to care – which of the tribes were our enthusiastic conspirators and which simply our victims.'

Montanus nodded dourly.

'I have shared similar concerns with my cousin, a man known to the Romans as Julius Classicus. He commands the First Nervian Horse, and like myself is descended from the kings who ruled our people before the man whose name he bears tore down our kingdoms and made us vassals of Rome.'

Kivilaz looked at him in silence for a moment.

'Prefect, I will be totally honest with you, and by association, with your cousin Classicus. My reward for twenty-five years of service to Rome has been a bitter dish. My brother was murdered, executed without trial. I was imprisoned, beaten and shipped off to Rome for my own execution, spared only by the suicide of Nero who would otherwise doubtless have ordered my death even while he played with his favourite catamite. His army of Germania procured my brother's death from a pliable legatus augusti, and in turn had their demands for my murder frustrated only by an accident of great events. I demand vengeance for my brother, and recompense for my own mistreatment!'

He fixed the Nervian officer with a knowing gaze.

'You men of the Nervii, you have shed no less blood than we Batavi for our would-be imperial masters. And for what reward? The same bitter dish served out to my people, more or less. Distasteful service to their empire, subjected to perpetual tribute and the rod and axe of their empire's "justice", and forever at the mercy of the whims of our rulers. And yet I, with little more strength than a single cohort of former imperial bodyguards, men cast aside by Rome when the need for them was deemed to be over, and with the righteous fury of my people and that of our allies the Cananefates, have brought such fire and terror on their forts and towns that they fear the name Batavi. And I have their huge, useless fortress encircled, slowly but surely starving them out and bleeding their strength with incessant attacks. But now that Vespasianus has won, it seems, I am issued with the pre-emptory order to cease hostilities and present myself for judgement on the crime of starting a revolt that this same Vespasianus requested of me through his intermediaries. And I tell you, in deadly seriousness, that I will not.'

He leaned forward, lowering his voice to something close to a whisper.

'Prefect, I know the truth of this rebellion against the Romans. And that truth is this: if we win, we will be free, with our own lands, freed from tribute and the tyranny of their centurions. And if we lose?' He snapped his fingers dismissively. 'In that case the situation will return to what it was before. I may die, of course, here or in Rome, but I was hardly expecting to live for ever. And my life is a fair stake in such a momentous gamble. Take that message to your cousin Classicus, and tell him that Kivilaz, war chief of the Batavi, would dearly like the opportunity to discuss these matters at length with him in person. Who knows, perhaps we might find a common cause?'

The Old Camp, Germania Inferior, November AD 69

'Gods below . . .'

Lupercus's muttered words sank into the silence without seeming to have been heard by any of the dozen men in the room.

'You're sure of this, Tribune Varro?'

The younger man nodded solemnly at Marius, aware that he was carrying news of the greatest possible import to the commander of the Old Camp and his officers. A tribune of the

Fifth Legion's defeated vexillation, and known to every man present, he had been selected by the victorious enemy general Antonius Primus to ride north to the legions on the Rhenus with the Treviran prefect Montanus, tasked with bringing them the news of the Vitellian army's total and catastrophic defeat.

'I was present at the battle, First Spear. I saw it all happen, and took part in the aftermath. And yes, we were completely defeated. A Gallic auxiliary prefect has been selected to deliver the same news to the Batavi leader Civilis, and I was ordered to bring it to you.'

Lupercus gestured to a chair.

'Make yourself comfortable, Tribune, and tell us your story, in your own words and not those prepared for you by the victors. What happened?'

Once all were seated, the young officer started his tale with news that, while troubling, was hardly a surprise to the legatus.

'The first blow we suffered was an attempt by Consul Caecina to surrender the army to Primus before we'd even met in battle.'

The legatus nodded grimly.

'Why Vitellius ever trusted a man who had so glibly changed sides from that of Galba to his own was never clear to me. Caecina was an opportunist, and no more worthy of his office than Otho was to that of emperor.' He gestured to the tribune to continue. 'When was this?'

'It was three weeks ago to the day, Legatus. In the absence of his colleague Fabius Valens who had remained in Rome on account of illness, he persuaded the legions' senior centurions to follow his lead and swear allegiance to Vespasianus while the troops were out of camp on the day's business, took down the emperor's portraits and sent a message to Primus that his army had agreed to a change of loyalties. Apparently he had been negotiating with the enemy in secret for weeks. If he had been allowed to carry it through he would have gifted Vespasianus with his rival's army, and enabled Primus to put his army across the Po unhindered.'

'And Vespasianus would most likely have triumphed bloodlessly in the space of an afternoon. What happened?'

The younger man smiled wanly.

'The legions mutinied on the spot the moment they discovered the plan, led by our own men of the Fifth. First Spear Decimus was particularly swift to draw his sword, as I recall it.'

'There's no surprise there. First Spear Decimus always was a most energetic man.' Lupercus shared an amused smile with Marius, who nodded his agreement with the air of a man who had suffered the rough edge of his senior centurion's tongue on more than one occasion. 'So what happened then?'

'Your colleague Fabius Fabulus was made commander in Caecina's place, unsurprisingly as it was his Fifth Legion that led the mutiny. I didn't have any feeling that he wanted the position, but then he wasn't given very much choice in the matter. As you say, First Spear Decimus wasn't a man to take no for an answer. The army marched for Cremona, the battlefield where we defeated Otho's army six months ago, marching eighteen miles a day and thirty on the fifth day, when it became clear that we were in a race for the town with Vespasianus's legions. We arrived at Cremona footsore and hungry, ready to make camp and prepare ourselves to fight the next day, but Legatus Fabulus made the decision to throw us straight at the enemy line despite our exhaustion.'

'Decimus's influence again?'

Varro nodded at Marius.

'Yes, First Spear. He persuaded the legatus that the enemy wouldn't be ready for us to attack so quickly, and that we were better risking a hasty attack at night with men already tired from a forced march than allowing Primus's men time to dig defences on ground that was already made difficult by ditches and vegetation, especially as our thirty-five thousand men outnumbered them by a good ten thousand. He argued that it would be in the finest tradition of the Blessed Julius's legions of which, of course, the Fifth was one, and that was that. We went in soon after dark, the Fifth and Fifteenth ordered to go straight up the middle with the legion detachments from Britannia and break the enemy centre, and we went for them like wild dogs with

Decimus in the front rank. We hit the Seventh Galbiana head-on and tore into them like heroes, and they only rescued their eagle from being taken by the loss of their own first spear and most of his leading cohort centurions. But the Eighth Augustan beside them held firm . . .' Aquillius nodded his approval with his customary lack of expression, drawing amused glances from the men who knew of his previous service with the Eighth legion. 'And Primus put his praetorians into the line to stiffen it. We were pushed back with nothing to show for the attack but a carpet of dead and dying men in front of us, theirs and our own.'

The young tribune paused for a moment, and Marius realised that his eyes were wet.

'I'm sorry, Legatus . . . it's just . . .'

To everyone's surprise Aquillius was the first to react.

'Take a moment, Tribune Varro. Battle affects everyone differently, and remembering the moment when men you knew died beside you can trouble you for the rest of your life. Better to let the grief flow.'

The young officer nodded gratefully, wiping a tear away with his hand.

'Forgive me. Two of my friends died in that fight, men with whom I had marched all the way from this fortress to Italy. After we'd won the throne for Vitellius at the first battle of Cremona we came to believe that we were immortal, and that no man could kill us, not that there would ever again be such a battle between Romans. Such hubris . . .' He wiped the last tears away, and his voice hardened as if the simple act of remembering the battle's events was armouring his mind against their lingering pain. 'One of them took a spear wound to his abdomen, low down, and even as he died he was still asking me if his penis was intact. I told him it was, but in truth both of his balls had been severed and his manhood was hanging by a strip of flesh. The other was hit by a scorpion bolt, a chunk of his bronze smashed deep into his body so that he vomited blood with the impact. I saw things I hope never to witness again, acts of bestial savagery the like of which I had only ever read about in the more lurid histories. And then, once we'd been thrown back by the praetorians, we suffered the indignity of a constant artillery bombardment, since the moon had risen and was illuminating us nicely, an unending barrage of stones and arrows that knocked us about quite badly. And killed the first spear.'

'Decimus is *dead*?'

The young officer nodded at Marius's shocked question.

'He was hit by a bolt while he was standing out in front of the legion shouting at the men to advance again. We'd already begged him to take off his helmet and make less of a target for the enemy artillerymen, but he was having none of it.'

The shocked first spear shook his head in bemusement as the news of his superior's death sank in, along with the realisation that he was now the most senior centurion remaining in the legion.

'From that moment the heart went out of the men, and while we didn't retreat we didn't go forward either, so it became a battle of skirmishes and confusion, with friend killing friend if they got the watchword wrong in the chaos, and bolts flying back and forth. It was nothing better than bloody murder, and we fought for the rest of the night as more of an unformed mob than a legion, it was just terrifying, if I'm honest. I did my best to provide the men with some leadership, but in the dark it was impossible to command any more of them than I could see by the light of the moon.' He grimaced. 'And I quickly realised that I'm no Decimus, as I tried to encourage men to advance to their deaths in those desperate hours. By the dawn we were no further forward than our starting point and we were totally exhausted. You have to remember that we'd marched thirty miles the previous day and then gone straight into battle with no food other than what we could snatch on the move, or what the people of Cremona brought out for us, so we were pretty much finished. And then, as the dawn came up, the enemy started making noise. A lot of noise.' He smiled wanly. 'It was the gods' last joke on us, as it turned out. We were astonished, of course, having assumed that they had to be as tired as we were, but they were actually shouting and cheering at each other, as if they knew something we didn't. We learned later that it was their Third Legion greeting the sunrise, Syrian sun worshippers to a man, of course, but the rest of their army thought that they were cheering the arrival of the reinforcements that they knew were on the way. That gave them heart, that and their commander going about encouraging them with humour and praise, and they came at us again in the grey first light like the spirits of the dead that littered the ground before us. It was too much.' Another tear glistened on his cheek, unnoticed. 'At first we fell back, men calling on each other to stand firm even as they inched away from the enemy line, only a few turning and running, and then in the space of half a dozen breaths the whole legion was running. And I ran with them. There was more resistance, but nothing that stood any chance of stopping them. The entire army was under their spears by nightfall of the next day, and Cremona was subjected to a sack that saw some of the most bestial behaviour imaginable, with no-one safe from rape and murder, not man, woman or child.'

The room was silent again for a moment before Lupercus spoke.

'We've seen battle of late, Tribune, and I can assure you that if it wasn't for these walls we would all have been running too, so we understand better than you might imagine. And now to practical matters. Where is the army camped, and in what strength? As you can probably imagine we're fairly keen to understand what progress is being made to relieve us from this siege.'

Later, with the tribune as thoroughly debriefed as the time allowed, the officers took stock of their position in the light of the information he had shared with them.

'A relief force formed of what's left of three legions is camped barely twenty-five miles distant, a day's march, and yet they won't risk coming forward, it seems? Are they cowards or just fools?'

The legatus smiled at Aquillius's indignant question.

'Neither, I suspect. From what Varro was saying it appears as if Flaccus was forced to relinquish control of the army to one of his legates until recently, which indicates that they're having problems with his being able to control his men. And let's face the facts, it's clear enough from what we've just heard that he favours Vespasianus over Vitellius, as do most of the men commanding his legions. I'd bet the contents of our pay chests against the coins in your purse that they've made a quiet collective decision to sit and wait for someone to take the throne before deciding what to do. Quite apart from their own concerns as to which course of action to take, they'll be mindful that Civilis is supposed to have risen up in support of Vespasianus, which means that now they know his mentor is likely to win the war they'll be even more inclined to wait and see what happens next.'

'So you're saying that a victory for Vitellius would have had them moving to relieve us, but a likely victory for Vespasianus does nothing better than freeze them in place for even longer?'

Lupercus nodded at Aquillius's baldly stated assessment.

'That's more or less the way I see it, First Spear. And given that it might take at least a month for Vespasianus's legions to work their way south to Rome and finish the job they started at Cremona, we're not likely to see anything constructive happen for at least that long. So tell me, how long do we have before the supplies run out and we turn to eating boot leather?'

Marius opened his tablet.

'We've enough flour left in the granaries to give us half a bread ration for the rest of the month. The salted meat will run out in less than half that time and the other supplies a week later, even at a reduced rate of consumption.'

The legatus nodded grimly.

'So we'll already be starving before news can reach the army of Vespasianus taking the throne. Which means we have no alternative but to get a message out to Legatus Augusti Flaccus making clear just how long we have left before we'll be forced to surrender. Holding back from advancing to relieve us in order to avoid the appearance of disloyalty is one thing, but doing so knowing it will result in the loss of a fortress and two legions is quite another.'

Marius nodded.

'You're clearly right, Legatus, although one messenger wouldn't be enough. We're going to have to risk losing several men to get just one of them through their lines.'

Lupercus frowned at him.

'That's unexpectedly *pragmatic* of you, Marius. But how do you think the men selected to make the attempt might feel about it? I can't imagine that the tribesmen will show them any mercy.'

The senior centurion smiled at his superior.

'Quite the opposite. They'll skin anyone they catch trying to get past them alive, in full view of these walls and outside of artillery range to prevent a mercy killing. I'd imagine they'll have men so adept with the knife that they can keep the victim alive for days. Which means that finding volunteers to run that sort of risk will be something of a challenge. Nevertheless, we have to try.'

'Surely none of them would be that stupid?'

Lupercus smiled at Aquillius's uncharacteristically cautious approach.

'Your colleague has a point, Marius. How do you expect to motivate them to take such an insane risk?'

'Greed. We'll need to appeal to their purses, rather than their sense of what's right. I've found that most men will relax their grasp on life somewhat if they believe that risking it might bring them enough money to be comfortable for the remainder of their time.'

'The remainder of their time?' Aquillius spread his hands disbelievingly. 'The remainder of their time is more than likely going to be short, mainly boredom with occasional outbreaks of terror, and end with some form of violent death or other. What use is gold here?'

His colleague smiled tolerantly.

'You're one of those men who had a broomstick up you from the day you joined, aren't you, Aquillius? You never saw the point of paying whores when you could do the job yourself for nothing, wine only kills your fitness and reactions, and the standard rations are perfectly adequate to keep you fit and healthy, eh?' The other man stared at him blankly. 'Most of the legionaries under our command aren't like that. They want to ride a soft body every now and then, pour rough red down their necks at every opportunity and eat something a bit better than the same old pork given the chance. And they don't think they're going to die here, in fact half of them are so young that they don't think they're ever going to die at all. Offer them a few gold coins to sneak out of here and through the enemy lines one dark and moonless night and they'll be falling over each other to be chosen.'

Aquillius looked at him disbelievingly, and Marius chuckled at his expression.

'I'll tell you what, brother, I'll get you as many volunteers as you need to whittle down to a handful of the men most likely to survive the attempt, then you can do the selecting and give them whatever training you think they need, given your reputation for being death in the night.'

The big man turned to Lupercus, but the legatus raised a pre-emptory hand.

'No, First Spear Aquillius, you may not request permission to carry the mission out yourself, and neither are you to quietly slip away when you think there's no one watching. Marius is right, and just this once I'll be the man making the decisions.' He nodded to Marius. 'There's a moonless night coming up, so let's aim to make the best use we can of that. Find your volunteers, Marius, and our colleague here can take a day or two doing his best to turn them into men who can vanish into the shadows at will. They may all end up staked out for torture, but I suspect that if we don't get word through to Hordeonius Flaccus that the Old Camp still stands but is in dire need of relief, and soon, then we may all suffer that fate soon enough.'

Germania Inferior, November AD 69

'You have the look of a troubled man, Centurion.' Alcaeus looked up from his contemplation of his fire, beckoning Banon to join him and preferring a cup of wine. The chosen man accepted it with a nod of thanks and took a sip. 'It's late. Surely you don't have guard duty again, you stood up all last night and that wasn't even your turn.'

His superior shrugged.

'It was better than sleeping. My dreams of late have been . . .'

'Troubled?'

The wolf-priest thought for a moment.

'Lively.'

Banon smiled at him across the fire.

'Lively? Mine have been somewhat lively too, of late, mainly concentrated on the fact that my woman's only forty miles that way.' He hooked a thumb over his shoulder. 'Which has made me more than a little restive at night, I can tell you.'

Alcaeus smiled at his friend's attempt to lighten the moment.

'I have dreamed, Chosen Man, not of the distractions of the flesh but rather of events to come. Of a battle. A blood-soaked confusion of man and horses, fought in the darkness with all the horror that we can bring to such a fight, and with the Romans running from our spears towards a wall that can offer them no protection. I see them falling back or dying on our spears, with no hope of being able to reverse the course of the battle given their abject terror.'

Banon nodded knowingly.

'You've dreamed about our fight to come with the legions at Gelduba. They'll have built a marching camp with a turf wall, because there's no timber to be had for miles around and the river's too dry for shipping wood, even if we didn't command most of the lower part of its course. So you've dreamed of our victory, have you? Have you shared this with Hramn?'

The other man nodded.

'Yes. But I have shared the dream in its entirety, Banon.'

He fell silent again, and after a moment his friend leaned forward to speak in a quieter tone.

'You dreamed of a victory, Alcaeus. What more is there to add?'

The priest's lips tightened momentarily before he shrugged.

'For your ears, and yours alone, old friend. I told Hramn the course of my dream . . . all of it. I told him of the darkness, and the blood flowing like water from our enemies' ranks, of the spears, and the horses, and the slaughter we were inflicting on them.'

'Yes? And?'

'And I told him of the sense of dread I felt every time I dreamed of that battle, Banon, something I cannot put a name to, something I have not seen, but it *was* there. I knew that if I turned my head to look to our rear I would see it, but something in me prevented me from doing so.' He shrugged. 'It's only a dream. Nothing more than the night-time imaginings of a tired mind.'

'And yet?'

Alcaeus looked at his friend in silence for a moment.

'And yet, Banon. I live in fear of it, not for the dream itself but for my own fear that I will find myself on that battlefield all too soon, under just those triumphant circumstances, and realise that if I turn around I will see the nameless thing, whatever it is, that haunts my dreams. And that if I do then our cause is lost.'

The Old Camp, Germania Inferior, December AD 69

'How do you rate their chances?'

Marius looked at the tight knot of legionaries crouched in the shelter of a canvas-covered bolt thrower while Aquillius gave them their last instructions. The centurion's frustration at not being the man going over the Old Camp's wall was evident in the terse way he was talking to the men who had survived the brutal selection process he had used to whittle down the thirty volunteers who had agreed to get a message through to the legions that Lupercus assured them would be close at hand.

'Honestly? If any of them get past the Germans I'll be delighted. But I have to give credit to Aquillius, he's found the best of them.'

The blue-chinned centurion had walked along the line of volunteers the previous day, scrutinising each man in turn with a stare clearly intended to intimidate, tapping each man on the chest with his vine stick and directing them either to step forward or backwards depending on what he saw in their eyes.

'Every man who stepped forward, fall out and go back to your centuries. If you can't even meet my eyes, then you're not going to do well when there are ten thousand barbarians ready to stick their spears up your arses.'

Waiting until the disgruntled legionaries had made their exit, he had ordered the remaining men to redress their line and then proceeded to the next test.

'All of you, on your bellies and lie *still!*'

Standing perfectly motionless at the parade rest, he had waited and watched as the baffled soldiers lay in silence, his face expressionless as he noted their every tiny twitch and shiver, as the ground's chill seeped into their bodies. After what seemed like an eternity he walked forward, tapping four of the remaining fourteen men with his stick.

'Return to your centuries! If you can't keep still for that short a time you won't manage it when there are barbarian patrols hunting for you in the cold and the dark!'

With the volunteers reduced in numbers to ten he slowly and deliberately unlaced the leather cord that secured the cheek pieces of his helmet and removed it, handing it to Marius with a wink.

'Right, let's see who's fit enough for this little game. Once round the fortress, and I'll give you a count of twenty before I come after you. Anyone I touch with this . . .' he'd raised the vine stick with a hard smile, 'will be returning to their century. Because, let's face it, at some point soon you're all going to need to run faster than you've ever had to run before.' Raising the vine stick he'd pointed in the direction he wanted them to run. *'Go!'*

After a moment's bemused silence, the first of them had taken off at a fast pace in the indicated direction, followed an instant later by the rest of the group as the realisation dawned on them that they had no option but to take to their heels.

'You're taking this very seriously.'

Aquillius had nodded at his comrade.

'Of course I am. Every man I send back to his century is

another man who won't die screaming with half his skin hanging off. And one or two of them just might have what it takes to get past the Germans, but if—'

'They can't run faster than you round the fortress with a count of twenty start then they'll never outrun the Germans. I did kind of get the idea of what you're doing. Surely you ought to be . . .'

But Aquillius had already started running, pursuing the volunteers with an evident relish that put another smile on Marius's face. After a lengthy wait, the first of them had rounded the final corner and run for the spot where the senior centurion was waiting, a tall and well-muscled legionary who was evidently at the peak of his fitness to judge from the way he stood breathing hard but with no obvious signs of discomfort. Another three men had crossed the line in his wake, each of them a little more exhausted than the last, and when Aquillius had pursued the last surviving soldier around the corner with barely a dozen paces between them he was still running hard, while the soldier had clearly been on his last legs, driven forward only by fear of the stern-faced officer behind him. With twenty paces left to run the man's fate had seemed sealed as Aquillius, sensing victory over one last victim, closed in with a final spurt of effort that had his vine stick inches from his quarry's back. Then, in the moment when it seemed the fleeing soldier's race must be run, he had thrown himself forward onto the road's cobbled surface, his out-flung legs catching Aquillius's boots and tumbling him onto the stones alongside him, then rolled swiftly back onto his feet and sprinted for the line while the centurion had regained his own footing with a thoughtful expression. Picking up his vine stick and stalking towards the five-man-group that was all that had remained of the original thirty, he had stared at the last man for a moment.

'You five have all passed my tests. You'll go over the wall tomorrow night, when there's no moon. You'll cross the open space between the fortress and their siege lines, wriggle through their fence of stakes, get across their ditch and then make a run for it, or just sneak away into the darkness if you've not been spotted. And may the gods reward your foolishness in volunteering for this suicide mission with success. That or a quick and painless death.'

Marius had waited until the five remaining legionaries were out of earshot before asking Aquillius the question that was on his mind.

'He tripped you. I expected you to punch the life out of him at the very least.'

His fellow officer had shaken his head, his expression unperturbed.

'Why punish him when he'd just displayed exactly the sort of skills they're going to need if they're to get through the German patrols?'

Lupercus nodded his agreement with Marius's opinion.

'He's found the best of them, that's clear. We'll just have to hope that at least one of them is good enough to get through to the relief force and give them the news that we'll be forced to surrender unless they do something.'

'You're assuming that they'll actually take some sort of action even if the message does get through.'

The legatus nodded.

'They'll have to. Hordeonius Flaccus can't afford to be the man who allowed the Old Camp to fall. And they've had more than long enough to march men up the river from the Winter Camp. Add in the legions from the other fortresses along the Rhenus and even the Batavi would have to think twice before trying to stop them.'

The first of the messengers went over the parapet, climbing down the knotted rope that had been secured onto the bolt thrower's heavy wooden frame, swiftly followed by his comrades. As the last one went to follow them down into the darkness, the man who had tripped Aquillius the previous day, the senior centurion took him by the arm and whispered something in his ear before gesturing for him to climb over the wall. The big man turned away from the wall with his face set in hard lines.

'Well, there they go. The next time we see them it's likely to be an unpleasant experience for all of us.'

Marius and Lupercus both nodded at their colleague's forthright statement, the former leaning forward to ask the question that was on both their minds.

'What did you say to the last of them?'

'I told him to get close to the big lad. The one with the muscles and the speed.' Aquillius grimaced, his face just visible in the darkness. 'But I told him to keep *just* enough distance that he won't realise he's being followed. And I told him that when the big lad gets discovered, as he undoubtedly will with all that confidence to lead him into making some mistake or other, to use the noise and excitement to make his own way through the Germans without being noticed.' Both men stared at him in amazement. 'I didn't spare him for tripping me because I liked the look of him, Marius, I let him live because that's just the sort of devious little shit that knows how to use another man's misfortune to his own ends. Let's hope he lives up to my low opinion of him, shall we?'

I I

Germania Inferior, December AD 69

'Are we ready to march?'

Hramn was standing stock-still as his body slave fastened the ties on his armour, but Alcaeus could see that his eyes were alive with the joy of their impending march south.

'Completely, Prefect. All cohorts are fully equipped for battle, every man armed with two spears and carrying three days' rations. All boots have been inspected and worn hobnails replaced with new, all blades sharpened and spearheads reseated if needed. Three thousand five hundred and fifty-four men including one thousand and seventeen horsemen are ready to march.'

The slave stepped away, and Hramn flexed his shoulders to make sure that the scale-covered jacket that would protect him in battle allowed him complete freedom of movement.

'Perfect. As ever, you have me turned out like a palace guardsman. Dismissed, and here's a coin to spend on that widow you've been seeing.'

Alcaeus caught the wink of gold in the air as the prefect flicked the aureus from his thumbnail to be caught expertly in mid-air by the slave, who was clearly used to the pre-battle ritual. Hramn shrugged at his raised eyebrow, leaning forward to stretch his calves after having stood motionless while being equipped.

'I do it every time we prepare to fight. After all, who knows what the day holds? And if I fail to return he'll end up as another man's property with all the uncertainly of such a change of ownership, so why shouldn't he enjoy a little pleasure before discovering his fate?'

He waited until the smiling servant had left his tent before speaking again.

'So they're ready, I presume? Really ready? I don't mean hobnails and bread.'

Alcaeus bowed his head.

'I understand. And yes, they're ready, Prefect. More than ready. They yearn for an honourable battle, an enemy who isn't hapless or cowardly.'

Hramn grinned.

'Or if they are cowardly, at least possessed of the good grace not to have constructed a fortress too strong for us to get at them once they've fled inside its walls, eh?'

'Yes. They see the risk, and they disdain it.'

'Good. You have them paraded?'

The wolf-priest smiled.

'Paraded and wondering what's keeping their prefect from telling them where we strike next, I'd imagine.'

'Very well. Let's put them out of their misery.'

The two men strode out onto the broad open field where the cohorts were waiting in perfect silence, their mail's polished rings a million tiny points of light in the rosy dawn glow. The breath of men and horses steamed in the chill of a winter morning, and Hramn took a moment to gaze across their ranks with the faint smile of a man finding himself married to his perfect woman.

'Men of the Batavi cohorts!' He paused for a moment. 'My brothers! I know that you have been frustrated for the past few months! You had a taste of glory at Cremona, a swift and glorious moment in the favour of Magusanus! But since that day both you and I have been frustrated from tasting the one thing we yearn for the most – the moment when we drive Rome's legions off their ground, tear into them like the wolves we are and utterly defeat them! But today, my brothers, that all changes! Today we march south with only one intention! Tonight, when the moon is at its darkest for the month, we will assault the Roman legions that have set up camp at Gelduba!'

He paused, allowing the impact of his words to sink in.

'Three legions, weakened by vexillations sent south to fight for Vitellius, their ranks packed with new recruits barely worthy of the title "legionary" when compared with the men we fought alongside in years gone by! Three eagles for us to capture, equalling the example set by Arminius! The imperial palace still echoes to an emperor's cries of grief when those three legions were lost, but soon we will give Rome a fresh mountain of bones and broken spears to mourn over! And when those three legions are shattered, scattered and destroyed, the only army north of the Alps worth more than a clipped silver coin will be *ours!*'

He nodded in satisfaction at the silent ranks of men before him.

'We may be fewer in number than those three legions, even in their weakened state, but every man here is worth five of Rome's legionaries on his worst day! And we will fall upon them from the darkness like their worst fear, bringing terror and death to them when they least expect it! Before the sun rises again your spears will have destroyed Rome's threat to our people forever!' He looked round at Alcaeus. 'Do you wish to speak, Priest?'

The centurion stepped forward, studying the men around him in silence for a moment before speaking.

'The Romans, as those of you who have fought alongside them will know, have a habit of bellowing challenges at their men! Are you ready for war, they ask! They shout the same question again and again, until the legionaries are heartened to fight for their legion's eagle! But that, warriors of the Batavi, is not *our* way! Every one of you is ready to fight! Every man here left the Island to join us ready to fight! Every man here knows that our existence as a people is threatened by Rome, and every man here will fight and die to remove that threat, if that death is to be the price of eternal freedom for our families! So when we fight today, when we tear into these legions like the warriors we are, we will not only do so for Magusanus, although I know he will watch us with pride and lend us his strength! We do so for our sons! For our daughters! We do it to ensure that they will never have to fear the loathsome depredations of Rome's swarming rapists! I tell you all, if we allow them the time to rebuild their strength with the men returning from the south then we will spend the rest of time under their boot, permitted to exist in return for subjugation and despoilment! And no man here can tolerate such an idea! So when our prefect orders us to attack there is only one question that we have to ask ourselves . . .'

He waited for a moment in silence once more, allowing the tension to rise.

'That question is this: how many Romans will we kill today? There is no need to state any number, because the answer, my brothers, is this – *all of them!*'

Hramn stepped forward and drew his sword, raising it to point at the dawn sky.

'We go to kill them all! Centurions, prepare to march!'

Germania Inferior, December AD 69

'Repeat the message to me.'

The slave who was about to buy his freedom by carrying out an act of treachery on the part of his master, recited the words he had memorised, eager to be away. The two men were mounted, having ridden south from Batavodurum that morning on the pretext that the older of the two, a highly respected man within the tribe, was travelling to inspect the progress of the siege around the Old Camp, but had halted five miles north of the fortress in readiness for their act of treachery.

'I am to ride to the Roman camp at Gelduba by a route that will avoid the risk of my being taken by our scouts. I am to report to Legatus Augusti Flaccus. I am to tell him that you have sent me with the warning that our cohorts are marching to attack his legions at Gelduba after dark tonight, and that he must immediately prepare to defend his camp or risk losing the war in a single battle.'

'Because if the cohorts manage to bottle up those legions in their camp, then they will slaughter every last man in that trap!'

The slave nodded.

'I understand, master.'

His owner waved a hand to dispel the need for servile respect. 'I am your master no longer. You will never be able to return here, you know that. From the moment you enter the Roman camp you will no longer be safe anywhere in our tribal lands, and neither will I, *if* your name becomes known, so keep it to yourself along with my own! Go south or west, make a new life for yourself with the gold I have given you, and never even think about returning here unless you wish us both to die. And a man in my position who is deemed to have betrayed the tribe will not be allowed to leave this life in haste, I know that to be a fact. Now, as we discussed, make directly for Gelduba and avoid all patrols, Roman or our own, because you can trust nobody. *Nobody!*'

The slave rode away to the east, the beginning of a long looping path that would take him around the army besieging the Roman fortress and hopefully to the gates of the relieving army's camp before nightfall, and his master watched until he was out of sight before resuming his ride south, talking quietly to himself as his horse trotted along the arrow-straight road that Rome had built from the fortress to the Island in happier times.

'Too many good men have died already, Kivilaz, for you to make matters a thousand times worse than they already are by slaughtering three legions and bringing Rome down upon us with enough vengeance to see our lands salted and our people sold into slavery like Carthage of old. Perhaps my treachery will be punished by the gods, but I cannot stand idly by and watch while you condemn the Batavi to extermination at the hands of a dozen avenging legions as the result of your lust to rule the Germans. Claudius Labeo was right, curse my stupidity for not listening to him when he told us that your chosen path for the tribe would lead to disaster . . .'

A squadron of horsemen rode into view from the south, and the traitor reined his beast in to wait for them. Their leader saluted respectfully, a man he knew by sight if not by name, and he returned the gesture with a smile of greeting.

'Twenty men sent to escort one tired old man into camp? Kiv must have a camp the size of a city if he's sending so many of you out on such a small errand!'

The decurion looked out across the open landscape before replying in respectful tones, using the title that was traditional in formal conversation with a man of the traitor's age and status.

'Father of the tribe, we were sent to escort you in from here. The Romans have been attempting to get messengers out, and patrols have been doubled to make sure that nobody gets through to the Romans at Gelduba. And it wouldn't do to have such a respected elder of the tribe killed for his horse by some desperate legionary, would it, sir? We were told to expect two of you though.'

The older man smiled at the question.

'My slave was annoying me so I sent him back to Batavodurum. And any Roman who tried to take my horse would soon enough discover that this tired old man has hidden teeth, wouldn't they?'

The decurion grinned back at him, nodding his agreement.

'True enough, Father. You stand as an example to us all of how a man should live and be prepared to die.'

Gelduba, Germania Inferior, December AD 69

'What are we waiting for?'

Egilhard turned his head and stared disbelievingly at Adalwin.

'Less than an hour ago by my reckoning you were complaining that we're walking into trouble, and that such a headlong advance into enemy territory could only end in disaster. Now you're complaining that we're not advancing into enemy territory. So which is it to be, fear of the unknown or boredom? I only ask because—'

'Get ready to move! We'll be on the march again shortly! And stop your bickering, there are men trying to sleep in the Roman camp complaining about the noise you're making!'

Banon's whispered command silenced the grumbling soldier momentarily, and Egilhard took his chance to check that each of his men was ready to resume the advance now that the swift meal the prefect had ordered them to take just after dusk, in preparation for the final advance to Gelduba, still ten miles distant, was complete. Lanzo had been posted forward into the darkness that had swiftly fallen across the land, placed thirty paces from the column's head to listen for any sign of an enemy presence, and the leading man went forward to join him slowly and quietly, but as he took a knee alongside the silent soldier the other man raised a hand to forestall any comment. Egilhard listened, guessing that his comrade was straining his ears to hear something or other, but after a long moment the other man shook his head in frustration.

'It sounded like a man running across the fields out there.' He raised a hand and pointed to the column's left. 'But too far away to see, and too faint to be sure, although I could swear I heard him trip, or fall, and curse before he carried on.'

'It could have been an animal.'

'Animals tend not to say "fuck" when they fall over.'

The two men were silent for a moment, but whatever it was that had caught Lanzo's ear was evidently no longer within earshot.

'What is it?'

Alcaeus had walked forward to join them and both men stood.

'Dancer thinks he heard a man out there.'

Lanzo nodded at the centurion's questioning stare.

'Moving in the same direction that we are, if I heard it right. And definitely a man, I heard his voice.'

The officer thought for a moment.

'Man or beast, we'll probably never know either way. If it was a man, if we couldn't see him then I doubt he could see us, so even if it was a scout of some kind we're probably still undiscovered. I'll tell the prefect but as far as I'm concerned there's nothing more to it than that. Get back to your tent party, both of you, we're going to push on. And both of you had better be in the mood for killing Romans, because I can feel it in my water that this is the fight that will determine whether we win or lose this whole war.'

Gelduba, Germania Inferior, December AD 69

'So tell us, soldier, what is the message that you were sent to bring us?'

The messenger stood shivering among the officers of three legions, a legion-issue cloak wrapped around his lean frame and held closed by one white-skinned hand while the other held a cup from which wisps of vapour curled, spreading the scent of the heated wine and honey that Antonius had ordered to be prepared for him. He had staggered up to the camp's gate three hours after dark, totally exhausted but driven on by some deep wellspring of energy that Antonius knew from experience only certain men could access when their strength would otherwise have failed. Vocula stood before him with a look of the most intent concentration, sensing, the senior centurion suspected, that his one opportunity to break the deadlock between his own urge to attack and his colleagues' reluctance to make any move north had finally presented itself.

'You actually escaped from the Old Camp on Legatus Lupercus' instructions? And you can prove that you're not simply a deserter desperate to avoid execution?'

The trembling legionary nodded respectfully at him.

'Yes sir. The legatus told us to . . .'

'Us?'

'There was five of us, Legatus, when we went over the wall. We was selected by Centurion Aquillius as the most likely men to be able to sneak through the long-hairs' lines and then find the legions coming to rescue us.'

'And you're the only survivor?'

'Seems that way, sir.' The legionary drank a sip of the hot drink, smiling at the taste. 'I heard two of the boys get caught, and the man in front of me went down fighting, took a few of them with him from the sound of it. I did like centurion Aquillius told me and used the excitement to get past them, while they was busy killing him.'

'The centurion told you to do that?'

Flaccus spoke from his place behind Vocula, his voice rich with amusement.

'That sounds exactly like the Aquillius I remember. What was it the legatus told you, Legionary?'

The messenger nodded gratefully.

'He told us to ask you, Legatus Augusti, if you remember the first parade of the Fifth Legion you saw. How the whole thing was a disaster, and how you thought he'd done it deliberate to avoid sending any more men south to fight for the emperor.'

'Did he now?' Flaccus smiled at the memory. 'Well, it's true, and if his intention was to give you something I'll remember to prove that you've left the fortress with his permission I don't suppose he could have chosen much better.' He glanced around at his colleagues. 'Gentlemen, I suggest you consider this man to be a messenger from Munius Lupercus himself. So what's your message then, Legionary?'

'Legatus Lupercus told us all to tell you that the Old Camp has been attacked by the Batavians and their allies. We fought them off, and when they attacked in the night too.'

'That must have been something to see. How many tribesmen did they bring against the fortress, Legionary?'

'So many that they made the ground beneath our walls shake, Legatus, and we killed so many that the crows were too heavy to fly by the time they was done! Thousands of them! And they tried to bring a ram against our south gate, but we burned it out with fire arrows, and then a siege tower but we burned that out too!'

Vocula nodded.

'What else did the legatus ask you to tell us?'

The soldier thought for a moment, taking another sip from his cup.

'The traitor Civilis came to the fortress before the attack and spoke to the legatus, Sir. He told us that we should swear allegiance to Vespasianus, like him and his men have . . .'

Vocula chuckled darkly.

'No doubt they're all committed followers of Titus Flavius Vespasianus, and the moment that the civil war is settled either way they'll lay down their arms and revert to being the empire's loyal servants! Was that all, Legionary?'

The soldier swallowed the rest of his drink.

'The legatus also told us to tell you that the Old Camp is low on supplies, Sir. There's enough food for another week if we eat like usual, so perhaps we can last two or three on half rations, but after that we'll have nothing left to eat at all.'

'I see.'

The legatus nodded to Antonius, who ushered the legionary away with orders for him to be fed and given a bed, returning to the room just as Vocula rounded on his colleagues.

'You see! While we sit on our backsides there are good men fighting and dying for the empire barely twenty-five miles away. Munius Lupercus must be at his wits' end with wondering how long it could possibly take for a relief force to make its way north and relieve his legions! And the worst thing of all? That bastard Civilis is professing to be taking a hand in the war for the throne! The bloody nerve of the man! He's no more a supporter of Vespasianus than I am!'

He looked around the room with an expression of incredulity.

'And here we are, doing nothing much better than playing with ourselves! Well, I for one have had enough. You men can sit here and do nothing to rescue two trapped legions until Saturnalia if you like, telling each other how very *wise* you are not to get involved in anything that might smack of loyalty to Vitellius, but by all the gods I'll have nothing more to do with it, or with you, if that's all you have to offer!' The legatus was silent for a moment, and when he spoke again it was in a quieter, more measured tone, as he turned slowly to look at every man in the room. 'I'll take however many men are willing to come with me and relieve the Old Camp myself, and I'll use Vitellius's name to get them moving if I have to. You *gentlemen* can all stay out of it, unless you decide that doing something right might make a nice change from this ridiculous game that we've played over the last few weeks. Anybody who wants to join me in the advance to relieve the Old Camp should—'

The room's door swung open without warning, and a centurion stepped through with an apologetic nod to Antonius.

'Begging your pardon, gentlemen . . .'

Vocula beckoned him into the room.

'What is it, Centurion?'

'There's a messenger, sir.'

The legatus frowned at him.

'Yes, we've already seen him.'

The centurion shook his head apologetically.

'No, sir, *another* messenger. There's a man just arrived at the camp's southern entrance asking to see the Legatus Augusti, sir. He says he won't give the message to anyone else. We searched him, but he's not carrying anything so whatever it is must be in his head.'

Vocula and Antonius exchanged glances, then the legatus nodded decisively.

'Bring him in, Centurion. Let's hear what he has to say.' He turned to his superior. 'Another message from your friend Civilis perhaps?'

Flaccus shook his head, seemingly untroubled.

'I doubt it, unless he's considered Prefect Montanus's tale of Vespasianus's victory and decided to make peace after all.'

Ushered into the office, the messenger looked about him with undisguised uncertainty at the gathering of so many Roman officers.

'You're a Batavi?'

He shook his head at Vocula's question.

'I am Bructeri. Make slave in war with Marsi when I was young man. Now I slave to Batavi, and given freedom to carry message to Legatus Augusti.'

Flaccus stepped forward.

'I am the Legatus Augusti. What is your message?'

The German looked at him for a moment, then decided to trust his instinct that this was indeed the intended recipient of his message.

'Message from my master. Batavi cohorts marching south to attack Roman legions after darkness come over land.'

'I presume that you were sent by—'

Vocula rode over Flaccus's knowing question with the urgency of a man who saw the jaws of a savage and unexpected fate closing around him.

'When will they attack?'

The messenger looked at him in puzzlement.

'March this morning at dawn. Attack this night.'

'But . . .'

Flaccus's confusion went unnoticed as Vocula started barking orders.

'Legates and first spears, get your legions out of their tents and into their armour! Now! Send them to the western gate by century as each unit is ready to fight and we'll form a defensive line as they arrive! Cavalry are to muster to the northern gate, but tell Tribune Gallio to find me at the western side before he does anything stupid! *Move!*'

He caught Antonius by the arm, holding him back as legates and centurions ran for the door.

'I'm going to find my sword and helmet, and then I'm going to command the defence. While you're getting the legion tipped out of their barracks make sure your centurions understand that we might well be fighting on the retreat back into the camp before we know it, so make sure they know to have their men in hand when that moment comes. We both know how likely it is that the First will be able to manage the manoeuvre with any dignity, and the Sixteenth is an unknown quantity.'

Antonius nodded and was gone, leaving Vocula and Flaccus alone in the room.

'So you're getting what you wanted after all, eh, Dillius Vocula?'

Staring at his superior for a moment, the younger man sighed, shaking his head with a wry expression.

'Hardly, Legatus Augusti. All that time we've sat here waiting for a victor to emerge in the war for the throne? If we'd just gone forward and challenged the Batavians and their ragbag allies they would probably have melted away and allowed us to relieve the Old Camp, because they know they can't face us in a straight fight, not with three legions and all the Nervians, Trevirans the other Gallic auxiliaries you called to join us. But now here they are, coming at us in the one way that tilts the odds in their direction, in the dark and without any room for us to manoeuvre, and I know which dog I'd be backing in this fight if I were a neutral! So you'd better pray that I'm wrong, because if they manage to break into this camp they'll destroy us to the last man, those that don't manage to run away. And let's face it, you're not built for running, are you?'

'Hear that?'

A horn was sounding in the camp, reduced to a tinny but still recognisable blare by the two miles of open farmland between the leading Batavi cohort and their objective. Another joined it a moment later, then a third, and suddenly the night was alive with trumpet signals. Alcaeus and Hramn exchanged glances at the column's head, the prefect's face a slash of white teeth in the night's gloom as he grimaced at his deputy.

'They know we're out here, it seems. No matter, we're close enough for it to make little difference, if we get among them before they have time to form up properly.'

'Our plan was to assault the camp while they were still all in their tents.'

'Plans change, Priest! And there's no time for discussion, only to act!' He turned and bellowed an order at his men. '*Battle march!*'

The column surged forward, crossing the open country at a pace close to a run, and Hramn barked a swift order to Alcaeus as he turned back towards the formation's rear.

'At half a mile from the camp get them into line and ready to attack. I'm going to talk to Bairaz!'

The Batavi Guard's new commander grinned when he saw Hramn stalking towards his men in their place at the column's rear.

'Someone's beaten us to it, from the sound of it?'

'Yes. Which means that the legions will be coming out of that death-trap of a camp as fast as they can, if their commander has an ounce of sense. Take a position on the right-hand end of the line and wait for the moment that they break, then hook in from the right and ride them down.'

The cavalryman saluted and turned back to face his men.

'Decurions, to me!'

Hramn ran back up the length of his command, reaching the foremost cohort just as Alcaeus barked the order for them to switch from column of march to battle line.

'I'll say one thing for Old Scar . . .' He stood panting for breath and watching the meticulous precision with which each century turned to their right, hurrying to extend his army's line in readiness for battle. 'He understood that if a man can't perform battlefield drills in the pitch dark, the day will come when he'll die as a consequence. I think our former allies are about to find that out the hard way. We break their line, Bairaz and his guardsmen cut them off from their camp, and the rest will be as easy as your fight at Bonna. Except they won't have the security of twenty-foot walls to hide behind this time!' He grinned at Alcaeus wolfishly. 'This is going to be bloody.'

The centurion nodded slowly.

'I know.'

Hramn shook his head.

'Forget your dream, Priest. It's time for us to defy omens and make the gods take notice of us. We'll give them a river of blood as a sacrifice, Roman blood, and they will know that it is our destiny to be the masters of our own fate. Just make sure your men are ready to spill that blood.'

'What do we have so far?'

Antonius turned to find Vocula beside him, lacing his cheek guards closed as another century ran up and joined the line under the directions of a handful of their legion's centurions.

'Perhaps five cohorts' worth. They're all intermingled, of course, but that might be an advantage if it stops the First Legion taking to their heels the moment it gets bloody!'

Vocula was still considering the statement when a horseman rode up, saluting briskly as he looked down at the two men.

'Legatus Vocula! Reporting as ordered!'

'Ah, Gallio.' The legion commander pointed out to the battle-field's right-hand side. 'You're my tactical reserve! Take your men two hundred paces out to the right and form up behind the line ready to attack. I'm putting the auxiliaries out there, and if they run I'll need you to try to turn them back. If that fails, you'll have to make a decision as to whether to take their place or fall back as well.'

The younger man grinned down at him.

'We'll put our spears to them, Legatus, never fear! And if we have to I'll take my men into the enemy like the very hounds of Hades!'

Vocula raised a hand.

'Exercise the appropriate caution, Tribune. You're no use to me if you get chased away by the Batavi infantry, and you're no use to me dead either. I want those bloody horses back, young man, you understand!'

The young officer saluted again, turning back to his command and shouting the expected response over his shoulder, leaving Vocula staring after him as he vanished into the darkness.

'We will do what is ordered and at every command we will be ready!'

'Do you think he'll obey that order, Legatus?'

Vocula smiled ruefully at his first spear.

'I think he'll have forgotten most of it before he's rejoined his men. Riding at the head of three hundred cavalry with another five hundred Treviran horse under his command? The boy must think he's invincible.'

Antonius nodded briskly.

'Forgive me for asking, Legatus, given that an hour ago my own plan was for nothing more challenging than a last inspection of the camp followed by a plate of something hot and vaguely edible and a cup of wine, but what's your plan?'

Vocula laughed out loud.

'Plan, First Spear? You seem to have mistaken me for the army's commander!' He raised a hand as Antonius opened his mouth to comment. 'I know! The army's commander is sitting back in the headquarters building wondering if he's going to have his throat opened by a Batavi warrior before the sun comes up, and the other two legates might as well not be here for all the good they're likely to be when the blood starts flying! But as to a plan, under these circumstances I can't see much further than holding them off when they attack and retreating in good order back into the camp if they manage to push us off this ground. Any ideas you'd like to add to that?'

Antonius shook his head.

'I'd got no further. Legatus. Most of these men are too unsteady for us to risk any sort of manoeuvre in the darkness in any case, and with three legions mixed up there's no command that I can think of beyond holding a line that I'd trust them to get right. I told my centurions to concentrate our men of the Twenty-second towards the centre of the line where possible, so if it comes to a retreat we might have some chance of maintaining an ordered line to cover the rest of the army, but—'

Suddenly men were shouting in the front rank, pointing out into the darkness at something the two officers couldn't yet see. Vocula strode forward and pushed through the line until his view of the darkened landscape to the west was clear, inhaling sharply as he realised what it was that had caught their attention. No more than a hundred paces distant from the defenders' confused formation the Batavi cohorts had marched out of the night's gloom and halted their advance to dress their line, what little moonlight there was gleaming softly on their helmets and spearheads as their ordered ranks shifted slightly to ensure that each man had another at each shoulder. Their shields were presented as an unbroken surface of wood and iron from one end of their formation to the other, and over the top of each one helmeted heads regarded the Romans with evident calm, the shouting and cursing that the legion centurions were using to get their men into position strikingly absent in the formation facing them.

'Gods below, Antonius . . .'

The first spear nodded, neither man able to avert their eyes from the enemy in front of them.

'Yes Legatus. We are about to discover what happens when the finest shock troops in the empire decide to take their iron to three times their number of raw recruits.'

'*Second century, prepare for battle!*'

The tent party shivered momentarily, every man behind Wigbrand transferring his spear to his shield hand and reaching out to lightly grip the mail collar of the man in front of him. Egilhard took a pace forward from his place at their rear only to find himself held back by a firm grasp at his own collar.

'No you don't! I was waiting for you to do something heroic.'

He turned to find Banon at his back.

'I can't ask them to—'

'Do anything you won't do yourself? Have you seen that lot over there?' The chosen man pointed across the gap between the two armies at the enemy auxiliaries struggling to form line in anticipation of the Batavi assault. 'Nervians, from the look of them. And if they perform like the other tribes we've met so far, they'll fight for a while and then scatter like chaff, once they realise that we're going to kill every last one of them if they hang around long enough. So behave like Grimmaz would have done, put your strongest man in the front rank and save yourself for the moment when the enemy are nicely paused to break and run. That's when you'll want the deadliest man you have in front of them, bloody-handed and as desperate to prove yourself to your men as you like, but until then you can either behave like a leading man or disappoint Lataz by getting yourself demoted back to being nothing more than a mule with a quick sword. Which would be a shame, wouldn't it?'

Egilhard nodded grimly, pulling free from the chosen man's grip.

'Lanzo!'

The response was instant, that of a man knowing what was expected of him.

'Leading man!'

'You know the drill! The best spear starts the fight!'

The soldier turned and grinned appreciatively before bulling his way forward into the front rank, clapping a hand on Wigbrand's shoulder and taking his place, raising his voice to be heard over the general chatter of men readying themselves to fight.

'Fuck me, Achilles, but there's a lot of the bastards! You sure you shouldn't be the man at the point of this spear?'

Banon leaned forward and muttered in his ear.

'This is the part where you say something to give them all a laugh.'

Egilhard nodded, swallowing his nerves and forcing a note of brusque amusement into his reply.

'I'm as worried as you are, Dancer! Anyone stupid enough to stand against us must be totally fearless!'

A soft laugh rippled across the tent parties to either side, and Lanzo's was edged with genuine respect.

'Fair enough! I'll leave a few for you though, we all know you've got a reputation to keep up!'

Alcaeus's voice stamped across the soldiers' laughter with the harshness that made the hair of the young soldier's nape stand up.

'Batavi . . .' Every man tensed, readying themselves to go forward. *'Advance! To! Contact!'*

Centurions and watch officers bellowed the command as an almost instant echo, and the cohort was abruptly in motion, stamping towards the Roman line at a deliberate pace intended to cause the maximum possible terror in the enemy's ranks before the horror of their slaughter began. From his place at the formation's rear Egilhard could see little of the men awaiting them, but Lanzo was calling out a continual commentary of disparaging comments in Latin intended both to encourage and inform the men behind him.

'There's one of them already pissed himself! Yes, you! You with the wet feet and the shaking spear!'

'That's why you put him in the front rank, eh?' Banon's voice was close to his ear. 'Because he's the best man you have, the sharpest, the quickest, the nastiest. The man your boys will follow into a hedge of enemy spears. You're learning fast, Leading Man. So tell me, what comes next?'

Alcaeus's voice rapped out again.

'*Halt!*'

The cohort was barely thirty paces from the Roman line, front rankers dispassionately staring at the men facing them and essaying practice thrusts with their spears. Egilhard answered Banon's question with growing confidence.

'They've not thrown their spears because if they do their swords will be too short to reach us. Which means we have all the time we need. Which means the barritus.'

The front rankers, knowing what was expected of them from long practice, had already started the susurrating chant, putting their mouths close to the rear of their shields to amplify the sound, and Banon was in Egilhard's ear again.

'They know us, of course, so they know to expect this . . .' He leaned in closer, lowering his voice to little more than a whisper. 'And Hramn knows it too. Be ready.'

'That must be their barritus, I presume?'

Antonius nodded, looking out over the enemy line at the ranks of motionless enemy warriors as their voices rose and fell in the hypnotic, booming chant.

'They'll come at us any moment now, Legatus!' Raising his voice to be heard, he shouted a command over the noise of the Batavi warriors. '*Any moment now! Get ready!*'

Vocula looked at Antonius questioningly, raising his own voice to be heard over the enemy warriors' eerie echoing challenge as the first spear's command was repeated by the centurions to either side.

'Surely they'll make this noise of theirs for a while yet?'

The first spear shook his head emphatically.

'Not this time, it'll only give us more time to get ready for them! And our men are already shitting themselves, praying for the barritus to never end! If I were their general I'd give it a moment or two and then—'

A voice rose over the barritus's swelling roar, a bellow of command whose intention was unmistakable.

'*Batavi! Advance! With! Spears!*'

With a sudden roar the enemy warriors were in motion, stamping towards the Roman line at a swift march pace that put them toe to toe with the camp's defenders in a dozen heartbeats. Their front rank was a flicker of barely visible spear blades that reaped dozens of hapless legionaries, the enemy warriors striking low with their butt spikes to cripple the men who were stepping forward over their wounded and dying comrades to take their places. The ranks of legionaries facing them visibly recoiled, the front ranks compressing back into the men behind them in their alarm at the speed and horror of the attack, their spears little more than a row of iron spikes to be pushed aside by the advancing enemy warriors as they stepped forward and thrust again. Fewer defenders died this time, the legion men using their shields to stop the iron blades darting hungrily at their faces, but the Batavi second rank were into the wounded with equal savagery, stabbing down with their butt spikes in the ruthless manner that a century of accumulated battlefield experience had made second nature. The legions' line was already being pushed off its ground, and while no men were running yet Antonius could sense that their collective breaking point was already dangerously close. Vocula leaned in and shouted a question over the battle's tumult.

'Can we hold them?'

The first spear shrugged, looking up and down the length of the legion's line as more men straggled out of the camp under the shouted encouragement of their centurions.

'I don't know! It all depends on how quickly we can reinforce—'

With a sudden flurry of running men, the Nervian auxiliaries on the line's right-hand end were broken and running, their standard held aloft triumphantly among the Batavi front rank while their officers cursed and beat them without effect, the auxiliaries fleeing heedlessly for the illusory safety of the camp. Gallio's cavalry stood in their way, spears ready to punish any man foolish enough to try to run through them, but the auxiliaries simply parted and flowed around them, intent only on escape. Without having to be told what to do the young tribune had his horsemen in motion, cantering forwards towards the victorious Batavi left-wing cohort that had inflicted such a catastrophic defeat on the Roman defence, and both men held their breath as the eight hundred riders careered into the enemy line at a canter, their long spears reaching out to reap the lives of the unlucky and unwary.

'Here!'

Lanzo thrust out a cohort standard, pulled from the twitching fingers of its bearer as the man wailed in fear and agony at the gash in his thigh pumping his lifeblood out onto the darkened turf. Even by Batavi expectations the swathe he had cut through the hapless auxiliaries had been swift and brutal, stabbing and shield punching his way deep into the enemy cohort's heart with his fellow warriors pushing forward on either side to keep the enemy from isolating him. As the standard had fallen, any remaining urge to resist had left the auxiliaries just as Hramn had predicted, and their sudden headlong flight for the enemy camp had left the first cohort staring at empty ground between themselves and their objective.

'*Horses!*'

A line of horsemen was cantering towards them out of the darkness, scattering the remnants of the broken Nervians like chaff as they came forward in a perfectly formed line with their lances held ready to strike.

'*Battle drill cavalry!*'

Alcaeus's barked order was taken up by centurions and watch officers along the first cohort's line, their men stepping into positions so well practised that no conscious thought was required as they switched to the formation the wolf-headed centurion had demanded of them. Front rankers knelt, shields grounded and spears pointing up at the height of a horse's chest, while the men behind them stepped forward and raised their shields to form a

wall of brass-bound wood seven feet high, resting the weight of
their raised boards on the iron bosses of the front rank's protection and thrusting their spears through the gaps between them.

'Here they come!'

The horsemen spurred their mounts at the Batavi line with
their spears ready to thrust out, but as they reached the line of
wood the beasts baulked at the prospect of the defenders' seemingly impenetrable wooden barrier. As the riders spurred their
mounts forward, trying to get them to collide with the shields
and provide them with the chance to thrust down with their long
lances into the men behind them, the front rankers thrust up into
the horses' vulnerable bodies with their long spear blades. A chorus
of equine screams rent the night air as the riders realised, too
late, the murderous trap into which they had ridden, those men
with unharmed mounts backing fearfully away from the evilly
sharp spears flickering out from the Batavi line while dying animals
kicked and bucked against the pain, unseating their riders and
spreading chaos as they blundered into the ranks of their
unwounded fellows, and horsemen thrown from dead and dying
beasts were unceremoniously put to the sword by the implacable
Batavi facing them.

A horseman staggered to his feet within a hand's reach of the
tent party, dazed by his heavy fall from his stricken mount, which
was noisily kicking in its death throes behind him while he stared
uncomprehendingly at the warriors with whom he was literally
face to face. Lanzo drew his spear back, ready to kill the man,
only to be frozen in his stance by a barked command from
Egilhard.

'No!' The soldier looked around at him in bemusement, while
the horseman's puzzled attempts to focus on the men before him
would have been comical under any other circumstance. 'He's no
threat! And we're not animals! Bring him in!'

Pulled inside the line of shields, the captive blinked in confusion,
belatedly putting a hand to his sword's hilt, and the young soldier
realised from his ornately decorated bronze breastplate that he
was a tribune.

'It's too late for that . . .' Stripping away the man's swordbelt, Egilhard tied it around his own waist with the hilt on his left, pushing the dazed captive at Adalwin with an order to keep him alive. 'He's worth money, you can see that from his armour.'

The horsemen were backing away, their losses and the capture of their tribune having ripped the heart from their brave assault on the Batavi line. Banon strode down the century's line shouting for the tent parties to reform.

'Battle drill spears! Get ready to move! We'll be into them on the flank any moment!' Catching sight of the captive, he took in the magnificence of his armour and helmet, nodding to Egilhard with new respect. 'A good move, young Achilles! That youngster looks like a man who'll be worth a good few gold aureii to release! Now get your shit on a pile and get ready to attack – they're on the retreat, so now's the time to finish them!'

'We must pull back, Legatus!'

Vocula nodded grimly, stepping back as the men in front of him retreated another pace in the face of the relentless Batavi advance, their ability to fight all but gone under the incessant threat of their enemies' probing blades, capable of little more than defending themselves with their battle-scarred shields. The path of their slow but seemingly unstoppable retreat was marked by corpses, dead men who had fallen to Batavi spears and then, as the enemy pushed their comrades away from the spot where they lay sprawled, calling out in agony for help, had been summarily butchered by the successive Batavi ranks. Order was being maintained by the hard core of their centurions and watch officers, but the legionaries were increasingly looking to their rear.

'But what if they rout?'

Antonius shrugged.

'They'll rout anyway, soon enough! We need to break contact with these animals and get back into the camp!'

The legatus nodded grimly.

'Very well! But they'll all have to retreat at the same time! That by-the-numbers stuff isn't going to work with these bastards knocking at the door!'

The first spear reached out and shook his trumpeter by the arm, dragging the man's attention away from the scene of horror that was playing out only a few paces in front of them.

'When I shout for you to blow, sound the retreat! Do it before I'm ready and you won't have to worry about the enemy because I'll gut you and leave you to die slowly myself!'

The man nodded at him, evidently terrified, and Antonius put his whistle between his lips before stalking away to his right with his vine stick and gladius raised across each other, blowing long blasts to call his officers' attention to him. His hasty orders to the centurions who had gathered around him at the camp's gate had been very clear on the likely need for them to have to retreat back into the fortress.

'If we sound the retreat, you *have* to keep the men around you under control! If they break and run we'll all die! I want a steady fall back, and no man can be allowed to step out of the line! If one of them gets away from his position without paying the price then they'll all be running a heartbeat after they see it. And if they all run then we all die, every one of us! You have to keep them in the line, gentlemen, or we'll all pay the price. So if you see this . . .' he raised stick and sword to demonstrate his proposed signal, 'then step back with your sword raised, and your chosen men, and their leading men too, and be ready to kill the first man who runs, or we'll all be dead men!'

Looking down the legion's rear he saw enough centurions holding their vine sticks aloft to show that his signal had been seen to know that he couldn't delay the moment any longer.

'*Trumpeter! Blow! Sound the retreat!*'

A thin line of men had stepped back from the legion's line, swords drawn and ready, beckoning the legionaries to retreat as the trumpet blared out the signal to fall back, other trumpeters taking up the call, the naked threat of their blades just enough to keep their men in place as they stepped back towards the camp's gate. Suddenly there was clear ground between legion and Batavi, ten and then twenty paces, the enemy still advancing in their usual manner and not yet alert to the opportunity opening up in front of them.

'Faster!' He waved with his sword, stepping back as fast as he could to encourage his officers. 'Get them back before the bastards realise what we're doing!'

The soldiers needed no encouragement, and more than one turned to run only to find a hard-eyed watch officer or chosen man in his face with sword raised. Antonius realised that disaster was being averted by a hair's breadth, the danger of the legions turning tail and running for their lives kept at bay by the soldiers' collective fear of the men behind them. Vocula was alongside him, his face taut.

'It's working! It's only bloody work—'

'*Cavalry!*'

A centurion to their left was pointing out into the darkness beyond the furthest extent of the line, and the two men realised that the threat they feared the most had struck their disorganised and terrified army at precisely the worst moment. A wall of thundering horseflesh washed towards the Romans out of the darkness, impacting the quailing centuries on the line's far left and shattering them instantly, Batavi guardsmen leaning out of their saddles to spear the hapless legionaries as they turned to run. The army's entire left flank disintegrated in a heartbeat, the enemy cavalry's brutal impact too much for even the threat of the line of officers behind them to be anything more than a gauntlet to be run by men intent on escaping the pitiless spears and swords that were reaping a grim harvest of those men too slow or simply incapable of running, frozen in their places by dread.

'They're running! They're all running!'

The entire Roman line was in retreat, their orderly formation lost to a melee of terrified legionaries fighting to get away from the twin threats of the infantry at their backs and the Batavi Guard's unexpected cavalry attack deep into their left flank. Alcaeus's voice rang out over the din of the enemy rout.

'Advance with spears! Double pace!'

Egilhard pushed his way through the tent party, slapping a hand on Lanzo's shoulder as the cohort hurried forward in swift and unthinking obedience to his command.

'My turn! You can guard the prisoner!'

But in the moment that his back had been turned the tribune had turned and fled, evading Banon's wild attempt to grab him and haring away into the night, leaving the chosen man cursing before turning back to the fight. The cohorts stamped forward at their fastest pace that wasn't a run, putting down the occasional legionary who ran in his panic into their line but for the most part herding the hapless soldiers back through the camp's gate and over its walls. A few hundred of the Romans had recovered themselves under the lash of an unseen officer's tongue, his bellowed commands for them to stand and fight finding some small part of them that was able to resist the terror advancing on them from all sides, and they offered the advancing Batavi combat with the desperation of men who knew their cause was already lost but had steeled themselves to fight, no matter that the likely outcome was death. Egilhard nodded his respect as he killed his first, putting his spear's blade through a legionary's throat at full stretch and then fending off the man's comrade as he raged forward with his unevenly matched gladius to die on the spear of the man next to him. Lanzo had refused to go back to the tent party's rear, remaining instead at his leading man's shoulder and stabbing out alongside Egilhard, their two spears seemingly twinned to their deadly purpose as the two men danced forward, hammering a deadly rhythm against the legionaries' shields and killing any man too slow-witted to recognise their threat and defend himself.

'Change over!'

Both men ignored the command to rotate back to the line's rear, both intoxicated with the savage joy of the fight, their aching muscles fired by the burning fury of murder that had taken them in its grasp and thrust them forward into the enemy, cleaving a bloody path into the Roman line. Banon, realising that his men were lost to the red mist that could overcome men whose senses were overloaded by the stink of blood and death, tensed himself to push through the line and pull them both away from the fight before a mistake born of their exhaustion led to disaster.

In his place at the century's rear, his deputy's sudden movement from his usual place five paces back from the line caught Alcaeus's eye, but as he turned to see what it was that had his chosen man stepping forward into the ranks of their men, a movement to his left snatched his attention. In the moment that it took for him to realise what was happening his sword hung loosely in his hand, as the stuff of his nightmares coalesced out of the darkness and fell on the Batavi line's rear with the speed of a striking snake. Turning to fight, he screamed incoherently as his friend died without ever knowing who or what it was that had taken his life.

12

The Old Camp, Germania Inferior, December AD 69

'Something's happening out there.' Legatus Lupercus stared out over the Old Camp's eastern wall with a frown of concentration. 'I just wish I knew what it was . . .'

Fires were burning across a broad swathe of the land to the south, perhaps ten miles distant from the fortress. Marius stared out at the smoke-tainted horizon with an expression of equal frustration.

'Fire. The universal signature of an advancing army. Someone's burning out farms as they advance, but is it our legions coming north or their cohorts going south?'

Aquillius raised a hand to point at something closer to hand.

'Whichever it is will become clear in good time, but in the meanwhile perhaps whatever it is that the Germans are trying to communicate to us is of more immediate relevance?'

Both men turned to look at the object of his comment to see a small column of men who were obviously Roman prisoners being marched along the line of the siege trench, barely inside the range of the fortress's bolt throwers, a number of cohort standards being carried proudly behind them.

'Well at least we now know where it was that the cohorts vanished to five days ago.'

Lupercus regarded the bedraggled captives for a moment before speaking.

'And I suppose we're intended to take the inference that we were on the losing side of whatever engagement resulted from this unexpected parade of spoils. And yet . . .'

'And yet, Legatus, it would be just as credible for these men to have been captured in a battle that the Batavians lost, and for Civilis to be displaying them in a last-ditch attempt to persuade us to surrender while only a dozen miles away the relief force is methodically destroying everything in its path as they advance victoriously.'

Lupercus nodded at Marius.

'Exactly.'

The column turned and marched dispiritedly towards the Old Camp's walls under the watchful guard of twice their number of Batavi soldiers, and Lupercus met Aquillius's questioning expression with a shake of his head.

'No, First Spear, you may not have the bolt throwers shoot at them. Those are Romans—'

'Roman *prisoners*, Legatus. They have forfeited their right to life by allowing themselves to be taken, rather than fighting to the death like men.'

The legatus's smile was wintry.

'Romans nonetheless.'

They watched as the column marched into hailing distance, a rebel centurion stepping forward to pronounce the message he had been sent to deliver, although not the wolf-helmeted man they had become used to as Kivilaz's emissary.

'These captives, and the standards they allowed us to take from them, are all the proof you need that your legions have been defeated in their attempt to relieve you! We assaulted their camp five days ago and drove them away with so much loss of life that a pit was dug to contain their bodies for the lack of enough wood to burn them! Your lives are now ours to command, Romans, and—'

'*He's lying! We beat th—*'

The captive who had interrupted the litany of victory went down under the blade of the closest of the soldiers gathered around them with their swords drawn, the Batavi leaning over him to deliver the death stroke, but the legionary's sacrifice had sufficed to confirm Lupercus's suspicions.

'I suggest that you take these men away from here now, Centurion, before I'm tempted to forget that they are my comrades and trade their lives for yours, you honourless bastards! Go, before I have my artillery shred you so brutally that even your own mother wouldn't recognise your shattered corpses!'

They watched as the prisoners were marched away, leaving the body of the man who had sold his life to break the enemy's attempted illusion lying on the churned earth in pools of blood that had filled a dozen of the deeply indented boot prints across which he had fallen.

'So if they were lying . . .'

Lupercus nodded slowly at Marius's inference.

'Then those fires are our legions on the advance. Although if it took Hordeonius Flaccus five days to follow up on a victory over the Batavi then I hesitate to even consider the state that they may be in. Very well, gentlemen, I suggest that you ready your cohorts for action, because the relieving force may well need all the help we can offer.'

Germania Inferior, December AD 69

'Watch officers! All watch officers report to the prefect!'

Lanzo looked round at Egilhard.

'That means you.' The younger man shook himself out of his reverie, getting to his feet with a bemused expression, and his comrade smiled wanly. 'I know. One minute you're a new recruit, then you're a leading man, and before you know it you find yourself in poor old Hludovig's boots. I warned Grimmaz that no good would come of this war, as I'm sure you remember, but it's an evil wind that brings nobody a little benefit, isn't it?'

The freshly promoted soldier looked at his boots for a moment.

'If I could . . .'

Lanzo raised a hand.

'I know, Egilhard. Trust me, I know. I feel exactly the same way about being appointed leading man in your place, given that the tent party consists of poor old Wigbrand, that idiot Beaky, Levonhard, and a man so scarred by the loss of his twin that it's all he can do to follow orders. But that's what we volunteered for when we followed Kiv on this quest for vengeance on Rome disguised by the mask of a fight for freedom, isn't it? We all knew in our hearts that Rome wouldn't take this revolt lying down and that we'd end up paying in blood for a few months of glory and slaughter. And if you think this is bad, just wait a while. Once they get their shit into a tidy pile and send half the empire's legions to put us down hard, then we'll look back at this moment with fond affection. Now go and see what it is that the prefect wants of us.'

The young soldier joined the stream of men heading for the headquarters tent to find Alcaeus waiting for them, a body of some five hundred men gathered behind him. Their expressions mirrored his own downcast mood, the cohorts still reeling from the disaster that had overtaken them at the very moment of victory over the legions at Gelduba. Poised to deliver the killing blow, with the blood of their victims so liberally spilled that the camp's watchtower fires had been reflected in its pools and streams, they had been assaulted out of the darkness to their rear by two cohorts of Vascones, battle-hardened men summoned from Hispania to join the relief force whose unexpected intervention in the battle had torn victory from their hands and replaced it with the bitter fruit of defeat.

'We have reinforcements from the Island! Prince Kivilaz called for volunteers to replace our battle losses, men who have completed their service and young men almost ready to join us! And these men behind me have volunteered to join our fight for freedom!'

On the surface his centurion remained the man he had been before the battle, but the soldiers of his century could see the signs, small but clear enough to men who knew him, that some essential part of his spirit had been torn away by the sudden and complete defeat that had resulted from the Vascones' unexpected arrival on the battlefield. His effortless command of his men was slightly diminished, as if he were going through the motions of a role in which he no longer quite believed. Egilhard's practised eye took the measure of the men standing in ordered ranks behind him, a mix of recently retired soldiers and youths a year or two younger than the usual recruitment age, shaking his head at the thought of having to take untrained soldiers and men lacking in the necessary fitness into battle.

'Before any of you muster the courage to ask me what in Magusanus's name I think I'm doing asking you to take these men into your centuries, think on this: we lost enough men at Gelduba to form four whole cohorts and have two hundred men to spare! We desperately need reinforcement, and these men have had the courage to volunteer themselves to serve the tribe despite their obvious disadvantages of age! So you *will* show them the appropriate respect for having made the decision to leave their homes and families to join us in our time of need! Does any man here have a problem with that?'

He waited for a long moment before continuing.

'No? Good! Very well, come forward in numerical order, starting with the first cohort! Every century will receive ten men!'

Egilhard walked forward but as his colleague from the first century turned away with his reinforcements he found Alcaeus waiting for him with a sad smile.

'I've a surprise for you, Watch Officer.' He beckoned a group of ten men forward, and Egilhard turned wearily to look them over.

'But . . .'

'Yes. Divide them among your tent parties as you see fit.'

He looked at the prefect for a moment before speaking, his voice taut with emotion.

'Thank you, Centurion.'

Beckoning the recruits to follow him, he led them away back to where his comrades were waiting, calling for his leading men to gather around.

'Reinforcements from the Island. We'll divide them among us and—'

'Egilhard . . .' Lanzo was staring at the men behind his friend in puzzlement. 'Isn't that . . . ?'

'Yes it is!' One of the older men stepped forward. 'Here's old Frijaz, back to show you children the way it's done! When the call went out for volunteers Lataz and I knew we had no choice but to step forward, and of course the boy here wasn't about to be left behind!'

The assembled watch officers stared at the two brothers, both men dressed in the equipment they had taken with them on leaving the cohorts years before, while Egilhard's younger brother Sigu was wearing a mail shirt that hung from his skinny frame.

'But he's no more than a boy!'

Lataz folded his arms and stared hard at the man who had spoken.

'He's fifteen. One year short of being ready to serve. Three years younger than the watch officer there.' His eyes gleamed with pride as he turned to look at his older son. 'He's been training with Frijaz and me for the last three years, and if it worked for Achilles I can't see it being a problem for his brother.'

One of the older leading men nodded sagely.

'I remember you two old bastards from my younger days. You were decent men, always did your part when it came to a fight, and good tent mates too from what I heard. I say we welcome these men back like the fucking heroes they are for walking away from their farms and families, and double so for a man who's brought a son with him. And you . . .' He looked at Egilhard with an expression that brooked no argument. 'No splitting them up to try and show how fair minded you are, right? Family men should serve together, so that they can look after each other. You can put the three of them in with Lanzo and I'll take The First One instead. Perhaps a change of tent party will help him get over the loss of his brother.'

A rumble of muttered agreement greeted his statement, and Egilhard bowed gratefully to their collective will.

'Agreed. And thank you.'

He took the three men off to one side, nodding at Lanzo who turned back to the tent party's fire with a smile.

'So this felt like a good idea, did it?'

His father stared at him, raising a hand to forestall any comment Frijaz might have to make, while Sigu stared in awe at the brother who had gone away to war only a year before and was now almost unrecognisable as the boy he had been.

'What choice did I have, eh, son? Kivilaz and Hramn managed to push you men into a meat grinder and get half of you killed in one night, which means that unless we want the Island knee deep in Romans we all have to do our part.'

'Did that have to include Sigu?'

Lataz shook his head with a wry smile.

'Which just goes to show that you know absolutely nothing about being a father, for all your skill with your iron. Do you really think I could have left the boy with his mother and sisters while this tired old whore-monger and I went off to war? How much do you think you'd want to be in his boots if I'd done that, eh? The man whose father went to war with Rome and left him behind? He'd carry that for the rest of his life.'

Egilhard shook his head.

'Instead of which . . .' He looked away for a moment, then shrugged. 'It is what it is, I suppose. Here . . .' He started unbuckling the sword belt around his waist. 'You'd better have this back.'

Lataz raised a hand.

'Not a chance! That sword's been passed to my oldest son, and it'll stay with my oldest son. Every time I hear the blade oath I'll know that Lightning's in the best possible hands to bring honour to our family. This old thing will be good enough for me.'

He patted the hilt of his gladius, and Frijaz snorted derisively.

'A man who has been sadly abused by the term "whore-monger" managed to steal that sword from a legion camp when nobody was looking, only for his brother to cunningly get him pissed and then take it off him in a rigged game of knuckle bones.'

'Rigged! You were so shit-faced that I could have told you black was white and you'd just have grinned at me! And whose idea was the game in the first place?'

Egilhard left his father and uncle bickering and turned to take stock of his brother.

'Brothers, eh? Look.' He decided not to try to sweeten what he was about to say. 'You think you're ready. You can fight with a sword and shield well enough to keep an old man like Frijaz in his place. You know the spear drill. How hard can it be, right?'

Sigu shrugged.

'You seem to have done alright.'

Egilhard grinned at him, unable to contain his joy at seeing his younger brother even while consumed with fear for his safety.

'Come here you idiot!' He wrapped the protesting boy in a bear hug, crushing him tight against his armoured chest. 'We'll get you through this.' Holding his disgruntled brother out at arm's length, his expression turned thoughtful. 'Hey, Dancer!'

The leading man answered without turning away from the pot suspended over the fire.

'Watch Officer, sir!'

'We need a tent name for the boy here. Those two old farts can make do with the names they were given back before Nero was even a bulge in his father's tunic . . .which were what, soldier Frijaz?'

The older man looked up at the sky for a moment before answering, as if seeking divine assistance.

'Knobby and Stumpy. Watch Officer. *Sir.*'

'Yes. You're Stumpy, as I recall, and Soldier Lataz is Knobby?'

His uncle's eyes narrowed.

'Yes. And thank you for reminding me.'

Egilhard grinned back at him, the hard, confident smile of a man making sure they both understood their relative positions in the century's rigid hierarchy.

'You know what they say, Soldier Frijaz. If you couldn't take a joke . . . '

'Yes, Watch Officer. I shouldn't have joined. Thank you for the reminder.'

His nephew nodded, turning back to Lanzo and gesturing to his brother.

'Sigu here doesn't have the benefit of their great age. You're his leading man, so you'll have to come up with something for him.'

His friend stood and walked over to them, looking the boy up and down.

'Well of course, given that your brother's tent name is Achilles, a name he earned by his deeds in battle . . .' The boy looked at him expectantly. 'I think the best possible name we could give you is—'

Trumpets blared out across the camp, their brassy notes at once familiar to every man, and Egilhard was bellowing the order his men were expecting before their call to action had died away.

'Stand to! Prepare for battle!' He turned back to Lataz, hooking a thumb at Lanzo. 'This is your leading man! Make sure that Sigu doesn't stop a spear before we get a chance to saddle him with a name he'll hate for the rest of his days.'

The Old Camp, Germania Inferior, December AD 69

'You're . . . leaving us here?' Lupercus was as tired as Marius had ever seen him, leaning forward across the Old Camp's planning table on his knuckles with an expression of incredulity. 'We've just resisted an enemy siege for the best part of three months, killed thousands of barbarians and lost hundreds of our own men, and now you tell me that you're going to march south again? And that you're going to take a thousand of my best legionaries with you to bolster your numbers! Am I supposed to take that seriously, colleague?'

Vocula nodded firmly, his features taut in the face of his colleagues' understandable amazement.

'I don't have much choice in the matter, Munius Lupercus. Consider the matter from my perspective.' Pointing down at the map table he raised a finger. 'Firstly, my three hideously under-manned legions are still recovering from the beating they took five days ago at Gelduba. The Batavians had us on a spit and half cooked, and if those auxiliaries from Hispania hadn't appeared in their rear when they did there'd be nothing left of all three other than a few hundred prisoners waiting for their turn on the altar. They're in no condition to go north from here and take the war to the rebels on their own ground, and I'm not even sure if I could make two of the legions involved advance a step further, never mind fight again.'

Lupercus opened his mouth to protest but Vocula cut him off with a second raised finger and kept speaking.

'Secondly, those same three legions are a mutiny waiting to happen. My colleagues and the legatus augusti have managed to mismanage them to the point that they regard us all as no better than traitors to Vitellius, and they're putting the blame for *his* defeat squarely on *our* shoulders. And since that defeat means that they won't be receiving the donative that Vitellius promised them when they made him emperor, they're not happy about it. Not happy at all. To be frank with you, colleague, I have a maddened dog by the collar and it's all I can do to avoid the bloody thing turning on me, which I'm doing by exercising discipline of the most ferocious kind to keep them in their place. But that will only work for so long.'

He raised a third finger.

'Winning a battle when we had the besieging forces between our two armies, and demoralised from their losses at Gelduba was one thing. They didn't even really fight, in point of fact, just melted away when Civilis managed to fall off his horse and give them the impression he was dead. The tribesmen ran first, and once they were gone there was no sense in the Batavi hanging around to face us on their own, especially with your men sallying out to join us. Which makes that horse's fall a piece of luck from the gods themselves, because a bloodless victory was pretty much all we had in us by that point. And a bloodless victory against a demoralised enemy is one thing, but undertaking a pursuit into country that will be swarming with that same enemy, on their home ground and itching for revenge for their humiliation, that's quite another. I estimate that nothing less than three full-strength legions will be needed to secure the approaches to the Batavian homeland, and another three if we're going to cross the river and teach them a proper lesson. And full-strength legions are something I don't have the luxury of possessing.'

He raised a fourth digit.

'And lastly, any such campaign into the north will need more food and supplies than I can muster out of the Rhenus fortresses, or even easily transport, given our loss of control over the river to the tribes.'

'But you managed to bring up enough food to keep what's left of my legions fed for another three months?'

Vocula sighed tiredly.

'Mainly by good fortune, given the evident unwillingness of my men to escort the supply convoys north. Trust me, Munius Lupercus, I'm not happy about any of this, but as I'm quickly discovering the hard way, command seems to be mainly about choosing the lesser of two evils. Leaving your two legions here forces Civilis to keep the Old Camp invested, for fear of you breaking out in his rear if he pushes on south as he must, if he's to settle this war before the legions from the south can join the fun. And I need to take my men back to Novaesium and regroup, gather more auxiliaries from Gaul . . .'

Aquillius snorted quietly, and the legatus turned to look at him.

'Something to say, First Spear?'

The big man stepped forward and saluted, unconcerned at his superior's ire.

'It has been my recent experience that our allies are not to be trusted when it comes to facing this enemy on the battlefield, Legatus.'

Vocula nodded, conceding the point.

'I can't argue that you're not right, given the history of this rebellion. But there's a major difference now, First Spear Aquillius. For the first time since this war started we have denied the enemy their customary advantage of having the most battle-hardened and experienced soldiers on the battlefield. With their cohorts not only having been given a good beating for the first time, but reduced to a shell of what they were before Gelduba, it's my estimation that our Gallic allies will find it somewhat easier to face them in battle from now on.'

'Yes, Legatus!'

Aquillius nodded curtly and stepped back, his face carefully composed.

'And now, if you'll excuse me, gentlemen, I need to check on my legions' preparations to march.'

As he left the room Lupercus looked at his senior centurions with a shrug.

'I'd say there's a man with the weight of the world on his shoulders, and if it wasn't for the fact that most of that weight is actually on my foot I might even feel some sympathy with him. But given that his orders mean that we'll have to stay here until he can muster enough of an army to come and pull our chestnuts out of the fire – again – I'm afraid that I'm suffering something of a lack of compassion for him.'

Aquillius's expression didn't change, but his disgruntled resignation to whatever fate it was that now awaited them with the departure of the relief force was evident.

'The legatus is a good man. I was talking to his man Antonius earlier, and he was clear that he's the only reason why that army hasn't already mutinied, but one man can only do so much. Add to that the fact that the Gauls are more likely to stab us in the back than join an army intended to invade the Batavian homeland, and I'd say the chances of our being relieved before the supplies run out again aren't very good.'

Marius nodded.

'And my men are starting to guess what's going to happen. I've already had half a dozen centurions ask me when we're going to start making preparations for the march south, and if they're asking the question then I'm quite sure their men will be equally concerned. And it's what form that concern might take that's my major worry.'

The Old Camp, Germania Inferior, December AD 69

'What's happening here?'

Marius was the first senior officer to reach the scene of what clearly threatened to become a full-scale mutiny, and at the sound of his voice the half-dozen centurions who were angrily remonstrating with the men before them jumped to attention, the oldest of them taking it upon himself to explain the situation, pointing to the men of the Fifteenth Legion, one thousand of whom had been paraded at the rear of Vocula's army to march south to Novaesium as commanded. The first spear's eyes narrowed as he realised with a start that considerably more of the garrison's strength than the selected legionaries were standing on the parade ground ready to march. Gesturing to his officers to step aside, he paced forward to stand toe to toe with the closest of the men thronging the open space.

'The men with orders to march south with Legatus Vocula all have tablets stamped with that order, to prove they're not deserting. Show me your tablet.'

The soldier shook his head, clearly terrified that the discussion could end in his execution.

'I . . . I can't, First Spear!'

Marius leaned closer, his eyes narrowing as he stared straight into the legionary's ashen face.

'If you're not authorised to be here, soldier, then what the *fuck* are you doing here?'

The hapless infantryman was literally shaking, his eyes darting to left and right as if in search of an escape.

'I can't do it, First Spear!' A tear trickled down his cheek, and his right eye was visibly twitching. 'I can't take any more! We thought we were rescued, but now the army's marching south and leaving us here to die! I just can't . . .'

He fell silent as Marius drew his gladius, the look on his face making his intentions all too clear, but as he raised the blade a familiar voice behind him stayed his hand.

'A moment, colleague?'

Turning, he saw Aquillius waiting ten paces behind him with an unfathomable expression. Men around the terrified soldier groaned audibly at the sight of a man with a reputation for spectacular displays of casual brutality, sure that such a harsh disciplinarian was bound to support Marius's evident rage at their attempted desertion, and their protest was enough to light his temper to its full fury.

'*Silence!* Centurions, any man making the smallest noise of protest while I'm speaking with my colleague is to be summarily executed! If a mouse has a shit on that parade ground, I want to be able to hear its turds hit the ground!'

Stalking over to where Aquillius stood he sheathed the sword and spat on the ground in disgust.

'Those fucking cowards! That a legionary from my command could be so . . .'

His colleague inclined his head in question.

'Terrified? Exhausted? Driven to the end of his rope?'

Marius gesticulated furiously as he sought a rejoinder to the softly voiced question.

'Spineless!'

The hulking centurion smiled at him.

'Don't tell me you don't wish you were marching south with them. I know I do.'

'We all do! But we haven't all shat ourselves and rushed down here to try to crawl out of here on our fucking *bellies!*' Aquillius shrugged, and Marius frowned at him uncomprehendingly. 'You're not suggesting that we allow them to . . .' His frown deepened. 'You *are!* You actually think we should let them—'

'How long do you think it'll take for Civilis to have his men back in place and this fortress back in his grip in all but name?'

Marius shrugged bad temperedly.

'Days.'

'I agree. No more than a week, probably far less than that. And when the time comes that the barbarians are banging on our gates again, do you really want men like *them* manning the wall beside you?' Marius stared at him without reply, and the big centurion laughed softly. 'I know. When I put it like that we both know that the risk of having a coward in the fortress is greater than just allowing him to leave with his tail between his legs. What if he fails to take on an enemy warrior coming over the wall, and in doing so condemns us all to death? An ineffective soldier is worse than no soldier, as I see it, because he'll consume as much food and water as a man who's still got command of himself but when the time comes to fight he'll let us all down.'

'So you *are* saying we ought to let them all go?'

Aquillius shook his head.

'No. But I am saying that any man whose courage has genuinely deserted him should be allowed to leave. It's either that or we execute them all here and now, and even I can see that the impact of that might be less than positive. Shall we find out who those men are?' He strode forward a few paces and then called out to the men thronging the parade ground. 'Any man with a pass to leave with the army, sit down and hold it up to prove you're not lying!'

He waited while the men with authorisation sat, leaving a long pause in which those who remained standing looked at each other nervously.

'Any man who lacks the courage to join me and my fellow centurion here in defending this fortress can sit down as well . . .' Some of the remaining legionaries began to sit, only to be frozen in place as his voice whiplashed across the parade ground. '*When* I'm finished with you! And *not* before!'

He strolled along the side of the untidy sprawl of legionaries, his voice effortlessly reaching the furthest part of the parade ground.

'You men still standing, take a look at the men around you. Some of you are broken, useless as soldiers because you lack the bravery to fight. Some of you started that way, right from the day we recruited you, which was our mistake, born of desperation to replace the men who went south with Vitellius. Others have been battered into that state of mind by the things they've seen and done. And there is no logic to it. What will utterly break one man's will to fight will leave another untroubled. And by the opposite logic there are also men who've been broken by the events we've fought through, but who refuse to admit it. For every one of you that lacks the strength to fight on, there will be another man back in the fortress whose will to fight is gone but who won't admit it, either to his tent mates or to himself.' He shrugged, turning about and strolling back along the formation in the opposite direction. 'And lastly there are more than a few of you who *could* fight on but are choosing to hide among their broken comrades, let's be clear about that. You know who you are. And yes, you *could* walk out of this fortress today without anyone trying to stop you. If you're not willing to fight, then I don't want you here. This fortress will be better off without you. Those of us still in possession of our manhood will be happy to see you leave, because for one thing, if you stay then you'll be nothing better than a ration thief, eating food that could keep a real soldier going for another day. And I for one don't want to find myself defending a section of wall with men who aren't ready to kill so that we can all survive. So those of you who aren't broken but who don't think they have it in them to stay with the rest of us, you can sit down.'

Not a man moved, and Aquillius allowed an uncomfortable silence to build while he paced along the crowd's edge.

'What? Not one of you is willing to admit that he could stay on but chooses not to? Very well. Here's an idea. Is there one man here who has the nerve to admit that he's not broken and was looking to escape, but has the balls to walk out here and take my hand as a comrade? No punishment, no hard words, just a welcome back into the company of men who can hold their heads up.'

For a moment Marius was convinced that not one of them was going to pick up the challenge that his brother officer had thrown down, but then, in a moment of decision that drew a flurry of interest, a single man stepped out of the throng and tentatively approached Aquillius, who put out a hand and took the nervously offered clasp with both hands, then turned to face the crowded parade ground with the hand raised above his head like the arbiter of a prize fight declaring the victor.

'A warrior brother who has rediscovered his courage! A man who knows that his weakness was almost his undoing, but who had the balls to put it behind him and step forward! Is there one more man like that, with the bravery to admit to himself that—' Another soldier was moving, accepting the first spear's clasp before shamefacedly joining the first. Another stepped forward, then two more, and suddenly there were dozens of men queueing to be welcomed back into the fold by the senior centurion, some meeting Marius's eye as they marched past him, while others stared at the ground in only partially assuaged shame. At length the last of them were gone, and Aquillius stared across the remaining men who remained standing.

'Any more? Does anyone else wish to recognise his own bravery? No? Very well. But before I have your comrades who have permission to leave this place stand and join you, let's be clear. Those of you who are broken have my sympathy. You didn't choose to be wounded that way, it chose you. I wish you all the best in defeating that fear, and finding a place as a soldier elsewhere. And those few of you who remain, who might have fought on but choose instead to run? I hope your gods find it in their hearts to allow you the chance to regain your pride – because no man will consider you as anything better than a dog on the street unless you find some way to restore the honour that you've chosen to discard. Not even if you live to be a hundred. I can assure you of that truth.'

He turned to Marius.

'Shall we go and prepare to defend this fortress once more, comrade, with the brave men who remain despite their fear?'

Novaesium, Germania Inferior, Saturnalia AD 69

'What was the fool thinking?'

Vocula looked out of the slightly opened Novaesium headquarters' window at the chaotic scene in the street outside, shaking his head in amazement at the sudden and catastrophic loss of discipline that had overtaken the fortress he still nominally commanded. Soldiers were roaming the torch-lit darkness in packs of twenty and thirty men, most of them clearly inebriated, and the atmosphere was verging on open violence as they surged through the streets shouting encouragement at each other and curses at their unseen commanders. Antonius had reinforced the guard on the building fourfold with men of his own first cohort whose loyalty he knew to be unshakable, but it was clear that even that many men, standing with their swords drawn and ready to fight if need be, would hardly deter a drink-fuelled mob of disaffected soldiers if the rioters' tempers boiled over.

'The legatus augusti did what he thought was right, and—'

Vocula turned on his colleague Gallus in fury, his patience snapping with the man's inability to see the situation running out of control.

'What he thought was *right*? And you're enough of an idiot to take his side in the matter?' He stabbed a finger into the stunned legatus's face. 'You think he had the right to follow the dictates of his conscience when it came to paying these men enough money to get them all pissed for a fortnight? We knew well enough that the local tavern owners were sending waggons south to Bonna and Colonia Agrippinensis to fetch in more drink, and women, when it became clear that our esteemed colleague was going to pay out Vitellius's donative, once the soldiers had found out about it! We knew that we'd be causing a temporary suspension of discipline, given all these men have been through! But at least they were going to be getting some small measure of what they'd been dreaming of – gold from *their* emperor! Gold sent here by Vitellius, something to justify their attachment to the man and allow them to move on to Vespasianus with some hint of pride.'

He shook his head at the darkly humorous irony of the defeated emperor's gift to his German legions, sent north before his fate had become clear with the disaster at Cremona, being the source of such blatant unrest. A shipment of gold from Rome, intended to be paid out as a donative to allow the men who had put him on the throne to celebrate Saturnalia properly, the money had arrived just in time for the feast, and had initially been the source of much rejoicing by men whose year had been eminently forgettable and who had seen a chance to lose themselves to orgiastic celebration for a few days.

'And then, just when it looked as if the money would guarantee us a week of peace while the legions drank and whored their way through the contents of their purses, that fool Flaccus went and announced that the gold was being issued to celebrate *Vespasianus's* accession to the throne. Doing what he thought was *right*! And now look at them! Two solid days of drinking and they've turned to sedition of the grossest kind! If my first spear didn't have the best of his men guarding this headquarters and the commanding officer's residence, they'd be in here already, and the beating they gave you after that fiasco with the grain ship would have been nothing compared to what they would have done to us when they found us. They're a mob, Herennius Gallus, and mobs tend not to respect rank once they're on fire with anger!'

The office's door opened and one of Antonius's centurions put his head into the room.

'Your pardon, sirs. If I might have a quiet word with the first spear?'

In the corridor he dropped the respectful mask, his voice taking on an urgent tone.

'We have to get them out of here *now*, Antonius. The mood out there's getting rougher by the minute, and they're fetching weapons from their barracks.'

'There's no chance we could put them down?'

The other man shook his head decisively.

'No chance at all. The First are the largest part of it, them and the men of the Fifteenth we brought out with us from the Old Camp, but the Sixteenth are pretty keen now that they can see there's nothing to stop them from taking part, and even some of our own boys from the less reliable cohorts are chewing at their ropes to join the fun.'

Antonius nodded slowly.

'The First have been on the losing side too many times, and they blame Flaccus for every damned battle they've managed to lose through their own idiocy or legatus Gallus's incompetence. And the men of the Fifteenth are consumed with the guilt of having survived their siege while their comrades have been left to rot behind a wall of Civilis's men, now that the siege has been renewed. You think they'll run wild?'

'I'd put a year's salary on it. And I think they'll be at it any moment now. You need to get those gentlemen to safety, and quickly, or they'll find themselves swinging by their necks from the roof beams.'

The first spear looked at the corridor's roof in thought for a moment.

'Very well. Have your men ready to leave, and warn them that we may have to fight our way out of this mess.'

'I already have. And they'll fight. But if the legates are with us we won't get more than twenty paces.'

Back in the office he found the officers waiting in uncomfortable silence, Vocula clearly having told his colleagues exactly what he thought of their support for Flaccus's decision to link the long-awaited donative with Vespasianus's victory.

'My men believe that the legions will be in open revolt very shortly, Legatus.'

Vocula straightened his back, nodding at his subordinate.

'In which case we may well have to accept the revenge that they will visit upon us for all of our perceived slights and failings. Would it be better for us to fall on our swords, do you think? The thought of being hacked to pieces by a crazed mob of drunken legionaries isn't the most dignified of exits I can imagine.'

Antonius shook his head.

'I have a less drastic idea, Legatus. As long as you can sacrifice a little dignity this evening we might all come out of this with our lives.'

The scene in the street outside the headquarters was more chaotic than that Vocula had seen from the upstairs window, a swirling mass of legionaries, some blind drunk and almost incapable of standing up, others bright-eyed with incoherent anger and eager to unleash their spleen on any target that presented itself. More than a few of them were armed, their bright iron reflecting the light of the torches that illuminated the fortress streets. The centurion nodded to the legionaries gathered around the door as he led the group out into the street, tucking his vine stick into his belt and drawing his own gladius, its familiar weight in his hand a comforting reassurance.

'We're going to double time it for our barracks, so air your iron! Anyone tries to stop us, put your shields through them! Anyone shows you their iron, put them down the hard way! Give me that shield!'

They advanced into the melee twenty men strong, their tight formation and fixed determination clearing a path through the mob's disordered bodies and unfocused anger. A soldier staggered up to the leading soldiers and goggled at the centurions behind their shields for a moment before slurring a noisy challenge.

'You're . . . fucking *officers!*'

The centurion lunged forward with his borrowed shield, punching out with its iron boss to flatten the man even as he turned to call out to his comrades, but the damage was done. A dozen legionaries and more were suddenly intent on the party, some of them armed and all of them distinctly hostile.

'You cunts! We'll—'

Antonius stepped through the protective line of his men's shields, knowing all too well that their illusory security would be torn down in an instant if hundreds of enraged legionaries descended on them, the rasp of his sword's blade against its scabbard's iron throat a familiar and distinctive warning note as he squared up to the speaker.

'You'll what? Kill us? You want to kill me, feel free to try, sonny! You'll be coming with me on that ferry ride! And you . . .' he looked at the man on the soldier's right, then the man at his other shoulder. 'And you! So make sure that's what you want, before you open the lid on this box! We're soldiers, just like you, and all we want is to get out of here before it goes to rat shit and you start killing each other! Want to try to stop us?'

The legionary who seemed to be their leader blinked hard, struggling to focus through the effects of the amount of beer he'd drunk.

'Who're . . . who're *they*?'

He was pointing past Antonius at the men in the middle of his escort, the legates looking about them in evident fear of their lives as the mob's chaos swirled around them, kept at bay only by the flimsy protection of a line of shields. Their usual finery had been hastily stripped away and discarded, high-quality wool and burnished bronze replaced by the roughly spun and less than pristine tunics of the slaves Antonius had ordered to relinquish them moments before.

'They're slaves! *My* fucking slaves! They cost me a small fortune and I'm not about to leave them to you lot to have your fun with! Now make your minds up, either fight or get out of my *fucking* way!'

The soldiers' decision hung in the balance for a long moment before they stepped back, suddenly deferential in the face of an aggressive and seemingly unblinking authority figure of the type whose commands they had been conditioned to obey from the first days of their training. Antonius stepped back into the square of shields, shooting his centurion a glance that was an unspoken order, but as the latter barked at his men to march, Gallus pulled at the first spear's sleeve.

'Flaccus? What about the legatus augusti?'

Antonius slapped his hand away in only partially feigned amazement at the legatus's inability to recognise his danger.

'Get your fucking hands off me, slave, or I'll have your back opened up like a butchered pig! Detachment, march!'

They ground into motion again, bulling their way through the crowd of men, and Vocula muttered in his ear loudly enough to be heard over the hubbub surrounding them.

'*Can* we do anything for Flaccus?'

Even as he spoke, the mutineers pressing at the gates of the commanding officer's residence broke through the heavily outnumbered guards, flooding into the building in such numbers that no resistance was possible. The centurion whistled for them to join his party, and as they did so he ordered his men forward at a swifter pace still, smashing their way through the crowd gathered around the gates and cowing any resistance to their passage with their raised swords.

'Faster! This is going to turn really nasty once they have him!'

As they passed the gates, Antonius caught a fleeting glimpse of the grossly overweight senior officer being dragged out into the building's central atrium by a pair of red-faced legionaries, his face a crumpled mask of terror as a third man stepped out of the crowd that had packed into the enclosed space with a sword held ready to strike.

'Gods below!' Vocula was fighting against the press of soldiers trying to hurry him along. 'I have to do something!'

Antonius took him by the back of his tunic and thrust him forward.

'There's nothing you can do! Once they've gutted him they'll be ready to do the same to anyone they can get their hands on that looks anything like an officer!'

The legionaries around them were moving faster now, in the relatively empty streets whose previous occupants were temporarily crowded into the residence.

'We should run, Antonius!'

The first spear nodded, and at a barked command from their centurion his men started running, the rattle of their hobnails on the street's cobbles momentarily drowned out by a huge cheer from the building behind them as whatever game the mob had been playing with the hapless Flaccus came to its inevitable bloody conclusion.

'Keep running! We'll take refuge in the barracks until this all blows over!'

Vocula nodded his assent, but to Antonius he bore the look of a man who would spend the rest of his life looking over his shoulder.

Marsaci tribal land, December AD 69

'Why are you doing this? You're of the Batavi tribe, are you not?'

Dragged in front of the leader of the small army that had ridden out of the mist to attack their village less than an hour before, the settlement's chief elder stared at the man before him with undisguised amazement. Equipped in the segmented armour worn by Rome's legionaries, he carried a helmet fitted with the cross-mounted crest of a centurion to differentiate himself from the men who served under him who had little to mark them as being anything other than legionary soldiers. Frowning at the leader of the men who had laid waste to his small settlement in a matter of minutes, he nodded slowly as recognition dawned upon him.

'I know you, you command the horsemen who camp close to the Batavi city of Batavodurum! We have offered you hospitality in the past when you have patrolled through our lands, so how is it that you come to us with fire and destruction when the rest of your tribe is away to the south from what we are told, seeking to end Rome's rule over us along with the men of our own cohort who fight alongside you?'

The roof of the village's hall collapsed in a shower of sparks as its timbers gave up the unequal struggle with the fire that had been put to the structure soon after their arrival, the wash of orange light illuminating the features of the man to whom he was speaking. He smiled, opening his hands as if to accept the elder's identification of him.

'I am indeed the man of whom you speak. As to why I am here, and the reason why your houses and farmhouses are burning, you should send word to Prince Kivilaz of the Batavi – or *King* Kivilaz as he will no doubt decide to be known – to inform him that you people of the tribes who support the Batavi in their war with Rome are suffering Rome's vengeance. You are not the only village to have discovered the hard way that to support the Batavi is to accept responsibility for their crimes, deeds which will bring Rome down upon you like an ill-tempered giant. For the time being Rome is content to have armed myself and these other men, dissenters from

Kivilaz's war on Rome who made their way south when this struggle began, and therefore natural recruits to my cause when Legatus Gaius Dillius Vocula decided to spare my life and send me to take some small part of Rome's revenge ahead of the day of reckoning.'

'You fight for Rome?' The old man stared at his village's tormentor in rheumy amazement. 'But you are Batavi!'

The other man nodded.

'I am. And proud to be so. When Rome has put *King* Kivilaz in his place then I will be happy to serve my people in any way the Romans see fit to allow, having proven my alliance with the empire through punishments of the allied tribes. And even if Rome decides that I should be put aside, seeing me as unreliable for having fought alongside Kivilaz for a short time, I will still be proud to have played my part in the defeat of a revolt which, allowed to continue unchallenged, can only result in further destruction of our once proud tribe. And your own. And as to all this?' He waved a hand at the burning hall and other structures to which fire had been set by his followers. 'This is ultimately for your own good, a small punishment now to save you from the full wrath of Rome's revenge later.'

The old man stared at him for a moment and then spat at his feet.

'You will be cursed by your own people, forever outcast. And I curse you too . . .'

The armoured man smiled at him again.

'A curse, if it is to be effective, must surely have a name. And the name to scratch onto that little sheet of lead is that of Claudius Labeo, once prefect of the First Batavian Horse and now simply a freedom fighter, bearing arms against the accursed family that, if Kivilaz succeeds in his plan to destroy Rome's legions on the great river, will undoubtedly preside over the destruction of our proud tribal name forever. For my part I'll accept a curse from every man, woman and child in your tribe, if it means I can help to spare you Rome's full retribution.'

He turned to look at the hall's flaming wreckage as it collapsed inwards.

'And it seems that my work here is done. Don't forget to make it clear to the Batavi who did this. And tell them for me that this is just the beginning. I will bring fire to my own people before very long, and perhaps an awakening to the fact that they have been duped into a war that they cannot win.'

Colonia Agrippinensis, Germania Inferior, December AD 69

'Welcome, Kivilaz of the Batavi.'

The Batavi prince walked forward into the circle of men who had gathered in a private house in one of the wealthier districts of Colonia Agrippinensis, its doors heavily guarded by men of the First Nervian Horse, stripped of their armour but still armed with their long cavalry swords. Bairaz, commander of the greatly depleted Batavi Guard, which had lost over two-thirds of its strength at Gelduba and was now little more than their prince's bodyguard, waited silently at the room's entrance. He watched as his master strode into the meeting of Gallic tribes like a man born to lead them all, despite his apparent deference.

'My thanks for your hospitality, Julius Classicus of the Nervii.'

Classicus stepped forward and clasped hands with his guest. A big, imposing figure, in whose deportment and mannerisms the Batavi prince saw another man of his own stamp, he greeted the Batavi prince as an equal, another member of tribal nobility who, before Rome's hegemony over the Gallic tribes, would have commanded his people by reason of his heredity rather than the empire's indulgence.

'When a man of your stature sends the message that he has a subject of mutual benefit to discuss, it would be remiss of me to do anything other than extend the hand of friendship and listen to your ideas. After all, when my cousin Montanus returned from the north and told me of your views on the matter of ceasing your war on Rome, I must admit that I found myself feeling a good deal of sympathy with your position.'

Kivilaz bowed, looking around him at the men Classicus had brought to their meeting.

'These are the men of influence in your tribe?'

'These men are elders of the Treveri, my kinsmen the Nervii, and of our hosts the Ubii as well, and of the Lingones whose rebellion was so cruelly crushed by Rome only last year.' The Nervian prefect raised a hand and indicated one of his comrades. 'This is Julius Tutor, a prince of the Treviran former royal family and appointed prefect of the riverbank by Vitellius before he left for Rome. And this . . .' he turned to another man who seemed to have been blessed with a somewhat self-regarding expression, 'is Julius Sabinus of the Lingones, a descendant of the divine Julius himself. His great-grandmother was a fine woman of the royal line, and it's well known that Caesar had a wandering eye, which in this case is reputed to have alighted on our colleague's ancestor and found her ripe for the taking.'

Sabinus inclined his head in greeting, evidently happy to be the subject of such prurient speculation given its association with the military strongman who had effectively opened the door to empire for his adopted son Augustus. Classicus gestured to an empty chair in the innermost circle of men, and continued speaking as Kivilaz took his seat.

'The news of your desire for continued war with Rome reached us at a most opportune time, just as the events in Italy that resulted in Vitellius's death were communicated to us. It seems that in their eagerness to deal out harsh justice to Vespasianus's brother Flavius Sabinus, who had taken refuge in the holy temple of Jupiter on the Capitoline Hill, Vitellius's desperate supporters committed the most ill-advised act in Rome's eight-hundred-year history. They set fire to the Capitol, it seems, to smoke the fugitive out of his refuge, and in doing so destroyed the temple of Jupiter as well.'

He paused, looking around him at the gathering, men nodding their heads sagely.

'As Gauls we are of course fully conversant with our history, and we know of that moment in time when it seemed as if our people would conquer Rome once and forever. But even back then, in the days when Brennus made the Roman army flee for

their lives, that most magnificent of temples was spared destruction, for fear of the god's anger. Perhaps this was our ancestors'
only error, but it was a fatal mistake, for Jupiter has guided Rome's
fate on an upward path ever since. No matter how bloodily her
legions might initially be repulsed, the god's favour has ultimately
guided the Romans from being little more than a dungheap city,
forever squabbling with its neighbours, to an empire that long
since forced upon us the surrender of our freedoms. The destruction of this most holy building by Rome's own rulers is a sign,
our priests tell us, that Rome's time in the sun is at an end!'

He looked around his audience, clenching a fist for emphasis.

'But I disagree! This is no mere portent of disaster! When the
Romans took fire to the most holy of places in their entire empire,
the seat of the gods' favour, they tore down in a single night what
it has taken their ancestors eight hundred years to achieve. By
this act of sacrilege, they have forfeited their most powerful god's
support. The power of empire is being wrested from Rome even
as we speak, and it is placed within our reach, if we are only bold
enough to reach out and take it! As we must, if we are to maintain all that was once good in Rome for the benefit of our own
peoples!'

Kivilaz nodded magisterially.

'I can see the reasons for your confidence. It is evident to me
that the moment has come for the Gallic tribes to take their
rightful place and cast off Rome's yoke. After all, at every turn
enemies afflict the empire, weakening it to the point where it is
ready to topple.'

Classicus nodded enthusiastically.

'Indeed! Everywhere Rome's enemies are on the march, we hear.
In the east the Jews have risen, and are fighting for their liberation!
The legions in Moesia and Pannonia are besieged in their winter
quarters and even the Britons have sensed their moment, it is said,
and are even now laying waste to that province's cities! Some
among us counsel caution, to wait and see if these rumours of
war and disaster for Rome are well founded . . .' He looked around
the crowded room. 'But I say that the time has come to *strike!*'

He slapped a fist into his palm with a crack.

'The Romans are riven by discord! Rome itself is under siege by enemies within! The legions are beset and preoccupied with their own wars on every frontier! Rome is finished! All we can do now is to act decisively and without hesitation to bring a swift end to this war, and usher in a new age of peace, safeguarded by our mutual strength! All we have to do is rise, my brothers, and close the Alpine passes with our armies, preventing them from reinforcing the pathetic, terrified remnant of their once mighty legions of the German frontier. And once we are sure of our freedom we can decide the limits we wish to set upon our power, not Rome!'

Kivilaz nodded.

'Well spoken, Julius Classicus. And what of those remnants of their legions? What of the men cowering under the close watch of my people in the Old Camp, the Fifth and Fifteenth legions in name if not in actual strength? What of the pitiful, demoralised army that squats in Novaesium, overcome with fear at having murdered their own general, the First, the Sixteenth and the Twenty-second Legions? And what of the single, terrified legion that occupies the Winter Camp far to the south? What should we do with them, when the flood tide of our uprising races like a tidal wave up the river and across Gaul, washing against the roots of the mountains and sweeping away Roman rule for ever?'

Classicus nodded, acknowledging the question's importance.

'The Old Camp will fall to you soon enough, when the legions trapped there realise that there can be no rescue for them. And the single legion in the Winter Camp will all too soon be overwhelmed when the tribes on either side of the river rise against them. As to the survivors of Vitellius's army in Novaesium, our intelligence is that they are torn apart by dissension, mutinous and ripe for the taking, and yet it is our opinion that to take arms against them might yet provoke them to useless but bloody resistance. Rather we plan to seduce them by alliance, and once they are with us to deal harshly only with their commanders, the gentlemen of Rome who have led them into the disaster they now face. The legionaries will ally with us, we calculate, in recognition that their best hope of avoiding punishment for their mutiny is to be part of a strong Gaul, united against all external threats in a new empire.' He looked into Kivilaz's eyes with a knowing smile. 'Where you seek to build an empire of the Germans, free of Rome's influence and control forever, we intend to build a Gallic empire, allied with you to protect all our peoples from Rome, by combining to close off their routes into our territory forever. Let the Romans do what they wish in Italy, their days of dominion over Gaul and Germany are over!'

He took a pair of wine cups and passed one to Kivilaz, raising the other in a toast.

'To the Gallic and German empires! If we stand united, then no power in the world will be able to push us off our own land!'

Later, with agreement reached as to their respective courses of action, Kivilaz took the hands of Classicus, Tutor and Sabinus, declared his undying support for their uprising, and took his leave escorted by his decurion Bairaz and the dozen carefully picked men of the Guard who had escorted him into the city from their camp beneath its walls.

'Do you believe all that stuff about the empire being under attack at every point, Kiv?'

The prince shook his head briskly as they walked through the city's empty streets with their watchful escort both in front and behind them.

'No more than you, cousin. But if it suits Classicus and his comrades to believe it, or even just to have their people believe it, that's sufficient for me. Nor do I care overly about their evident desire to build an empire as Roman as Rome itself, for all the good that decadence will do them. All I do care about is that Rome's long reach is about to be cut off at the elbow, and what strength remains to them north of the mountains will wither and die soon enough when it becomes clear that the gold to pay the legions will no longer be forthcoming. After all, we have two legions bottled up with no hope of rescue, and three more sit and bicker over the murder of that Janus-faced fool Hordeonius Flaccus at

Novaesium, not even strong enough to prevent us from riding south past them to meet the Gauls. What hope do you think they'll have once the Gallic auxiliaries show their hand? They'll surrender just as quickly as will keep their hides intact, and then we'll see how long the Old Camp holds out. All in all, I'd say that the days of Rome's empire in the north are at an end, crushed under the weight of two new empires, one of the Germans, the other of the Gauls. What price their threats of retribution now?'

Historical Note

Researching the *Centurions* trilogy was a fresh challenge for a writer who has, over the course of writing nine previous stories in the *Empire* series, become a little blasé about the historical background, events, military units and tactics, weapons and armour and just about anything else you could care to name about the late second century. To find oneself suddenly over a hundred years adrift of one's chosen period of history was in one respect easy enough – after all, not that much changed over the period in many ways – and yet a bit of a head-scratcher from several other perspectives. The revolt of the Batagwi tribe is on the face of it a simple thing – Romans upset tribal mercenaries, who then rise up and teach them an almighty lesson as to how to manage subject peoples and their armies – and yet the history, and the story that can be teased out of those dry pages left to us by the primary sources Tacitus and Cassius, is far more complex than anything I could have predicted.

To start at the beginning, the Batagwi – Batavians to the Romans – were one of the German tribes subjugated by Caesar in the wake of his rampage through the Gauls, and quickly became a firm ally of what was to become the empire. Providing Rome with a military contingent that sounds like it would have been the match of any legion – eight part-mounted, five-hundred-man infantry cohorts and a cavalry wing – they were a powerful blend of German ferocity in battle with Roman equipment and, to some degree, Rome's military ethos and tactics. In return for this disproportionate contribution to the imperial forces, they paid no taxes to Rome, an indication of just how valuable their contribution was deemed to be. Their role, to judge from the relatively scant sources, was in the long tradition of shock troops that has continued into the modern era in formations like the Parachute Regiment and the US Marines, hard men trained to high levels of physical competency and tactical aggression and, by consequence of both that conditioning and their collective underlying social backgrounds, lacking some of the instincts to self-preservation that can hamper soldiers from risking everything in pursuit of victory in the moment of decision that occurs on all battlefields. The best equivalent for us to consider with regard to the Batagwi tribe's contribution might well be the Gurkhas, Nepalese soldiers who have fought with great honour and bravery for the British empire and its post-colonial army, and whose bloody reputation has resulted in their mere presence in the order of battle proving fearsomely intimidating to Britain's enemies on many occasions.

Parented for decades by the Fourteenth Gemina Legion, it seems that the Batagwi cohorts did a good deal of the initial dirty work on one battlefield after another, as at the battle of the Medway in AD 43. Their sneak attack at dawn across the seemingly unfordable river seems to have destroyed the British tribes' chariot threat before the battle commenced, and allowed the Fourteenth, under the improbably young Hosidius Geta, and the Second Augustan under the future emperor Vespasian, to establish the bridgehead from which victory would eventually result. Incidentally, for those readers with an interest in the cursus honorum and its age restrictions, the historical record is a little confused with regard to Geta, and the legatus in question might have been an older brother, although age restrictions on command tended to be relaxed by a year for each child born to a family – so we can consider legion command at the age of twenty-four (it was usually no younger than thirty) as improbable but eminently possible, under the right circumstances. The most startling aspect of all this is that on more than one occasion the Batagwi used an organic amphibious capability – and by organic I mean without the assistance of any third party such as a naval unit – to cross rivers and narrow coastal straits and turn an enemy flank by appearing where they were least expected. How did they do this? Swimming while wearing their equipment which, weighing around twenty-five kilos, would obviously overwhelm even the strongest of swimmers in short order even before the encumbrances of having to carry a shield and spear are taken into account. It's possible that the latter were carried by means of some kind of improvised floatation device, but we cannot discount the possibility that fully equipped infantrymen were carried across the water obstacle and straight into battle by means of the cohort's horses being used to literally tow them across. This seems to have been what Cassius Dio is describing in *The History of Rome:*

The barbarians thought the Romans would not be able to cross this [the River Medway] *without a bridge, and as a result had pitched camp in a rather careless fashion on the opposite bank. Plautius, however, sent across some Celts who were practised in swimming with ease fully armed across even the fastest of rivers. These fell unexpectedly on the enemy . . .*

This was probably as innovative and disruptive to an unprepared enemy as massed parachute drops were (under the right circumstances) in the twentieth century, and the Batagwi seem to have been viewed as Rome's best and bravest shock troops, capable of doing the impossible and turning a battle to Rome's advantage by their unexpected abilities. For a long time this guaranteed them the highest possible status as an allied people, ruled not by a governor but instead by a magistrate voted into office by the tribe's most exalted citizens, the *noblissimi popularium* (the ruling class, literally 'most noble countrymen'). This tended to mean, one suspects, that they were pretty much guaranteed to take a Roman perspective on the behalf of a self-interested ruling class of families, themselves granted citizenship in perpetuity by the early emperors, in the pursuit of a Roman foreign policy that sought to ensure an alignment of the empire's ambitions with those of the tribe's rulers.

This relationship went even further than the battlefield, for in 30 BCE Augustus recruited an imperial bodyguard from the

Batagwi and the other tribes that dwelt in the same area, Ubii, Frisii, Baetasii and so on. Where the Praetorians guarded the city and in particular its palaces, the *corporis custodes* protected the emperor himself, and were trusted for their impartial devotion to the task of ensuring his safety and deterring assassination attempts that might otherwise have been considered by the praetorians themselves (and for which they later gained an unenviable reputation). Disbanded briefly at the time of the Varus disaster in AD 9, they were swiftly reinstated when it became clear that the tribe had taken no part in Arminius's act of outright war, and the Batagwi played a full role in the suppression of the tribes to the north and east of the Rhine that was to follow. They remained at the side of a succession of emperors until late AD 68, when the new emperor Galba made what appears to have been the fatal mistake of dismissing them for their loyalty to Nero, thereby leaving himself open to assassination by an improbably small number of praetorians.

It is important to understand just what this meant to the Batagwi, and why they took the dismissal quite as badly as they undoubtedly did. The bodyguard were, of course, a source of enormous kudos to the tribe and their local neighbours, and a significant source of income to boot, but the importance of their place in Rome went deeper than simple national pride – the influence of their position close to the throne on the tribe itself cannot be ignored. Exposed to Rome, the hub of empire and meeting point for dozens of nationalities and cultures, it was inevitable that the guardsmen would have had the blinkers of their previous existence removed to some degree, and that they would have been eager to share their new experiences and learning with friends and families. Anthony Birley argues in *Germania Inferior* (in an article entitled 'The Names of the Batavians and the Tungrians') that many guardsmen would have been likely to have been given new Latin or Greek names on their entry into service, as their own names might be unpronounceable for a Roman, and the perpetuation of these names into the Batagwi mainstream as proud parents sought to rub a little of a brother or an uncle's fame off on their new offspring must have been inevitable, which is the reason why some Batagwi characters in *Onslaught* have apparently anachronistic Greek names that are in fact entirely valid for their time and place. The guard effectively came to define the Batagwi's significant status within the empire, a source of enormous prestige at least within the tribe itself. This in turn justified the degree to which they had subjugated their culture to that of Rome, including the incorporation of their religion into the Roman framework, their god Magusanus, as was so often the case with local deities, being deftly spliced with the Roman version of Heracles/Hercules to create a new and mutually acceptable deity. The guard had come to define the Batagwi to a large degree, and when they came home for good late in AD 68 it must have seemed as if the tribe had been cast aside by the previously doting parent regime, with immense impacts on both the Batagwis' own self-esteem and indeed their relationships with the other local tribes who were equally impacted by this inexplicably sudden and shocking change of fortunes.

Of course the split with Rome was more complex than just the overnight loss of their prestige. It went far deeper than the sudden thunderbolt of late AD 68, and had been growing ever more obvious to those with eyes to see it over the previous years. The Batagwi and their allies the Cananefates, the Marsacii and the Frisiavones had to some degree, if the Roman commentators are to be believed, simply got too big for their own boots. In effect, it seems, they had made the age-old mistake of believing their own propaganda (or at least that of their Roman allies who called them the 'best and bravest', in itself possibly a play on the Germanic origins of the tribe's name, 'Batagwi', which might well have meant 'the best'). They had taken, we are told (admittedly by Roman historians whose sources and motivations may not be entirely unbiased), to strutting around telling anyone who would listen how important they were to Rome, had fallen out with their former parent legion the Fourteenth Gemina – possibly because the legion was lauded by Nero as his most effective after the Battle of Watling Street and the defeat of the Iceni, while the

Batagwi had presumably gone relatively unrecognised – and had thereby contributed to the increasing disenchantment with what was later portrayed as their overbearing behaviour. Rescued from internal exile of a sort by the onset of war between the German army of Vitellius and Otho's loyalist legions – having previously been posted garrison duty standing guard on the Lingones in eastern Gaul ostensibly to prevent a recurrence of the Vindex revolt (a failed uprising that had ultimately led to Nero's suicide) – they had immediately (if we believe the primary sources who were of course propagandists with their own agenda) taken up where they had left off, telling all and sundry how they had mastered their former parent legion and how critical they were to the success of the war against Otho. It is doubtful if they were much loved by either legions or generals, but rather tolerated for their ability to turn a battle given the chance to do so.

In late AD 68, and at about the same time as the returning men of the bodyguard, Gaius Julius Civilis ('Kivilaz' in the book, this being entirely my own invention and in no way attested by any source) returned from captivity, trial and acquittal in Rome. Civilis's Roman name identifies him as the son of one of the tribe's original noble families – a prince and successful military commander – but he was a man with an unhappy recent past. Charged with treason for having allegedly participated in the Vindex revolt, his brother had been summarily executed and Civilis himself sent to Rome to face the same charge. Freed by Galba – who had after all benefited hugely from Vindex's apparent folly in rising up without an army worthy of the name – he went home and was promptly re-arrested by the army of Germania Inferior under the emperor-to-be, Aulus Vitellius on the same charge. Freed once more, by a canny emperor who realised the risk posed by potentially hostile tribes in his own backyard while his armies were for the most part far distant in Italy, Civilis seems likely to have discerned the inevitability of a third attempt to make the charge stick, once Vitellius had no further need to tread softly around the Batagwi at the war's end.

And if the quasi-judicial murder of his brother and the threat hanging over his own head weren't enough to motivate him to revolt against Rome, the opportunity to seize power in a political system that must have seemed to be sliding away from the *noblissimi popularium*'s control, as more and more men of common rank achieved citizen status through their military service, may also have been too strong a temptation to be passed up. Whatever the reason, Civilis roused his people to revolt and the bloody events that will be completed in the next book. *Retribution* came to pass.

There are some other smaller subjects to discuss while we're looking at the historical backdrop to *Betrayal* and *Onslaught*.

As you will already have realised (and if you've not read this book yet, be warned that this is a spoiler of sorts), it's fairly clear that the man with the most to gain from a Batagwi revolt was actually not Civilis, given that Rome was always going to stamp the rebellion flat eventually, but rather Titus Flavius Vespasianus, Vespasian as we know him. When the Batagwi and their allies rose up and started killing Roman soldiers, the effect was to plant a dagger in Vitellius's back at the worst possible time, dragging his attention away from Vespasian's army as it advanced into Italy and preventing him from drawing any further reinforcements south from Germany to bolster his cause. It's worth making the point that there's no evidence that (another spoiler) Pliny the Elder was Vespasian's emissary to the Batagwi, but rather my invention based both on his previous military service in Germania Inferior and the fact that he was a friend of the emperor-to-be who rose to a position of significant responsibility after the latter's victory. Perhaps I'm taking two and two and adding them up to make seventeen, but given Civilis's time in Rome it's far from impossible that Pliny and Vespasian's son-in-law Cerialis – a man we're going to be seeing a lot more of – found an opportunity to make mutual cause, or at least to form a friendship that later translated to that alliance of convenience.

And onto Gaius Aquillius Proculus (more spoilers here), blue-chinned, dead-eyed warrior of Rome – at least in this fictional version of the revolt. What a gift for a historical novelist looking for a charismatic protagonist. All we know about him is that a phalera – a medal, worn with several others on a chest harness – with his name and legion engraved onto its reverse, was discovered in the remains of the cavalry fort close to Batavodurum, and that, as Tacitus tells us, he was a centurion of the first rank – presumably a *primus pilus* – of the Eighth Augustan who led the initial resistance to Civilis's uprising (another spoiler: that failed in the face of treachery from both Tungrian auxiliaries and the fleet). He then disappears from the historical record, but not from this story!

And lastly, Claudius Labeo. To be frank, if Labeo hadn't existed I would have invented him because – as we're going to see in *Retribution* – not only is he a complex character who's going to bring out the very worst in Julius Civilis, but he was a major player in the events towards the revolt's end. I think it's safe to say that he represented everything in his tribe's ruling class that Civilis disdained and revolted to overthrow, and which must have been one of his major motivations in making his bid for independence from Rome.

As usual, your comments and criticisms are very welcome, whether via my website's comments page or social media. I endeavour to answer all posts quickly, but writing and work sometimes get in the way, so please continue to show the usual patience and don't be afraid to nudge me if I'm slow responding. And now I'm off to start writing *Retribution*.

Anthony Riches

A CHANCE TO WIN A PIECE
OF ROMAN HISTORY . . .

For your chance to win a Roman silver denarius,
go to Anthony Riches' website

WWW.ANTHONYRICHES.COM / COMPETITIONS

and answer the following question:

Q: WHAT COLOUR DID THE BATAVIAN LEADER
JULIUS CIVILIS DYE HIS HAIR BEFORE
LAYING SIEGE TO THE ROMAN
FORTRESS OF THE OLD CAMP?

Plus, for the unique opportunity to win a solid
gold Vespasian aureus, answer the second of three
questions to be found in the pages of each book
in the Centurions trilogy - three books, three
questions and a valuable piece of Roman history
to be won!

Q: FIND THE THIRD BEFORE A DYING
ENEMY DROPS HIS WEAPONS

Find the first question in *Betrayal: The Centurions I*
(and on Anthony's website), and look out for the
last of the three questions in *Retribution: The
Centurions III* (April 2018), for your chance to
win this unique and evocative prize.

UK only. For full competition terms and conditions please
go to www.anthonyriches.com/competitions